THE FALLON LEGACY

by Reagan O'Neal

A TOM DOHERTY ASSOCIATES BOOK

THE FALLON LEGACY

Copyright © 1982 by James O. Rigney, Jr.

A Tor Book

Published by Tom Doherty Associates
8-10 W. 36th St.
New York City, N.Y. 10018

First printing, May 1982

ISBN: 0-523-48029-6

Printed in the United States of America

Distributed by Pinnacle Books, 1430 Broadway, New York, N.Y. 10018

*To Miss Ruby Glover,
who gave me the tools.*

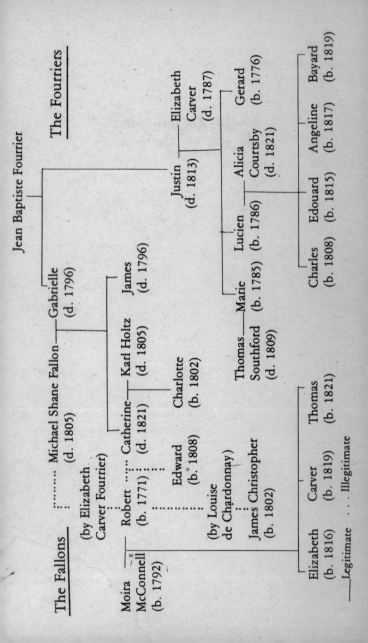

BOOK ONE

Charleston
1822

I

Robert Fallon's high cheekbones and hooked nose, gifts of a Black Irish ancestor, and his piercing blue eyes normally gave him a piratical air some thought odd for a Charleston merchant. He was six feet tall, and muscular despite his half-century. Of late, however, worry lay on his face. It was only January, but he knew already that 1822 would be a hard year. The papers piled on his study desk showed clearly that once again there would be little if any profit.

He fingered the black band on his coat sleeve. It was two months since cholera had flared on the Sea Island plantations, two months since his alluring half-sister had died. If her death had eased some strains, it had brought others. Her children, for instance. Charlotte, nineteen, blonde and pretty, was no problem, but Edward, almost fourteen . . . Edward was a special problem.

Reminding himself that he was to meet that morning with the executors of Catherine's estate, he decided to check the morning mail before leaving. The top letter was from New Orleans. He ripped it open.

My Dear Mr. Fallon,
    I take pen in hand as representative of Le Garde, Thibodeaux, La Fontaine and Smith, attorneys at law and executors of the late Esteban Lopes . . . .

The late Esteban Lopes, he thought in shock. Lopes had been a close friend, and a business associate. They had gone in the path of violent times together, before Robert had settled to being a merchant. He read on.

. . . Among his papers were documents indicating he had undertaken certain sales for you, and was soon to forward the sum of seventy thousand dollars in gold. Unfortunately, his estate is remarkably small, and quite unable to come near such an amount. I regret to inform you of this, but it is my duty to say that Le Garde, Thibodeaux, La Fontaine and Smith have no connection with any dealings that you may have had with Mr. Lopes, and can in no way be held accountable for these monies. If you wish to bring a claim against the estate . . . .

He let the letter drop. A friend was dead, and to his horror he could only think of the seventy thousand dollars. That money had been meant to cover projects already begun. At the foundry Kenneth Graham, his young Scottish engineer, was attempting to duplicate the process for making English steel. He'd had a new steamship, *Comet*, built for the express purpose of trying to make a profitable steam crossing of the Atlantic, something no one else had yet done. Damn it, he needed that money desperately. It was a good thing he was finally meeting Catherine's executors. He was certain to be made trustee of her estate for the children. That would tide him over, and the money could be repaid in a few years, long before the children were old enough to receive control.

Abruptly he made a grimace of self-disgust. Was he that desperate, had he sunk that low, to risk their inheritance?

Loud voices outside his door pulled him out of his funk. He went out to find the hall filled with gabbling children and maids. Albert Varley, the butler, a tall, thin man with blue-black skin, was trying to restore some semblance of order.

"What in blue blazes is going on here?" Robert shouted. Silence fell, all of them staring at him as if he had appeared by magic.

Edward was the first to recover. "Nothing, sir. It was an accident, sir." Fallon blood had given him high cheekbones and blue eyes, but on him the eagle nose had softened its curve, and his hair was silky brown ringlets.

He had too much of his mother's looks, Robert thought, making him *too* handsome, almost pretty. "You up to some mischief, Edward?'' he said. Please let it not be Edward this time, he thought. He loved the boy, but sometimes . . . .

"Yes, he is," Elizabeth said loudly. Not yet six, she stepped defiantly out from her mauma's side, but one hand clutched the stout black woman's skirt. Named for Robert's mother, she had inherited the first Elizabeth's violet eyes in a pretty heart-shaped face beneath midnight curls. "Chloe was hurt, papa."

Chloe was one of the cook's assistants. Edward took on a sullen expression as Robert eyed him. "What happened to Chloe?"

"Just wanted to scare her," Edward muttered. "Just wanted to make her jump."

"There was a brick, sir," Albert said carefully. He was young for a butler, only thirty-five, and educated beyond a butler's station. Moira had found him doing odd jobs for barely enough to stay alive, and hired him. Robert was under no illusions about Albert's first loyalty. "It . . . fell, sir."

Robert waited. Another fit of silence seemed to have taken everyone. Only the two smallest children in their maumas' arms were unaffected. Thomas, a year old, waved a chubby fist at him and gurgled, while Carver, at three, grinned and held out his arms. Each boy had a falcon's beak of a nose. Robert was briefly thankful, for Elizabeth's sake, that the nose seemed to pass the female Fallons by.

Finally he said, "I take it this brick fell on Chloe?"

"That it did," Moira Fallon said, bustling into the hall. She was a small woman, slenderly built, with finespun black hair and an upturned nose. At thirty, ten years of marriage had given her a quiet dignity, but now her normally clear gray eyes flashed and an ominous touch of brogue was in her voice. "I'll be talking to you about this alone, husband."

The children scurried out, maumas herding them, Edward's young valet at his heels.

"In my study," Robert said resignedly. This wasn't the first discussion they'd had about Edward, and it was making out to be as unpleasant as the rest.

He held the door for her, then settled in a wingchair while she paced before the fire. "He dropped a brick from the second-floor porch," she said without preamble, "and hit Chloe as she was coming down the back stair. She's a gash down the side of her head, and if the brick had been an inch to the right, it would've killed her. It's a wonder she didn't break her neck tumbling down the stair."

"Why, I'll blister . . . ." He drew a deep breath. Punishment did little except make Edward more sullen. "Boys sometimes do rough things," he said awkwardly. "You'll find out when Carver and Thomas are older."

"Will they be tripping a friend down a well, breaking his leg?" she said conversationally. "Will they be talking another friend into trying to ride a stallion in rut? There was a broken arm out of that, and a fractured jaw. Will they be putting a coral snake in the butler's bed?"

"He thought it was a king snake, Moira. An easy enough mistake to make. Besides, Albert wasn't hurt."

"Robert, that boy is a bastard by birth and by temperament. I will not have him in my house."

"You seem to forget I'm a bastard, too. If my father hadn't taken me in—"

"You weren't Michael Fallon's bastard by his half-sister!"

He flinched. "For God's sake, how many times does that have to be brought up? You know I've never made excuses, but she could reach inside me, twist my thoughts till I didn't know what I was doing. God knows I tried to break away, but she . . . . It was Edward gave me the strength. The horror of it. That gave me just enough strength to flee Charleston."

"I know," she murmured. Her slender fingers brushed his brow.

"Pacific typhoons and Malay pirates seemed no more than fitting payment for . . . . And then there was you. You gave me the strength to return to Charleston, the strength to resist Catherine's witch-powers. Don't you see, Moira, it'd be all too easy for me to turn my back on Edward, but I can't. The only expiation I can make is to try to make certain he grows up to be a fine man. Don't you see? I must.''

There had been a moment when he thought she might be relenting, but that moment had passed.

She drew a shuddering breath. ''It's out of the house I want him, Robert. It isn't his birth, or maybe it is, but there is something frightening about him. He does things, and people are hurt, and he doesn't care. He scares me, Robert.''

''You're letting your imagination run away with—''

''I know what I feel! He must go!'' She had rounded on him with her fists clenched, and he found himself on his feet facing her.

''I say he stays!'' He knew his face was carved in stone.

''In that case, husband,'' she said coldly. ''We must attend the Alyards' party tomorrow night. We have already accepted. But I will thank you to move your things into one of the guest rooms.'' She slammed the door behind her.

Why wouldn't she understand, he thought. She knew it all. About James, too, his other son. Long before he met her, he had been going to marry Louise de Chardonnay, just as soon as he returned from a voyage to France. Only the Barbary pirates had intervened, and after two years in a North African quarry he returned to Charleston to find Louise had borne him a son, James. Almost to the last she had waited, then, sure he was dead, she had married Martin Caine and gone to Louisiana. He had never been able to find the boy—man, now, if he was alive—though he kept New Orleans lawyers on retainer to try. Surely Moira could understand that he couldn't abandon Edward, too.

The chiming of the clock reminded him of his appointment, and with an oath he hurried to get his hat and walking stick.

James DeSaussure's offices occupied a two-story brick building on Meeting Street. A discreet brass plaque near the door proclaimed that James DeSaussure was an attorney at law. He was also something of a banker, or moneylender, for merchants, factors, and planters of sufficient solvency, something that wasn't mentioned on the plaque.

The door was opened by a stooped, chocolate-brown man in the black suit of a butler who ushered Robert inside and took his curly-brimmed beaver and gold-headed stick. "Mr. DeSaussure is expecting you, sir."

Robert followed him upstairs. The room looked more like a drawing room than an office, with a fine Turkey rug on the floor, Chippendale chairs scattered about, and a fire burning beneath a carved marble mantel.

"Thank you for coming, Mr. Fallon." DeSaussure's bass voice belied his size. He was a small man, almost delicate, with tiny hands and feet, and deep-set eyes that gave him the appearance of timidity. The appearance was misleading. DeSaussure had twice faced his man on the field of honor. "You know Oliver Huger, don't you?"

Huger, a dark-complected, frog-faced man with tiny ears and thick lips, jerked a nod. "Mr. Fallon." He regarded Robert unpleasantly.

"A chair, Mr. Fallon?" DeSaussure said. "We can do our business over a glass of wine, certainly. Madeira? Or Port?"

"Madeira," Robert said. He sat, taking the glass De Saussure handed him, and waited for them to begin.

"First," DeSaussure said, "let me apologize in advance. Your sister's will is still in probate, of course, but I fear I must tell you that you are not to be the trustee."

"Not!" A little of the wine slopped onto Robert's wrist.

"Looking forward to that, were you?" Huger said.

Robert's voice chilled. "What do you mean by that, sir?"

"Oliver, please," DeSaussure said. "Mr. Fallon, I fear Oliver, in his rudeness, has stumbled on your sister's fears. Forgive me, but your business difficulties are not exactly secret. Apparently she feared some, ah, temptation."

"Ridiculous!" But it was close enough to his own earlier thoughts to make him angry. "And it's damned offensive!"

"My apologies," DeSaussure said gravely. "It was your sister's reasoning, sir, not mine."

Robert acknowledged the apology with a short nod. "Is

this why you wanted to see me?"

"Oh, no, Mr. Fallon. As you're no doubt aware, your sister divided her property roughly into two equal parts, one to be held in trust for her daughter, Charlotte Holtz, and one for Edward Fallon, her adopted son. These will be turned over at age twenty-five, unless either makes a marriage without the trustees' consent, in which case the bulk of the legacy will be divided among that legatee's children when the youngest reaches twenty-five." He paused. "The children, I fear, are the problem."

"Problem?" Robert said. "They're safe in my house, taking lessons from a tutor I hired."

"Exactly," Huger broke in. "Picking up your strange ideas against slavery."

"Be quiet, Oliver," DeSaussure said. "I objected to the way Mrs. Holtz cut you out of her will, Mr. Fallon. Not mentioning you would be one thing, to specifically state you were to receive nothing . . . ." He spread his hands. "Are you certain that won't color your attitude toward the children in time?"

"Of course not! I love those children."

DeSaussure nodded thoughtfully. "There's nothing in the will to exclude you having the children. Though you realize it would be impossible to give you anything from the estate toward their support."

"I wouldn't take it if offered," Robert said. He wanted nothing of Catherine's. Nothing but the children.

"I still say," Huger began, but DeSaussure cut him off.

"It's settled, then. And I think the children are in fine hands."

If only Moira was as easy to convince, Robert thought. Damn the woman! Damn her!

II

On leaving DeSaussure's office Robert went to the Fallon and Son warehouse, on the East Bay Street end of Carver's Bridge. It was nearly a hundred years since Thomas Carver, his mother's father, had built the wharf, last in the city to be called a bridge. His father had built that into the shipping company, back in the days when hundreds of ships filled the harbor on any given day. Now the ships came in scores, and most of the American flag vessels were out of New York and Boston. By God, perhaps he couldn't turn the tide by himself, but he could try.

He saw *Comet*, her tall stack rising between foremast and mainmast, tied up to the wharf, and hurried up to his office. Graham was waiting for him, sandy hair matted and his coat open over a sweat-soaked shirt.

"What speed did you make?" Robert asked as soon as he came in.

"Ten knots," Graham answered. He had a thick Scots accent. "She willna' do more, sir."

Robert settled behind his desk. "I need twelve, Mr. Graham, if I'm to compete with the English packets." He tried to moderate his tone. Graham did his best, in the foundry as well as with Olympic. "Can you get more pressure in the boilers?"

"It isna' possible, sir, not and leave a safety margin. I dinna' want to be scattered over half o' creation. If you mean to put *Comet* into service to England, it isna' the speed, it's the water, and the fear, that's the problem."

Robert nodded angrily. It was two years since *Savannah*

14

had crossed the Atlantic, but people were still afraid of steam when there was no riverbank handy to swim to if anything went wrong. *Savannah*'s thirty-two cabins had been empty, and if she sailed again they still would be. "What are you doing about the water? This condenser of yours—"

"It isna' efficient enough, yet, sir. Ideal would be to recover all the steam as water. We'll ne'er make that, o' course, but we must come close to cross the ocean."

"Then do it, Mr. Graham. And I want twelve knots if you have to swim behind and push."

"I may have to," Graham muttered.

A knock on the door prevented Robert's explosion. "Come," he growled.

Morton, the warehouse foreman, stuck his long, bespectacled nose through the door. The Georgian had a pen behind his ear and a sheaf of papers in one hand. "The shipping lists, sir," he said. "You said you wanted to see them directly you came in today."

"If you dinna' need me, sir," Graham said, "I'll get back t' the ship."

"All right," Robert said. "Let's see those lists, Mr. Morton." The two men slipped past each other, Morton taking the chair in front of Robert's desk, Graham closing the door behind him.

"*Lady Charlotte*," Morton said, "crossed the bar at ten this morning, sir, bound for Liverpool in cotton. *Olympic* sailed for Georgetown immediately after. If she manages to get there without the steam works blowing up, she'll return in cotton and rice."

"I can do without the comments," Robert said sharply.

Morton cleared his throat. "Yes, sir. *Nomad* made harbor this morning from the Baltic. Here's the manifest."

Robert snatched the paper. Swedish timber and German leather. Not a treasure, by any means, but every cargo that came in staved off collapse that much longer. "Excellent, excellent. What other arrivals?"

"None, sir. And if I might speak of it, *Hunter* is a month overdue."

"A month is nothing in the China trade, Morton."

"Still, sir, the effects of her loss must be—"

Robert's palm cracked on the desk like a gunshot. "*Hunter* will make it, Morton! *Olympic* will make it!" God, his last two China ventures had disappeared in typhoons. He couldn't afford another. "What else do you have?"

"Nothing, sir. Oh, yes. Ben Miller and that big Turk are downstairs. Do you want me to send them up?"

"You kept them waiting? Morton, you're a fool." He hurried out of his office, leaving Morton with his mouth open.

As he made his way out of the half-empty warehouse, he tried to get his temper under control. He knew he was striking out at everyone in sight, and on small provocation. Coming onto the wharf and seeing the two men was like losing half of his worries.

"Ben! Kemal! Damn it, it's been months. If I just wasn't so busy."

"It's all right, captain," Miller said. "We understand." A balding bear of a man, he'd once been Robert's bosun. Kemal, near six and a half feet, his dark head bald as an egg, was silent; he had no tongue. The three of them had escaped from the Barbary pirates together and been together ever since. "The wife keeps my nose to the grindstone, anyway."

Robert raised an eyebrow. "Married life paling after five years, Ben?"

"On the balance? No."

"On the balance?"

"Well, captain, you have to understand my Alice is a God-fearing woman. She stopped me chewing twist, and I can't smoke except outside. I don't take a drink except when she doesn't know about it. She can raise an awful fuss for a little woman."

"Good Lord, man, has she made you over complete?"

"Maybe she has, captain. But there's good food on the table when I come in at night, no matter how late. She worries when my feet get wet, and babies me like I was dying if I get a cough. There's something about sitting in front of my own fireplace with my arm around the wife that's like nothing I ever knew before. Then too, if not for her prodding me, I'd still be running a sailor's grog shop, instead of the Atlantic Hotel, with fine planters and such. On the balance, captain, the good outweighs the bad by a long margin."

"And you, Kemal," Robert said. "Martha still treating you all right?" When they had all left the sea, Kemal had bought McCaffrey's Coffee House, and married the widow McCaffrey.

Kemal grinned and nodded vigorously, but Miller let out a whoop. "Martha? She practically worships him, captain. Four years and a nipper, and they're still on their honeymoon." Kemal nodded agreement.

At least *their* marriages were doing well, Robert thought. "Not like old times, eh? No barroom brawls. No one shooting at us."

"Maybe the earth swallowed Gerard Fourrier up," Ben laughed.

Robert felt a chill. It was a name he tried not to remember, the name of his half-brother. When he was a mistreated sixteen-year-old boy, he'd thought his name was Robert Fourrier, till his mother, who had been Elizabeth Carver, told him of Michael Fallon on her deathbed. The man he'd called father, Justin Fourrier, had only let him live to torment her, and with her death he had had to run. He had only crossed Gerard's path once since then, that he knew, but men had died because of it. And worse. Much worse.

Miller sniffed and cleared his throat. "Sorry, captain. Didn't mean to bring him up. Reason we came—well, Kemal had just stopped by the hotel for a minute—is this." He pulled a folded and sealed paper from his coat pocket and handed it to Robert. "Lady asked me to deliver that." Small grins had appeared on both their faces.

A scent of roses drifted from the cream-colored paper. His name was written there in a feminine script full of curlicues. He stared suspiciously at the two men—they were grinning broadly now—and ripped it open.

My dearest Robert Fallon,
    You do not know me, but I know much of you. Fear

not. I have no spies. Dominique You has told me many tales of his exploits with you and the brothers Lafitte. I could not be in this so delightful city and not meet you. Tonight, at nine, I am having an intimate *salon*. Do say you will come.

Until Tonight,
Lucille Gautier

He frowned at them in turn. "Is this a joke?"

"No joke, captain," Miller said. "She took my best suite of rooms three days ago. Pretty girl, young, with a bit of a French accent. Wears expensive clothes cut to show her figure, and captain, does she have a figure."

"You know what this is about?" Robert fingered the note.

"Not exactly, captain. Only, she said when you came tonight you was to be showed right up to her rooms. She slipped me a ten-dollar gold piece to make sure you're not disturbed after that." He was having difficulty containing his mirth, and Kemal was openly making the sounds that served him for laughter.

"Damn it, Ben, I don't even know this woman. Who is she? She claims she knows Dom. Hell, she's staying at your hotel. What do you know about her?"

"Nary a thing but what I've told you, captain. She rented a carriage from Dawson's, but she has her own driver and footman. Big black fellows. I'll tell you this, though. She has as fine a brace of tits as I've seen in many a year. Captain, a man can't be married enough to pass those by."

Robert shook his head impatiently. The size and shape of Lucille Gautier's breasts mattered little to him. He had enough trouble with Moira without a young woman bold enough to send notes like this to strange men. He let it drop into the water.

"Let's find a drink," he said. When the three of them had settled in Vell's Tavern, up the street from the Bridge, he raised his glass. "Gentlemen, I give you women. God save us from them."

III

The room was neat, but it seemed slightly off. The size, the plainness of the mantel, the finish of the wainscoting, all marked it for the dining room of an artisan or shop-keeper, but the furnishings—table, chairs, sideboard, chest-on-chest, and pier table—all could have gone into any mansion in the city.

The furnishings were only wood, no matter how fine they looked, no matter that he'd made every stick himself, Jeremiah Carpenter thought. You'd think a wife could understand that.

Sarah pushed through from the pantry and set a cloth-covered bowl of biscuits between the eggs and the ham. She was a tall woman, full of breast and hip. Near twenty years of marriage had put few extra pounds on her; her dark face was as smooth and unwrinkled as the day they first met. She sat and shook out her napkin without look-ing at him.

"A man who has a fine home, and a fine daughter," she took up where she'd left off, "shouldn't involve him-self with the wrong sort of men."

Jeremiah tried to change the subject. "Where is Leonie? Isn't she coming down for breakfast?"

"She's been gone an hour or more. Over to Mrs. Tobias's to help with the baking. Denmark is a personable man, I suppose, but—"

"Why," Jeremiah interrupted, "is she always running off to help with cooking or sewing or some such damned fool thing? She has her chores to do right here, and her studies. I'm not paying hard-earned money to Thomas Bonneau so she can waste her time." He was a greyhound of a man, slender except for broad shoulders and big hands, and four inches over six feet.

Sarah stared at him with her soft brown eyes. He sometimes wondered if she could read his mind. He didn't believe in all that voodoo mumbo-jumbo, but there were times . . . .

"It's time for us to talk about Leonie, Jeremiah. She and I have talked it over, and we can't see any reason for her to continue at Bonneau's school. It's a waste of time and money."

"What?" he said incredulously.

"It wouldn't be long till she's getting married—pray God—and what she'll need to know then is how to cook and clean and mend and sew and a hundred other things. It won't do her one bit of good to be able to parse a sentence, or say who the Cham of Tartary is."

"Damn it, woman! My daughter isn't going to grow up the way I did, ignorant and scraping to live until I was a man grown. She's not going to marry some buffoon who'll burn her books because he thinks they're magic and give her a baby a year till she dies. I want more than that for my daughter."

"You want! You want!" She jerked to her feet, face hard across the table. "What about what Leonie wants? Just because our sons died in the cradle doesn't mean you can make Leonie into a substitute."

He found himself on his feet to face her. Her voice had risen with every word she spoke, and his now rose to match it. "I want to make her more than a drudge. More than somebody's servant. More than just another black to be spit on."

"More? She can't be more. A woman can't be much, and a black woman can't be anything. Leonie can be a wife and have a husband to take care of her, or she can be a spinster and live on charity in her old age. That's all there is, Jeremiah. There's no point educating her above her station."

"Her station!" he erupted. "Her—"

"Well, well," a smooth, deep voice cut in. "You folks just argues to beat the band, don't you?" Billy Carpenter had all of his brother's height, but in him the breadth of shoulders and size of hands were matched with thick arms and a deep chest.

"You just come barging in without knocking, Billy?"

"In my own brother's house?" the other said expansively. "I sure do." He grinned nastily at Sarah. "You gots to watch that arguing with your husband. He liable to take a stick to you."

"I'd better see how things are in the kitchen," Sarah said to the fireplace.

Billy barely moved aside enough for her to pass. "Why don't you gets me a plate while you's out there?" he called after her. The door swung shut in his face. "You expects me to eat off the table?"

"Why don't you get a job?" Jeremiah said, without any hope. "I taught you how to read and write and cipher so you could get decent work and earn your way."

"I gots plenty money." The chair Sarah had vacated creaked as Billy dropped into it heavily. He scooped more eggs and ham on top of what she'd been eating, and shoveled it from there to his mouth. "I gots plenty ways to get money," he said around a mouthful.

"Dice and cards," Jeremiah said scornfully. "I suppose you've got a fighting chicken tucked away somewhere." Billy grinned at him and belched. Jeremiah tossed his crumpled napkin on the table and rose.

"What's matter, brother? You ain't eating?"

"I'm not hungry anymore."

Jeremiah's walk down Bull Street to Denmark Vesey's small single house was depressing that morning. It was a street of mixtures and melding, black and white on the cobblestones without distinction, except when a black man stepped aside to let a white man by, a white man who didn't notice him and wouldn't, unless he failed to step aside.

Mansions stood next to modest houses, rich whites living next to black artisans and shopkeepers. Even the poorest house was painted and kept up. Denmark said the whites

insisted on it, so they wouldn't have to look at poverty.
Denmark said the only reason the whites let blacks live
near them was so their servants would be close to hand.

The thought of Leonie living in one of those houses,
trudging each day before dawn to a white man's house,
bowing and scraping and curtseying, burned at him. Yes,
sir. No, ma'am. Right away, ma'am. I'm sorry, sir. I'll do
better next time. Home again, bone-weary in the stark
moonlight. And the only hope of escape—some white
man looking on her curve of hip and swell of breast, putting her in rooms with fine clothes that she'd take off for
him so he could . . . . No! In the name of God, if there
was a God, there had to be something else for Leonie.

He turned into the small garden of 20 Bull lost in his
own fears. A shape reared up in front of him; the breath
caught in his throat and he threw his hands up defensively.

"What the matter, Jeremiah? You done look like you
seen a haunt."

The shape resolved into a skinny, balding black man,
his seamed face fitting any age from forty to sixty. William
Paul didn't know his age himself, closer than five years.
Jeremiah let his hands fall, and took a shaky breath.

He'd recruited William himself, six years earlier. Denmark had given him hell about it; William was just too
much of a coward to do more than stand watch in Vesey's
yard during meetings or sometimes run a message.

"I'm all right," Jeremiah said finally. "I was just lost in
my thoughts."

"Oh. I understand." It was clear he didn't, but he
wouldn't question Jeremiah. He almost worshipped the
man who'd told him one day he could be free. "Jeremiah,
I carved a comb. Out a piece o' turtle shell. You reckon
maybe it be all right if I give it to Leonie?"

"I'm sure it will. You come on by the house this evening, and we'll have a cup of coffee. You can give it to her
then. I know she'll love it."

"I reckon. You know, I likes makin'g them little things
for her. I wish there was something I could make you. You
the onliest one'll even talk to me more than sayin' 'go
there' or 'do that'." He hung his head. "They don't like

me 'cause I scares easy."

"There's nothing to be frightened of," Jeremiah said gently. "Are the others here, yet?"

Williams' grin returned. "Yes. I hear he got him another one." Vesey's appetite for women was a source of amazement and a certain humor tinged with pride among his followers.

"Think he'll marry this one? How many wives does he have, anyway? Five? Six?"

"Seven, I hear. He won't marry this one, though. She be free, so I hear tell. He don't never marry none as ain't slave. Don't have to worry 'bout them complaining about nothin' that way."

Jeremiah frowned. Vesey orated often, long and loud, about his wives being slaves, about the fact that his children, the children of slave mothers, would themselves be slaves. He always explained why he had to marry again: because his last wife had been carried upcountry, or because her master turned him away, but he always had a slave wife, and sometimes two or three, close by. Lately Jeremiah had begun to grow almost as cynical as William. Perhaps Denmark needed those slave wives. Then he could point to them and tell other slaves that he wasn't just a freeman living high on the hog. He was oppressed, too.

Jeremiah puffed his cheeks out disgustedly. He was getting as bad as any of them. Do whatever's needed, do anything, use anybody. He thought of Leonie. Bad as the rest or not, for her he'd do what was needed.

"You keep a close watch, William."

He crossed the long, dim porch. The front door was unlatched; a murmur of voices drew him to the parlor door. He opened it and stepped in.

Six sweaty, anxious men jerked toward the door, some half-rising before they froze. Only Denmark's face, fine featured and pale as most whites' beneath a graying cap of kinky curls, was calm.

"You're late, Jeremiah," Vesey said. As if his words had confirmed Jeremiah's identity, the others sank back one by one.

"Sorry." He took a seat beside Peter Poyas. He'd

known the stocky ship's carpenter for twenty years.

A stranger was sitting up beside Denmark, a stooped, emaciated fellow with bushy whiskers as black as his face. He shifted constantly, quick, darting movements broken by moments of absolute stillness. He turned suddenly to stare back at Jeremiah, coal-black eyes with only a thin rim of white. His face was expressionless, then suddenly flashed into incredible malevolence. As quickly as it came, the evil was gone, leaving only a bushy-whiskered old man. Jeremiah was shaken in spite of himself.

"Now that Jeremiah's here," Vesey said, "we can get down to business." He opened a bible in his broad hands, and raised his voice in the ringing thunder of a hellfire preacher. "And the children of Israel sighed by reason of the bondage, and they cried, and their cry came up unto God by reason of the bondage. And God heard their groaning, and God remembered his covenant with Isaac, and with Jacob. God make it so with us. Amen."

"Amen," the others echoed. Except the strange old man, Jeremiah noticed.

"To begin with," Vesey went on in a more normal, if deep, voice, "I mean to introduce Jack Pritchard." He indicated the whiskered man. "He's a good man for our cause." Jeremiah tried to remember where he'd heard the name. "As to our purpose—"

Jeremiah snapped his fingers. "Jack Pritchard. Gullah Jack!"

Vesey watched Jeremiah anxiously, Pritchard defiantly.

"The Gullah Society," Ned Bennett said in a strangled whisper, and Gullah Jack's eyes swiveled to take him in, and Rolla Bennett next to him. Ned was dark and muscular, Rolla slight and coffee-colored. They weren't related, taking their common last name from their owner, Governor Thomas Bennett.

"Good you know the society," Jack said, getting to his feet. Despite his shortness and his stoop, he seemed to loom. "Good you know you don't cross—"

"I ain't afraid of no society," Peter Poyas barked.

Jeremiah found himself able to speak again. "You're a fraud, Jack. You've convinced the ignorant you have some kind of powers, that you're a witchdoctor, but there's nobody here afraid of you, or your society." He knew he was lying. Except for himself, Poyas and Vesey, there was terror on every face. A belief in magic, or fear of a knife in the back from a society member who did believe, it made little difference. He hurried on before he could begin thinking about knives and how many society members there were rumored to be. "We don't need your kind, Jack."

"You not afraid of Jack?" Jack fumbled in his coat pocket, and despite himself Jeremiah's palms began to sweat. "I show you be afraid, damn so."

"Jack!" Vesey shouted. "Jeremiah! Both of you shut up and listen. Jack, damn it, stop whatever it is you're doing. Do you hear me?"

Jack turned angry eyes on Vesey. Slowly the scowl faded from his chameleon face, replaced by a broad grin. "Sure, Denmar'. I ain' hurt him."

Vesey faced them, hands high, some of the preacher showing through. "Listen to me, all of you. Listen to me carefully. We've come too far to turn back. Too far to let our dream go glimmering. We need Jack. We need the society. Scores of men will do whatever they're told, carry messages, obey orders, without wondering what's in the message or why they have to do a certain thing, just because the order came from Gullah Jack." It was the first time since Jeremiah's first outburst that the full name had been said. Vesey seemed to sense his mistake, sense the chill going through them. His voice took on an edge of anger. "Do you want to give it all up now? You care that little for men who wear chains, men with the same skin as yours? Cowards! Go on! Run! Hide! Grovel for the white man! Lick his boots! Let him take your women! Maybe he'll throw you an old coat!" He stopped, panting, sweat dripping from his face. Their eyes clung to him. He put their worst shames and fears into words, but they couldn't stop listening. They wanted more. He was cool water in their desert lives, and if they had to take bile with it occasionally, they thought it small price. "Well? Why aren't you leaving?" Jack stirred uneasily.

"None of us would abandon you, Denmark," Jeremiah

said quietly. "Good God. You taught me to read and write."

"None of us is going," Rolla said. "But that Gullah Soc—" His eyes bulged as Gullah Jack flashed a demon's grimace. As quickly as it came, it was gone, the grin back in place. Rolla's mouth hung open; he snapped it shut, and hurriedly wiped sweat from his face.

"Denmark," Jeremiah said, "we don't need the Gullah Society for what we plan. There are enough of us already." The plan, painfully worked out, was simple. On a night yet to be determined, a ship would be seized in the harbor, and two hundred slaves from the city would board it, to sail with the morning tide before they were discovered. Such a mass escape would make every newspaper in the world, dramatizing their cause for all to see.

To his surprise Vesey smiled a lazy smile. "Do you know how many ships sail on an average morning? I'll tell you. Five. Ten. Why have one shipload escape when we can free ten shiploads? Imagine it. Two thousand slaves with their bonds broken at one time."

"Madness," Rolla Bennett breathed.

"That's the word," Jeremiah agreed. "If we tried to reach half that many slaves in this city, we'd all end up dead."

"Ah," Vesey smiled. "But we don't get them all from the city. That's where Jack's messengers come in. They can reach the plantation slaves."

"You're going to bring that many people into Charleston in *one night?*"

"It just takes timing, Jeremiah. Everything must be timed perfectly."

"Nothing is ever timed perfectly. Something always goes wrong."

"These men will do it perfectly, because they'll die as slaves if they don't."

"The ships," Jeremiah said desperately. "We can't take that many ships."

"If we can take one and hold it all night, we can take five. Or ten." Vesey's voice was calm, powerful. He radiated confidence.

Jeremiah looked around. The others all sat watching. Abruptly he realized they were leaving it to him and Vesey. If he could argue Vesey out of it, it was done with. If not . . . . But depsite himself, he was half convinced. It was insane, but it was grand. Still . . . . "We can't be sure how many ships will be sailing," he said slowly. "Not in time enough. Sometimes there aren't even five ships. I've seen days with three, or even two. So it all falls back to finding enough for two. That's the most we can count on. That might be manageable."

"We'll find two thousand," Vesey said. "We'll wait till there are as many ships as we need."

"Wait! We make that many people wait more than a day, two at most, and we'll have fifty men boasting to their neighbors about how they're escaping, and another fifty so scared they'll run to the whites for protection."

Vesey grinned delightedly, as if Jeremiah had come exactly where he wanted him. "Not this time. No one will loosen a lip."

Jeremiah knew Denmark had his perfect answer ready. "Why?"

"Jack, man! Their tongues will shrivel in their mouths if they talk. Society members will recruit them, and his magic will keep them silent." He stepped closer to Jeremiah, his voice dropping, the words for his ears alone. "Over twenty years we've labored, but the beast still lives, and thrives. The beast must be killed, and we must use anybody, any means, to kill it. Think, Jeremiah. No more threes and fours. Two thousand people free. Think of it!"

It was madness, but oh, God, it was grand. "I almost think you could do it," he whispered.

"I *can* do it. *We* can do it." Jeremiah felt the power of the man enfolding him. Denmark raised his voice. "Believe in me, Jeremiah. Believe in what we're doing. That's all I've ever asked."

"I do believe, Denmark. God help me, but I do." The others' tension drained away palpably. "My God," he laughed suddenly, "if you manage this . . . no, when you do it, you'll put your name in the history books."

Vesey dismissed the idea with a snort. "I don't care

about history books." He strode back to the front of the room. "Peter, where's that map? I'll show you how we're going to stand fat Charleston on its ear."

IV

"Mr. and Mrs. Robert Carver Fallon," the butler announced over the sound of violins playing something French. "And Miss Charlotte Fallon Holtz."

The Alyard mansion had a ballroom, but the gaiety spread across the black-and-white marble floor of the entry hall to a large drawing room on the other side, its doors flung open. Dancing women spun and dipped, their dresses a pastel garden in spring. The men were stiffer, the black of their tight suits almost overpowered by the eye-aching white of shirts and gloves, high collars and intricately knotted ties. The couples danced together, yet they danced separately, fingers laid gently on wrist, sometimes not even eyes touching, as they wove their intricate figures.

Around the walls stood men red-faced from too much wine and laughter at their own jokes, and women flushed from dancing and enjoyment, their voices competing with the violins, violas, and cellos.

Slim, redhaired Anne Alyard rushed to greet them. "My dear Moira, how splendid you look. That green silk is just wonderful for you! And Charlotte. Oh, my dear, if you only knew what I'd give to have your pale, clear skin. Now I have someone for you to meet, Charlotte. You, too, of course, Moira, but especially you, Charlotte. I'm sure Robert will excuse us. Won't you, Robert? Of course you will."

The three women moved away, arms linked, heads close, their murmurs fading into the music that filled the house. Robert took a drink from a passing servant and wandered through the crowd, nodding to this casual acquaintance, speaking to that one, kissing a hand or two.

Across the room he saw someone he wanted to speak to: John Calhoun. He had known him since Calhoun was a gangling boy come to study law in the offices of Robert's friend, Langdon Cheves. Though two months shy of forty, he had been Secretary of State under Monroe for five years. With him was William Johnson, a Justice of the United States Supreme Court and William Mortimore, a Charleston merchant, both long-time friends. Unfortunately the group included Colonel Robert Hayne and James Hamilton, Intendant of Charleston. Calhoun and Johnson claimed Hayne was basically sound, but his friendship with Hamilton marked him in Robert's mind. Hamilton was an opportunist of the first water, and there were few who didn't know it.

"Ah, Robert," Calhoun said as he approached. "Join us." Calhoun's dark hair, touched with gray at the temples, was thrown back from his high forehead in a mane, and his deep-set eyes were merry.

"Delighted," Robert said, as Johnson and Mortimore added their urgings. Hayne's nod was barely civil, and Hamilton's smile was a grimace. "Not dancing, gentlemen?"

Johnson lifted his eyes to heaven mournfully. "In a just world, Robert, only women would be allowed to dance."

"Then this isn't a just world," Calhoun laughed. "If Robert's wife meets the rest of our wives, we'll all be dancing the gavotte whether we will or not."

The others laughed at that, Hamilton more heartily than the rest. The Intendant was a tall man, of medium build, with a long nose and wide mouth.

"We were speaking of Florida," Hamilton said to Robert when the laughter was done. "Washington is finally getting around to putting in a civil government." His manner was so smooth Robert was sure he was being led into a trap.

He spoke in what he hoped was an offhand fashion. "Now that Florida's bought, it's late for discussion. Let's talk of something more interesting. For instance, I'm backing Khamsin at three to one against all comers during Race Week.''

"I'll take five hundred of that," Mortimore said in his soft Virginia drawl. His long face rarely broke into a smile, but there was always a twinkle in his dark eyes. "I'm sorry, Robert, but three to one? I have Sea Dancer entered, you know.''

"I know, Glenn. But that won't save your five hundred.''

"What kind of name is that for a horse," Johnson grumbled. "Khamsin. Some sort of foreign name, eh?''

"Arabic," Robert answered. "It's a hot desert wind in North Africa.''

Hamilton's smoothness had slipped as the conversation slid away from him. "Just a moment, Fallon. You talked enough against buying Florida. Why so reticent now? Florida will be a glowing jewel in our Southern crown.''

"Florida will be a glowing nothing," Robert said. "Monroe gave up our claims on land south to the Rio Bravo del Norte for a useless spit of coral. And mark my words, the land the Spanish call Texas will be valuable one day.''

"Valuable!" Hayne laughed. His face was heavy, with a broad nose and thick lips. "Half oceans of sparse grass, the rest equally divided between desert and jungle. Why, there's gold in Florida.''

"Then the Spanish have been keeping it a good secret," Robert said drily. "There's nothing in Florida but Indians and runaway slaves.''

"You don't believe we have a right to recover our property?" Hayne asked. His voice was smooth and dark.

Abruptly Robert understood. If Robert were to argue his opposition to slavery, and thus to retaking runaway slaves, Calhoun would have to publicly oppose him. Anything else would be disaster for a Southern politician. The entire thing was to force a wedge between him and Calhoun, malicious mischief meant simply to strike at him. A glance at Calhoun showed he understood as well. His look asked Robert not to press it.

"Fifteen millions in tax money," Robert said carefully,

"is a damnable amount to pay for a worthless piece of land. Then, too, there'll be the expense of putting down the Indians. Not to mention dead soldiers."

Hayne snorted. "General Jackson will put those Seminoles in their place quickly enough."

"I doubt that," Calhoun said with a grateful smile to Robert, "Jackson will bury his ambitions in the Florida swamps."

Hamilton's eyes flickered uncertainly. Hayne didn't seem to realize the conversation had been diverted. "Why, Jackson will finish it in a year with a few hundred Regulars and some of those backwoods militia of his."

"The Spanish had more than two hundred years," Calhoun replied, "and the situation gets worse by the day."

Hamilton shot Hayne a warning glance, but the Colonel pressed on. "You sound as if you agree with Fallon, that Florida isn't worth it."

"It isn't," Calhoun said shortly.

Hamilton grabbed Hayne's sleeve. "I think I see your wife beckoning, Colonel. You'll excuse us, Mr. Calhoun, Justice Johnson?"

Hayne blinked. "What? I don't see . . . oh, very, well. If you'll excuse me, gentlemen?" The room milled as dancers left the floor and others took their place. The two men melted into the crowd as the music took up again.

"Hamilton," Calhoun spat, "is a pisspot, willing to let any man who'll carry him along use him. I wish to hell Hayne could see him for what he is."

"Easy, my friend," Johnson murmured. "Public figures are not allowed the emotions of ordinary men."

"If I can't speak my mind among friends," Calhoun began, then shook his leonine head. "You're right, of course."

"It will go no further," Mortimore said. "I assure you."

"I'm not sure I understood what you meant about General Jackson's ambitions," Robert said. To his surprise Calhoun studied him before replying.

"You know Jackson?" Calhoun asked finally.

"I've met him. I served under him at New Orleans."

"Yes. I'd forgotten that. What do you think of him?"

"He's the best general this country's seen since the Revolution," Robert said promptly.

"But as President?" Calhoun prodded.

Robert hesitated, remembering the hawkfaced, autocratic man who brooked no opposition. "A nation isn't an army," he said slowly. "I'm not sure he realizes that."

"Ah," Johnson beamed, like a teacher whose pupil has gotten a difficult question.

"You believe General Jackson aspires to the White House?" Mortimore asked.

"It's taken as a fact in Washington," Calhoun said. "And that will add the West to the sectional struggle. Three-way fights are always worse than two-way. God send an end to it."

"You ask for a perfect world," Johnson said sadly. "There will always be sectionalism. Always."

"But surely," Mortimore said, "the answer is in the Missouri question, the compromise. Free states formed from the Western lands might make their own section, but the slave states will surely follow the rest of us."

"If there are any more slave states beyond Missouri," Robert said. "The right to say whether a state is free or slave now lies with Congress. They can repeal the compromise tomorrow. And I can't see the Northern states sitting by while the South gains the upper hand."

"Not many people see that side of the compromise," Calhoun said. "And far from letting us gain the upper hand, the North wants to keep us subjected."

"Hold on," Mortimore exclaimed. "We're hardly subjected."

"Aren't we?" Johnson asked. The old man sighed heavily. "Have you looked at the ships that come to your docks? How many are out of a Southern port? What goes out of Charleston? Cotton, a little rice, less tobacco. You can count the manufactories in this state on your fingers. And the same is true for most other Southern states. So long as we have nothing but agriculture, the South is a captive market for the North, and they can do with us as they will."

"So the answer lies with Fallon's foundries and steamships?"

"It does," the old judge agreed. "In part, it does."

"Another part," Robert said, "lies in getting rid of the slaves."

"You don't ask much," Mortimore said drily.

"The price of them is too high," Robert insisted, "and you know it. Forget morality, if you will. Buying slaves, raising slaves, caring for slaves too old to work, all take money. That's what we have too little of. We have credit bulging in our pockets because English and Yankee mills want our cotton, but if all the debts were called in the whole state, maybe the entire South would be bankrupt."

"You understand a great deal," Calhoun said, "but you don't understand it all. Do you think anyone in this state will give up his slaves willingly? The only way would be by command from Washington, and I'll fight that as long as I have breath. The precedent of it would make the South no more than a Northern colony. And that would bring civil war."

"Surely not," Mortimore laughed. "The very idea is ridiculous."

"Unfortunately not," Johnson said. "Think on it, man. How would it be done? Sell them? Where? Simply turn them free? Most of the men in this room would be paupered by that."

"The children could be freed," Robert said. "Let it end with the people already slaves. That would satisfy—"

"That would satisfy no one," Johnson broke in. "A Panglossian solution that would anger everyone, and leave everyone feeling cheated. It might be the fastest way to disaster of all."

"Then how do we get out of it?" Robert said.

Johnson shook his head. "I'll be damned if I know." He gulped his brandy and grimaced.

"All I know," Calhoun said, "is that the South shall not be crushed, and this nation shall not be torn apart. There must be some accommodation, some middle ground we can all live with. There has to be. We shall find it."

"Gentlemen?" said a low, musical voice. A dark-eyed young woman laid a confiding hand on Robert's arm. Her pale lavender dress was daringly cut, a lace-edged diamond exposing the inside curves of rounded breasts. She turned her beautiful face—a face a sculptor might title classic beauty, Robert thought—to each of them. "I do hate to interrupt when your faces are so long. I know that means your talk is of the most important." The stranger's words had a slight French accent. "But I shall simply die if I cannot speak to Mr. Fallon right this moment. Alone?"

Calhoun hid a smile, while Mortimore made no effort to hide his. Johnson, however, bowed as gravely as he ever did in a court. "I'm sure, my dear, that your claims take precedence over ours. Take him away. But be careful, for he is a veritable rogue."

She dropped a curtsey to the jurist. "I will be ever so careful, sir. Come, Mr. Fallon." She took a firmer grip on his arm.

"Tomorrow?" Robert said to Calhoun.

"Yes, tomorrow. I have to get back to Washington soon."

The girl pulled him away and into the flowing pattern of dancers. He sidestepped down the floor, facing her at arms' length, the tips of her fingers resting on his palm. Her smile was radiant. "*Mon Dieu!* I do believe you do not remember me."

"I'm afraid I don't," he said ruefully. They spun and began to sidestep the other way.

Her laughter was glass bells in a breeze. "That is because we have never met. You would be surprised how many men would have claimed to remember. I was testing you."

"I'd be surprised if you knew enough men to make a judgement. You can't be more than—what?—twenty? And do you realize you haven't even told me your name?"

They had reached a point in the dance where she curtsied and he bowed deeply. When they straightened he realized that her face had changed. The coquetry, the fluttering foolishness was gone. "I am Lucille Gautier," she said, and the patterns of the dance spun them apart, to opposite sides of the room.

He studied her as best he could between the moving dancers. She offered the same smile to every man who took her hand and passed to the next. No, not quite the same smile. The smile she'd given to him was warmer. Damn Moira, anyway.

Lucille flowed back to him, her eyes sparkling on his face. "May I call you Robert? I know such a great deal about you that I feel I have that right. Let me see. I know there is a dragon on your left forearm, put there by heathen Chinese. I know you have an ivory-hilted sword you took from the governor of Derna, in North Africa. I know you enjoy women, and cards, and horse-racing, but not dice, or cockfighting, or bear-baiting."

"You've studied me. To what purpose?"

"I did not study you at all. Do you not remember what I said in my note? Dominique You told me all about you. You really should learn to remember the contents of *billets-doux*."

The dance was going to separate them again. Instead, Robert took her hand and, when they reached the point where the couples separated and doubled back, they continued on off the dance floor. He procured two glasses of wine from a waiter and found a place for them against the wall.

"Why would Dominique tell you about me? And why this . . . well, pursuit, for lack of a better word. I'm old enough to be your father, girl, and don't think it doesn't hurt to say that."

"Lá! Dom is always ready to tell a girl a story about daring deed. About you, Robert. Dominique You is . . . colorful." Her slender fingers caressed the stem of her wineglass in a vaguely disturbing way. "I like colorful men."

Robert laughed. "That was long ago and far away. I'm a merchant, getting older and less colorful by the day."

"Some men never get old," she said. "I was born in New Orleans, but when my father died, my grandmother took me to Europe to live. London and Venice, Rome and Vienna, Paris and Florence. When my grandmother died I went back to New Orleans, to visit the city of my birth." She sighed. "It was disappointing, after Europe, Just another provincial American town. But there was Dom. He was not provincial. And you, you are also not provincial. I found I could take passage for Europe as easily from here as from there, so here I am. To take a look at you." She lowered her eyes, running a fingertip around the rim of her glass.

"I'm hardly a natural wonder," he said drily. "Now that you've had your look, what do you intend to do?"

"I will remain in Charleston for a time. Perhaps we can have a glass of wine together from time to time."

"I'm a married man," he said gently. "In Europe it may be different, but in Charleston married men don't meet with unmarried young ladies."

"Has no woman ever told you that you are indeed a natural wonder, Robert Fallon?" Before he could speak she set down her wine and tugged him toward the dance floor, where another set was beginning. "Come, let us dance."

He saw Moira in passing, with Mortimore, with Calhoun, even with Judge Johnson, though how she'd coaxed him onto the floor he couldn't imagine. Charlotte seemed more interested in ratafia than in dancing, or perhaps it was in the tall young man who kept fetching it for her. A Pinckney, Robert thought, or a Simons.

Lucille was aware of her own beauty. As she moved with him across the floor, floating to his touch like down on the air, laying her hand on his wrist, stroking his cheek with a laugh, so quickly he almost wasn't certain he had been touched, he realized that her movements, while graceful and discreet, consciously showed off the curve of her breasts, seeming large for her slimness, a slender arm and delicate wrist, her tiny waist above the womanly swell of her hips. Fully clothed and fully decorous, she was as tantalizing as another woman would have been naked and abandoned.

"Robert?" Moira's touch on his arm made him start. He had been standing against the wall, he realized, waiting for Lucille Gautier to finish dancing with some young buck so he could lead her out again. "Are you all right? You seem preoccupied."

"I'm fine." He managed a laugh. "You know I'm not much for parties." He saw that Charlotte was behind her. "Are you two ready to go? Finished with your young Pinckney, Charlotte?"

"Simons, Uncle Robert," she said shyly. "Peter Simons." A flush rose in her pale cheeks. "And he's not mine. He's just . . . brought me ratafia."

Moira eyed her shrewdly. "He'll do quite nicely, dear. And I didn't notice him taking ratafia to anyone else." Charlotte's flush deepened, and Moira smiled. "It's all right, child. I won't be embarrassing you any more. Yes, Robert, we're ready to go."

They gathered wraps and cloaks, and made their good-byes to the Alyards while their coach was being brought round. The horses' breath made white plumes in the night, and their hooves had a chill ring on the cobble-stones. Robert settled back next to Moira. Charlotte sat across from them.

"Who was she?" Moira asked quietly.

"She?" Robert said. "Who?"

"The young girl you danced with eight times." She flicked a glance at Charlotte and dropped her voice still lower. "The one who walked like she had no clothes on. Who is she?"

"I suppose you mean Lucille Gautier," he said. "I suppose I did dance with her two or three times."

"Eight times."

"For God's sake," he growled, "you're always after me for not dancing. Tonight I danced."

She retreated into an angry silence—more for Charlotte's sake, he was sure, that anything else—and he sighed for the long night. God, but everything was mounting up. Lopes. The business. Edward. Now this. Lucille Gautier, he decided firmly, was one problem he would do without.

V

Moira counted the knives in the ornate knife-box one more time, then locked it with one of the keys at her belt. Robert objected to the box, but after the slave revolt in Camden six years earlier she put every knife in the house in it. None came out without her knowing who had it and when it would be returned. Their servants might be free blacks, but she would take no chances. Hadn't an entire village of runaways been found near Georgetown only six months earlier? There were reports free blacks had sold them food and clothing.

She began her morning rounds of the house in a good mood. Albert was overseeing two of the younger maids polishing silver. Not the best silver—that was entrusted only to him—but the everyday. Another maid was waxing the sweeping staircase that arced down into the entry hall, while the last was helping the housekeeper turn bedding.

In the kitchen—a brick building separated from the main house for fire protection—she frowned at the sight of Chloe beating batter in a bowl, the half-healed scar pink on the brown of her face. Edward had been good for two weeks since that. She was half hoping it had frightened him enough to straighten him out, and half afraid it would. He was a child of evil, no matter how angelic he could look when he wanted to, and his very presence made her stomach twist. That the things he did were caused by the taint on him, she had no doubt, but she couldn't find it in herself to forget it, or forgive him for it, because he reminded her of Robert's part in that taint. Were he suddenly to seem just another boy, no more destructive or violent than the next, Robert would never be forced to send him away. Her morning's good mood was abruptly gone.

"All you gals line up!" came a shouted growl from outside, and Hannah, the cook, banged through the door, her fat cheeks gleaming like oiled coal. She waved a wooden spoon in one ham-sized hand. It wasn't used for stirring, but as a symbol of authority, and to smack the bottoms of kitchen maids who caught her displeasure. Chloe and the other two kitchen maids scurried to put down what they were working on and form a line, big eyes mesmerized by the waving spoon.

"Ma'am," Hannah said to Moira, dropping as much of a curtsey as her bulk would allow. "I gots to get these here gals straight. Every last dried apple we got done walk off. And I going to find out who done it." The last was delivered with a savage swipe of the spoon that brought low moans from the maids.

"Perhaps that won't be necessary," Moira said. "I'm sure these girls will tell us what they know. Won't you?"

"Don't know nothing about no apples, ma'am," Chloe said, not taking her eyes off Hannah's spoon. The stout girl next to her only shook her head, and the third, tall slender Iris, stared straight at the floor, mumbling.

"What was that, Iris?" Moira said. "I didn't hear."

"Ma'am," Hannah said, "you go on up to the big house. I bring this Iris girl up in a little bit, and she say everything she know."

Iris threw one terrified look at the massive cook and spoke out loudly. "I doesn't know nothing 'bout no apple. I just seed young mast' Edward going down there three, four time is all."

"Master Edward ain't take no three bushel apple," Hannah said ominously. "You Iris girl, and the rest of you, get on to the storeroom. I find out about them apple."

Moira clapped her hands as the kitchen maids began sniffling. "All of you be quiet. Hannah, I want to talk to Edward before you do anything. If I find he has nothing to do with this . . . ." She felt sick at the shining reprieve in the kitchen maids' faces. For all she knew, one of them had stolen the apples. She could barely admit to herself that she wanted it to be Edward.

"Ma'am," said Hannah, "what that boy goin' to do with so many apple? These girl, they—"

"No, Hannah. No." She couldn't say any more.

She rushed back to the main house. In the front drawing room she collapsed on a sofa. Stealing dried apples, even three bushels of them, was a small thing compared to the commotion he usually raised. But it would be a sign that he hadn't changed. God, it was horrible. She wanted him gone so badly that she wanted him to break things, to hurt people. She just wanted him out of her house.

Albert coughed diffidently in the doorway. She didn't raise her head. "Yes, Albert? What is it?"

"There's a note, ma'am," he said hesitantly. "For you. It was brought by a street urchin, ma'am. One of those boys in dirty rags who hang around the docks."

"And it's for me, Albert?"

"Yes, ma'am. He said distinctly, for Mrs. Robert Fallon, ma'am."

Taking the paper, neither expensive nor cheap, she broke the large lump of blue wax sealing it. She read the first few lines.

"You may go, Albert. I don't want to be disturbed for a time." She was astonished at her control, at the calmness of her voice.

When he was gone she opened the note again. The letters were made from straight lines, as if the writer had used a ruler to disguise the hand.

TEN YEARS AGO MOIRA FALLON AND CATHERINE FALLON HOLTZ MURDERED JUSTIN FOURRIER. THEY THREW HIS BODY IN THE RIVER DURING A HURRICANE. SOMEONE SAW IT. IF MOIRA FALLON IS WILLING TO TALK, SHE SHOULD GO TO THE FISH MARKET AT THREE O'CLOCK AND BUY THREE GROUPER.

She crumpled the paper savagely. No one could have seen the killing. Not murder, she thought. Self-defense. The memory of the night still brought nightmares. She had stepped into the drawing room to find Catherine, naked, held at gunpoint by a Justin Fourrier who had left the bounds of sanity. Moira was to have been next.

It had been she who wielded the heavy silver candlestick that crushed his skull. God, his blood had been so red. She'd wept, but it had been she who stiffened Catherine's backbone when she discovered Fourrier was dead and panic had her by the throat. Charleston thought Fourrier a respectable man. At best discovery meant the destruction of their reputations, a smearing of the Fallon name. There were always more than enough who would make their own stories to fit the innuendo. She had pleaded, bullied, driven Catherine to help her fetch a mule from the stable, while a hurricane beat at Charleston's rooftops, to help her take the body to the docks.

Justin Fourrier's corpse had been disposed of by tides and the harbor sharks. But a blackmailer soon appeared. Jasper Trask, an oily slaver. He had been watching their house that night, watching Fourrier for his own purposes, but he was quick to see where his profit lay. The nightmare hadn't ended until Trask died at the hands of a confederate later that year.

Now it seemed it hadn't ended at all. But who? And why so cautious? Trask's cronies would not have waited so long.

A deafening shriek echoed down the hall, followed closely by the sound of china smashing. Immediately a babble arose, maids' voices overlapping one another, and in the midst Edward's voice, protesting. Moira rushed out.

At the back of the entry hall, Albert knelt amid shards of crockery, carefully feeling the arm of a maid who lay moaning. The other maids stood in a knot, rags held to their noses, all talking and none listening. A heavy, stomach-wrenching smell hung in the air.

"What in the name of heaven?" she gasped.

"Chamberpots, ma'am," the butler said, rising. "I told the girl not to bring down more than one at a time, but she had three when . . . ." He gestured helplessly.

Edward stuck his head from behind one of the maids, and Moira started. His entire face was red. Rouge, she realized. Her rouge.

"Ma'am," Albert said, "I believe Patience's arm is broken."

"Oh, my God," she sighed. "Edward—"

"I didn't mean to hurt her, auntie," he broke in. "I was just playing red Indians." He waved a massive hunting knife.

The knife was too much. It was all too much. She couldn't cope with this boy, not him and a blackmailer, too. She snatched the knife, and it was all she could do not to shake it at him. He took a wary step back from her anyway.

"You never mean to do anything, do you?" she spat. "But someone always gets hurt, don't they? And you smile your smile and no one knows you for the little monster you are. You'll kill someone one fine day, and what will you do then? Smile? Say you didn't mean it?"

"What's going on here?" Robert called from the front door.

She whirled on him, stopping him in his tracks with the glitter in her eye. She shook the knife in the air as if it were bloody evidence. "He's broken Patience's arm! He's smashed chamberpots all over the rug! Good Turkey carpet that we'll never get clean! The smell will be in here for weeks! He's smeared my rouge all over his face, stolen apples, run through the house waving his great knife. It's a wonder no one was stabbed. I'll not wait till he murders us in our beds, Robert Fallon. Do you hear me? I want him out of this house. I want him out! Out!"

His face was as icy as the harbor wind. "I thought I had come to sit quietly with my wife before dinner. The foundry with all the furnaces going is more peaceful than this. I will not be shouted at in my own house. Good day, madam." He bowed stiffly and as quickly as that was gone, the slam of the door behind him ringing down the hall.

Moira took an involuntary step after him, protest and plea half formed on her lips. She had to tell him about the blackmail. She needed him. The hunting knife dropped unnoticed to the carpet.

"Get a doctor for Patience," she ordered dully. As she spoke she walked slowly toward the drawing room, not looking at them. "Clean up this mess as best you can, and do something about the smell. Take Master Edward up to his bedroom and get him clean. He'll be remaining there except for lessons until further notice. Oh, yes. I'll need someone to go with me to the fish market. I want to be there by three o'clock."

"The fish market, ma'am?" Albert was plainly surprised. "The best fish go early, ma'am. There won't be much left but—"

Moira shut the drawing-room door behind her, cutting him off. Then she began to cry.

VI

Robert stormed out of the house in a cold rage. A chill breeze and the gray damp of the just-finished rain suited him well. He walked the cobblestones unheeding of the splashes of passing coaches and wagons.

What did she think she was doing, shouting at him like that, waving a knife like a madwoman, issuing commands? Did she think he'd get rid of the boy if she shouted loud enough, if the boy broke enough dishes or ruined enough rugs?

A ragged urchin, pale face obscured by dirt, darted from a protected corner in split boots that were too big anyway. He wore mittens worn through on the palms, and carried a small tray of roasted walnuts. He couldn't have been more than ten.

Robert took a twisted paper of nuts and pressed five dollars into the boy's hand. The urchin stared at the gold piece as if wondering what it was. "I ain't . . . I mean, sir, well, they're a penny," he mumbled.

Robert tucked the spill of nuts into his coat pocket. "Keep it."

The boy's eyes widened, and suddenly he began to run. "Thanks, mister," he called over his shoulder.

Probably afraid he'd change his mind, Robert thought. "Come to Carver's Bridge in the morning," he shouted. "There's a place out of the weather for you."

He subsided, uncertain if the boy had heard or not. That one was too young, but he couldn't see one of the ragged street children without thinking of his other illegitimate son, James. Louise had been a good woman. She'd have cared for him as best she could, but she could have died a month after leaving Charleston. That Martin Caine she married could have abandoned her and her other man's child. The boy himself could have died . . . .

He would have thought Moira would understand.

A passing coach, brasswork shining and leathers polished, drew over toward him, and he moved closer to the side of the street.

"Mr. Fallon." Lucille Gautier put her head out of the coach window, the leather curtain held to one side. A fine shimmering net covered her hair, mocking the coverings other women used to protect themselves from the rain. "Come, Robert. You cannot walk in this damp. You will catch your death." She swung the door open invitingly.

Moira hadn't thought of the damp. What was it Miller had said? He put up with all his wife's faults because she made him change his clothes and warm his feet when he got damp. "Thank you, Miss Gautier."

"Lucille."

"Thank you, Lucille." He settled across from her with a smile. "Perhaps you could drop me at the Bridge."

A blustery wind rocked the coach, whistling round the curtains. Lucille shivered. "No, Robert. This is no day to work in a drafty warehouse. Felipe, my driver, is also my butler. Come to my rooms, and I will have him prepare a hot toddy, and you can put your feet up in front of a fire."

"Your rooms," he said doubtfully.

"Your wife should not have let you come out in this. She should have made you sit in front of the fire with your pipe."

He hesitated, looking at her smiling face. There would be no smiles at home. Moira would have her back up, and no matter how much he tried, so would he. The night would be spent in bitterness and recriminations.

"I'd be pleased to have one of Felipe's hot toddies," he said.

Lucille knocked on the roof and the carriage moved forward.

The wind whipped off the Cooper River carrying hints of ice. It picked up droplets from the cobblestones of Queen Street and hurled them as half-frozen slush at the handful of shoppers in the long, open shed of the fish market. The shoppers were all black at this late hour, when prices came down. Among the sellers were a few whites, most looking as if thoughts of packing up were close, as the need for a sale warred with having to sell to blacks.

Moira walked through the market with her back as rigid as if she were going to her own execution. Lead weights in the hem of her cloak held it against the clawing wind. One mittened hand held her hood in place, kept her face in shadows.

Close on her heels followed Albert, bundled in a heavy coat with the collar up, one hand on his hat, the other clutching a basket. He had insisted on coming with her himself.

"What kind of fish do you want, ma'am?" he asked.

"Grouper."

"*Grouper*, ma'am? I don't know what Hannah will say if we bring back—"

"I want grouper," she said tiredly.

Two of the fishmongers nearby heard her and dashed forward, a wiry, gray-haired black man reaching her just ahead of a tall, skinny white man.

"Fine grouper," the black man said, thrusting a bulging-eyed gray-green fish forward. "Fine grouper for a fine lady. Twenty cent. Don't get no better, no cheaper."

"Eighteen cents," the white man said. His long nose twitched as he cast a sidelong glance at the other fishmonger. He held his fish by the lower lip so its mouth yawned wide enough to take a man's head.

"Seventeen cent for the fine lady."

"Fifteen cents."

"Fourteen cent for the fine lady."

"Twelve cents," long nose said grimly.

" 'Leven cent for—"

"God damn it," the skinny man shouted. "You can't sell for eleven cents. My children go hungry if I sell for twelve. You're just trying to drive me out!'' His nose twitched, and he suddenly seemed to fold in on himself. His eyes darted, to Albert, to the other fishmongers, everywhere but at Moira. ''I'm sorry, ma'am, for the way I spoke,'' he said hurriedly. ''I . . . I'll pack up my fish and go. There's no need to call the constables.''

''Stop!'' Moira said imperiously as he turned away. ''Why do you think this man is trying to drive you out?''

He kept his head down, studying her from a corner of his eye. ''Because it's true, miss. Whites, free blacks, all being forced out. Soon there won't be any but slaves left fishing, or selling fish.''

'' 'Leven cent?'' the other fishmonger said hopefully.

''Ma'am,'' Albert said, ''you shouldn't be in this cold any longer than necessary. I can finish here if you want to go back to the coach.''

She ignored them, concentrated on the skinny fishmonger. For the moment she could think about this man's troubles and forget her own. ''Are you claiming that the *slaves* are plotting to force you out of fish selling?''

''Yes . . . no . . . it's not the slaves, miss. It's their owners. Some send a boat out just so they'll have fresh fish if it's wanted. They tell the slave to sell whatever isn't needed. The price doesn't matter, high or low, so long as it's all sold. It's just better than throwing them away. Go down the market, where it's all slaves selling, and this grouper's twenty cents. If I set up there, or a free black, then it's eleven cents, or ten, or nine, or whatever it takes to sell lower than me.''

''What's your name?''

''Frank Hill, miss.''

''And how many children have you, Mr. Hill?''

''Four, miss.'' He shifted his feet, wanting to be on his way.

''Tomorrow morning, Mr. Hill, you will come to the Fallon house, on East Bay above the Battery. I may have help for you.''

''Help, miss?''

''I'll expect you at eight o'clock sharp, Mr. Hill.''

"Yes, ma'am." Hope struggled onto his face. "Eight o'clock. I'll be there, ma—"

"I'll take those three grouper. At twenty cents. But don't think that means I'm a soft touch."

"No, ma'am. I wouldn't, ma'am."

"Eight o'clock, Mr. Hill." She handed him the money. "Albert, put those grouper in the basket."

She walked out of the fishmarket as erect as she had walked in, but happier. In making her offer to the fishmonger, in his desperate hope, she had found her courage again.

Whoever was behind this blackmail, she was going to find him, and bury Justin Fourrier once and for all.

Robert laughed as Lucille Gautier pressed him down in a chair before the fireplace and lifted his feet to a leather footstool. Her suite consisted of sitting room and bedchambers for herself and her maid. The coachman and footman were housed above the stables.

"What are you doing?" he protested as she knelt by his feet, tugging off his boots.

She set them near the fire, close enough to dry, but not close enough to scorch. "*Mon Dieu!* You cannot warm your feet in wet boots. I will make the toddies." She patted his feet as she got up.

"Where's Felipe?"

"I told him to go to his room and dry off. Do not worry," she laughed. "I will not poison you."

Indeed, Robert thought later as they sipped the hot mixture of sugar, brandy and water, it was a very good toddy. He had been surprised when she made one for herself—it wasn't a woman's drink—but she said she'd gotten as cold as he. She sat on the edge of the footstool, looking at him through long lashes. It should have seemed demure, but it was far from it.

"Very good," Robert said. He drained the last. "I think I'd better go, now."

"I will take your glass." She bent across him, reaching for the glass, and stopped with her face on a level with his.

Soft brown eyes seemed to fill her face; her lips were parted slightly.

It seemed the most natural thing in the world for him to kiss her, a hand cupping her face. She made only a faint murmured protest as his lips met hers.

He got to his feet, lifting her in his arms as he rose, and her head sank against his chest with a contented sigh. He carried her into the bedchamber and lay her on the big fourposter.

They undressed each other. He smiled gently at the way she fumbled at times with his clothes, seeming proof of her innocence. Her breasts were satin mounds, too large to be held in one hand, yet firm, shimmering slightly as she trembled. He laved a pink nipple with his tongue, and she tangled her fingers in his hair, pulling his head tightly against her breast.

She cried out when he entered her, cried out again later, full of surprise and delight, as she came, and then again still later. His hands and mouth roamed her satin skin till she moved uncontrollably. Her fingers clawed at his shoulders; her heels drummed a tattoo on his back. More than once her small white teeth drew blood on his chest. Through it all her throaty moans continued, for him not to stop, to never stop.

After, he lay on his back, her breasts pressed into his ribs, her head on his shoulder. She shivered, and he drew the feather comforter up over her.

"I will see you again?" she said hesitantly.

He nodded. "I have a house on Montague Street. I rent it, but it's standing empty now." He heard her breath catch. "It's not a big house, but there's a stable with rooms for Felipe and the footman, and I can find you a housekeeper."

"No," she said softly, and he was surprised that his feelings went beyond disappointment. "Felipe will be my butler, and I will find my own housekeeper."

Sudden guilt racked him. Moira was a loving wife, and if he hadn't always been faithful, he'd never actually taken a mistress. They argued, true, but they had always argued. Only now the arguments were all the time. Damn it, a man deserved an oasis of peace in his life.

"Done," he said harshly. "Done."

Moira slept fitfully, tossing and waking to find the other side of the bed still empty. She was up before her maid came to help her dress, and hurried downstairs as soon as the last hook was fastened. Albert was just closing the front door, a note in his hand.

Her breath caught when she saw the note. The blackmailer already? She had no plan.

"From Mr. Fallon, ma'am," Albert said.

Cooling relief enveloped her. He was all right. Almost immediately it was replaced by anger. How dare he remain out all night without so much as one word? She ripped open the note coldly.

Dear Moira,

Please accept my humblest apologies for last night. I encountered Kenneth Graham, and he told me about a problem at the foundry I should see to. We kept men working all night, and I am afraid I did not realize the night was going until it was gone. I must go straight to the Bridge for an important meeting. I will be home for dinner.

                                                              Love,
                                                              Robert

The paper crumpled in her fist. Him and his foundry. He paid more attention to his business than he did to his family. This wasn't the first time he'd rushed off without a word.

Elizabeth came marching in from the back of the house, her mauma trailing at her heels. "Mother," she announced, "you must tell Samuel to saddle Gem. Gem is my pony, and I want to ride him." There was indignation in her violet eyes.

"It's too wet for you to be riding," Moira said.

Hannah appeared with her spoon in one hand and a chicken dangling from the other. "Ma'am, you gots to come back here and look at these chicken. That man done send us scrawny little biddies again."

Elizabeth tugged at Moira's skirt, then put both fists on her hips. "Mother," she said forcefully, "I wish to go riding."

"You take that tone of voice with me, and we'll see if you still want to ride after a taste of a stout switch."

"It would not be proper," Elizabeth said, "for a lady to be beaten."

"I'll remember that when you start acting like a lady," Moira said drily. "Now, Hannah—" Elizabeth tugged at her skirt again. "What is it, girl?"

"May I at least climb up in the hayloft and watch Samuel curry the horses?"

Moira bent low and whispered conspiratorially. "Only so long as your father doesn't catch you. He wants you to be a proper lady, you know."

"I know," Elizabeth said solemnly, and they shared a smile. "Thank you, mother. Come on, Agnes."

As the girl scurried off, towing her mauma, Moira turned back to the cook. "About these chickens—"

This time a knock at the door cut her short. "I'll get it," she said when Albert appeared.

There was a plump woman on the front steps, no more than five years older than Moira, but plain of face and plain of dress. It took Moira a moment to recognize the gray-clad woman as Alice Miller. Her face was set in lines of worry and doubt.

"Mrs. Fallon, I'm sorry to bother you this way. I truly am, but I wouldn't do it unless I had to talk to you. Please?"

"Why, certainly, Mrs. Miller. Won't you come in?"

The woman stood head down, seeming overawed by the surroundings. She darted an anxious glance at Hannah and Albert. "Could I speak to you alone, please?"

"Certainly. Albert, we're not to be disturbed." She led the way into the drawing room and shut the door. "What is it, Mrs. Miller? Is there some trouble?"

Alice Miller wrung her hands. "I thought long and hard on it. I even prayed. I . . . well, I wouldn't want a woman under my roof if she came to me like I'm coming to you, but I had to come. It wouldn't be right, otherwise."

"I don't understand any of this, Mrs. Miller. Why *have* you come?"

"There is, or was, a woman staying at our hotel. My husband's and mine. Her name is Lucille Gautier, or so she says."

"I think I've heard the name." But where? It was only vaguely familiar.

"Yesterday afternoon your husband went up to her rooms. I don't hold with such, truly I don't, but if I caused a scene with him my Ben would have a fit. He didn't come back down until this morning. I went right up there and told her she had to leave. She had the nerve to laugh at me. She said Mr. Fallon was giving her a house."

Moira sat calmly, but every word struck her a blow. She pressed both fists into the pit of her stomach, hard, to keep from fainting or screaming or throwing up.

"Thank you, Mrs. Miller," she whispered. Her voice would go no higher.

"I know you hate me, Mrs. Fallon, and you have cause. Truly you do. But I had to tell you. I had to do what I thought was right. You do understand that, don't you?"

Moira looked at the woman rubbing her hands in a washing motion, her face on the edge of tears. She didn't hate her. "I understand, Mrs. Miller."

"I . . . I suppose I'd better go now."

"Yes," Moira said softly. "I suppose." She barely heard the door open and close.

If someone had asked her, if someone had dared ask her, if Robert were faithful, she'd have said yes without thinking. She wouldn't have thought, she knew, because thinking would have made her doubt that answer. At fifty-two Robert looked a dozen years younger, hard-muscled and handsome, a dashing corsair to set feminine hearts aflutter. But there had never been proof, never the certainty that her suspicions had any basis in fact.

God damn him! She wished she loved him one ounce less so she could kill him. God damn him to hell!

She got up slowly, as if protecting brittle bones. In the hall Hannah still waited with her chicken, and Margaret, the housekeeper, had questions about the use of some damask material. Even Albert was there, waiting his turn. She held her head up, imitating a strength she did not have. Whatever happened, she would not give in.

"Hannah, I'll see you in the kitchen in a few minutes. Margaret . . . ."

VII

Robert peered out the window at the sky above Montague Street before going to the mirror to tie his tie. The first week of April had been all rain, though milder than the icy showers of February. He could walk to his meeting with Oliver Huger, though he wasn't certain if he should keep that appointment. The meeting would be a turning he couldn't reverse.

Lucille shifted on the bed, muttering in her sleep. He smiled ruefully at her tousled reflection in the mirror. He should have been paying more attention to business these past weeks, but Lucille had a fire in her that, once kindled, could not be extinguished.

His eye fell on the letters lying below the mirror. They were why a meeting with Huger was necessary. The lawyer's reports from New Orleans. Esteban Lopes had completed the sale of Robert's Mississippi properties only the day before he died. The gold had been moved to his house, to his private strongroom, and was to have been shipped the next day. No trace of the money could be found. The lawyers minced around the edges of saying Esteban had used the money himself. He had been having business reverses for months. How he could have disposed of so much gold in the one day before he died, they did not suggest.

The biggest surprise, perhaps, was how little they had discovered concerning Esteban's death. Robert had just asked because Thibodeaux was so sketchy. Beyond stiff pronouncements of natural causes the lawyers had run into a brick wall, but they were certain there was more that wasn't being told. Again they did a lawyer's dance around saying anything direct, but their inferences were clear enough. They thought he'd committed suicide.

It all added up to men who didn't know Esteban Lopes —else they'd not have presumed suicide—disguising the fact that they didn't know where the gold was, either.

"Are you off again?" Lucille asked sleepily from her nest in the sheets.

"Yes. I might be back this afternoon."

"Might be. *Zut*! I never know when you are coming. I fix my face and hair, dress in my best, and sit by the fire because you went home to your wife." He put on his coat. Her voice changed, became wheedling. "At least tell me what business takes you from me. Who are you meeting?"

"Oliver Huger."

"A merchant?"

"No, a lawyer. And a banker of sorts." He bent to kiss her. "And that's enough about business. You always ask, and I know you must be bored to tears by it. You don't have to pretend an interest."

"Everything about you fascinates me," she crooned. "I want to know everything."

"Well, suffice it to say this meeting with Huger is important." He laughed. "It might decide whether I can continue to afford you."

She sat up in bed, her breasts swaying slightly. "What do you mean?"

"Nothing. A bad joke." He grabbed the reports and hurried out before she could go on.

That had been a very stupid thing. Mistresses who thought the money might run out were not known for remaining, nor for keeping silent about the reasons for their leaving. More rumors about Fallon and Sons he didn't need.

To his surprise Kenneth Graham was waiting in the front hall.

"Your hat and stick, sir," Felipe said.

Involuntarily Robert exclaimed, "What on earth are you doing here? How did you know to find me?"

"The boiler on *Comet* burst wide open, sir," Graham said excitedly, then abashment overtook him. "I didna' mean to embarrass you, sir, but I had to let you know. There were stories about . . . ." He drifted off lamely.

"What was the damage?" Robert said. Hang the rumors. This was important. "Was anyone hurt?"

"There wasna' anyone hurt. She split down one side while th' pressure was building. All we had was a bluidy great mass of steam and a piece of iron stuck in the bulkhead. At full pressure she would ha' blown the whole ship apart."

"Damn! It'll take a year to get another boiler from England."

"That may na' be necessary, sir. I think I can build another right i' the foundry, better than the one that burst. We can ha' it installed in two months."

"Two months," Robert breathed. "And better, you say? Will it give me twelve knots?"

Graham blinked. "That I canna' say, sir. Not until she's in the ship and we've actually had a run."

"Then get cracking, man. We're already another two months behind schedule."

He hurried Graham off, and climbed into the carriage waiting in the drive. Rumors, Graham had said, but he had no time to worry about them. For now he must concentrate on Oliver Huger.

Huger's office on Broad Street was almost a copy of DeSaussure's, but without the good taste. The furniture was an expensive jumble of styles, the carpet gaudy and the curtains drab. The brandy he gave Robert was indifferent.

"Now, Fallon," Huger commenced once the formalities were over, "what exactly is it you want?"

"What do I want?" Robert said as if he couldn't believe the question. "Haven't DeSaussure and Pinckney made that clear? They said they were arranging the loans through a syndicate of friends, and I assumed, since you were involved with them on other things . . . . Perhaps I presumed too much." He made as if to rise and go.

"No, no. Sit. Sit, please." Huger licked his heavy lips

worriedly. He was just the sort of man to believe his friends would make deals behind his back and cut him out. It was the sort of thing he would do. "James has been hurried of late," he said carefully. "Not much time for details, you see. Why don't you fill me in?"

Robert let his reluctance show. "I don't know why he wouldn't have . . . oh, very well. DeSaussure has arranged a syndicate to loan me one hundred thousand dollars for expansion of the foundry, with the syndicate holding a note on the foundry."

Huger's eyes bulged even more. "One hund—! I don't believe it!" He added a perfunctory, "No offense meant."

Robert leaped to his feet. "I don't believe you know anything about this. In which case, sir, I don't care what you believe. Good day, sir."

"A moment!" Huger interposed himself before the door, waving Robert back. "A moment, please, sir. If you will just listen a few minutes . . . . " It's true I'm not part of DeSaussure's syndicate."

"Then why should I remain?" But Huger took his pause for assent and pushed forward a chair. He sat.

Momentary doubt clouded Huger's frog-like eyes. "James must believe your foundry is a better investment now than he did two months ago."

"Since you aren't in the syndicate, I don't see what business that is of yours." The hook was set. DeSaussure never made an investment without long investigation; the same could not be said of Huger.

"We are both businessmen, you and I."

Robert reflected that Huger would call out anyone who publicly named him businessman. Now greedy sweat beaded his face. "We are."

"And businessmen must look for the best deal. Isn't that right?"

"That's true," Robert said slowly.

Huger rubbed his hands together briskly. "Then this what I propose . . . ."

When Robert left Huger's office a broad smile lit his face. In his rush to cut out the men he thought had cut him out, Huger had insisted the papers be signed immediately. The fat lawyer had commited himself to form a syndicate of ten who would circumvent the laws that limited loans from the Bank of South Carolina to one man to two thousand dollars and in turn lend the money to Robert. He had his hundred thousand.

He began to laugh out loud.

"It won't work." Jeremiah studied the map on the wall of Vesey's dining room and shook his head. Circles and arrows showed the planned movement of escaped slaves down to Charleston and their gathering places prior to being put on the ships. "I just won't work."

"Damn it," Peter Poyas snapped, "you are the most always-find-something-wrong man I ever met."

"It gots to work, Jeremiah," Monday Gell said. The wiry harnessmaker sweated with the fear that it all might be called off. "It gots to."

Gullah Jack twitched his whiskers and fingered a bundle of white cock feathers, muttering under his breath. Jeremiah thought it was a curse.

Vesey ran his fingers over his tight-curled gray hair and leaned back in his chair. "What's your objection this time?" he asked tiredly.

"Everything," Jeremiah replied. A storm broke from the gathered men, each trying to talk at the same time. "Let me finish. Let me finish!" He waited until they fell silent, all but Gullah Jack who fingered the white feathers more furiously, muttering with a beady eye fixed on him. "In the first place, the plan calls for two thousand people. I was doubtful, but I agreed to go along."

"That right," Ned Bennett broke in. "You agreed. Why you messing about now?" Rolla nodded fiercely.

"Because if all the numbers we've been hearing are right, how many people at how many plantations, we've got over three thousand ready to come in from the country alone. And another four or five hundred here in the city." Despite his best effort a pleading note crept into his voice. "For the love of God, the whites aren't fools! The Arsenal is full of militia, and they keep a watch in the steeple of St.

Michael's. It would've been almost impossible to keep them from discovering the people we planned for in the beginning. And we keep getting more! Doesn't anybody pay attention to what they're told?''

"Militia come, we kill them," Gullah Jack announced. "I give the men a *juju* to put in they mouth, can't no bullet touch them. We kill them militia they come."

"Is that what it's coming to, Denmark?" Jeremiah asked wearily. "A pitched battle with the militia? Denmark, there'll be dead blacks piled in the streets."

"What if the militia can't raise no alarm?" Poyas asked. Everyone looked at him curiously, and he shifted in his chair. "I mean, suppose somebody climb up in St. Michael's steeple and knock that watch on his head?"

"Ain't enough," Rolla said. "Sometimes the militia send they patrol out to the streets the way they suppose to."

"But if they couldn't," Vesey said thoughtfully. "They don't expect any trouble at the Arsenal itself. There aren't more than a hundred men there, and they don't keep their muskets ready to hand. Most will be asleep. Men who moved fast could seize the building before the militia knew what was happening." He got up and drew at a circle at the corner of Meeting and Broad Streets, across from St. Michael's. "Yes, I think we'd better seize the Arsenal."

"More killing," Jeremiah said. "And useless."

Vesey rounded on him. "Damn it, Jeremiah, blacks are being killed by inches every day by these whites you don't seem to want to bruise."

"If we have to kill militiamen," Jeremiah said carefully, "I'll kill militiamen. I want this escape as much as you do. More. But what happens while we seize the Arsenal? Have you asked yourself that? All it takes is one man, raising an alarm, and every white man in the city will dig out a shotgun or a rifle. We might hold them off in the Arsenal, until they get cannon over from Fort Moultrie, but what about our brothers we're trying to get away? That's our purpose here! Not some kind of backwards Santo Domingo. Not watching our people shot down like dogs."

"If we could dramatize our cause by our deaths," Vesey began stiffly.

"God damn it, Denmark, think! Think about every slave revolt you've ever told me about. Do you remember Gabriel, in Virginia? He had a thousand blacks ready to fight, and there was never a mention of it. Not in the North, not anywhere. If we want the word spread, we need the escape. Dead niggers ain't worth nothing!"

There was silence. Gullah Jack had stopped his mumbling. He watched Jeremiah as if he had just seen something new, and dangerous. Finally Poyas nodded.

"You right, Jeremiah. He right, Denmark. Ain't going to do no good us dying proud if nobody ever hear about it."

"If we could keep the whites from joining forces." Vesey sounded doubtful about it himself, but he went on. "There are guns enough in the Arsenal for us to send out our own patrols. We could force the whites to stay in their homes, or at least keep them from getting together. Maybe they could be taken prisoner."

"The whole city!" Jeremiah said incredulously.

"Need more guns than the Arsenal," Ned Bennett said.

"They's five hundred stand of musket in Duquercron's store on the King Street Road," Poyas said. "Some of the people coming down the Neck could get them."

"And Shrirer's store over to Queen Street," Monday Gell added. "It be full of musket." Others began to speak up with more suggestions.

"Now wait a damned minute," Jeremiah broke in. "You put hundreds of armed men in the streets and you're asking for another Santo Domingo. I don't want anybody massacred, black or white."

"Leastways blacks got theyselves free in Santo Domingo," Poyas muttered.

"Are you ready for that?" Jeremiah asked savagely. "Damn it, Peter, are you? Are you ready to murder women, and children, and old people, people who never hurt you, just because they're white?"

Peter refused to meet his eyes. Another long silence

descended on the room, until Vesey spoke. "I think this meeting is about over. You all go on home. We'll meet again next Tuesday."

Jeremiah stayed in his chair while the others filed out. Vesey took the map from the wall and rolled it.

"Denmark, I don't like where this is headed. There's no way you can control those men once they get guns in their hands."

"A few people will probably be hurt," Vesey agreed. He hid the map and his journals behind loose bricks in the fireplace.

"A few, Denmark? You're talking hundreds dead."

"Damn it, Jeremiah, even back when we were talking about one ship and maybe a hundred runaways we thought somebody might be killed."

"This is different."

"If it's all right to kill one to get a hundred free, isn't it all right to kill fifty to get five thousand free? A hundred for ten thousand? Damn it, you have to trust me to handle things the best I can. This isn't some children's story where everybody lives happily ever after."

"What happened to the old days, Denmark? God, I'm so tired."

"They're gone, like all old days. We handed out pamphlets and got nothing. Southern trash whipped us like dogs when they found the words on us, and Northern scum patted our woolly heads and told us to wait for a reward in heaven. I'm tired, too, Jeremiah. Tired of waiting." He held up a knotted fist. "This will set us free. This and nothing else. Now are you with me or not?"

"You taught me how to read and write, how to talk properly, how to damned near everything. If it wasn't for you I'd be one of those ignorant fools shaking when Gullah Jack looked at me crosseyed. I'm not going to leave you now."

"Good man." Vesey put a hand on his shoulder. "And don't be on Gullah Jack so hard. Many believe in him, men who'll perform miracles because they believe he protects them. Go on home, smoke your pipe in front of the fire."

VIII

Outside Vesey's house Jeremiah stopped and stared. The man talking to William Paul was his brother, Billy. Anger stirred and bubbled in his weariness like hot porridge. He had arranged a job for Billy; why wasn't he at work?

Billy met him with a lazy grin. "Hi, brother. I was just showing William here how—"

"What in hell are you doing here? You're supposed to be at Mr. Morrison's." William took one look at Jeremiah's face and bent to his raking.

Billy grabbed Jeremiah's arm, pulling him out of the yard and down the street. "You knows I ain't much for lifting and hauling, 'specially for no fat white man." He looked over his shoulder toward Vessey's house and slowed his pace. "I 'spects it's just my nature to keep on playing them cards and dice, Jeremiah."

Jeremiah wrenched his arm free. "What are you dragging me along for? And why are you looking back at Denmark's house like you expect somebody to come after you? You didn't do anything back there, did you?"

"Why doesn't you let me ask the questions, big brother? What you doing with that light-skinned Vesey nigger? What kinda trouble you getting yourself in?"

"Trouble?" He couldn't stop himself from looking around. No one on Bull Street was paying the least attention to them. A boy ran past rolling a hoop.

"Don't play the fool, Jeremiah. You the educated one. Ain't nobody don't know Vesey always talking bout ab'li-tion and such. White folks got that man marked.''

"There aren't any laws against talking." Bitterness tinged his voice.

Billy snorted. "Talk! You think I ain't seen it always the
same ones? You, and Peter Poyas, and Ned and Rolla Bennett, and Jack Purcell, and Monday Gell, and that Gullah
Jack with his witch talk. White folks don't like meetings
like that.''

"We know what we're doing, Billy." He touched his
brother's arm. "I know you're worried about me. Sometimes I think papa wouldn't like how much we've drifted
apart.''

"Got to look out for you," Billy muttered. "I's the one
born to be hung, not you." His sober look faded; he
barked a laugh. "I gots to be going. You take care yourself, brother." He started up the street.

"Wait," Jeremiah called. He didn't have many close
times with Billy, and he didn't want this one to end.
"Why don't you come to dinner? Sarah's fixing a good
hen. And if you don't want to work for Morrison, I can
always use another hand at the shop.''

"Sure you can," Billy laughed. "No, I gots to see
Bacchus Hammet. He got him a fighting chicken he think
is something. I going to show him different. You take
care." And he was gone around the corner.

Jeremiah made his way home slowly. There was a futility
to talking with Billy. Some time when he himself was
young, his foot had been set on a ladder called respectabil-
ity. He didn't know when. Vesey teaching him. Michael
Fallon insisting he learn a trade and setting him up a shop.
Billy had refused the ladder, and Jeremiah couldn't get
off.

Sarah was in the front hall, dusting furiously, when he
came in. She pushed back the kerchief that kept her long
hair out of her face and shook the feather duster at him.
"You better talk to your daughter, Jeremiah.''

His heart sank. Leonie was 'his' daughter when she was
in trouble. "What's she done?"

"She's been taking sewing lessons from Elfie Pringle.
But Elfie says Leonie hasn't been to her in a week." She

suddenly looked frightened. "Jeremiah, she refused to my face to tell me where she's been going. I put her in her room till you came home."

"I'll talk to her." He started wearily up the stairs.

"Your dinner'll be ready when you come down. Leonie isn't getting any. Refusing me to my face!"

He knocked on Leonie's door, and when there was no answer went in. Lying across her bed, Leonie twisted to watch him with big eyes, wary as a fawn. She had none of what he considered his plainness, but rather had all of Sarah's beauty magnified. He thought again of the future for a beautiful black girl. He wanted to cry.

"Leonie, your mother tells me you haven't been seeing Elfie the way you're supposed to."

Her chin came up. "I am seventeen, after all, a grown woman."

Damn it, he wouldn't let her go astray. Not her and Billy, too. "Don't you take that tone with me," he snapped. "You're still not too grown for me to take a strap to your backside. Now, where were you?"

She gasped. He'd never raised a hand to her in his life, but at that moment he was capable of it, and she knew it. "I . . . I was reading poetry. The azaleas have begun blooming, and it's too warm and pretty to spend all day inside, sticking embroidery needles in my fingers."

He sighed. It was a reasonable explanation for a girl like Leonie, full of the juices of life. "What do you want out of life, child?"

The question seemed to surprise her. "Want? Oh, I don't know, papa. Pretty dresses, and dancing, and poetry." She seemed to realize that wasn't what he wanted to hear. "Papa, I want to get married, eventually. And to teach, if my husband will let me."

"Teach." That had a satisfying sound. "As for the marrying, do you have a boy in mind? I haven't heard you mention anyone."

"I won't marry a boy, papa," she said firmly. "I want someone settled, an older man with his own shop or business."

He smiled at her seriousness. "You seem to have this all

planned. There aren't many men like that who aren't married already.'' Perhaps there would be in Haiti. She could hold her head up there.

"I'll find one," she said airily. "Perhaps a widower."

"Perhaps. But until you get married, you'll do what your mother says. I don't want you to miss any more lessons. A girl who wanders around . . . well, she can get the wrong sort of reputation."

"Papa!"

"Don't you papa me. And don't you miss any more lessons, either. You understand?''

"Yes, papa," she said dutifully.

He nodded to ratify her agreement. If he didn't get her away from Charleston she'd get her pretty dresses and poetry, and he didn't want to think about how. Pray God Vesey's plan worked.

"Ma'am?"

Moira opened her eyes at the sound of Albert's voice. She had fallen asleep on the drawing-room sofa over a volume of Keats. Nights had brought all too little sleep of late. "Yes, Albert?''

"A note came for you, ma'am." He held out a folded piece of ordinary paper sealed with a lump of blue wax. "A boy left it and ran before I could question him."

Her hand shook as she took it. In the weeks with no communication, she had begun to hope the blackmailer had died, or given up. "You may go, Albert."

He remained. "Ma'am . . . if you'll forgive me, I remember another note like this, delivered the same way. It seemed to cause you some . . . anxiety. I just want you to know, ma'am, that if I can be any help, any way at all, I'd be glad to."

"Thank you, Albert. There's nothing . . . ." But help she might well need. "Wait, please." She took a deep breath and broke the seal with her thumb.

PUT FIVE HUNDRED DOLLARS IN A BASKET WITH OLD FLOWERS ON TOP LIKE TRASH. PUT THE BASKET IN THE BUSHES AT THE CORNER OF SOCIETY STREET AND EAST BAY, IN FRONT OF

DUNN'S WAGON YARD. TODAY. IF YOU SET ANYBODY TO
WATCH, ALL WILL BE REVEALED.

Five hundred dollars, she thought bitterly. More than a
year's wages for an overseer. Two for a chief clerk. Once
she'd paid that for a ballgown and thought nothing of it.
Now, with Robert's businesses barely hanging on, she had
to scrimp and cut corners. She had given Hill, the fishmonger, less than half as much—after promising, she had
felt bound—but a brooch from her jewelry chest had gone
to the moneylenders to pay for it. Very well. She had more
jewelry. But she would finish this blackmailer once and for
all. *If you set anybody to watch* . . . .

"Yes, Albert, you can help greatly. First get me a basket . . . ."

Moira clutched the basket as the carriage threaded its
way among high-wheeled cotton drays. The street wasn't
paved here, and the heavy wagons had worn deep ruts that
tossed the carriage like a boat at sea.

She had gotten the money from a Yankee who quoted
scriptures about improvidence, told her to pray for help in
her time of suffering, and gave her a tenth of what the
pieces were worth. The carriage lurched to a stop in front
of a brick wall where faded letters proclaimed DUNN'S
CARTERS & HAULERS, the words half obscured by thick
oleander bushes. A handful of unshaven men squatted at
the corner, staring curiously. She stared back. After a
glance at the quality of her carriage and a few muttered
words among themselves, they moved around the corner.
The wagon drivers on the street were too engrossed in cursing each other and moving their wagons ahead to pay her
any mind.

"Ma'am," the driver said, "you sure this the right
place? Ain't no proper place for you."

"This is the place, Josephus." There was no point in
putting it off. She climbed down, thrust the basket well
under the bushes, and straightened. No one seemed to
spare her a second glance. Three black men in patched
clothing were slouched against a wall up the street. She

didn't look at them again. The one in the middle was Albert.

"Take me home, Josephus."

Back at the house she marched straight to her sitting room. Waiting wasn't hard, she told herself. It was merely letting the time pass. She rang for a maid and ordered tea. It came. She let it sit, the silver pot and the tea in it growing cold. She chose a novel and sat, not reading, not turning pages. At a knock on the door she leaped to her feet, the book falling unnoticed.

"Come."

Albert slipped inside, closing the door behind him. "I'm sorry, ma'am," he said simply.

The room seemed to sway. She sank back. "He got away?"

"Yes, ma'am. It was another street boy. He took off across a fence, through someone's back yard. Even if I could've kept up, he'd have seen me."

"My God. He might not even be . . . . He could have just seen the basket and taken it."

"No, ma'am. He went right to it. Somebody who saw you put it there told him where to look."

"I suppose there's something to that," she said bitterly. She poured a cup of the tea. It was room temperature, acrid and slightly slimy tasting.

"Ma'am," Albert said carefully, "I don't know who's causing you trouble, but I'm sure Mr. Fallon could get it straight in a minute."

"No!" Let Robert come from Lucille Gautier's bed to save her? Never! "Not a word to him. Do you understand? I'll deal with this myself." If only she knew how.

IX

Robert walked the rough planks of Carver's Bridge, watching the lighters load. There were only two ships tied to the tall pilings, a New England brig and *Spray*, a Fallon coasting schooner. The rest of the moorings were taken by lighters, little more than barges to take cargo out to ships that were only in for the change of a tide. *Comet*'s berth was empty. She'd been towed to the foundry wharf, up on the Neck, in readiness for her new boiler.

All seemed to be going well at last. Through most of April, Huger had been reluctant to honor his agreement, afraid that instead of beating DeSaussure. he had beaten DeSaussure to a disaster. After all, it had been an article of Huger's faith that industry wouldn't work in the South. The South was meant for agriculture, for cotton and slaves.

Robert had never threatened. He'd simply stated that Huger had agreed to form the loan syndicate. Huger always worked his mouth violently, mopped his face, and promised that all would be ready in a few days. They both knew that if the document became public, say in a suit for default, Huger was ruined in Charleston. Many men loaned money in Charleston, but gentlemen were never public about it. He'd be held up as a common usurer, and one who'd gone back on his word. A sin compounded. Ten days before, though, Huger had finally shown him papers signed by some of the syndicate and agreed that he could have the money by the first of June.

Domestically things were not going as well. Moira was ever more cold and distant. He'd tried patching things up—he'd even considered dropping Lucille, though, of course, Moira knew nothing of her—but his every approach had been met with withdrawal. Damn her, if she was trying to drive him away she wouldn't be doing it better. He spent more and more time on Montague Street, less at home.

"Mr. Fallon." Morton came down the wharf, his spectacles almost to the end of his nose, his ubiquitous pen in hand. "There's a John Lafflin in your office, Mr. Fallon. He said you might remember Grande Terre. I don't—"

Robert broke into a run, heedless of Morton's startled shout, scrambled up the stairs to his office, and threw open the door. The man seated beside his desk, sipping his brandy, was heavier than he remembered, athletic slimness become prosperously stout, but the years had not made him unrecognizable.

"I'd never have thought when I woke," Robert panted conversationally, "that this afternoon would see Jean Lafitte in my office."

"Sssh!" Lafitte hissed. "Not with the door open, my friend. There are too many people who do not remember the patriotic services that I and Dominique and *mon oncle* Renato gave to this country. I am John Lafflin, please."

Robert shut the door and accepted a glass of his own brandy from the other man. "I thought you were in a place called Campeche. Galveston Island, in Mexico? Rogues and scoundrels gathered from all over the Caribbean." He didn't wait for an answer. "Damn it, Jean, it's good to see you again! How the hell are you?"

Lafitte shrugged. "I am as I always was. But Galveston is finished. My fine *Maison Rouge* burned, and all my corsairs scattered. Your good President Monroe took exception to me, me who never harmed an American ship and did great service to the United States. If it had not ended, he would have sent your Navy."

"A bad business, Jean. But what of Dominique and Renato? Is Beluche as fat as ever?"

"*Mon oncle* has not lost a pound," Lafitte laughed. "But he is respectable, now. Renato Beluche is the Admiral of this fellow Simón Bolívar. A hero. And Dom lives quietly in New Orleans, dabbling in politics. He and Girod, the mayor, last year they have a plan they think nobody know about—to rescue Napoleon Buonaparte and bring him to this country. Only two days before sailing did they receive word of the Emperor's death.''

"Good God! That doesn't sound like quiet living to me.''

"Perhaps not," Lafitte mused. He swirled his glass, staring into the amber brandy. "However, I did not come here, risking a rope, to talk with you of old times. You know that Esteban Lopes is dead?''

"I know," Robert said bitterly. "He had seventy thousand dollars in gold for me that seems to have disappeared.''

"Ah," Lafitte said mysteriously. "Another circle that brings us all together again. It is part of the pattern, I tell you. Fated.''

"What are you talking about, fated?''

"I also had some money with Esteban when he died, and it, too, is gone. A small matter of some three hundred thousand dollars. The way he died—what do you know of that?''

Robert blinked. Three hundred thousand dollars? "Natural causes, I was told. The lawyers I had investigating did report officials were reluctant to say anything, but they thought that meant Esteban committed suicide. I'll never believe that.''

"Suicide! Pah! He was murdered. The officials do not wish to say anything because they fear it was done by voodoo.''

Robert laughed. "Voodoo! Ghosts and goblins and . . . .'' Lafitte's face was patiently solemn, a man listening to someone who didn't know what he was talking about. "You're serious.''

"I am. I do not mean Esteban was killed by black magic. I think me there was poison. But the *jujus* were left with the body, and those fine men who are so sure there is no voodoo are so afraid he was actually killed by it they look no further. Natural causes, pah!''

"But—''

Lafitte tapped the side of his nose slyly. "Before Campeche was done, I found in my quarters a bundle of white feathers tied around a thorn and daubed with some foul paste. You think I do not recognize this thing? It is a *juju*. If such a thing is placed beneath the bed of a man, that man will die, or so they believe. I think me if Campeche did not end, I, too, would have been found dead with *jujus* laid around me."

"There has to be a connection," Robert agreed, "but—"

The door banged open and Oliver Huger staggered into the room, his eyes staring from his head. He practically threw himself across the desk, clutching at Robert's hand. "For the love of God, Fallon, there's no need to pull us both down. It's ruin. Fines. Public ridicule. You're as guilty as I am, you know. Perhaps not in the letter of the law, but the spirit. As guilty as I."

Robert watched the man in disbelief. Huger was almost in tears. "What's happened? Pull yourself together."

"Pull myself together?" His voice rose on every word. "Pull yourself together? I'll—" For the first time he saw Lafitte. Veins throbbed in his forehead. "Who is this? What—"

"I will wait outside," Lafitte said.

Robert nodded. "Just for a moment, please, ah, Mr. Lafflin."

Huger chewed his lip until the door closed behind Lafitte, then reputed. "This morning I received a letter, stuffed under my door." For a second his voice teetered on panic. "It detailed everything, Fallon. The technicalities we're using to get around the law. Everything! It said if the loans went through, it'd all be made known to the authorities. Letters to the papers. It might not mean prison, Fallon. They wouldn't put a man of my position in prison, would they? But I'd be ruined, just the same. I'd have to leave the state. You'd be ruined, too. Don't forget that. No one will trade with a merchant who's broken the banking laws. I don't know who you showed that agreement to, but whoever it was . . . . You do understand, don't you? The agreement is finished. And by your own stupidity.

Who *did* you show it to?''

The agreement was finished? Perhaps *he* was finished. ''I didn't show it to anyone. Our agreement's never left my pocket.'' He took it out and tossed it across the table. No matter what he did, it was worthless now. ''Here. I won't be needing this, it seems.'' Huger's thick lips hung slackly. ''I've no reason to ruin you, Huger.'' Robert sighed and scrubbed his face with his hands. Back where he started from. ''Would you mind going?''

''Why, no.'' Huger hesitated, then snatched the agreement. ''I'll be going right now.'' He put his hand to the door, and it was jerked open by Glenn Mortimore, out of breath. Lefitte peered over his shoulder.

''Come quickly, Fallon,'' he panted. ''Your foundry's on fire.''

Shockingly Huger giggled. ''I knew it was a bad investment.'' Everyone stared at him; he fled.

''Well?'' Mortimore pressed. ''My carriage is in the street.''

They clattered downstairs in a knot.

X

The smoke was visible before they reached the Neck, two tall plumes of it. Mortimore's driver drove like a madman. He rounded the turn into the foundry grounds on two wheels. Robert leaped out while the horses were still fighting the reins.

The tall smokestacks atop the three-story brick foundry stood amidst flames like stork's legs among rushes. Their tops were shrouded by the billows of smoke. The glass in yet another window broke and fell under roaring fiery fingers clawing through the opening. Streams of water from the foundry's three pump carts hissed and disappeared into the building without effect.

The stables were a bonfire two hundred feet long. No one was even trying to save it. A stench of burning meat drifted from the squat structure; Robert hoped it was horses.

Graham came over to him, coat off, shirt sooty and dotted with spark holes, face smudged. A livid welt ran across his forehead.

"Was anyone hurt?" Robert asked. "Was anyone killed?"

Graham shook his head, coughing. "No, sir. A lot o' minor burns, and one broken arm, but no more. Eight horses in the barn we couldna' get out. That's the worst."

"At least no one died."

Part of the foundry roof fell, geysering sparks and precipitating a fall of ash. The fall of everything. Robert's bleak thought was interrupted by Graham.

"I fear I'll be a week or two late o' what I said wi' the boiler."

"How can you possibly finish?" James gestured angrily at the burning building.

"I dinna' ken how this fire can be so hot as what the furnaces are used to. Once we dig the rubble away, I'm wagering the works will be as sound as ever. The fittin's are done, stored in a shed the bastards didna' get. Put a piece o' canvas up to keep the weather off, and I'll finish."

"Bastards? What do you mean?"

"You dinna' know?" Graham said incredulously. "It was set. One o' the yard men saw the stable afire, and we all came runnin'. But i' the confusion someone fired a barrel o' waste in the foundry. He was seen runnin'. By the time I realized what wa' happenin' the fire was in the timbers o' the second floor."

"Are you sure it was set?" James asked. "Fire'd be easy enough to start on its own in a foundry."

"Captain Holden surprised another, sir, tryin' to fire th' *Comet*. He put a ball through the blackguard, but the man got away, leavin' a bag o' combustibles and a slow match. The captain's goin' o'er the ship now to make sure he didna' start a fire before he was found."

Robert's hackles rose. It was too well done to be the work of a madman. Someone had tried to destroy him, was trying. But who?

"Robert," Mortimore said, "your friend's been talking to me." He gestured to Lafitte, standing by the carriage. "He says somebody's trying to kill you. He sounds serious."

With a crash more of the stable collapsed, leaving two drunken walls standing like candlewicks in the flame. Robert followed Mortimore. The heat from the foundry reddened faces even as far back as the carriage.

"I say a name to you," Lafitte said as he walked up. "Cordelia Applegate."

Robert gaped at him. That was a name from the past indeed. An unpleasant one. Three times their paths had crossed, and in those three crossings she had charged him with rape when he abandoned her bed, tried to blackmail him into murder, and succeeded in blackmailing his sister, Catherine, into spying for the British at New Orleans. It had been she who killed Jasper Trask. "There's nothing more we can do here," he said. "Let's ride, and talk away from the heat."

As the carriage left the flames behind, he told Mortimore the story, judiciously omitting Catherine's spying and who Jasper Trask really was.

"My God," Mortimore breathed when he was done. "Do women like that exist outside Greek legends?"

"Cordelia Applegate is real enough," Lafitte said. "And she knows voodoo, and believes it, I think. When she escape after the battle, she don't go to the British, like everybody think. She hide with a *mam'bo*, a voodoo priestess. She is one evil woman, and I think me that the evil of voodoo attract her like a fly to carrion. She stay more than a year, and when she leave, she believes."

"Extraordinary!" Mortimore said. "I swear, bad as you make her sound, I think I'd like to meet this paragon of evil."

"No, you wouldn't," Robert said. "Jean, if you knew where she was, why didn't you do something? I know you couldn't kill a woman, of course, but—"

"But I don't know she is there until she is gone three years. I do not turn my back on a viper like that one, Robert. I hire lawyers, I let word be spread that money will be paid for information about her. I have left instructions for these lawyer's reports to be sent to you. I care where this woman is, and will be, not where she was, so I do not remember all the names and places. No matter. Always I learn where she was last year, or two years ago. I tell you one thing, though. There is no thing about that woman that is not touched by blackest evil."

"I'm convinced. Three meetings with her are three too many for me."

"Ah, but you still have your life, my friend. This one is not so lucky for the men she, ah, befriends. This Mr. Applegate was a man in Kentucky or Tennessee. He die, along with two, three other men, and they say it is murder. Cordelia, she take the money and come to New Orleans.

Some time after you two meet, she marry again, but this husband, in one year he put a pistol in his mouth and . . . pft!''

"I think you're right, Robert," Mortimore said. "I don't want to be in the same city with this woman."

Lafitte nudged him in the ribs. "Sometimes she don't win. This fellow who put the pistol in his mouth, his mother managed to sell off almost all the estate and disappear. You remember those old houses Cordelia used for hideouts? That was all she had left. That old woman pick her clean."

Mortimore shook his head. "For all you know, this Applegate woman could be dead. She sounds as if she led a rather violent life."

"Cordelia Applegate doesn't kill easily," Robert said.

"She is alive," Lafitte agreed.

"If you two believe she's behind this, we must turn Charleston upside down to find her."

Lafitte snorted. "*Mon Dieu!* Our gentle Robert has singed her tail feathers a time or two. She don't get so close as the same city unless he is already dead."

"I wish she was that scared of me," Robert said. "She could be here, or her agents. It could even be Gerard Fourrier."

"Another enemy?" Mortimer asked. Robert nodded.

"A name I don't hear in a long time," Lafitte said. "But he has no quarrel with Esteban or me. It would be too much coincidence."

"We must institute a search of the rougher parts of town," Mortimore said, "where the sorts of men who could be hired to start fires might be found. The constables . . . ."

Robert lost Mortimore's words in a cloud of thought. The carriage was into the upper city, on the cobblestones of Meeting Street. Coincidence, Lafitte had said. In one day he had been pushed to the brink of disaster. It would be too much of a coincidence if Huger's letter didn't have the same source as the fires. But how could anyone have known about the agreement? It was all a jumble. Voodoo. Cordelia. New Orleans. *I was born in New Orleans,* a low, musical woman's voice seemed to say. *I want to know everything.*

"I think I know where to find those men," he said grimly. "Glenn, would you have your driver take us to Montague Street?"

"Surely. But what's there?"

"My mistress's house," Robert said, and gave instructions to the driver.

Lafitte chuckled under his breath, but otherwise an embarrassed silence fell as the carriage made its way through the city. Azaleas in full bloom could be seen over high garden walls. Many of the walls were getting a fresh coat of whitewash from black men with white-streaked buckets at their feet and broad, dripping brushes in their hands.

A block from the house Robert commanded, "Stop." When Lafitte produced a brace of pistols, he took one without asking and started for the house. The others scrambled down and followed.

"What if she refuses to see us?" Mortimore asked uncomfortably. "I mean, a scene . . . ."

Robert stopped. "She'll let me in." He looked up at the white house, its windows framed by dark green shutters. "She wouldn't keep a wounded man in the house. He'll be in the stable." Cracked oyster shells crunched under their boots as they made their way up the drive.

"If he's there," Mortimore muttered. "I mean, we're doing all this on no real evidence at all. Your own . . . well, you know what I mean."

"We'll know in a minute."

The green-painted stable door creaked softly as he pulled it open and stepped in. From a stall halfway down the stable Felipe straightened, staring at them in disbelief. Robert cocked the pistol and raised it smoothly.

"If you move a muscle I don't tell you to, I'll put a ball between your eyes. Get your hands on top of the stall where I can see them."

"You making a mistake," the man said, but he lifted his hands as directed. Sweat beaded his face.

"He isn't wounded," Mortimore said doubtfully.

"Let's see what's in the stall," Robert said, then added,

"And keep your hands right there," as Felipe twitched. When he'd moved far enough to see into the stall, he could see another black man, lying on the straw, clutching a bloody bundle of rags to his shoulder. "The footman."

"An accident," Felipe said hastily. "Miss Lucille bought a pistol, and—"

Robert motioned sharply with his gun. "Shut up. Jean, you and the others tie these two up, then come in. I'll be with Lucille. Don't disturb us till I call."

"Lucille," Lafitte mused. "A pretty name . . . ." He subsided as he caught the look of Robert's face.

Robert slipped the gun into his pocket as he approached the house, dusted off the worst of the ashes. He put his head into the brick kitchen behind the house. The cook was there, and the maid.

"You have the rest of the day off. Go now."

They looked at him strangely, but they knew who paid the bills. In minutes they were gone. He went in the back way and climbed the stairs. It was after four, and Lucille was a woman of habit. She would be in a perfumed bath, even with a wounded man in her stable. He swung open her bedroom door and stepped in.

Her enameled porcelain bath tub was in the middle of the rug, and perfume was heavy in the air. Lucille stood near it, a large towel held before her, her hair pinned high on her head. She wet her lips with quick motions of her tongue.

"This is a surprise, Robert. I did not expect you." She shrugged into a peignoir, belting it loosely, and stepped into high-heeled mules. "I will ring for wine."

"Did you meet Esteban Lopes in New Orleans?" He thought her hand trembled on the bell pull.

"I do not believe I know the name, Robert. *Mon Dieu.* You know my short history in New Orleans." The peignor opened in a double V down the front, barely covering her nipples above the belt, below it flashing open as she walked, displaying the silken length of her thighs and the dark patch at their juncture. All desire for her should have been gone; he lusted after her more strongly than ever, and hated it.

"Strange that of all the people I know in New Orleans, Dom is the only one you've ever met."

"Not so strange. New Orleans is not a village, after all."

"Still . . . . What about Cordelia Applegate?"

"What can be keeping Denise with the wine?" She took a few agitated steps toward the door, then took hold of herself with a strained laugh. "But I forget myself. I have brandy here already. You would prefer brandy, would you not?"

"Brandy will be fine."

She seemed hesitant about turning her back on him. Finally she turned to a decanter on a table. Casually she moved between him and the table. He couldn't see her pour. "Here you are," she said, turning. "You will not mind if I do not join you? For me brandy is much too strong this early."

He set the glass on a table next to the room's only chair. "Is it merely a sleeping potion? Or poison?"

The last word wasn't out of his mouth before she lunged at him, and he realized that despite his watching she'd gotten a knife, its blade no longer than a lady's hand, but long enough to reach a man's heart.

Desperately he grabbed for the knife hand, felt the icy burn of the blade across his palm. Then his hand closed on her wrist. She clawed at his face, but he batted her hand aside. He twisted her other wrist until the small dagger fell to the carpet.

He dropped into the chair, pulling her to her knees between his thighs and clamping his legs around her, trapping her arms. He caught her chin, pulled her head against his chest, twisting her face up. With his other hand he picked up the glass.

"Did you intend to kill me, Lucille? It's time to find out."

As the glass slowly approached her face, a whine started deep in her throat, fought its way past clenched teeth and lips compressed to paleness. Her head jerked frantically away. "Please," she whispered. "Mother of God, mercy!"

He sighed, suddenly weak. Carefully he set the glass back on the table. He wasn't sure if he would have made her drink it. He wasn't sure he wanted to know.

"That glass is evidence to send you to the gallows. If you hope to save that pretty neck you'd better tell me—"

Savagely twisting, she got a leg free and kicked at the table. His hand darted for the glass, too late to keep it from toppling over the edge. There was a self-satisfied smirk on her face.

"You little bitch," he said conversationally. "You'll still tell me everything I want to know."

"*Salaud!*" she spat. "I will see you in hell before—" She ended with a squawk as he flipped her face down across his lap. He rucked up the bottom of her peignoir, exposing the satin curves of her buttocks. "What are you doing?" she asked incredulously.

"This," he said, and brought his hand down with a sharp crack.

"Aaah! *Bâtard!* I will kill you! I will see you rotting in hell you bastard pig sister raping—*Oh, mon dieu, aidez moi!*"

Vile curses, pleas and screams flowed from her as he continued. Her nails dug into his leg. She tried to sink her teeth into his calf. He ignored it, as he attempted to ignore the honeyed flesh he held writhing on his lap, the long slender legs kicking wildly, the rounded breasts that quivered enticingly as she struggled. He concentrated on turning her bottom the same color as the flames of his foundry. Sometime later he realized her words had changed.

"I will talk!" Her whole body shook with her sobs. "*Ah, Dieu! Miséricorde!* I will talk! I swear!" He noted he hadn't fallen far short of his goal with her behind.

He rolled her off his lap. She hit the floor with a thump and a cry, and tried to soothe her buttocks with both hands. There was a tap at the door.

"Fallon?" Lafitte called. "You sure you're not ready for us yet?"

"Come on in. All of you."

Lucille's eyes had darted hopefully to the door at the knock. Now she scrambled to get her peignoir back about her as the men trooped in. She began to rise, but at a shake of his head sank back. Still she made it look as if she merely chose to kneel on the floor.

"Begin with Cordelia Applegate," he said. She hesitated. "I can always let them watch this time. You make quite a show."

Her face colored, a mixture of rage and humiliation. If she had that knife now, she wouldn't miss. She followed Lafitte with her eyes as he rummaged the chests and cabinets.

"She will see you rotting in hell," she said arrogantly. Mortimore joined Lafitte's search as he listened. Only Robert kept his eys on her.

"No more foolishness," Robert said. "Where is she?"

"I do not know." He reached for her, and she shied back frantically. "I swear! I do not know! My instructions came by letter in New Orleans."

He sat back with a noncommittal expression. It fitted what he knew of Cordelia's methods, but despite everything that had happened Lucille was too much in control of herself for him to be sure.

"I don't find any letters," Lafitte said, turning from a chest-on-chest, "but I find this." His hands were filled with small vials and packets. "White cocks' feathers. Thorns. Maybe I whip up a *juju* make you tell everything you know."

"You?" she sneered. "You hold powers in your hands you cannot begin to comprehend, white man. Some of those powers are loose in this city. All of you will be burned away in fires of rage you are too stupid to even know are being lit."

"Cordelia," Robert said flatly. "Keep to Cordelia."

"Wait a minute, Robert," Mortimore said thoughtfully. "She called him white man." He caught her chin, twisting her face up. "She could be a quadroon."

"Only an eighth," she spat. "But an eighth outweighs all the rest, does it not? How do you like it, white man Robert Fallon? You have been crooning and snuggling with a nigger wench!"

"Black, white or green," Robert said, "I'll blister your hide if you don't start talking about Cordelia Applegate."

"I know nothing of her! I was hired by a man I never

saw before, and my instructions came in a letter. I know no
more.''

"Did you get instructions about Esteban Lopes by letter, too?''

"I do not know Esteban Lopes,'' she said sullenly.

"Robert,'' Mortimore said, "I think it's time to turn
this over to a magistrate.''

"No,'' Robert replied. Mortimore looked at him
wonderingly; Lafitte nodded. "Setting aside the scandal of
having my own mistress arrested, what charge will hold
her? She tried to poison me, but there's no proof except
my word. Even if we convince a magistrate Felipe and the
footman set the fires, I wouldn't put it beyond her to talk
her way free. And I want her to hand until I find Cordelia
Applegate.''

Mortimore looked around in bewilderment. "How? If
you don't take her to a magistrate . . . .''

"Ben Miller has small rooms behind his hotel for
patrons who want to lock up their slaves at night. Dressed
in a coarse shift and locked in there, no one will pay any
mind to anything she says. I'll have plenty of time to find
out what I want to know.''

"God,'' Mortimore breathed. "I'd heard you were a
hard man to cross. Now I believe it.''

"You will not hold me long,'' Lucille said abruptly.
"The black hands you despise will strike you down, and I
will walk free through your blood.''

"Your friends won't help you this time,'' Robert said.
"Glenn, what's the furthest port you have a ship sailing
for in the next twenty-four hours?''

"The Baltic. Russia. But what has that to do with anything?''

"The footman just signed on that crew. Felipe's sailing
on a vessel I have bound for India. And that,'' he said to
Lucille, "takes care of that, doesn't it?'' She stared back at
him with glittering eyes.

XI

The eighth of May was a bright Wednesday, but the cloudless sky and flower-perfumed air didn't fit Jeremiah's mood. There was little more than a month to the day they'd been planning for, and the closer it came the less he could sleep, or eat. There were strange undercurrents at the meetings of late, and not knowing what they meant disturbed him.

He turned into Vesey's yard, nodding to William Paul, on watch again with his rake. Paul called to him as he reached the steps.

"Jeremiah. Listen, Jeremiah, I hears you done been talking dangerous. You better watch yourself, lessen some of these young bucks thinks you going back on them."

"I was working with Denmark while they were sucking sugar tits, and I'll stil be with him when they've run back to their mothers."

"I suppose. 'Spect I shouldn't be talking bout it nohow." The wiry man scratched at the walk with his rake. "Denmark got him a new gal."

Jeremiah recognized an attempt to make amends. It must have been difficult for him to say he thought Jeremiah was making a mistake. "Is he going to marry this one? That'd be number eight, wouldn't it?"

"I don't reckon he going to marry her none, way he sneak her in and out. I don't even get a glimpse. I figure she already got a man. Must not be much of one, though. Sometime Denmark, he forget to shut the window, and I hear that gal squealing like a shoat stuck in a fence. I tell you, he putting a working to her.''

He cut short Paul's story as gently as possible and hurried in. The others were all there, but the meeting hadn't begun yet. Vesey still had his Bible in hand, and the map hadn't been hung on the wall. He frowned at the big leather-bound ledger resting on the table. That meant Vesey was bringing in another recruit today. That was something he didn't entirely approve of, all this new ritual with recruits. He nodded to Peter Poyas as he took his seat. Instead of nodding, Peter frowned worriedly. Vesey opened the Bible.

''Today's reading is from the fourteenth chapter of Zachariah. 'Behold, the day of the Lord cometh, and thy spoil shall be divided in the midst of thee. For I will gather all nations against Jerusalem to battle; and the city shall be taken, and the houses rifled, and the women ravished; and half of the city shall go forth into captivity.' God make it so. Amen.''

''Amen,'' the room echoed, as always excepting Gullah Jack. For once, Jeremiah, too, was slow in responding.

''And now,'' Vesey continued, ''let us bring our new brother into the fold.'' Jeremiah thought Vesey looked at him oddly when he said it.

It took only seconds to prepare. The curtains were pulled and extra hangings draped over them, casting the room in darkness. The men moved into the shadows along the walls. The ledger was opened, and two dim candles, barely bright enough to cast a pool of light around the book, were set on either side. Vesey stood beside the book, while Poyas left the room and returned with the recruit, a tall well-muscled man with a black bag over his head. Mystery, Vesey often said. They must be given mystery and fear.

''Do you come before us of your own free will?'' Vesey intoned. ''Do you swear eternal hatred of the white race, and your readiness to die for the freedom of your brothers?''

''I swears,'' came the muffled reply.

''Know then that the book of our number is before you.

When the covering is removed from your head, you must pick up the pen and make your mark immediately, for your protection and ours. If one is betrayed, all are betrayed. If one hangs, all hang. You must sign or die.''

"I sign your book.''

Peter Poyas whipped the sack from the man's head, and Vesey immediately presented a cocked pistol to his face. "See your fate if you betray us. The fate of you and those you hold dear. Treason will not be allowed, and death . . . .''

Jeremiah blanked out the words in his shock.

"I understands,'' his brother Billy said, picking up the pen.

Jeremiah couldn't believe it. He had introduced Billy to Vesey years ago, hoping to instill into him the ambition and dignity he'd gotten from the older man. Billy had drifted away in a matter of months, bored with talk about abolition when there were card games to be played and girls to be talked into the bushes.

Billy finished the laborious process of printing his name and looked around the room at the sinister shapes lining the walls. "My brother here?''

"There's no need for you to know,'' Vesey replied. "Nor for you to ask. Asking questions you shouldn't, knowing things you shouldn't, these can get a man's throat cut some dark night. Take the convert out.''

Poyas took Billy out the way they'd come. The rest busied themselves getting the windows open again. It was already too late in the year for closed rooms.

"Denmark,'' Jeremiah said while everyone was still wiping sweat from their faces, "that was a pretty violent reading. Spoils, houses rifled, women ravished.''

"The rest of us had a meeting,'' Vesey said quietly.

Jeremiah looked around. The others' faces, even his friends', were stony. He wet his lips. "A meeting without me?''

"We decided there's no way to gather all the folk without fighting. Some of those country people are so used to obeying whites, if they were told to give up their muskets, they might do it."

"We make certain every group, no matter how small, has somebody trustworthy with it."

"It won't work, Jeremiah."

"Then we go back to the first plan."

"Be reasonable. There are six thousand men ready to descend on this city, forget about the women and children, like it's the gates of heaven. For our own protection we have to kill all the whites capable of fighting us . . ."

"No, Denmark."

" . . . and all the blacks that might help them, the ones who duck their heads when whites pass by."

A sick emptiness filled Jeremiah. "Our own people, too!"

"If they help white folks," Gullah Jack snapped.

Jeremiah looked around the room. Poyas, the Bennetts, even Monday Gell, all met him with impenetrable eyes. "Not this, Denmark. After all we've done, it can't come down to murder." Vesey didn't answer.

Jack snorted. "I see one nigger step in the gutter and duck he head when white folk pass—" He lunged toward Jeremiah, a dagger a foot long suddenly in his fist.

Vesey's fist met him in mid-lunge, smashing him into the wall. Jack stared up menacingly from the floor, blood from his mouth and nose trickling into his whiskers.

"Don't you ever threaten that man," Vesey told the crumpled man quietly, and a current of menace ran beneath his quiet so strongly that Jack's face blanked in amazement. "He was carrying pamphlets to the plantations when he was nothing but a snot-nosed pickaninnie. He taught people to read and write when they would have flogged him for it, guided runaways to safety when he knew he'd hang if caught." He drew a deep breath, straightening to his full height. "Don't ever let me hear of you threatening him again." He whirled suddenly on Jeremiah. "And you. I suggest you remember Luke eleven twenty-three. You'd better go now. We have things to discuss I don't think you want to hear."

Jeremiah left the house. To abandon Vesey would be to abandon a lifetime. But the course Vesey was on was impossible for Jeremiah to follow.

Suddenly he remembered the verse Vesey had commended to him. Luke eleven twenty-three. He who is not with me is against me.

He quickened his step.

XII

Robert worked through the mail on his lap, aware of Moira's disapproving look from across the sitting room. It wasn't for the mail—though she thought he should attend to that in his study—it was merely his presence. He had hoped his being at home more might make a difference in their relationship, but she actually seemed more irritated with him than anything else. He decided on another overture.

"We have an invitation to the Manigaults' dance tonight, don't we?"

"Yes," she said, bending over her embroidery hoop.

"We haven't been dancing in some time. You could wear that sapphire necklace I brought you from France."

She threw the hoop down on the sofa, getting to her feet. "I . . . I don't want to wear it. And I don't want to go dancing. The least you could do is ask before you begin planning what I'll wear."

He stared angrily as the door slammed behind her. Damn the woman! Now she'd argue over something as innocuous as a necklace.

Lafitte was two days gone, still fearful his identity would be discovered. Mortimore had been strangely taken with the pirate—with "John Lafflin," rather. He'd had "Lafflin" three times to dinner.

Lucille still sat in a cramped, dusty room behind the Atlantic Hotel, insisting she'd told him all she knew, even trying her physical charms. That gave him hope he still might discover something. She must be desperate to try

89

that after what had happened. God knew he couldn't torture her, and there was a limit to how long he could keep her locked up. But then, he couldn't just turn her loose, either.

He opened another letter. Thomas Ferguson, Attorney. The lawyer Lafitte had hired to search for Cordelia Applegate. This must be the report.

> My Dear Mr. Fallon,
>   As with the previous reports made at the behest of Mr. John Lafflin, I am forwarding to you a summary of the further information secured concerning the Gautier marriage . . .

For a moment he could only stare. Gautier? Previous reports? Hastily he dug through the rest of the mail. There was a fat packet bearing Ferguson's name. It held summaries of all the reports made for Lafitte. He scanned until he found the Gautier name.

> . . . marriage in November 1801 between Cordelia Applegate and Charles Marie Claude Gautier is recorded . . . .

Gautier. He turned back to the original letter.

> . . . Gautier marriage, in particular the reasons and methods of its end. Marianne Louise Gautier, Charles's mother, was not Claude Francois Gautier's wife, but his property, a mulatto slave, though it apparently pleased Gautier to carry out the deception on his neighbors. This enabled Marianne to "inherit" as Gautier's widow, though by law, of course, both she and her son were part of the estate.
>   When Cordelia Applegate Gautier learned her husband was a quadroon, by what means I have not yet discovered, she had already had a child, sex not recorded, and so was apparently unable or unwilling to escape the marriage. There were rumors at the time of her husband's suicide that she had killed him, but the facts do not bear this out. What is certain is that shortly after his death his mother began signing over properties to Cordelia. We can only speculate that blackmail was involved. Discovery would have cost "Madame" Gautier her "freedom."
>   As you know, Marianne managed to transfer nearly

worthless properties to her daughter-in-law, while selling the rest, and disappeared with the child. Apparently she was involved with Satanist and witchcraft cults in several European capitals, though I have no details as yet. Her death in 1819 was mysterious and was probably related to the cults. No trace has been found of the child.

I Remain, Sincerely Yours,
Thomas Ferguson, Attorney

Stuffing the letter into his pocket, he hurried out of the house.

When he reached the back court of the Atlantic Hotel, it was in turmoil. Lucille stood in the middle of the slate-paved yard, surrounded by Ben Miller, Lionel Kennedy, and a burly man with side whiskers who had her wrist in his calloused fist. All three men were trying to speak at once above her head.

Miller noted his arrival with a relieved look. "Captain, they're trying to take the girl."

"Are you mixed in this, Mr. Fallon?" Kennedy said. He was a man who could get lost in a crowd of two. Robert thought it was that had driven him to become a magistrate, and to desire more.

"I left this girl here," he said. "Why are you taking her?"

"I'm taking my property," the burly man said. He was nearly bald, and had lost the top of his left ear. "Name's Tobey Wheeler. I bought her, straight and clear, and I'm taking her. I got papers." He jerked her arm to punctuate each sentence; fear and uncertainty were plain on her face.

"As Mr. Wheeler says," the magistrate said tightly, "he has papers." He produced them from his pocket with an acerbic look for Wheeler. He wasn't a man to like having even the smallest of his prerogatives usurped. "These state that Tobey Wheeler purchased a runaway slave girl, Lucy, who sometimes calls herself Lucille, or Lucille Gautier, from a Mr. Claude Gautier of New Orleans. There's a description. Um. Pretty, light-skinned, big breasts, good shape. The clinchers, though, are the moles. Two little ones, an inch apart, high up inside her left thigh. We found them." Lucille colored and looked away.

Robert remembered the moles. Despite his knowledge of her, the sick look in her eyes convinced him this was no escape attempt. But what, then? "You say you bought her from a Claude Gautier?"

"That's right," Miller assented. "She run twice before, and Gautier figured he'd had enough. I'd been watching this bit shake her hips around New Orleans for a long time, though, so I bought her 'in the woods,' as they say, and run her down myself."

"There seems to be a problem," Robert said slowly. The letter in his pocket didn't disprove Wheeler's story, but he was sure she was Cordelia's daughter, not a slave. "A friend of mine, Mr. John Lafflin, left the girl in my keeping as his property. I certainly can't let her leave Charleston until he returns to straighten this out."

"A fine gentleman, Mr. Lafflin," Miller said, picking up quickly.

A small doubt appeared on Kennedy's face. "There are these papers, Mr. Fallon. She does meet the description, and she's answered to the name." Wheeler's brow was drawing down thunderously.

"If Mr. Wheeler will consent to remain in the city until Mr. Lafflin returns," Robert said, "I'd be willing to leave the girl in his possession."

"Stay here?" Wheeler said warily, but his face cleared slightly.

"Of course, I'd pay for your food, lodgings and so forth, since your inconvenience is at my request." Robert paused, not wanting to say too much too fast.

"You pay the bite and I keep the girl? Don't see no reason why not."

Robert nodded, and added casually, "I'll want to talk to her from time to time. Not that I mistrust you, but I need to keep an eye on my friend's interest."

"I don't know," Wheeler began doubtfully, then suddenly brightened. "Sure. Sure, you can talk to her all you want. Only you'll have to wait a few days. I ain't had my fill of her, yet, or rather, she ain't had her fill of me, if you get my meaning." He guffawed loudly.

"We get it," Kennedy said drily. "If this business is

concluded . . . . Mr. Fallon.'' He hurried out, and
Wheeler followed almost on his heels, with a shout of his
own over his shoulder, pulling Lucille behind him.

As soon as they were gone, Robert said, ''Ben, I want
that man watched day and night.''

''Captain, I couldn't tell you while they were here, but
that Wheeler, if that's his name, was one of the Baratari-
ans.''

''One of Lafitte's men?''

Miller nodded. ''He was always in trouble with the La-
fittes and Beluche. Got a mean streak in him, bad.''

''Lafitte's treasure,'' Robert murmured. He ignored
Miller's questioning look. ''Put a man on him quickly,
Ben. One or the other of them is going to lead me to
Cordelia Applegate.''

When the door shut behind her and Wheeler, Lucille
dropped her frightened pose and stared at the dirty room
distastefully. The bed was unmade, a cockroach ran across
the grimy wall, and it smelled of stale sweat. ''Could you
not have found a better place?'' She glowered at him
where he stood by the door. ''Fetch me a bath. This place
is no better than the pigsty where I was, but at least I will
be clean before we go.''

He shook his head wonderingly. ''Just who do you think
I am?''

''Fool! You are from Cordelia, of course. How else
would you know so much of me? I played the part very
well, eh? Now let us stop these games and—'' She cut off
in a squawk as he gathered the front of her coarse shift in
one fist and swung her in an arc. At the end he jerked,
flimsy seams popping, the entire rag coming away in his
hand. Naked, she flew sprawling across the bed.

''First rule, girl. You don't call me fool.''

She was too stunned even to cover herself. She had been
sure he was her rescue. She wet her lips. ''I will scream if
you—''

''Go ahead, girl. Folks know I'm staying here with my
wench. Might ask me to keep you quiet.'' He chuckled,
but the amusement didn't reach his eyes.

"What . . . what do you want?"

"Well, now, that's a story. I was watching this man, you see, name of Esteban Lopes, cause I knew he'd got a lot of money to keep for . . . for somebody. I figured maybe me and a few friends might relieve him of it. Only, 'fore we could, he come up dead, and the money come up gone. But I'm a thinker," he said, tapping the side of his head with a finger. "I remembered me a big-titted wench what was hanging about Lopes, and what disappeared the same day he died. Same day the money went. Weren't as hard as I figured, finding out about you, tracking you down. Funny the way I found you, ain't it? What happened? They find out you ain't white and sell you for breaking some law? That must of burned you some, you with all that gold hid away somewheres and can't get to it. I figure you ought to be right grateful to me. So you just tell me where old Lafitte's gold is, and I'll take, say, half for my trouble and be on my way." He was still grinning, but his eyes remained cold.

The man was a fool, she thought. He'd made a story out of bits and pieces, convinced himself it was the truth, and stupidest of all, he seemed to think she'd trust him. "That seems fair," she said. "But I will take you to the gold, not tell you where it is. We must return to New Orleans. Let us leave at once."

"You'll tell me," he began thunderously, then swallowed the rest of his words. His jaw knotted and worked, then shaped a semblance of a smile. "I don't see no call to go yet. Let this Fallon pay my way a bit. Relax."

"Fallon is not as he seems," she said urgently. "Listen to me. We must go—"

He moved like a cat, catching her jaw in his hand before she could twitch, lifting until her eyes were level with his, her toes dangling in the air. He produced a leather strap in his free hand and held it where she could see it. She clutched his thick wrist desperately with both hands.

"I reckon we do this the hard way. I never was much for all that talking anyway. Now I don't need your butt, girl, so it don't matter none to me if I got to whip it clean off. You understand me?"

She couldn't open her mouth, but she managed a mumbled, "Yes."

"Good." He stroked the strap up and down her cheek. "Good. Now you're going to talk to me about all kinds of things. You going to tell me things you ain't never told another soul. Mainly, you going to tell me about gold. Lafitte's gold. And if you so much as open your mouth about leaving, or this Fallon, or any other kind of foolishness to try to get me off the gold, I'll skin you like peeling a rabbit. Understand that?"

She managed another, "Yes," and he tossed her onto the bed. She worked her jaw, wondering if he'd broken it.

"Might as well find out what kind of woman you are," he said, beginning to unfasten his pants.

"Listen to me," she said desperately as his hairy legs came into view. "You must listen to me about Robert Fallon."

"You didn't believe me," he said sadly, and picked up the strap.

XIII

By the final week of May Jeremiah had reached his decision. That Sunday, he stood adjusting his coat before the mirror with care. "Sarah, what would you think if we left Charleston?"

She looked up in surprise from her sewing. "Why on earth would we do that?" They were in their bedroom, she sitting by the window.

"A fresh start, Sarah. Some place where nobody expects you to step out of the way because you're black."

"And where might that be?"

He shrugged. "New York. Boston. Maybe Jamaica, or even Haiti." Haiti might be possible, even if Denmark went through with his plans.

"But Jeremiah, you have your own shop here."

"I can start a new shop. We have to do it, Sarah. We have to."

"Why, you sound as if you've already made up your mind."

"I have." He took a deep breath. It was time to take the first step. "Tonight, at church, you'd better say goodbye. Monday I'm selling what I have in the shop. I'll collect as much as I can of what's owed me, and book the first passage available to New York. Once we're there we can decide if we want to stay. By week's end we'll be gone from Charleston."

Her face crumpled in distress. "But, Jeremiah, this is too sudden. Our friends. Leonie. We can't just root her up. We have to talk about this."

"There's no time to talk!" He softened his voice. "Sarah, believe me, there's no time. I want us out of this city. I want you to start packing today, now. When Leonie gets home she can help. I have to go tell Denmark."

"Jeremiah, you're not in some kind of trouble?"

"No," he smiled sadly, "I'm not in trouble. I have to go now."

He cut off her questions with a quick kiss and left. That he felt he had to tell Vesey made him feel worse than ever. It wasn't just that he owed him an explanation. With Vesey's talk of violence, that verse he'd flung at him the last time he left Vesey's home, it was a matter of safety. All he could do was leave before the streets filled with blood, and convince Vesey that his going wasn't a betrayal.

On Bull Street he stopped at the sight of a familiar face going up Vesey's step. What was Leonie doing at Vesey's house? He watched the whitewashed house. She didn't come out. Unwelcome thoughts entered his head. Oh, God, she didn't come out.

William Paul started up in surprise when he came into the yard. "What . . . Jeremiah, what you doing here?"

He brushed past the skinny man.

"Jeremiah," Paul said desperately, "you got a minute? I hear there going to be a army come from Santo Domingo . . . Jeremiah? Jeremiah, come on and let's sit."

Jeremiah banged open the door, Paul's voice fading behind him. He took the stairs two at a time. The door to Vesey's bedroom was cracked, and a moaning woman's voice rolled through.

"Oh, God, yes! Yes, Denmark! Oh, God, Denmark, yes!"

He pushed his way in, the room kaleidoscoping around him. The creaking bed. Vesey's pale tan buttocks rising and falling. The slender brown legs wrapped around Vesey's waist. The girl's head tossing on the pillow, hair fanned, mouth slack.

"Oh, God, harder! Use me, Denmark! Harder! Oh, God, yes!"

"Leonie!" he screamed, and threw himself forward in a clumsy dive.

Vesey twisted desperately, but the girl was oblivious, hugging him tighter, and Jeremiah's momentum took them all off the bed on the far side. His hands locked around Vesey's throat. He ignored the other man's frantic blows.

"Son-of-a-bitch!" he sobbed. Why wouldn't Vesey die? His struggles were becoming weaker, but he still fought. "Son-of-a-bitch!"

Abruptly strong hands were pulling him off Vesey. He twisted, fighting to get back to the man slowly lifting himself from the floor, but Paul, Peter Poyas, and Gullah Jack held him. Leonie wept in the corner, hiding her nakedness with a sheet from the bed.

"You bastard!" Jeremiah spat. "I believed in you! Bastard!"

"I know it was wrong," Vesey said, hastily pulling on a pair of pants, "but I'm going to marry her. Believe me, Jeremiah, I—"

"You mother-raping bastard son-of-a-bitch!" Jeremiah began to sob and couldn't stop. "There aren't enough women in this city? You had to take my daughter? My daughter!"

Vesey hesitated, looking at the girl crumpled in the corner. "We can't talk now. Take him some place quiet. We can't let this jeopardize our plans. Jeremiah, I'll explain later. I will."

"Bastard!" Jeremiah spat as they dragged him out.

He let them pull him out of the house. When they realized he wasn't going to fight any more Gullah Jack walked ahead, while Paul and Poyas held his arms. They turned toward the shed at the rear of the property.

This was the end of hope, he thought. Vesey would keep him locked up until after the uprising so he could . . . so . . . because of Leonie. Sarah and Leonie would be in the city when it happened, their souls tainted by what they would see and hear. God forbid by what they might do. He had to have that hope left at least.

Abruptly Jack whirled. Jeremiah had just time to see the long blade of the dagger before it slammed into his chest. He stared at the hilt against his coat in disbelief. There was no pain, just an incredible feeling of heaviness.

Jack's face gleamed with triumph. "Like Vesey say, this nigger ain't going to jep'dize nothing." He stuck his face so close to Jeremiah's that his whiskers brushed the other man's face. "You still sneering, ed'cated nigger? When Vesey tired of that wench of yours, I going to jump her myself."

"Sarah," Jeremiah whispered. Then there was no breath and no time.

William Paul jumped back as Jeremiah sagged, letting Poyas lower the body to the ground. "He ain't mean this! Vesey ain't mean kill him!"

Poyas knelt, holding Jeremiah in his arms. He didn't look up.

"I say kill him," Jack replied. "He ain't mess up nothing now. You best help me get this body hid 'fore somebody see it."

"Peter, you going to squat there on your knees? He done kill Jeremiah! Ain't you going to say nothing?"

Poyas shivered. "I say we better hide him 'fore somebody see."

Paul's mouth worked. "I guess," he managed.

Paul didn't look at Jeremiah's face as they carried his body down the garden to the back of the woodshed. He had held his arm, but he hadn't known what was going to happen. He kept telling himself that.

They dug the grave behind the slope-roofed shed. Paul began to sweat. Poyas laid Jeremiah in gently, and put his kerchief over his face.

"What you sweating for?" Jack asked when the last shovelful of dirt had been replaced.

"I hot," Paul mumbled. Poyas said nothing. He hadn't sweated.

Jack nodded slowly, nostrils flaring as if to smell for fear. "Denmark, he got a soft spot for this nigger, and he got too much on he plate to get more worry now. You better don't say nothing." Suddenly he grabbed a handful of dirt from the grave, sprinkling it in the air and mumbling while he fixed them with a malevolent glare. "You talk, your tongues shrivel in you mouth.''

Paul nodded dumbly; Poyas kept his silence. Jack swiveled his head between them, sniffing, then nodded and disappeared up the yard.

"He going to kill us," Paul said once the bushy-whiskered man was gone. "We don't tell Denmark, he kill us to make sure we never do. We don't got to say the words. You can write printing.''

"Shut up," Poyas growled.

"What you mean shut up?''

"Denmark find out, he kill that Jack with he bare hand. Them country folk, they figure Jack dead, that white hangman alive, you know who they be scared of most. Just one go to the militia and we all hang. We don't tell Denmark nothing.''

"But that Jack he kill us both," Paul protested.

Poyas put a hand on Paul's shoulder. "Don't you worry none. Three of us disappear, Denmark he get 'spicious, and Jack know it.''

"What we going to do, Peter?''

"Come all that burning and shooting," Poyas said grimly, "somebody going to get a musket ball in he bushy whiskers." He rounded on Paul violently. Paul tried to duck back, but Poyas had his shirt in both fists. "You keep you mouth shut, understand? You don't say nothing to Denmark nor nobody. We take care of it our ownselves, you and me, when the time's right.''

"Sure, Peter. I keeps my mouth shut.''

"All right," Poyas said. He released his grip on Paul's shirt. "Just you remember it.''

Paul watched Peter walk up the yard. He was almost as scary as Gullah Jack. Either one would kill him if he crossed them. Abruptly he remembered he was alone beside the unsanctified grave of a man he'd helped murder. He hurried out of the garden, leaving his rake where it lay. He needed to be a long way from that grave.

It was plain enough even to him, he thought. If he let Denmark know, Poyas would kill him. If he didn't, Jack would kill him. What to do? God, what to do?

Peter realized he'd walked all the way to East Bay. He

was at Fitzsimmons Wharf, below the fish market. On a lazy Sunday afternoon there wasn't any work going on. There was no one on the wharf at all except for one black man near the end, leaning on a piling and idly watching the ships. Paul thought he recognized him. Peter Prioleau, a slave of Colonel John Prioleau. He was one of those Vesey warned against, one of those content with their chains, who took old clothes and were grateful for food handed out at the kitchen door.

Suddenly a plan was in his head, fullgrown. He could try to recruit Prioleau, who didn't know him, telling him Gullah Jack was the rebellion's leader. The whites would hang Gullah Jack, and he'd be safe. Maybe he could find two or three others, to make sure somebody ran to his master.

He walked down the wharf, reminding himself to be careful. He didn't want to end up being flogged or hung. He leaned against the next piling down from Prioleau. Not far out a schooner was anchored, a flag at the masthead with the number ninety-six on it. He pointed at it.

"I seen a lot of flags with seventy-six, but I ain't never seen one with ninety-six," he said.

Prioleau looked at him. "I guess I ain't neither." There was no glimmer of recognition on his face.

Paul was satisfied. He took a deep breath. "Something serious going to happen in this city . . . ."

XIV

There were rain squalls the last Thursday in May, and Robert remained in his study, going over Graham's reports on the work at the foundry. Graham wanted money he'd be hard pressed to provide without selling the cotton mill. And there were the lawyer's reports on Cordelia Applegate. Somewhere in there had to be an answer to Lucille.

She still refused to say anything, even when he hinted he might help her get away from Wheeler. And hint was all he could do, for the burly man loomed smiling in the room whenever they talked, making his own heavy hints that he had to make certain Lucille's charms were enjoyed by him alone. They were in a room above a grogshop because the tavernkeeper where they had been before had told Wheeler to leave. Lucille's screams were disturbing other patrons. She hadn't told him anything, though, or he'd be gone. As it was, Robert wasn't sure how long before Wheeler decided to risk the constables' pursuit and carried her off to where he could get down to real torture.

He was on one of Graham's reports when there was a tap at the door. "Come," he said, and Albert entered.

"Mr. Fallon, one of the stableboys, Henry Elkins, came to me with a story you should hear."

Another problem, Robert thought. "Have him in, then."

Albert opened the door and motioned a muscular black youth into the room. "Tell Mr. Fallon what you told me, Henry."

Henry shifted from foot to foot as if afraid his boots

would damage the Turkey carpet. He crumpled his hands, and his eyes flitted around the room as he spoke hesitantly.

"This fellow come up to me whilst I was fishing this morning. I was give the morning. I weren't shirking. Anyhow, he talk about the weather, and the fish, and then he say there going to be a big uprising of slaves in the city, and I should ought to be in it. He say there thousands coming in from the country, and they going to kill all the whites. He want me to come put my name in some book. I get scared, so I come tell Albert." He shrugged uncomfortably.

Slave uprising. It was what every white feared, whether he let himself admit it or not, whether he opposed slavery or kept five hundred hands at cotton. It wasn't to be credited that rebelling slaves might distinguish between those who opposed slavery and those who supported it. A white skin would be a signal for the knife, and not the most ardent abolitionist wanted his throat cut in the cause of freedom.

Robert raised a questioning eyebrow at Albert. "I believe he's telling the truth, sir," the butler replied.

Robert nodded. "Henry, I'll have a gold piece for you this evening, and I may want you to tell your story to some other men."

The stableboy's face brightened at the mention of gold. "Yes, sir."

"Albert, I'll want my carriage brought round immediately. I have to see the Intendant about this."

"Yes, sir," Albert showed the boy out, then paused. His face worked for a minute before he spoke. "Sir, I have to tell you. I came to you because of the massacre talk. If it had just been an escape, I wouldn't have."

"I never expected you would," Robert said quietly.

After a moment Albert bowed. "I'll see to your carriage, sir."

It was after four when Robert lifted the brass knocker on James Hamilton's front door. A frightened black butler let him in. The house was crowded with worried men. Governor Bennett stood on the landing above the entry hall with

Colonel Hayne, Bennett nodding as Hayne put some point across with gestures. A half-dozen militia officers occupied straight chairs along the wall, and Hamilton himself had his head together with John Prioleau. They both looked up at Robert's entrance.

"Mr. Hamilton," Robert said, "Colonel Prioleau. Either you've already heard my news, or I've come at a strangely opportune time."

"What news?" Hamilton said impatiently. "We must leave in a few minutes for a meeting at City Hall."

Robert kept a rein on his temper and his dislike. "One of my servants was approached this morning by a man who claimed he was recruiting for a slave uprising."

Hamilton nodded irritably. "Probably William Paul. He approached one of the colonel's blacks last Sunday, though the colonel didn't report it until today. I must say you're more prompt."

"I didn't know until today," Prioleau said testily. "I was out of town, and I'm afraid my wife thought it was just foolishness."

"Well," Hamilton said, "we have it in hand now. The Colonel's man recognized this William, and he'll be questioned at the Council meeting."

"I've met William Paul," Robert said. One of Jeremiah's friends, he recalled. "Hard to believe he'd be mixed in anything like this."

"You'd be surprised to find out a nigger's black," Hamilton snapped. "I'm surprised you didn't wait till we all had our throats slit in our beds before you said anything."

"Here, here, Hamilton," Prioleau said hastily. "No call for that kind of talk."

Robert spoke levelly. "I'd like to bring my stableboy, Henry, to give evidence to the Council. He might be able to identify William Paul, if he's the same man."

"We have our identification," Hamilton said, "from Colonel Prioleau's Peter, and the Council meeting isn't open to the public." He was politely correct to the point of insult. "If you'll excuse us now, Mr. Fallon, we have the business of discovering how far this rot has spread." He climbed the stairs and joined Bennett and Hayne.

Prioleau shrugged helplessly. "I'm sorry, Fallon."

"And I, Prioleau."

When Robert reached home Ben Miller was waiting in the entry hall, and Sarah Carpenter, bonnet tied firmly under her chin and hands clasped on her lap, sat on a straight back chair against the wall. "Wheeler's changed rooms again, captain," Miller began.

"I'll see you in a minute, Ben," he said. "Mrs. Carpenter, what can I do for you?"

She stood up, clutching her skirt uncertainly. "Mr. Fallon, I have to talk to you. Please? Jeremiah always trusted you, and I don't know who else to talk to."

"Of course, Mrs. Carpenter. Would you step into my study?"

"He's gone, Mr. Fallon," she burst out. "Jeremiah's gone!"

"Gone! You mean he's dead?" He cursed his tongue inwardly as her face twisted. Her knees wavered, and he helped her back to a chair. "Ben, get Albert to bring some tea."

"I'm all right," she managed. "Please, I don't want tea. I want you to help me find Jeremiah."

"Tell me what happened."

She produced a handkerchief from her reticule to dab at her eyes. "Last Sunday Jeremiah said we were leaving Charleston."

"Leaving? Did he say why?"

"No, sir. He just said, say goodbye to my friends because before the week was out we'd be on a ship for New York. Then he went off to tell Denmark, Denmark Vesey, that we were going. He didn't come back." She squeezed her eyes shut and took a deep breath before continuing. "I went to Vesey, he's an old friend of Jeremiah, and Vesey said he'd come, and that he'd agreed to put off leaving and go upcountry on some kind of errand for him. For Vesey, I mean. Vesey said he was surprised Jeremiah hadn't sent me a note, but I wasn't to worry because Jeremiah'd be back shortly. Only it's been a week, Mr. Fallon, and all Vesey says is Jeremiah'll be back soon, but I haven't had a word from him. I . . . I went to a magistrate, Mr. Kennedy, but he wasn't much interested." She looked away. "He thought Jeremiah had run off with a woman, and I ought to forget about him and get a new man."

"That sounds like Kennedy," Robert muttered. "Jeremiah's probably so far upcountry he has no way to write you. Did Vesey say what the errand was?"

"No, sir. Something about wood. Mr. Fallon, I don't know what to believe."

"You can believe Jeremiah's all right. I promise you I'll find him and get word back to you. And a letter."

"You will? Thank you, sir. Thank you so much. I'd better be going now. I've taken up too much of your time."

"Won't you at least have that cup of tea?" Robert asked gently.

"No, sir. I have to go."

Once she was gone, Robert looked at Ben, and the other man didn't need to hear the question. "I've heard of Vesey, captain. He's supposed to be a troublemaker, but blacks respect him."

"I don't like this story of Jeremiah going off without even a word for his wife, Ben. Can you set somebody to keep an eye on Vesey? If there's been dirty work done, the only way we're likely to find out is to follow Vesey till he makes a slip."

"I'll get on it right away, captain."

Robert scanned the Friday newspaper for word of the City Council meeting and found none. He had to concede it was just as well Hamilton wasn't letting any news out. He'd feared an official panic, with blacks arrested on suspicion and whisper, and hung on the assumption they wouldn't have been arrested if they weren't guilty. It had happened before, in other places.

In the mid-afternoon, Albert announced Glenn Mortimore.

"Glenn," Robert said, rising as Mortimore entered the study. "Good afternoon."

Mortimore seemed distracted. "Robert, there's something going on at City Hall. There's a clerk there who—''

''—told you about the special Council meeting last night.'' He smiled at Mortimore's confusion. ''Sit down.'' They settled in facing wingchairs.

''You know? I didn't think there were half a dozen men outside the Council who knew.''

Robert explained his trip to Hamilton's house the night before. ''But he wasn't interested,'' he concluded. ''This morning I couldn't even get in to see him.''

''Then you don't know about the arrests?''

''Arrests! Who've they arrested, Glenn?''

''I only know of two,'' Mortimore drawled cautiously. ''Peter Poyas and Mingo Harth are the names I got. They were arrested this morning, then released.''

''Good. If they let them go, perhaps Hamilton's going to keep his head.''

''I hope so,'' Mortimore said doubtfully. He paused a moment, working uncomfortably toward something. ''*Hunter*,'' he said finally. ''She's—what?—five months overdue? I suppose you've given her up for lost.''

Robert shook his head. ''A family tradition my father started. Fallon and Son never gives a ship up till there's proof she went down.''

''Commendable sentiment, Robert, but hardly sound business.''

''I'm *not* a sound businessman, Glenn. I dream too much, and I believe in men instead of accountants' ledgers.''

Mortimore straightened as if that were the opening he needed. ''Listen, Robert, may I presume to talk to you a little about those dreams and those ledgers? You've become a friend over the past few years, and I . . . well, I'd hate to see . . . you understand.''

''I understand.'' He laughed mirthlessly. ''I suppose I can stand hearing from a friend what everyone in the city must be saying. Though I think I know it already.''

''Perhaps you do.'' Mortimore hesitated. ''Fallon and Son would be one of the finest shipping firms in the country if it weren't for the drains you put on it. Forgive me, Robert. I know you were one of the first to see what steam could do, and one of the first to put steam vessels into the coast trade, but you've sunk enough money into *Comet* to build a dozen coasters, without a penny back on it. Now you're trying to rebuild the foundry.'' He took a deep breath. ''Forget the foundry for now. Put *Comet* into the coast trade, so you'll at least get something out of it. Let somebody else be first with regular steam traffic across the Atlantic. Put your efforts to the mill and shipping, and in five years or so you can start again with the foundry. It's a sound enough business, in the long run. And if somebody else solves the steamship problems before you do, you can copy him and be in competition with him a year later. Damn it, Robert, it's time to stop dreaming and be practical.'' He sat back, watching Robert.

Robert had sat quietly through Mortimore's words. ''I'm my father's son,'' he said now. ''I don't know what drove him, or even what drives me—some legacy in the blood. My father dreamed dreams other men thought impossible. He was a bondservant, the next thing to a slave, and he dreamed of being a shipowner and a planter. He dreamed of a new country when other men thought that insane. My dreams are steamships crossing the oceans, and a South that doesn't have to buy its very pins and needles from the North. Maybe I'm as crazy as he was, but I'll accept that. Proudly.''

''So you're going to press on, even though it's all about to come tumbling down.''

''I am, and it won't.''

''Face facts, Robert. The rumors are rampant. You had some sort of loan arranged, a large private loan, and it fell through. You must be in deep difficulties. Robert, I'm trying to help you. Even if you went to every bank in the city, the legal limits on loans would keep you from borrowing enough to keep everything going. Retrench. Save what you can. Rebuild the rest later.''

A slow smile built on Robert's face. ''Every bank in the city,'' he murmured.

''Wouldn't be enough,'' Mortimore said.

''But there are banks in Columbia, and Savannah, and Norfolk, and New Orleans, and . . . Glenn, I'll go to as many banks as it takes, borrow what I can from each, until I have what I need. If it takes fifty loans from fifty banks, so be it.''

"You're mad! Paying back all those loans would keep you in debt for years. And think of the interest! You'll have to pay at least three percent! Money that should go for expansion will go to the banks, and you'll have to borrow more to expand. It'll take you twenty years to get out of debt if you ever do.''

"Twenty years from now, my sons will be running things. They can see if they have the legacy of fire in their blood. If not, well, my father started at the bottom, and so did I. My sons will be strong enough to do it, too, if need be.'' Perhaps James already had.

"Good God,'' Mortimore said softly. "In a way you really are mad. You'll gamble their futures on your dreams.''

"Living's a gamble, Glenn. Do you know how my father got his start? He scraped together enough to salvage a ship the owner thought was lost for good. I got mine by scrimping till I could buy a half interest in a brig and put her into the Caribbean trade, fighting off Spanish *picaroons* out of the Hispaniolas, selling guns to revolutionaries in South America, with them ready to cut my throat if I turned my back. I'll give my boys what I can, and prepare them to face life as best I can, but if they have to make their own gambles some day, so be it.''

"You're a hard man, Robert Fallon.''

"Perhaps I am,'' Robert mused. "But if I wait ten years, or even five, it may be too late, for Charleston, for my sons, for everyone. The foundry would have to start from the beginning, competing against other foundries that could already duplicate English steel and guard the secret as close as any Sheffield foundry. The factories will be in New Jersey and Massachusetts, and the steam ships will run from New York and Boston. Charleston will be a backwater port for Yankees to buy cotton and sneer at the pretentions of tenant farmers who remember when they were aristocrats. Because that's all they'll be, with what isn't owned by Yankees controlled by them. I don't think my sons would want to live here then. I hope not."

"I wouldn't say any of that in public if I were you. You'd have to refuse a dozen challenges."

"It's the truth."

"That won't stop the challenges," Mortimore said drily, "or the bricks through your windows." He eyed Fallon for a moment. "By God, if you're a madman—and I'm not sure you aren't—maybe it's madmen we need. I'm with you. What can I do to help?"

"Perhaps a few letters to your friends in Virginia. Introductions, character references, that sort of thing."

"You have them. If we don't find ourselves hip deep in axe-wielding slaves."

"I doubt we will," Robert said. "If anything, it's just a few dozen men in the country, the way it was at Camden. It's crazy to think they'd try anything against the city."

Mortimore eyed him wryly. "You can call anything crazy?"

"Maybe not," Robert laughed. He got to his feet. "Let's talk of something more pleasant. What do you think of going up country for a bear hunt this fall . . . ."

XV

By the sixteenth of June all Charleston knew that a slave uprising was afoot. Peter Poyas sweated, though the Sunday morning was unseasonably cool, and wondered how long it would be before more arrests came. He walked into Vesey's yard, flicking his eyes by habit to where William Paul had always been with his rake, and went on in. If some of those arrests should by chance be men who knew more than Paul had . . . .

The others were already there. Vesey was sweating, too, Poyas noticed. Jack Purcell sat silently in a corner, while the Bennetts started to their feet when he came in. Monday Gell looked ready for his own funeral. Only Gullah Jack seemed untouched by fear. His eyes worked back and forth from man to man, burning with fervency as he fingered his crude dagger.

Poyas had pieced together some of what Paul had done from the questions he had been asked. Now he wondered if it had been from fear of Gullah Jack. He dismissed the idea.

"About time you got here," Vesey said. He hauled the map out of the hiding place behind the bricks and thrust it into the fireplace.

"You think we got trouble now?" Poyas said. "I know a boy belong to Captain Harrison, and he say most every militia company is gathering at ten tonight."

"Shit!" Vesey said. He pulled more papers out and threw them after the map. The others stirred uneasily, muttering. Gullah Jack kept fondling his dagger.

Poyas was shocked. It was the first time he'd ever heard Vesey say more than a hell or a damn. "What we going to do?"

"Ain't quitting," Gullah Jack spoke up. "That what you want, ain't it, Poyas? Quit, and be safe, and suck on you mama's tit."

"Be quiet," Vesey snapped. He bent to light the papers in the fireplace. "No one's quitting anything. We just move everything up. Everyone was supposed to move at midnight. Now I want everybody in place at nine. The militia thinks it's going to be waiting for us. We'll be waiting for them."

"With what?" Ned Bennett wanted to know.

Gullah Jack broke in. "You getting scared? You remember, all them run back to they mama's tit going to get they throat cut."

"You leave me alone," Ned protested. "I ain't sure I wouldn't rather risk you than get myself hung or shot by the militia."

"You carry my crab claw *juju* and believe, ain't no bullet touch you."

"Damn your—"

"Both of you be quiet," Vesey said. "Nobody will hang. As for being shot, sometimes that risk has to be run in a revolution."

"Risk?" Ned said. "I take a risk, but this ain't risk. Half our people in the city scared to twitch till they see the men from the country, and all we got so far is thirty men come from Jim Island last night with nothing but a half-dozen butcher knives between them. We ain't got musket or pistol but for sixty, seventy. They going to be guards on all them store on the Neck where the musket be, and they going to be ready at the Arsenal, too. That ain't risk. It cutting our own throat."

"Then we'll kill the guards!" Vessey shouted. He pounded on his thigh with one work-gnarled fist, visibly controlling his temper. "Jesse Blackwood is ready to ride. I'll have him pass the word for the country people to start moving now."

"You think the whites going to let them just come in?"

Peter asked. Gullah Jack glared at him, and he glared back.

"They'll come a few at a time, just like we originally planned. Peter, the whites aren't ready for us. The country will sneak in by handsful, the city will rise, and the whites'll still be waiting for ten o'clock. One last thing. I want Jeremiah to write a note for his wife. She is on my doorstep every morning almost."

Poyas shook his head. "He ain't going to write no note." Gullah Jack's chair creaked.

"Damn it," Vesey muttered. "If he won't, we'll have to lock his wife up with him. That ought to bring him around."

"Jeremiah dead," Poyas said. Gullah Jack's knife caught the light as he shifted it from hand to hand.

"Dead," Vesey breathed. "Jeremiah's dead?" His voice gathered strength. "I told you to keep him somewhere safe. I didn't say anything about killing. Who did it? I'll have his head!"

Poyas' eyes flickered to Gullah Jack, poised on the edge of his seat. The truth would end it all. But Vesey still believed there was a chance. "He did it his ownself," he said. "He was in a barn up on the King Street Road. He jump out the loft with he hand tied, break he neck. I bury him in the marsh, cause we can't afford to have that body found."

"No," Vesey said. "No, we can't have that."

"Stop this tear dripping," Gullah Jack growled. "He'd've sold us all and he got the chance."

"He was a great man, and the first black martyr to our revolution. We'll erect a statue to him. He'll be a hero for our children."

"We better put up the statue later," Poyas said. "Right now we got other things."

"Yes. Of course. In a minute I'll get Blackwood off. Remember, most of the whites have already left the city for the summer. Even if the militia was waiting, they couldn't stop us. Now get to your tasks."

Robert was glad the fever gripping the city hadn't penetrated his house. On the way to church at St. Michael's he'd seen men in the streets with guns, waiting for something to happen. Anything. And the rumors were there, too. At the stroke of noon—or midnight—by St. Michael's bell—or St. Philip's—every black in the city would rise. It wasn't the city blacks at all. An army of five thousand runaways—or ten thousand, or twenty thousand—had gathered near Georgetown, waiting to march on the city.

He'd told Moira and the children they would all spend the day indoors, but now, in his study, he began to think the men in the street had at least a touch of the right idea. He was almost certain the mass rising of hundreds, even thousands, of slaves wasn't going to happen. It was even possible no one was involved at all beyond William Paul. Still, it might not be a bad idea to have his guns loaded.

From upstairs a ringing gunshot echoed through the house. He dashed into the hall, through the milling, chattering servants, and took the stairs in giant strides. The door to Edward's third-floor room stood open. Albert was already there, a musket in his hands. Edward and Elizabeth stood defiantly in the middle of the rug, she with a pistol gripped in her fist. His valet and her mauma huddled on the far side of the bed.

"What in hell is going on here?" Robert asked.

"It was an accident," Edward piped up. "I was showing Bets how to work the musket, but when I let it off cock my hand slipped." He pointed to a hole in the wall between two windows. "See. It couldn't have hurt anyone."

Moira hurried in, face white. "Are the children—" She dropped to her knees and hugged Elizabeth to her. "You're all right, my little darling. Thank God, you're all right."

"Of course we are, mama," Elizabeth replied. "We're going to defend ourselves if the slaves come."

"Edward," Robert said, "what have I told you about loading guns without me around? You and I are going to have a talk I don't think you'll like." The boy dropped his eyes. "Albert, would you take that musket, and the pistol, back downstairs, please?"

"No!" Moira said. "What if the slaves do come? All the

women were talking about it at St. Michael's this morning. They say there are thousands of them ready to cut our throats in our beds." Her eyes drifted to Joseph and Agnes. "They even say some free blacks are in it, too. I want a gun. Let Edward have one, too. And Elizabeth's old enough to defend herself, if it comes to that."

"What about the babies?" Robert said. "Carver at least is big enough to pull a trigger if he uses both hands. Albert, take the guns downstairs." Albert took the pistol from a pouting Elizabeth and left with both weapons. "As for you two, if I hear of either one of you handling a loaded firearm without me present, you won't sit comfortably for a week." Edward looked abashed; Elizabeth stiffened indignantly.

Robert took Moira's arm and led her out of the room. She waited until they were in his study with the door shut before she spoke. "And will you be taking a switch to me if I want to protect myself?"

"If you want to act like a child, I'll treat you like one." He ran his fingers through his hair. "What did you think you were doing up there? The children are scared enough without seeing you in a panic. I thought you were stronger than that."

"I can only be strong by myself so long," she retorted.

"I haven't meant to leave you alone. I haven't wanted to. God, sometimes I feel like a man in quicksand. Every time I move to get out, I sink deeper. I'm sorry, Moira. I've never meant to hurt you."

She walked into his arms, laying her head against his chest. Amazed, he smoothed her soft black hair.

"Damn you, Robert Carver Fallon. All you have to do is say you're sorry, and I melt inside. Damn your eyes for the hell you put me through."

"It hasn't been by choice, Moira. Somehow, I always thought you'd be there, no matter what. I promise you I'll stop spending so much time with other things. We'll go up to Tir Alainn for the fall."

As he spoke she stiffened, finally drawing away. "There always are other 'things,' aren't there?"

"Moira, I love you."

"I know you do. And I love you. From the day I first saw you, striding up that Belfast street like a pirate, Kemal and Miller in your footsteps like a pair of great dogs. I'll not lose you, Robert. I'll put a pistol ball in your head before I'll lose you."

"It won't come to that," he laughed.

She gave him an unreadable look. "I'd best go look at the children." There was a tap at the door. She opened it to let Albert in, slipping out at the same time. "Sir," the butler said, "Mr. Mortimore is here. And Mr. Miller."

"Show them in. But first." He dug out his key ring and detached one key. "This is the spare key to the gun cabinet. Load everything. Pistols, shotguns, everything. Don't let Mrs. Fallon know you have a key. If the situation gets bad enough, and I'm not here, tell her you found a key and distribute the guns to whoever you think is most trustworthy."

"Sir, you must be forgetting I am a black man."

"If I didn't trust you, I wouldn't give the key to you."

Albert tucked the key into his waistcoat pocket. "Thank you, sir. I'll show Mr. Mortimore and Mr. Miller in."

Mortimore and Miller bustled into the study, the merchant in the lead. "Robert, I met Miller on the steps, you must listen to what he's found out."

"The uprising?"

"No, captain," Miller said. "Wheeler's dead. His own knife in his back."

"Damn! Lucille?"

"Gone, sir. One of the watchers thought he saw a pretty wench come out of the alley by the grogshop, but he was supposed to watch Wheeler, and he knew the girl was kept tied, so he didn't think anything of it."

"We should have turned her over to a magistrate," Mortimer said.

Robert ignored that. "What we have to do is find her."

"Captain, that might not be so easy. If she just fades in among the blacks, she can plain disappear. I know a few blacks who'll ask questions for me, but not enough to find her if she wants to hide."

"Money," Mortimore said. "She won't have any. That

should make her easy enough to find.''

Miller shook his head. "She cleaned out Wheeler's pockets, sir. There wasn't a penny in that room, and with you picking up his tab, captain, he had to have a tidy sum. He never went nowhere else.''

"Ben," Robert said, "you'll have to do your best.''

"All right, captain. I just hope we have better luck than with Vesey. He hardly ever leaves his house. All his friends come to him.''

"Who's Vesey?'' Mortimore asked. "Does he have anything to do with the girl?''

"Something else,'' Robert said, and explained about Jeremiah's absence and his wife's worry.

"Do you think this touches the uprising?''

Robert laughed. "Next thing you'll be like the old women in church this morning, thinking everything is involved in that mess.'' He sobered. "If he did kill Jeremiah, I'll knot the rope around his neck myself, but it'll turn out to be for some ordinary reason. I've learned Vesey is a lady's man. It's possible he wanted Sarah. She's a good-looking woman.''

Mortimore had listened impatiently. "I'm not the only one who thinks a great deal is involved. Half the city thinks every black in the state is awaiting a signal to start killing whites. Everyone's on tenterhooks about what the Committee will do next.''

"The other half of the city,'' Robert rejoined, "is saying their people are faithful old family retainers and couldn't be involved in anything like that. You can't go by what people say. What's this about a committee?''

"Oh, Christ! That's why I came over. To see if you'd heard. But when I met Miller on the steps . . . . The City Council has appointed a Committee of Safety and Vigilance under our old friend Kennedy. It was announced just a few hours ago, but they've already arrested eight, ten blacks, maybe more, including four of the Governor's slaves. I hear Bennett's up in arms over that, claiming the entire thing is a farce and there isn't any uprising planned. He was speaking out of the other side of his mouth yesterday.''

"Human nature, sir," Miller said.

"And not our affair," Robert said. "Not until they find
an uprising, or cause one. Our business is to find Lucille
Gautier. Once we do . . . ."

Leonie sat naked before the mirror in Denmark's bedroom and examined her reflection with satisfaction. Her
dark skin was soft. Velvet, Denmark called it. Her breasts
were high and firm, her waist tiny above the flare of her
hips. Denmark had many women—she wasn't deaf; she
heard—but none had her ripe seventeen-year-old body or
her exuberance at the newly discovered delights that body
could give and receive. She'd succeed where the others
failed, make him want only her. And she had a secret
weapon, for when the right time came.

She'd been terrified the day her father discovered them,
afraid he'd kill her, afraid he'd kill Denmark, afraid Denmark would kill him. When her father was dragged out
she'd screamed at Denmark, clawed at him. He'd slapped
her to stop her shrieks, then taken her on the floor. She
fought him, pounding with her fists while her legs wrapped around him convulsively. In that flood of passion
when she didn't know if she loved him or hated him she
was certain their child had been conceived. The child that
would finally bind him to her, and convince her father to
accept Denmark as her husband.

She hoped her father returned soon from wherever Denmark was keeping him. Vesey had explained that he had to
be kept away—on a farm in the country, she thought—
until he calmed down, that there were plans she shouldn't
worry her pretty head about, plans that her father might
wreck because of what he'd found.

From the living room below, disturbingly hollow voices
rose. All day men had come and gone, and voices had
growled at her through the floor, but Denmark hadn't
come up, though she'd stayed naked to delight him. She
pulled on the peignoir he'd given her, lace that offered
glimpses and hints of the supple body beneath, and went
downstairs. He had told her never to interrupt one of his
meetings, or even to come downstairs while one was in

progress, but if she could catch his eye from the door perhaps he would come back to the bedroom with her and relax.

She cracked the living-room door. Voices hammered at her. She stopped with her eye to the crack. In the mirror on the wall she could make out the dim shapes of five men around the table. The curtains were drawn, casting the room into shadows, and the chest-on-chest against the far wall seemed to loom over them.

"I tell you, ain't no way I could get through," Jesse Blackwood said. A slender, pale-skinned man, he stood at one end of the table leaning on his fists. Vesey sat at the other end, with Monday Gell and Jack Purcell on one side, and a man it took her a minute to recognize as Gullah Jack on the other. He had shaved off his whiskers.

Vesey looked around the table. "Tell us again what happened." His voice cracked.

"I done told you twice," Blackwood began, then took a deep breath. "I rented a horse with the two dollars you give me. I had the pass you forged in my pocket. First two patrol I meet on the Neck, they don't even look at me. I expect they take me for white. Third patrol had a man name Tyler McCoy in it, and he recognize me. They say all passes suspended, and I better get back to the city."

"And you did what you was told," Gullah Jack sneered.

"There was six of them. And they watch me."

Jack's face twisted. "They watch you? They watch you!"

"What else did they say, Jesse?" Denmark asked. He pulled out a handkerchief and wiped sweat off his face. "Did they mention any names? Say they were looking for anybody in particular?"

Blackwood shook his head. "All they say is, they catch my black ass outside the city again, they skin it and hang it in a tree."

Leonie frowned. Whatever Denmark was involved in, it seemed to be against the law. That didn't worry her as much as his involvement with that Gullah Jack, though. When he looked at her she felt he could see right through her clothes, and she knew he could concoct philtres to make her do whatever he wanted. She'd told Denmark about her fears, though, and he'd just laughed and called her a country girl. She realized Monday Gell was speaking, and she'd missed the first of what he had to say.

" . . . Ned and Rolla Bennett, too. I seen Poyas took, and Billy Carpenter with him. Paul got to have talked. They taking too many as is involved, else." She stifled a gasp at Billy's name.

"No difference," Gullah Jack said. "Don't make no difference at all."

"Oh, shut up!" Vesey said. "We can't get the country people in through the patrols, and the city people won't rise without them. The militia and the City Guard are alerted, and they've apparently got our names. What do you want to do? March onto the gallows for them?"

There was a moment's silence. Jack's face flickered through a dozen contorted emotions. "You giving up? We can drink white blood! We can—"

"We can do nothing," Vesey said. He stood, and his voice strengthened. "Not now. But even if they hang Peter and Ned and the rest, they'll lower their guard again. And we'll be ready."

"You pretty casual about them hanging Poyas and the others," Gell said.

"We don't have time for mourning," Vesey said "We all knew any one of us, or all of us, might die. Now we have to carry on."

Gell was persistent. "How we going to do that if they got our names? Every time somebody walk in the shop to get a piece of harness mended, I going to figure it the constables coming for me."

"Don't be in the shop," Vesey said. "Hide for a few days. All of us should, until we see if we're wanted. I'll send word to the country, and Gullah Jack, too, that the people there are to disperse and wait for a new time. It won't be long in coming. You watch. They let Peter loose once. They may let them all go if they keep their mouths shut. In a week we could all be together again, setting a new date."

"You forgetting about Paul," Gell said. "They ain't turning him loose no matter what."

"Paul was a fool! He deserves whatever he gets!" Vesey tugged at his coat, breathing deeply. "If there are any papers you haven't burned yet, do it. Anything that as much as mentions a name or anything out of the ordinary. Are you prepared to get word to your people in the country?" he asked Gullah Jack. Jack watched him through glittering eyes, unspeaking. Leonie shivered. Vesey seemed to take his silence for assent. "All right, then. Let's not waste any time."

As the men rose from the table Leonie scurried back up the hall and ducked into the closet beneath the stairs. She peeked through a crack at the men leaving, one by one and always peering through the window before opening the door as if to see what was waiting. Vesey was the last to come out of the dining room. She darted out to meet him.

"Surprise, my darling! I—"

He caught her hair in his fist, twisting her head back till she thought her throat would break, pulling the skin of her face tight. His eyes went from the closet to her and back again. "What were you doing? I told you never to come downstairs while I'm having a meeting! Do I have to pound it into your rump with a strap? Were you listening? Spying? What did you hear?"

"Nothing! I swear, nothing!" Her knees had turned to jelly. She had to clutch his coat with both hands to keep from hanging suspended by her hair. His eyes drilled into her. "I didn't know anyone was still here. I was going to surprise you when they started coming out, so I hid in the closet. That's all! I swear!"

After a minute he released his grip. She grabbed the newel post to keep from falling. "Go home," he said. "I'll see you in a few days." He hurried up the stairs without looking at her again.

When a little strength came back to her legs she followed. He had a horsehide traveling case on the bed, packing. Razor, shaving brush and mug, two clean shirts. She tried to take the shirts from him to fold them. He jerked them away and stuffed them in.

"I told you to go home, girl."

"I have to talk to you, Denmark."

"There's no time now. We'll talk in a few days." He rummaged in the drawers of a dark bureau.

"Why can't we talk now? What was going on down there? Why do you have to rush off? Is my father involved in this?"

He froze, pinning her with his dark eyes. "Were you lying to me, girl? Did you listen downstairs?"

"I told you—"

"I know, I know. Yes, your father's involved. And if you want to keep a rope off his neck you'll go home and keep your mouth shut. About me and about the meetings."

"A rope!" She rushed into his arms. "Denmark, it's your neck I'll keep silent for. If I was tortured I wouldn't say anything."

He took her by the shoulders and held her at arms' length. "Good God, girl. That body cries out for a man to hustle it into bed. Jeremiah should've understood I couldn't keep my hands off you, even if he was my brother instead of just my friend."

"He's still all right, isn't he, Denmark?"

He turned away, back to his packing. "He's all right. Put some clothes on before I forget why I have to go. And remember to keep your mouth shut."

She gasped. "I just realized. The uprising the whites are scared of. You're all in the uprising."

"God damn it, girl, I said to home! Go home!"

Shivering, she took off the robe and began to dress. She still hadn't told him about the baby, and now she realized she was afraid to. She began to weep silently. He didn't look around from his packing.

XVI

Billy Carpenter lay on the stone floor staring at the ceiling of his cell. It was stone, too. And the walls. The cracks in the ceiling looked like a map. He'd spent the week since his arrest staring at it. The only opening was a grill, a foot square, in the iron-bound wooden door.

At first he'd been glad to get a cell by himself, what with the others raving with fear and rage. He wasn't sure he could have stood even a little time in that stone box with one of them. Now they'd all quieted down, of course. An hour's fear made the anger rise; a week of it dried the mouth. Now he wished one of them was in with him.

He got stiffly to his feet and put his face to the grill, staring at the grill in the cell door across from his. The hall was empty, so far as he could see. "Poyas." He knew Poyas was in that cell. He'd seen him dragged in, kicking and screaming. "Poyas!" Poyas was chained to the floor, of course. What could he expect, attacking everybody who came close? "Poyas, damn it, answer me!"

The fool wasn't going to answer, and the other man in his cell was probably too scared. Billy sank back to the stone floor. He didn't know why he wanted to talk to Poyas, anyway. All the man would say was, "keep fighting," and "don't say nothing," and "die like a man." Didn't he realize the time for all that was past? At first Billy had thought Vesey might move the rebellion up and rescue them. He didn't know when that date was supposed to be—at his level, he was just to wait for orders—but now he didn't think it was ever going to happen. It was time to think about ways to get out on his own.

The wall had a pattern of cracks that looked like an island. An island with no cells on it. And no ropes.

Footsteps outside brought him to the door again. A slight black boy in his middle teens was pushing a broom down the hall in desultory fashion. "Hey, you!" Billy called. The boy stiffened, started to look, then quickened his step, keeping his eyes firmly on the floor. "Boy, you wants Gullah Jack to get you?" The boy stopped, raising frightened eyes to the grill. "I want you to get me something, boy."

"Ain't allowed to get you nothing," the boy mumbled.

"You want Gullah Jack to shrivel up you eyes in you head?"

The boy swallowed. "What you want?"

"Paper, pen, and ink. And somebody to carry a note."

"You ain't Gullah Jack."

Billy pressed his face against the grill, face distorted by the bars, teeth bared in a grimace. "I knows him, boy. You don't get me what I wants, you belly going to swell up like a pregnant woman till you busts. You don't believe me, you wait. You belly be hurting before dark."

The boy took off running. The heavy door at the end of the hall slammed behind him. Billy let himself drop. He'd done the best he could. It might still work.

An hour later a cloth bundle was pushed through the grill and fell to the stone with a thud. There was the sound of running feet. Quickly Billy unwrapped the bundle. A good pen, a bottle with a little black ink in the bottom, and two crumpled sheets of paper. The boy would be back, he knew. If he was scared enough to bring the pen and the rest, he was scared enough to come back. Carefully he smoothed out the paper, dipped the pen and began.

Jeremiah had taught him how to do ciphers and write with proper grammar and spelling, though he hadn't let him mess with the way he talked. His handwriting had been a complete failure, though, and finally Jeremiah had let him stick with printing, each letter carefully drawn with straight lines.

MRS. FALLON. I AM IN JAIL. YOU MUST GET ME OUT UNLESS
YOU WANT EVERYTHING KNOWN . . . .

Robert was at his desk, writing to a bank in New Orleans, when Albert showed Ben Miller in. He put the letter
aside. It was, he was beginning to think, a waste of time.
Why should a bank lend to even a prosperous merchant in
a city all the way across the country?

"Captain," Miller said as soon as the door closed behind the butler, "I have news."

"Lucille?"

"No, captain. Jeremiah Carpenter."

Robert poured brandy for both of them. "What news?"

"Only rumors, captain. But they were picked up by
three of the boys." He stopped to sip his brandy, and slipped further back in the chair. "They say Jeremiah Carpenter is dead. Some say Vesey killed him, and others just say
he's dead because Vesey wanted him dead. But they all say
Vesey was responsible, one way or another."

Robert set his brandy down without drinking. He'd
been almost certain Jeremiah was dead. Almost. But hearing that others thought so, too, made it more real, more
final. He might not be able to bring the man back, but he
could attend to his killer. "Is anyone willing to testify,
anyone who has something to testify about?"

"Small chance, captain. Right now everybody with a
black skin is afraid to go near a magistrate."

"Do you know where Vesey is now?"

Miller shook his head. "Matthew's following him, but
he changes where he sleeps every night. He's scared."

"I'll see him hang."

"How, captain? No magistrate's going to pay attention
to black rumors, and second hand at that."

"I still have enough influence in this city to get a man
arrested if I charge him with murder," Robert snapped.
"He'll talk once he's thrown in a cell, if only to claim self-
defense."

"I expect he will, captain."

"When will this Matthew report where Vesey's staying
the night?"

"Probably by eight o'clock."

"Good. Let me know as soon as he comes." The hotel-keeper rose to leave. "Ben, I want him. Bad."

"We'll get him, captain."

Moira was in the entry hall when the rap came on the front door. Albert was nowhere in sight. She opened the door herself. A slender black boy, perhaps fifteen, stood awkwardly on the steps, his worn coat wet from the unseasonal rain. Grim clouds roiling to the east told of worse to come.

"You Mrs. Fallon, ma'am?" the boy asked.

"That's right. You'd better step in out of that rain."

"Thank you, ma'am." He dug a folded, dingy scrap of paper from under his coat. "I was told to bring this. And I goes to wait for a answer." Water trickled down his face.

The once crumpled paper, folded carelessly, had no connection in her mind with the crisp, blue-sealed blackmail notes. She had no preparation for what she read.

MRS. FALLON. I AM IN JAIL. YOU MUST GET ME OUT UNLESS YOU WANT EVERYTHING KNOWN. I HAVE WRITTEN DOWN EVERYTHING, AND THE NAME OF ANOTHER WITNESS, AND GIVEN IT TO SOMEONE. IF I AM NOT RELEASED SOON HE WILL TAKE IT TO A MAJISTRATE. DO NOT THINK MY HANGING WILL SAVE YOU. HE WILL TAKE IT. THE WITNESS WILL TALK. GET ME OUT SOON, OR YOU ARE DONE FOR. BILLY CARPENTER.

She clenched her jaw to keep her teeth from chattering. Billy Carpenter? *He* was the blackmailer? How could he bring himself to do it? His brother was Robert's friend. God, he deserved to die. Regretfully she put a clamp on her emotions. Whatever he deserved, she couldn't risk his letter. Or his witness.

"Can you read?" she asked the boy suddenly. He shifted his feet and shook his head. "Are you sure? I'll give you a dollar if you read something I give you."

A pained expression crossed the boy's face. "I surely would like that dollar, ma'am, but I just don't know no reading."

She peered at him intently. He seemed to be telling the

truth. Lord, she was becoming suspicious of everyone. "That's too bad. I'll have a note for you to take back. Wait outside."

She left him dripping on the steps and hurried to the drawing room. Quite abruptly she hadn't wanted him in her house. Perhaps he was not more than a messenger, but perhaps he was Billy's companion in blackmail. Perhaps he was the other witness. The ridiculousness of that—he would have been five or six at the time—brought her to a fit of giggles. She had to bite her fist to stop. There was no time for hysterics.

She took a sheet of paper from the writing desk and printed hastily. If he saw fit to disguise his hand in such a fashion, so would she.

I WILL HELP. BE PATIENT, BUT I WILL HELP.

She didn't sign it.

When she pressed the note, along with two dollars, into the boy's hand, she asked, "Where is he exactly? Which cell?"

He backed down two steps. "In the back," he mumbled. "The second floor." Abruptly he ran, slipping at the foot of the stairs but rolling to his feet in a mud puddle and darting down the street. The rain was coming heavier, and he was soon lost to sight.

She shut the door and leaned against it. How on God's earth was she going to get him out of a jail guarded by half the militia in the city?

The rain had grown into a screaming storm by early evening, blacking the sky. The wind-hurled rain found its way past the upturned collar of Robert's caped overcoat as he hurried into the City Guardhouse, next to the Arsenal on Meeting Street. Ben Miller and Matthew half-ran in his footsteps. Miller, like Robert, held his hat against the wind; Matthew, a lanky young man with a dark beard, clutched a cloth cap.

Inside, a blue-coated sentry started at the apparitions bursting out of the storm, and raised his musket to high port. "Yes, sir? Can I help you, sir?" Three more of the

City Guard lounged at a table, playing cards.

"Let me speak to the officer in charge," Robert said. "I want to bring a charge of murder. A man named Vesey."

"Vesey? Vesey! Yes, sir. Halloran, get the captain! Tell him it's about Vesey!"

"Vesey!" One of the men at the table dashed out of the room. The other two hastily buttoned their tunics and put away the cards.

In a moment Halloran was back followed by a short whip of a man who stood so straight he at first seemed taller than he actually was. His tunic was buttoned up to his neck, gold buttons and braid at sleeve and collar gleaming. "I'm Captain Dove," the rigidly braced man said. "Can I help you, sir?"

"My name is Robert Fallon. From what your men have said, Captain, I can help you. I'm bringing a charge of murder against Denmark Vesey. It seems you're already interested in him."

Dove looked at the sentry. The man pulled his shoulders back another half-inch. Dove sighed. "Yes, sir, we're looking for Vesey. For three days now. Several of the men arrested have named him the leader in the uprising plans."

"It doesn't matter to me what charge you arrest Vesey on. I intend to see him hang."

"If he's the ringleader they say he is, he'll hang, Mr. Fallon. But first we have to arrest him."

"Then I suggest you and some of your men come with me."

Dove's composure cracked. "You mean . . . you know . . . God damn it, Halloran, get Sergeant Tillotson. Tell him I want a dozen men ready to go get Denmark Vesey in ten, no, in five minutes. Move, man!" The same man disappeared from the room again, Dove rubbed his hands together briskly. "Now, if you'll just tell me where Vesey is, Mr. Fallon."

"Matthew here will lead us. He knows the house."

"No need for you to go along, sir, in all this wet."

"No," Robert said sharply. "I'll be there when he's arrested."

The sergeant arrived with his squad, muskets tipped with bayonets, rain cloaks pulled grumpily around them. None liked the prospect of going out, even for Vesey. There'd been enough arrests the past week to blunt any feelings of breaking the conspiracy open.

The bearded man took the lead, with Robert, Dove and Miller on his heels. The guardsmen brought up the rear, a straggling line, trying to keep their musket locks dry beneath their cloaks.

The wind moaned through shuddering tree tops, and driven rain hit the skin like needles. White waves of spray were driven down slick streets, shiny in the light of the street lamps that hadn't been blown out. Then they were in streets lit only by the glow from windows. They turned down Wentworth Street. After two blocks Henry stopped, pointing to a squat house, its lights dimmed by drawn curtains.

"He'd better be right, Mr. Fallon," Dove muttered.

Matthew put fingers to his lips and whistled, low and mournful. Another man appeared from the shadows across from the house, shoulders hunched, rain dripping from the brim of his hat.

"Sam," Matthew said, "it's all right. Is he still here?"

Sam nodded. "Least, he ain't come out by the front door."

"But by the back?" Dove growled. "All right then. You two men around back. You two and you two, to the sides. And keep your eyes open for anything suspicious at the windows. If he manages to slip out he could walk right past you in this." The six men designated melted into the storm. "Well, Mr. Fallon, you ready to go in?"

For an answer Robert walked up the steps and used the knocker. With an oath Dove rushed to join him. The door was opened by a plump brown woman who peered at them with worried eyes. "We're here to see Denmark Vesey," Robert said.

"He ain't here," she gasped, and tried to swing the door shut.

Dove threw his shoulder into the door, bursting it open and sending the plump woman staggering across the plain hall. There was a scraping from a door to the left. Robert ran to it and threw it open. Denmark Vesey sat crouched in the open window beyond, one leg already out in the rain. Dove brushed past Robert with a cocked pistol in his hand.

"Denmark Vesey, I arrest you in the name of the sovereign state of South Carolina and the city of Charleston therein, on charges of conspiracy to cause an uprising among slaves."

At a muffled shout from outside Vesey looked out of the window, then carefully climbed back in. He smoothed the front of his coat with both hands. Rain poured in, puddling on the floor. "There's been some mistake. I admit trying to run may look bad, but after the last few weeks I'm afraid when I saw armed men breaking into the house I panicked. This is my wife's house, you see, and—"

"You're talking too much," Robert said. "The shadow of the gallows is on you, Vesey, and it's cracking you wide open."

Vesey's eyes were calm, but he continued stroking the front of his coat. "I'm surprised to see you here, Mr. Fallon. It is Robert Fallon, isn't it? Perhaps I shouldn't be. Jeremiah always thought you were something special, but you aren't so different after all."

"You mention his name again, Vesey," Robert said, "and I'll kill you with my bare hands." He saw something die in Vesey's face and knew he had been right.

"None of that, Mr. Fallon," Dove said. "He's in my custody, and if one single thing happens to him it'll be because a judge says so. You understand?"

"I gave him to you," Robert said.

"You did that," Dove conceded. "But he's in the custody of the law, now. We don't have lynch justice in this city."

"I can talk to him," Robert said. "I can talk. I want you to know, Vesey, that whatever they hang you for, it was killing Jeremiah Carpenter that put you on the gallows. And if they should somehow let you off with a jail term, I'll be waiting when you get out."

"Damn it, Fallon," Dove broke in.

"I didn't kill Jeremiah!" Vesey cried. "He was my friend!"

"Your friend," Robert sneered. "If your hand didn't kill him, it was your friends. Did you say, I'll shed a tear for an old friend, but this man has to die? Was it your henchmen who murdered him?"

"I didn't touch him," Vesey said. "I never touched him."

Robert thought if he didn't get away from the man he'd throw up. "You can have him, Dove. I don't want to touch him." As he strode out he could hear Vesey importuning the captain.

"This is all a dreadful mistake. I'm a respectable citizen, with property and a business. Why would I risk . . . ."

XVII

On the twenty-ninth of June the city's four daily papers broke the news of Denmark Vesey's death sentence, and the next morning, Sunday, Moira received another note from Billy. She sat for hours in the drawing room, stuffy with its windows tightly shut to keep out the bad summer humors, reading and rereading it.

MRS. FALLON. YOU BETTER GET ME OUT. VESEY IS TO HANG NEXT TUESDAY. IT WILL BE MY TURN SOON. IF I AM STILL HERE WHEN VESEY HANGS, I WILL TELL THE MAN WHO HAS MY LETTER TO TAKE IT TO A MAJISTRATE NOW. GET ME OUT IF YOU KNOW WHAT IS GOOD FOR YOU.

This time he hadn't signed it.

She'd thought of and discarded plan after plan since the first demand came. She had no political pressure to bring to bear, no favors to call in from men in high places. A plea to the governor would be met with sympathy for her kind heart, a pat on the head, and an admonition to let her husband explain why what she asked was impossible.

Fantastical plans had come in the small hours of the morning. Disguising herself as a man, a guard, and sneaking into the jail. Blacking her face and pretending to be a sweeper so she could get to the proper cell. The rest had been worse, and all impossible. She was one woman by herself. The thought of asking for Robert's aid had been sternly dismissed the instant it occurred. Not after Lucille Gautier.

Suddenly she sat up straight. One woman alone. Per-

haps she didn't have to be. She rang for Albert. When he
came she said, "Albert, you once said you'd do anything
in your power to help me. Did you mean it? Think before
you answer, because what I must ask may be more than
you're willing to do."

"Ma'am," he said carefully, "short of murder, I'll help
you any way I can."

"It might not be too far short of murder," she murmured. Now was the time to leap in or back away. She
took a deep breath and told him of Justin Fourrier's death
and Billy Carpenter's blackmail.

"So that's what was troubling you," he said when she
finished. "I'll do whatever I can, ma'am. But am I correct
in thinking you haven't told Mr. Fallon?"

"No, and you're not to breathe a word to him."

"Ma'am, I really think—"

"No!" She realized she was shaking, and clasped her
hands to still them. "Please, Albert."

"I promise. But what are we going to do then?"

"Break him out," she said. When he nodded, she
almost fainted from relief. "Who else can you get to help
us? I have a plan." She had several, all previously discarded because she needed men to carry them out. It all
depended on who he named, and how many.

"Frank Hill, ma'am," he said promptly. "He's the
only man I can think of we can trust in this."

"Hill? The name is familiar, but—"

"The fishmonger, ma'am. You gave him two hundred-
odd dollars."

"That seems an age ago. But would he become involved
in something like this? It was only a few hundred dollars."

Albert smiled. "Not much to you, ma'am, but the
world to him. I see him often. We haven't paid for a fish
in this house since. There were nights he and his wife went
to bed hungry, ma'am, so they could feed their children.
Now he has three boats, because of you, and he's prosper-
ing. If you asked him to feed Billy Carpenter to the sharks,
he wouldn't hesitate a minute."

"There must be nothing like that. If he dies, whatever
the cause . . . . Take me to Frank Hill, Albert. And hurry.

There isn't much time.''

"Where's Albert?'' Robert asked the maid who took his hat and walking stick. The butler never allowed maids to answer the door.

"He gone out, sir. With Mrs. Fallon.''

"Bring coffee to my study.'' Before he reached the study door, though, Hannah appeared at the back of the entry hall, her wooden spoon held rigidly as if to make up for her nervousness at being out of her realm.

"Mr. Fallon, that Sarah Carpenter here to see you, and she worry something fierce. She in the pantry.''

He didn't relish another meeting with Jeremiah's widow. Telling her Jeremiah had been killed by Vesey had been more than enough. She had collapsed in tears so deep there'd been nothing left for him but to go.

She was seated at the big table in the pantry. Someone, Hannah probably, had given her a cup of tea that she hadn't touched. She scraped her chair back when Robert entered, rising with a much older woman's hesitations and stiffness.

"Sit down, Mrs. Carpenter,'' he said. "Drink your tea. Are you all right?''

"She's gone, Mr. Fallon. Leonie's gone, too.'' Her voice quivered, and he realized she was way past the end of her resources.

"Gone where, Mrs. Carpenter? Do you mean she's left home?''

"Yes. No. I don't know, Mr. Fallon. It was yesterday, when the news of Vesey's sentence was in the papers. She started in about him being murdered by . . . ,'' her voice faltered, '' . . . by you folks. She was weeping and shouting. I couldn't take it. I slapped her face and asked her why she wasn't singing that her father's murderer was hanging. She slapped me back. She said I didn't know anything about Vesey, that he wasn't that kind of man, and she knew it for a fact. When I asked her how she knew, she started crying again and ran out of the house. I thought she'd come home in an hour or two, but I haven't seen her since. Mr. Fallon, she's all I have now. I don't want her to get hurt." She began to shake with sobs, collapsing back into the chair.

"She probably just spent the night with friends," Robert said. "Perhaps with some family you know."

"I went to all of them. Nobody's seen her. Mr. Fallon, there's a curse on us. Jeremiah dead. His brother's going to hang. Now Leonie's gone. I don't know what to do any more."

"His brother! Billy? Why would Billy hang?"

"This same Vesey thing," she sniffled. "They arrested him the first day." He handed her his handkerchief, and she dried her face.

"I had no idea. Billy's always been more interested in gambling than anything else."

She nodded vigorously. "He never even went to church except to please Jeremiah. Maybe the court will find him innocent. I don't think I could stand it if they said he was in with the men who killed Jeremiah."

"I didn't think he was a political man. But he might have done that to please his brother, too, mightn't he? Mrs. Carpenter, was Jeremiah involved with Vesey's scheme? Could he have been killed because he was going to turn them in? I can't see him going along with what's coming out of the trials, not with murder and rape."

Two hundred years of black servitude snapped her face shut. It might have been polished brown wood. "My Jeremiah was a good man."

He wondered if she meant too good to be involved with Vesey, or too good to turn him in. "I guess it doesn't matter, now."

"No, sir." She watched from behind that wooden face.

"I'll do what I can about finding Leonie, Mrs. Carpenter. And perhaps I can do something for Billy, too."

The wooden face cracked into flesh, and for a moment tears flowed silently. Then she was blankfaced again, only the dampness of her cheeks testifying to a loss of composure. "You destroy us with your kindnesses."

"What? I don't understand."

"I'll wager you don't, Mr. Fallon. You call me Mrs. Carpenter, and you called Jeremiah your friend, but you owned us as much as if you had papers on us. Your family, your father and you, made Jeremiah more than just another black man in the gutter. A word from you and we'd all be nothing again. We might have been on a long leash, but you held the end of it.''

"That's ridiculous!''

"When Jeremiah had troubles, he never had to work them out himself. You were always there to lift him out of it. And me, too. I ran to you when Jeremiah disappeared, and now for Leonie. You're the man who solves all our problems.'' Abruptly she stood. "I have to go, now.''

"I still want to help.'' He thought his words made her pause for a second at the door, but she kept moving, down the brick steps and around the corner of the house. He turned to find Hannah watching him, her face as blank as Sarah Carpenter's had been.

"Pardon,'' the cook said. "I gots work to do.'' She hurried out, disappearing into the kitchen behind the house.

"Has everybody in this city gone crazy?'' Robert yelled. "Are we all mad?''

Moira was surprised to find Robert waiting in her sitting room. He looked awkward and out of place among the room's satins and silks, velvets and damasks. She cast aside her bonnet and sat gracefully in a Chippendale chair. He stood with his feet wide apart, shoulders braced as if under a heavy weight. His face was unreadable. It abruptly occurred to her that he could have discovered the blackmail.

"You look serious, Robert. Is something wrong?''

"Can you help Sarah Carpenter? Without letting her know you're doing it? Maybe one of your friends could give her a job.''

"I thought you were sending her money.'' Her breathing hadn't quietened yet. Any mention at all of the Carpenter family was too close to Billy to suit her nerves.

"I don't think she'll accept it any longer.'' He grimaced. "Leonie Carpenter's apparently run away from home. And Billy's gotten himself jailed with the Vesey lot.''

"Leonie's run away?'' She was surprised at how steady

her voice was, but she couldn't talk of Billy, not to Robert, not even casually. "Whatever on earth for?"

"God alone knows," he sighed. "Or what Billy thought he was up to. Except for being Jeremiah's brother, I don't suppose he's worth the powder to blow him up, but I can't believe he'd go along with murder."

"Will you try to find the girl? It's dangerous for a girl as pretty as she. She probably doesn't realize."

He waved her concern away. "I'll do what I can, have questions asked. It's Billy that—"

"Are questions enough, Robert? She might have left the city."

"She's a girl," he laughed. "Still in her teens. We'll find her hungry and tired in somebody's shed. You mark my words."

"Perhaps," she murmured. "But what of Mrs. Carpenter? What skills has she?"

"Skills? How should I know? She kept a house. Cooking, sewing, that sort of thing, I suppose."

"That sort of thing. Robert, many a woman keeps house who can't do anything well enough to be paid for it. But never you mind. I'll discover what she can do. You must find her daughter. She can't lose her husband and Leonie, too."

"I'll find her,' he said, and there was weariness even in his determination. He walked across the room and touched her cheek gently. "Don't ever let me lose you, Moira."

"I won't," she replied. And was instantly troubled by what she was keeping from him. It wasn't fair that she should feel so, she thought. When he told her about Lucille Gautier, she'd tell him about her plans for Billy Carpenter's escape. She sighed. "Would you mind leaving me alone for a while, dear? I feel fatigued."

She listened to his parting murmurs in a welter of conflicting emotions. Guilt at keeping secrets from him. Anger that he forced her to keep secrets. Anxiety for her plans. By the time he was gone she did feel fatigued, but she rose immediately and rang for Albert.

"I'm sorry for the delay, ma'am," he said on entering the room ten minutes later. "Mr. Fallon wanted the carriage brought round."

"Did he say where he was going?"

"No, ma'am."

"No matter." There were only two days left, and no time for nonessentials. "Did you get the message delivered?"

"By that boy who works in the jail, ma'am. Just, 'Tuesday morning. Be ready.' "

"Good. And the militia uniform for Frank Hill?"

"The tailor was willing to promise delivery tomorrow."

"Pay him double, if need be, but make sure he has that uniform ready." She pressed her fingertips against her eyes. She would lie down, with a cool compress on her forehead and cucumber slices on her eyelids. Conscience pricked her. "Albert."

"Yes, ma'am?"

"You realize the danger of this?"

"I realize ma'am. Will there be anything else?"

"No, Albert. And thank you. Will you please send Matilda up to me?" She could feel the pressure as a pain behind her eyes. She really did need to lie down.

James Hamilton's butler disappeared deferentially from the entry hall of the Intendant's house. It was Lionel Kennedy Robert needed, but at the magistrate's house he'd been told Kennedy was with Hamilton. Gall bubbled in him at having to ask those men for a favor, and worse for having to face both at the same time.

The butler returned. "Mr. Hamilton will see you now, sir."

The two men were waiting on either side of the fireplace, elbows on the mantel like a painting of huntsmen after the kill. They seemed uncertain what sort of fox they'd found. Hamilton's thick brows were drawn together; Kennedy's nondescript features appeared even more so in surprise.

"Gentlemen," Robert said.

"We're busy, Mr. Fallon," Hamilton said. "We can only spare you a few minutes."

"I've come to collect a favor you gentlemen owe me."

"Owe you!" Kennedy burst out. "What favor do we owe you?"

"I showed you where to find Vesey."

Kennedy's jaw dropped. "The duty of any public-spirited citizen."

"And you weren't interested in the rebellion, Mr. Fallon. Oh, no, not you." Hamilton walked stiffly to the sideboard and poured himself a brandy. "As I recall, you were in a lather because Vesey supposedly killed some other black."

"That's beside the point," Robert said. "I still gave him to you on a platter."

"What is it you want?" Hamilton asked.

"You have a man in your cells, arrested in connection with the conspiracy."

"A black!" Kennedy exclaimed. "I should've known it."

Robert went on as though there'd been no interruption. "From what I know of the man, he's not likely to be any kind of leader, if he's involved at all."

"And you want special treatment for him?" Hamilton's voice was smooth.

"So far only ringleaders have been sentenced to death. Others found guilty—and I'm still not sure he will be—have been sentenced to exile. If that's the sentence, instead of shipping him out to Africa, turn him over to me. I'll see that he's sent out of the country."

"It seems to me you do want a favor," Hamilton said.

"For the love of heaven, Hamilton," Robert said, "you have the ringleaders. Do you really need to hang every black who was fool enough to listen to Vesey? Billy Carpenter couldn't lead a cockfight."

"We don't have all the ringleaders," Hamilton said. "There's a fellow calls himself Gullah Jack still on the loose that we know of, and we have suspicions about two or three more."

Kennedy stroked his chin. "Carpenter. Carpenter. Where have I heard that name?"

He walked to Hamilton's desk and began rumaging through a pile of papers while Robert seated himself. If they connected Billy's name to the man he'd charged Vesey with murdering, they might take a different view of the killing and of Billy. Their suspicion would put him on a gallows for sure.

"Here it is." Kennedy waggled a paper at them. "This Billy Carpenter is one of the cases we vote on tomorrow. He should be sentenced before nightfall."

"If you find him guilty," Robert said.

"What? Oh, of course. If he's guilty."

"Can you tell me if he's likely to be found guilty?"

"That's up to the jury, Mr. Fallon. No business of mine to interfere."

"Of course not. But as to the other thing. If his sentence is exile—and remember, if he's involved at all, he's a small fish—can he be put in my custody?"

Hamilton's long nose had begun to twitch. Now he leapt in. "Certainly not, Fallon. What you ask is highly irregular. I'm surprised at you."

Kennedy had been caught with his mouth open. He peered at the Intendant with considerable asperity. "Not at all, my dear Hamilton. Precedent. There is precedent. Several slaves sentenced to exile have been remanded to the custody of their owners for shipment out of the state."

"But this Billy Carpenter isn't Fallon's slave!" Hamilton said it as though he'd won his point, but the magistrate was still visibly rankled over being cut off.

"Still, we do owe Mr. Fallon something for Vesey, eh? If this Billy fellow is to be exiled, he's your responsibility, Mr. Fallon."

"A moment, Kennedy," Hamilton said, drawing the magistrate aside by his sleeve.

Their voices were muted, but once Kennedy's voice was raised in, " . . . my word, sir . . ." before sinking back to a barely audible murmur under the other's urging. Hamilton's gestures grew broader, while Kennedy alternately nodded and shook his head like a man giving ground slowly. Finally the Intendant stalked back to the fireplace looking like he'd gotten half a loaf when he expected a full one. Robert worried about which half he'd gotten.

Kennedy harrumphed and took a wide-legged stance. He was obviously over his pique at Hamilton and remembering how little he liked Robert. "This release in custody has precedent, it's true, but so does a time limit. Each man who's had his slave released to him had to have the black out of the state in twenty-four hours, and post a bond to it. Therefore, you must post a thousand-dollar bond to have this Billy shipped out within twenty-four hours of his sentence. If you fail, Billy will be remanded to custody and shipped into exile in the regular manner. And, of course, your bond will be forfeit."

The regular manner was a matter of public record, now. Exiles were to be put ashore in the clothes they stood up in, in some tiny African coastal village, where they'd be lucky not to be killed as strangers or die of the fever in a year.

"I have a ship sailing Tuesday for Jamaica and the Caribbean," Robert said. "If you can give me some idea of when a verdict is expected, I'll be there."

"The trials," Kennedy said portentously, "are not open to the public." Hamilton's smile was approving.

"I'm not certain I understand," Robert said.

"There's nothing to understand." The Intendant's voice was smug. "Verdicts are posted every morning for the public."

"They're posted at eight," Robert said incredulously. "How am I supposed to post a bond, take custody, and get him aboard *Dolphin* in time for her to make the morning tide?"

"That's your problem," Hamilton replied.

"Damn it, you're as much as making it impossible."

"I don't like your tone," Kennedy said. "You came here for a favor, and now you want to set your own conditions. Twenty-four hours is what the others got. If you don't like it, go home and let justice take its course."

Robert found himself back on the street in a haze of anger. Putting the sailing off till the evening tide was out of the question. If Hamilton had anything to do with when the court voted, the twenty-four hours would be up well before then. It wasn't likely Kennedy would press for a death penalty simply to spite him—as little integrity as the man had, he had more than that—just as he wouldn't go back on the letter of his promise. Only the spirit. The problem was doing half a day's work in under an hour. Just getting him to the ship in time was nearly impossible. The bond alone would take hours if Kennedy had anything to do with it.

Suddenly a smile creased his face. He climbed hurriedly into the carriage. "Charles Furman's house, Josephus. Quickly!" As the horses drew him clattering over the cobblestones he wondered about Leonie. When he left Furman's he'd have to get Miller started looking for her.

The high-wheeled cart thumped over ruts in the road, and every thump sent another jolt of pain up Leonie's spine. Her hands had begun to blister from sawing at the reins of the hammerheaded swayback between the poles, but neither pain bothered her. They were badges of her escape from Charleston, from a life where she could never be truly free. Her skin imposed one kind of slavery, her mother's words another.

Suddenly two mounted white men, roughly dressed and with rifles slung across their backs, were blocking the road. Patrollers, looking for runaways. "Look what we got here, Tyrell," one said. "A likely-looking wench. I ain't never seen her before. You think we ought to take her in to check?" His beady brown eyes ran over her like rough hands.

"Never heard of no runaway heading west," the man called Tyrell said.

Leonie smiled to herself. That had been her reason for heading west instead of north. The further north, the greater the chance of being held as a runaway, and the only way to prove her freedom would be through her mother. Then they'd drag her back as if she really were a slave.

She thickened her accent. "I belong to Miss Jennie Holt. She done send me over to Hammond to get some flower she want to plant." She checked the name of the next town every few miles. "I got me a pass." She fumbled the folded paper out of her dress and handed it to

Tyrell. A lap desk, folded and stowed under the straw in the cart, had provided the means of forging it.

Tyrell's whiskers moved as he mouthed the words. "Looks all right to me. Come on, Ezra. We got a lot of ground to cover yet."

"How do we know she didn't forge that?" Ezra asked. Leonie tried to keep her hands still on her lap.

"You think I can't tell something writ by a lady? Ain't no slave girl got a hand this fine."

"I think—"

"Ezra, you just want to scare this girl out of her dress and into the bushes. Well, you ain't going to waste time when you're riding patrol with me." He handed the pass back with a smile. "Don't you worry, girl. I ain't going to let Ezra hurt you none. Now you better get on your way. Folks is edgy what with all the doings over to Charleston."

"Yes, sir. It's horrible." She didn't have to fake a shudder. How many more had died? Denmark, certainly, or he soon would. "I'll certainly get on my way." She twitched the reins, and the swayback horse moved on up the rutted road.

XVIII

The second of July was a muggy Tuesday, a day when the sun came up behind clouds that trapped the heat but gave no promise of rain. A gallows had been erected on Blake's Lands, north of the city, and from before first light carriages had rattled on the cobblestones as people went out to the hangings. There would be picnics, and children playing games. A celebration with the proof before them that the danger was finally over.

Moira turned from the drawing-room window. "Go over everything one more time. There's no room for mistakes."

Albert and Hill stood in the middle of the Turkey carpet. Hill fidgeted in the blue of a militia corporal, and Albert continually tugged at the rough pants and shirt he wore, trying to find some way they fit.

"We enter the jail," Hill said, "with this letter you gave us. Then . . . ."

The carriage rolled to a stop at the Bridge, and Robert opened the door for Kemal and Ben Miller.

"Morning, captain," Miller said as he followed the bald Turk in. "You expecting trouble with this Billy Carpenter?"

"I want to be sure he gets aboard *Dolphin* with no difficulty. Does Morton have *Olympic* ready?"

"Aye, captain. She's—"

"Mr. Fallon? You be Mr. Fallon, don't you?" Robert swiveled his head at the boyish shout. A street urchin with

the inevitable dirty face and ragged shirt peered up at him
with a box clasped firmly beneath his arm.

"I am," Robert said.

"Lady give me a dollar to bring you this." He handed
up the box and looked hopefully for another tip.

It was a four-inch cube, ornately carved in arabesques. It
took a moment to find the thin line marking the lid. "A
lady, you say?"

"Yes, sir. She was about to take a boat out to a ship,
and she asked if anybody knew Mr. Robert Fallon to see
him, and I stood forward."

A sudden chill of caution took him, and he set the box
carefully on the seat next to him.

"Lucille Gautier?" Miller asked.

Robert nodded. "Let me have your knife, Ben."

Miller produced the heavy-bladed clasp knife from beneath his coat. Carefully holding a corner of the box,
Robert forced the blade under the top and twisted. With a
snap the lid flipped open, and from each side of the box
an inch-long needle suddenly projected. He stared at the
dark-stained point a finger's breadth from his hand and
shivered. Inside the box was a bundle of white feathers
tied to a large thorn.

"Mother of God," Miller breathed.

The urchin stirred uneasily. He couldn't see over the
side of the carriage. "What's the matter, mister? I delivered it just like she give it to me. I didn't do nothing to it."

Robert tossed him a dollar to quiet him. "I know, lad.
Did the lady say what ship she was taking?"

"No, sir. But I know the boat was from the *Mary J.* Out
of Salem, bound for New Orleans."

"Good lad. You come back here this afternoon, and
there'll be regular work for you."

He barely heard the boy's thanks. He knew the *Mary J.*
Another ship making the morning tide. He could get to
her, perhaps even put his hands on Lucille, but not if he
was going to get Billy Carpenter aboard *Dolphin.* Carefully he closed the lid; the needles retracted smoothly. "The
jail, Josephus. And hurry."

The forbidding gray jail loomed over Magazine Street

like a medieval fortress, with square towers and crenellated roofline. Armed sentries stood at the arched gate in the thick wall surrounding the yard to one side of the jail. As soon as the carriage stopped across the street from it, Miller hopped down and walked over to engage the guards in conversation. In moments he was back.

"The list isn't up yet, captain. They say what with the big hanging and all, it might be a little late."

"It won't be late. Kennedy and Hamilton will be just as punctual as the law requires, not a minute fast or slow. They want to watch me make a fool of myself struggling to get him out of the state before the deadline."

He climbed down and began to pace the cobblestones. Except for a small knot of young men from the newspapers waiting for the list to be posted, the street was nearly empty. Guards posted two blocks from the jail in all directions were discouraging traffic, and even people who lived in the area deemed it wisest to remain indoors.

Miller, watching him pace, finally said, "I haven't been able to find a trace of that girl, captain. She must have left the city."

Robert didn't stop his walking, nor take his eyes from the iron-bound gate. "Put out flyers, Ben. I promised Leonie's mother I'd find her."

"North, captain? She's likely headed for the free states."

A small door set in one of the gates opened. "That's right. North." A militia sergeant came out with a hammer and carefully tacked two sheets of paper to a post a few feet from the gates. The reporters flocked to it.

Robert pushed his way through, ignoring their protests. The two sheets were headed FOUND GUILTY and FOUND INNOCENT. Billy Carpenter's name was third down on the guilty list. Sentence: exile.

"Wait here," he told the other two, and went to the sentries. "I'm here to see Magistrate Kennedy. He should be expecting me."

"One minute, sir," the sentry said, rapping on the small door. It was covered with iron bosses. The sergeant who had posted the list appeared at the judas window, and, after listening to the sentry, opened the door.

"This way, if you please, sir," he said.

The thick stone walls held the coolness in the office Kennedy was using, as later in the day they would hold the heat. Robert was willing to wager the nondescript man would be gone long before his collar began to wilt.

"Ah, Mr. Fallon," Kennedy said with false joviality, "I see you've already perused the posting. Early bird, eh?" He didn't rise from his desk.

"Early enough. If you'll have Billy Carpenter brought out, I'd like to get him to the docks."

"Certainly. Certainly. Just as soon as we get the formality of the bond out of the way." He drew a sheet of paper to him, dipped a pen, and began to write with exaggerated care. "I'll have to get a clean copy made of this, of course, but I like to see to the wording myself."

Robert permitted himself a small smile as he took several folded sheets of foolscap from inside his coat. "The bond has already been posted."

"What?"

"Magistrate Furman was kind enough to see to it Sunday night. You'll see that cotton to the value of one thousand and eighty dollars was put up as pledge."

"Going behind my back," Kennedy muttered as he shuffled through the papers. "I'll tell you, I don't like it one bit." He drew out his pocket watch; Robert did the same. Eight ten. Robert could see the magistrate's thoughts. Ten minutes to get Billy out of the jail, another ten at least to get to the wharf. There wasn't a chance of making the tide for any ship that waited that long. "Everything does seem in order, though," Kennedy said finally. "Millrose! Have Billy Carpenter brought up here."

Robert could feel the minutes ticking away before Billy shuffled in, manacled hand and foot, flanked by a pair of guards. "I'll have the irons off him, please. Hello, Billy."

Billy flashed a grin that was half sneer. "I didn't reckon on getting out this way." One of the guards produced a key at Kennedy's nod and unfastened the manacles. Billy rubbed his wrists, still with the half sneer on his face.

"Any way of getting out is a good way," Robert said. He took the pass Kennedy handed him. "We'd better hurry, or you'll miss your passage." He ignored the magistrate's snicker and hustled the black man out.

He hurried down the stone steps as fast as he could, pausing only at the gate to show his pass. As he opened his mouth to call for the others to follow, there was a sharp crack, followed immediately by the whine of a bullet off of the gate's iron bosses. He dove to the cobblestones, dragging Billy with him. His cheek stung. He put up a hand, and it came away red.

The door in the gate clattered open, and a dozen more guards rushed out, shouting, to join those already waving their bayonet-tipped muskets about wildly.

"Where are they?"

"It's the blacks attacking!"

"Anybody hurt?"

"Him! Over there!" A number of hands pointed to Robert.

Miller and Kemal crouched, ready to move in any direction, studying the far side of the street amid the militia's confusion. A pistol had appeared in Miller's hand, and Kemal gripped a broad-bladed dagger. Billy leaped up to run.

"Get him in the carriage!" Robert shouted.

Billy wasn't a small man, but Kemal plucked him up and thrust him into the carriage. Robert followed close behind.

"It's that Gautier bitch again!" Miller shouted as he clambered in. "We have to finish her!"

"No time. Josephus, the Bridge. Drive, man! Drive!"

The carriage rattled down the street, leaving the militia milling behind them.

Albert stared after the retreating carriage, then looked down at the man he and Hill had jumped in the act of firing. Sallow complected, with a nose that'd been broken more than once, he lay in an alley down the opposite side of the street from the jail. A trickle of blood ran down his face from his scalp.

"Is he hurt?" Hill asked. He peered around the corner after the carriage.

"I think he's still breathing."

"I meant Mr. Fallon."

Albert shrugged. "I think so. They were moving too fast to see much. But he got Billy Carpenter out."

"That fellow was Carpenter? Why?"

"I don't know. I don't care." He peeked at the militia again. They were finally spreading out in a search. "We'd better get out of here."

"We can't leave him." Hill indicated the man on the ground, who chose that moment to twitch and emit a groan. The fisherman whipped out a pistol from beneath his coat, and Albert was suddenly gladder than ever they hadn't had to go through with their plan. "Listen," Hill said, jerking the would-be assassin to his feet. "You can go with us, or you can stay here." He cocked the pistol with a loud snap. "Which will it be?"

The sallow man eyed the gun unblinkingly. "I reckon I'll go with you."

Quickly the three headed down the alley, away from the militia.

In the carriage, Billy sat silently while Robert and Miller talked in low voices about how to track Lucille Gautier and Cordelia Applegate. When they drew to a halt before the warehouse, he finally spoke.

"What we doing here?"

"No time," Robert said, dashing up the wharf. "I'll explain on the boat."

Kemal and Miller dragged a protesting Billy down the dock after him and onto the *Olympic*, lying where he'd ordered with steam up and a trail of smoke lifting from her stack. "Take her out, Captain Holden," Robert shouted as soon as his feet hit the deck. To shouted orders from the quarterdeck mooring lines splashed over the side, and the paddlewheels churned the water to froth. *Olympic* accelerated away from the Bridge.

"What you doing?" Billy writhed in Kemal's grip, his face contorted by fear and rage. "You going to kill me?

You kill me, everybody know everything! I wrote letters! I can write, you know! I wrote letters!''

"Calm down," Robert said. "Why would I want to kill you? You've been sentenced to exile, man. I thought you'd rather be sent to Jamaica than some African village of straw huts."

"So?" Billy said cautiously.

"Mind your manners!" Miller growled.

Robert waved the old seaman to silence. "There are men in the city would like to see you sent to Africa just because I don't want it. They set a twenty-four-hour time limit after your sentencing for you to be out of the United States, then held up your release to my custody until they thought you'd miss the tide. They'd have the satisfaction of making me look like a fool at your expense."

"How you planning on changing that?" He relaxed in Kemal's grip, no longer fighting, and Robert motioned the big Turk to let him go. Billy took a nonchalant step away. "I still ain't hear you say how you going to change anything."

Robert frowned. He hadn't expected overwhelming gratitude, but neither had he expected complete contempt. "*Dolphin*, the ship that'll take you to Jamaica, sailed earlier. That's her ahead." He pointed to a bark under full sail for the harbor mouth. At the rate they were closing, they'd come up on her about the time she reached the harbor bar. "You'll transfer by sling. I have a letter of introduction to a man in Jamaica who'll help you get a job, and a hundred dollars to get you started."

"A hundred! I figure it worth a thousand to keep them letters from being sent."

"What in hell are you talking about?" Robert snapped. "What letters?"

Billy sneered. "The letters what made you get me out of jail. The letters that'll tell what your wife done to that old Fourrier. She already paid some, but I ain't got none of that now. You don't want them letters sent, you gets me a thousand dollar."

Robert listened in stunned silence, then abruptly something happened. "You son-of-a-bitch!" he howled.

Without knowing how he got there, he had his fingers locked in Billy's throat. "You bastard! Blackmail my wife! I'll kill you, God damn your soul to hell!"

Suddenly he was being dragged loose by Miller and Kemal. The crew watched in disbelief. "Easy, captain," Miller said. "It isn't worth it. There's witnesses."

"Don't you touch me again!" Billy choked out. "You touch me, I—" He was cut off abruptly by Kemal's huge hand closing on his throat and lifting till only his toes touched the deck. He clawed at the Turk's arm, but the grip didn't slacken.

"You want him dead, captain?" Miller said for Robert's ears alone. "Kemal and me, we'll rig his sling. He'll go right into the paddlewheel. An accident."

Robert shrugged free. Tugging the money and the letter of introduction from his coat he shoved the envelopes into Billy's trouser pockets. "I was your brother's friend," he said quietly. "That's why you're going to live. I owe him. To tell you the truth, though, you ain't worth a tenth of what he was. I'd probably be doing more for his memory if I was up at Blake's Lands seeing the man who killed him hang."

"You lie!" Billy managed to get past Kemal's grip. "Jeremiah upcountry. He come back, he cut all you throat."

"You're a damned fool," Robert said.

Suddenly he felt infinitely weary. He staggered to the bow and leaned against the rail, staring at the shape of the bark ahead. But he didn't see it. Moira had been blackmailed, and she hadn't come to him. Were their lives such shambles that she thought she had to face that alone? They weren't much better off than the Carpenters, destroyed and scattered on the winds. He had to hold things together. Somehow he had to.

"Captain," Miller called. "It's time."

He brought himself back to the ship. *Olympic*, quivering with the strain of her boiler, thrashed alongside *Dolphin*. The bark's rigging creaked as she rushed for a channel that already might be too shallow. It was certainly too shallow for the paddlewheeler.

A weighted rope, hanging from a yard, swung over from the bark. Miller grabbed it; Kemal hoisted Billy to the rail. The two men worked at tying the rope around his waist. Miller looked at Robert questioningly. He shook his head, and Miller turned back with a shrug. With a hearty push from both men Billy swung out and across. Hands on *Dolphin* grabbed him, and cheers went up from both ships.

"Both astern!" Holden shouted, and the wheels shivered to a halt, then thrashed in reverse.

Robert watched the other ship closely. The full spread of canvas hurled it toward where there should still be enough water for its keel. Closer. And then it was through. Another cheer went up, but Robert didn't feel like joining.

"Ahoy the deck!" the masthead shouted. "Sail two points off the starboard bow!"

"What of it?" Holden shouted back.

"It's *Hunter!* I'd recognize her anywhere!"

Suddenly Robert did feel like cheering. By God, nothing would beat the Fallons. Nothing could beat the Fallons. "Put her about, Captain! I've a need to get home."

"Mrs. Fallon," Hannah said, "that Albert say he got to see you out in the stable." Her mouth wrinkled disapprovingly. "He wearing some old rags from I don't know where."

"I'll go see what he wants," Moira said. She laid her unread book carefully on the sofa and left the drawing room with a conscious effort not to run. Something had gone wrong, her brain hammered. Albert should be on one of the fishing boats, leaving the harbor with Billy.

When she pushed open the stable, she gasped. Albert and Hill were both there, with a man she'd never seen before. Hill was holding a gun on him. She took a quick look to see if anyone else was in the long brick building.

"It's all right, ma'am," Albert said quickly. "I cleared everybody out before we brought him in."

"Who is he? What happened? Where's Billy?"

"Your husband got him out, ma'am," Hill said. "Then this fellow took a shot at him. At your husband, I mean."

She swayed and would have fallen if Albert hadn't steadied her. "Is he all right?"

"I think so, ma'am," Albert said. "They all got in the carriage and drove off. He looked all right."

"Please, God," she whispered. Suddenly she jerked the gun away from Hill and jabbed it at the sallow man. "Why did you try to kill my husband? Why, damn you? If he's hurt . . . ." She backed him up against a stall door.

He licked his lips and stared at the gun wide-eyed. She was more likely to kill him by accident than the men on purpose. "It weren't my idea," he stammered. "It was that woman. She paid me."

"What woman?" she grated. "A name, damn you!"

"She never gave no name. A fellow found me and said there was this woman wanted me. She give me a hundred dollars, and said there was another hundred if Fallon was dead today. Before God," he whined as her knuckles whitened on the gun, "it weren't my idea!"

She took a deep breath and regained control. All three men sighed with relief. "Where did you meet her? What did she look like? I want to know every scrap."

"She was pretty, kind of dark." He gestured in front of his chest. "And she had some kind of accent. A lady, by her clothes."

"Lucille Gautier," she breathed. What had Robert gotten himself into with that woman? "Do you have a place you can keep him until we find out what he knows?"

"I have a place, ma'am," Hill said.

She returned the gun to the fisherman and left them. Outside she met Hannah again.

"Mrs. Fallon, Mr. Fallon just this minute come in the door, and he want to see you something awful."

"I think it's time I saw him, too," Moira said.

When Moira entered his study Robert started toward her, then stopped. There was something different about her, a look of serene strength. He took a quick step and put his arms around her. "I just put Billy Carpenter on a ship for Jamaica." She sighed against his chest. "Why didn't you tell me what was going on?"

Her reply was a whisper. "Why didn't you tell me Lucille Gautier was trying to kill you?"

He grunted as if struck. "How—? Where—? No, it doesn't matter. She's gone, Moira. Sailed this morning for New Orleans. She came here to destroy me. She was responsible for the foundry fire. She tried three times to kill me. It's hard enough for a man to tell his wife he's made a fool of himself without him knowing just how big a fool he's been."

"And it's hard for a woman to ask her husband for help when she knows he's come from another woman's bed."

He winced. "She's Cordelia Applegate's daughter."

"Cordelia—" she began, then clutched herself tight to his chest. "She can't be coming back into our lives. Not after so long. Does everything have to go on and on, every enemy come back to haunt us?"

"Hush, darling." He stroked her hair, like fine black silk. "We'll outlast them all. We can survive anything."

"I believe we can."

"Our biggest trouble," he said, "will be surviving ourselves. I've watched one family disintegrate, Moira. I don't want to watch ours do the same. I'll make arrangements about Edward . . . ."

She covered his mouth with her fingers. "I've learned something about my own strengths, Robert. There's no need to send the boy away."

"Are you sure, Moira?"

"I'm sure," she said firmly.

"You're a surprising woman. I wonder if I'll ever exhaust your surprises."

"I still have one or two more. Including one in the barn."

With a laugh he scooped her up in his arms. "You have an infinity of them." He kicked open the study door and carried her into the hall.

"Robert, your back!"

"You wait till I get you upstairs, and I'll show you how

strong my back is.''

"Robert, the servants," she said, scandalized. "It's the middle of the morning."

"Let them think what they want to. Let the whole damned world think what it wants to." He took the stairs two at a time.

BOOK II

Louisiana and Texas
1822-1828

XIX

James Christopher Fallon strode across the broad veranda of Beaulieu, set on a hill with a view of the Mississippi through the trees, and rapped on the door. The September Louisiana air still smelled of summer. He stood an inch over six feet, with broad shoulders and a deep chest. He had been told his father, a sea captain killed by Barbary pirates, was the source of his blue eyes, and of the hooked nose and high cheekbones that made him look slightly dangerous even in repose. Even at twenty women gave him a second glance, and men thought twice.

Pompey, the gray-haired black butler, opened the door and smiled, "Good morning, Mister James. You bright and early this morning."

"I didn't even sleep last night, Pompey." He let the stooped man take his walking stick and curly-brimmed beaver hat. "I have to see Miss Helene."

"Yes, sir," Pompey chuckled. "I didn't expect you come this early to see Mr. St. Albin. She in the front drawing room."

"No," he said with an answering grin. Helene's father was full of boring tales that politeness seldom let him escape. He winked, and the butler laughed again.

Peter St. Albin had built Beaulieu after a European tour with his wife and five children. He'd been entranced by the interiors of Italian *palazzos*. The drawing room had gilt-and-lacquer furniture, a huge marble fireplace, and cupids and clouds painted on a blue ceiling.

Helene was seated on a sofa with her back to the door,

159

her pretty blonde head in a book. He looked over her shoulder and grinned. The book was upside down.

"Can you really read it like that?" he said innocently.

She snapped the book shut. "You're no gentleman, James Fallon, to go looking over a lady's shoulder that way."

He turned on his heel. "Then I guess I'd better go."

"No! I mean . . . oh, damn you, James Fallon. You sit yourself down." He laughed and took a seat next to her. She slid away from his arm. "I'll thank you not to act as if I'm one of those quadroon girls."

"Helene!" Thank God she didn't know he had said goodbye to one of those quadroon girls, Angélique Deseau, only the day before in the little house on Rampart Street where he'd kept her the past two years. "You shouldn't even know about such things."

"Women aren't fools," she said primly, "and we aren't blind." Her clear blue eyes looked at him through pale lashes. "It must be something important to bring you out so early. I know the hours you keep, gambling and carousing with that awful James Bowie."

"It is important, Helene. You know I love you, don't you?" Her smile was answer enough. "I want you to marry me."

"Why, James, you know papa thinks eighteen is too young for a girl to marry."

"Come with me to Texas. We'll build a grand new life together." He didn't notice the way her mouth hardened. "There's land to be had almost for the asking. Stephen Austin—I've told you about him—has already gone. He's promised me a good place in his colony."

"Always Texas! I declare, James Fallon, I don't see why you can't be satisfied right here. You'll inherit Greenwood, or most of it, and it's a fine sugar plantation, if not so big as papa's."

"I have three sisters, Helene, and Greenwood must provide them with dowries."

She blinked. "You mean you'll be cut off? I know Thomas Martin is only your stepfather, but he wouldn't do that."

"No, he wouldn't. But I don't intend to leave it up to him. I've told him what's right, and he understands." He wished his mother understood as well.

"You're not worried about your sisters. You just want some sort of adventure. I declare, I don't know what your stepfather thinks, letting you spend time with Indians and such. And that trip you took on the river last year."

"A lot of men travel on the river."

"On a keelboat? With those lowlife rivermen?" She sniffed. "You seem to delight in ruffians. Indians, rivermen, and now Texas."

"Stephen Austin is a respectable attorney, Helene, and he wants sober, industrious men."

"But you're a gentleman!"

"I'm a man," he said; but he could see she didn't understand. "Helene, if your father won't let us marry right away, we can still be betrothed. Your father can't object to your getting married at twenty, and in two years I'll have built a home you'll be proud of."

"Two years!" she wailed. "If we're betrothed, and you're gone, I won't be able to go to a single ball or *soirée*."

"But, Helene—"

"You're not the only gentleman who calls on me. Samuel Deschamps is the most beautiful dancer, and Beaumont Langford has written sonnets to my eyes, and—"

"But you love me."

She made a petulant *moue*. "I do. And if you stay, I'd much rather marry you than any of those others. But . . . two years!"

"Wait for me," he said quietly, "or marry me now and come with me."

"I'm coming down with a migraine. I think you'd better go, James."

He kept a tight rein on his anger. "Of course." He started for the door.

"And, James," she said to his back, "I don't think you should come back until you decide whether it's me you love, or Texas."

He slammed the door behind him.

As he galloped away from Beaulieu, his temper began to cool, and he slowed to a walk. When he saw Henry Cameron lying by the river with his hat pulled over his eyes, he drew rein. The free black man was five years older than him, as near as either could figure, and they had practically grown up together. It had been Henry who introduced James, to his father's delight and his mother's dismay, to the Indian villages. Louise Martin, a French diplomat's daughter, was horrified that her son preferred the company of a black and hunting in the bayous to the social company of young men of his own class. Thomas Martin, who had grown up in the mountains of East Tennessee, thought it just fine. A fishing rod stuck in the bank of Cameron's feet jerked.

"I think you've got a catfish, Henry," James called.

Henry lifted his hat from his handsome face. He was an inch taller than James, and almost as black as coal. "I reckon," he sighed. After a minute he drew the line in, tossed the fish on the bank, and threw the bare hook back in the river. "I ain't exactly down here for fishing. I just got some thinking to do, but it don't hardly seem right to be by the river without putting a line in."

"You have troubles, Henry? You sound worried."

"Women so contrary headed—why is that?"

"I don't know. Looks like we're in the same boat. I've got woman troubles, too."

"Marie Desalle don't want no part of me."

"Helene St. Albin just tossed me out on my ear."

"Least you don't have voodoo to worry about."

"Voodoo! You don't believe in that foolishness, do you?"

"You know better," Cameron said scornfully. "But Marie does. I won't have my wife mixed up in that, and she won't marry a man who doesn't believe. Trouble is, I love her so bad I can't think straight. How you figuring to solve your troubles?"

"I'm going to Texas," James said.

"Texas! The Indians out there'll kill you soon as look at you. And what I hear, the Mexicans don't like Americans one bit better."

"A friend of mine has permission from the Mexicans to start an American colony. Maybe you ought to come along, too. It'll be a good place to forget a broken heart."

"Sounds to me like a good place to get a broken head. I reckon I'll stay here."

"All right," James laughed, feeling better. "You take care." He turned his horse back up the river.

"You take care, too," Henry called after him. "And good luck in Texas."

It wasn't far to Greenwood, a three-story house of cream brick set amid giant pecan trees and oaks with limbs as thick as a man's body.

Crowel, the butler, met him at the head of the veranda steps. "Mr. James, where you been? Your papa and mama been wanting you all the morning." Three brunette heads appeared giggling at the door, and as promptly disappeared. His sisters, Barbara, seventeen, and the twins, Elaine and Eleanor, fifteen.

James peered after the girls in surprise. They invariably ran to greet him, pestering him unmercifully. "What's going on here, Crowel?"

"Ain't my place to say, Mr. James. Was I you, though, I'd get myself on in the study."

James hurried inside. The entire family was waiting in Thomas Martin's study. Thomas himself stood in front of the fireplace, feet planted wide and hands clasped behind his straight back. Louise, at forty a petite, still beautiful woman, didn't look at him. She was running her fingers over a blanket that covered the low table against one wall.

"We've been waiting," Elaine said accusingly, and Eleanor echoed, "Waiting." Both spoiled the effect by giggling. Barbara frowned condescendingly at her sisters. All three girls had their mother's beauty, though in the twins it was still masked by chubbiness.

"Have I fallen into some trouble I don't know about?" James asked.

Louise opened her mouth, but Thomas forestalled her. His hair was graying at the temples, his lean face tanned from long days hunting. "No, boy, no., Your mother and

I have had a long talk.'' He gave her a look that brooked no interference; her face tightened. ''We've decided that if you truly want to go to Texas, you should.''

''Think of the strange animals you'll see,'' Eleanor said excitedly.

''And wild Indians!'' Elaine squealed.

''James,'' Barbara said, ''you will come back, won't you? I mean, to visit us?'' She tried to keep her voice serene—she was very conscious of being an adult—but there was a tremor in her words.

''Of course, I'll come back,'' James said gently. He took Louise's hand, and for the first time she looked at him. He saw she had been crying. ''And you, *maman*? Have you decided I should go to Texas?''

She reached up to stroke his cheek. ''You are so much like your papa.'' She still had a faint accent more than twenty years after leaving France. ''He would not be bound by a woman's apron cords, and I gave you to raise to a man who also would not be bound. I have been foolish to think I could keep you here.''

''I won't be gone forever, *maman*.''

''Could you not at least stay until spring?

''Stephen will have given all the good land away by then.''

''The boy's right,'' Thomas said. ''He'd best be gone before the month's out.''

''But that's less than two weeks,'' Barbara protested. ''I've begun three shirts—oh, you weren't supposed to know—three shirts for your Christmas, James. I'll never have them done in time.''

''And me,'' Elaine said. ''I—'' her twin nudged her vigorously ''—we're embroidering two dozen fine lawn handkerchiefs—''

''*Two* dozen!'' Eleanor exclaimed.

''Well, if he's going away, he'll need more. You have to stay longer, James, so we can finish them.''

Barbara sniffed. ''The way you two sew, he'd have to wait a year.''

''*Silence!*'' Louise snapped. ''I will not have James' last days with us disturbed by your bickering.'' It was enough to bring the girls to chastened silence.

Thomas cleared his throat. ''Boy, I did my best to talk you out of this, but I can see you're set. And I reckon there's nothing left but to see you outfitted.'' He flipped back the blanket.

On the table lay a yager, a double-barreled rifle, between a pair of double-barreled pistols. All three weapons spoke of the height of the gunsmith's art, their fine-grained stocks inlaid with thin silver wire in scroll patterns.

''Man ought to have a good gun,'' Thomas explained gruffly, ''and that fine wire won't reflect the sun and give you away.'' Louise turned her head swiftly.

James put an arm around her shoulders. ''I'll be all right, *maman*. These are fine gifts you've given me. Thank you, *maman*. Thank you, sir.''

His stepfather waved that away. ''Now you intend to breed horses, if I understood you right.''

''Yes, sir. Good horses and mules are worth their weight in gold in the Western Lands. I've been talking to William Jenkens about buying one of his stallions. I should have enough left to buy about twenty brood mares, maybe more if I can get some wild mustangs.''

''I was over at Jenkens' yesterday,'' Thomas said, ''and while I was there I bought River Wind. I expect he'll be a good stud.''

''River Wind!'' The four-year-old was part Arabian and part Spanish Barb, and already considered one of the best studs on the river. James recovered his voice. ''Sir, I can't allow that. It's too much.''

''Too much!'' Thomas looked truculent. ''Boy, what kind of father would I be if I sent you off without any sort of inheritance? You'll do me the favor of taking the horse and the money—''

''Money!''

Louise put a hand on his arm. ''Thomas, you are so clumsy. James, it is much less than would be your inheritance. Only a thousand dollars. Now! I will not hear another word. *Zut!* You will take this horse, and this money. Do you hear me?''

''I'd give in, boy,'' Thomas said. ''She's put her foot down.''

James threw up his hands. ''Thank you.''

''Well. That's settled,'' Thomas said. ''Come down to the stables, boy. I'll show you your new stallion.''

James followed his stepfather toward the door. Behind them his mother said, ''And now, girls, if you are to have your presents ready in time, there is much sewing to be done. *Là!* Much sewing.''

As the two men passed the neat white cabins of the house servants, James stopped and turned to face the other man. ''I asked Helene St. Albin to marry me. She said she wouldn't. She won't wait, either.''

Thomas sighed sadly. ''James, Helene St. Albin would be a wonderful wife for you if you were staying here, but not for Texas. It'll be a rough life for years. Not what she's used to. Not what you're used to, either, for all I've tried to show you the harder side of life.''

''You and mother had nothing but this piece of land when we came here.''

''And for the first five years we lived in a two-room cabin.''

James remembered the rough log cabin well; as a little boy he'd loved to play in the dirt behind it. ''I'm willing to start with no more.''

''I know, boy. But is Helene?''

James did not want to answer. ''Jim asked me to come down to the Quadroon Ball tonight. I thought I might go.''

Thomas looked back over his shoulder as if he thought Louise or one of the girls might be there. ''I thought you'd said your goodbyes to Angélique.''

''I did.'' He laughed suddenly. ''She flew into tears and announced she'd die if I left, but she was already powdering her face when I left. She may be there—she'll hardly have found a new protector so soon—but that's not the reason I'm going. It'll be fun to dance where all the women are pretty, and Jim's a good companion for that sort of evening.''

"Well, just don't let him talk you into going down to Tchoupitoulas Street, or up to the Swamp. Young Bowie has a liking for bars full of rivermen. I don't want to hear your carcass has been dragged out of one of the canals." A twinkle appeared in his eye. "And if you do come home tonight, have some coffee at Maspero's first. Try to return sober."

"Don't you worry, sir. This is an evening of dancing. No more. Come on. Let's go look at River Wind."

XX

The Theatre d' Orleans, on Orleans Street, was the finest theater in North America, with an imposing two-story colonnade of arches across the front, but the exterior of the Orleans Ballroom, a large wing of the theater, was severely plain, squat and almost ugly. On this Thursday night in mid-September a steady stream of well-dressed men came up the narrow, muddy street and disappeared inside the ballroom.

James paid his two-dollar admission at the door and gave his beaver hat and walking stick to the attendant. It was twice the admission to the balls attended by young women of the finest families, but on nights when one of their balls conflicted with the *Bal du Cordon Bleu*, more than one young lady of excellent blood would sit the evening out for lack of partners.

"James!" James Bowie appeared out of the revelers, a glass of wine in one hand. He was much the same size as James Fallon, but with sandy hair and gray eyes. His clothes were impeccable, snowy shirt, intricately knotted tie, suit of dark superfine, but his raffish expression matched his reputation. He was always ready for fight or frolic, and some said he'd been involved with Jean Lafitte in smuggling slaves until Lafitte abandoned Campeche. "I didn't expect to see you here tonight."

"I didn't expect to come, Jim." He'd spent almost as much time with Bowie as with Henry Cameron.

"Helene doesn't like the idea of Texas, eh?"

James had to grin in spite of himself. "You're too damned smart, Bowie."

"Smart enough to know when to disappear. I'll go down and see if Rob Macklin wants to play a little poker."

Bowie faded back into the crowd, and James moved deeper into the ballroom, enjoying the pretty girls, exchanging an occasional flirtatious smile.

He had no intention of tarrying among the private reception rooms on the first floor, although at almost every door someone he knew invited him in. Invitations to play faro or the new game of poker were easily slipped, though, and he soon found himself in the second-floor ballroom.

Crystal chandeliers hung from the high, arched ceiling of the long, gaudily ornamented room. Paintings and statuary in niches decorated walls paneled in fine woods. Music drifted from an orchestra of liveried blacks. The whole room was just a setting, though, for the jewels, the girls in their colorful silks and satins. A quadroon was a quarter black, but some had as little as a sixteenth of black blood. Their complexions ranged from pale coffee to ivory whiteness. Without exception they were lovely. There was by far more of softly rounded shoulders and bosoms exposed than would have been allowed at any other ball.

Against the wall stood *les mères*, the girls' mothers, as resplendent as their daughters, but stout and dignified to a woman. Should a man wish to dance with a girl, or should he wish a more permanent arrangement, he approached her mother. No girl at the Quadroon Ball was a prostitute, but there was only one life that was both acceptable and tolerable for a girl who was fair enough to be white but declared by law to be black. A gentleman's mistress. The girls were educated from birth, taught the social graces, to dress and converse, to be beautiful and pleasing. The *Bal du Cordon Bleu* was the means by which they formed their *liaisons*, and their mothers were as protective and wary as any aristocrat.

Before going far he found his way blocked by a woman more beautiful than any women had a right to be. She should be made of marble and set on a pedestal, he thought. Her large chocolate eyes studied him boldly. Her white satin gown hugged the curves of her.

"Pardon, sir." Her faintly accented voice was musically alto. "Is your name by any chance Fallon?"

He blinked. The girls of the *Bal du Cordon Bleu* never approached strange gentlemen.

"Why, yes, it is. James Fallon. But I don't believe we've met before. I could never forget someone as beautiful as you."

She laughed. "Yes, you are a Fallon. You are from Charleston, in South Carolina?"

"No. My father, Robert Fallon, was of that city, but when he died my mother married again and . . . ." But why was he telling her all this? "Who are you? How do you know my name?"

"I was lately in Charleston, and I saw . . . a portrait of your father. A most handsome man. A man, I wager, used to having his way with women. Will you dance with me?"

She held up her arms, and he found himself leading her out. She glided like a cloud, making him feel as though he had wings.

"You still haven't told me your name."

"Call me Lucille." She lowered her head, but he could feel her watching him through her lashes.

"Lucille. Lucille what?" She laughed and pressed herself to him briefly. Her swelling breasts were, as Bowie would say, enough to make a man forget he'd been weaned.

"Just Lucille. Perhaps *l'ange* Lucille, James Fallon, come to whisk you to heaven."

"My dear, were I seeking a companion, I'd look no further. But I'm leaving for Texas before the month's out."

Her smile slipped for just an instant. "Texas," she murmured as if to herself. "But it is a large place." A sultry note entered her voice. "I do not seek a patron, James Fallon. My . . . my last friend left me with more than enough. I come here to enjoy the dancing. No more. But I think that one night in your arms would satisfy many of my dreams."

He shook his head. This was totally beyond his experience. "You do tempt me," he said slowly.

"Let me tempt you." Suddenly she was drawing him off the dance floor, and he was letting her. "Come with me now. My carriage is outside, my rooms only a short drive."

"I just have to tell some friends I'm going."

"Tell them later. When men delay, women change their minds."

"All right," he laughed.

In no time they had his hat and her shawl and were in the street. To his surprise, Henry Cameron was passing by as they came out. The black man looked at them and started. A boy ran to fetch Lucille's carriage.

"James," Henry said quietly, "can I have a minute?"

James looked at Lucille. She was tapping her foot; the carriage was already rolling toward them. "Tomorrow, Henry." The carriage pulled to a stop in front of them. He helped her in and followed quickly.

"But, James," Cameron called after them as the carriage pulled away.

James lost no time nestling Lucille into his arms and covering her mouth with his. Her kisses were hungry, to his delight. She darted a glance out the window, muttering that the driver was taking too long, before offering her lips again. He couldn't help a smug smile.

Her rooms were on Burgundy Street. She hustled him out of the carriage with, despite the lateness of the hour, a quick look up and down the empty street. She was not, he thought, as old a hand at this as she made out. His smugness increased.

The rooms were jewels—furnishings, rugs, paneling, all as exquisite as could be found in the city. Whoever her last patron was, he thought, he had cared for her. Lucille bustled about, not ringing for a maid, fetching glasses and a decanter on a tray herself. He took them from her hands.

"After. I'm drunk enough right now on you."

She reached for the tray with a forced laugh. "Careful! You will drop it."

"I'll be careful." He set it down, and pulled her into

his arms. "Later." He scooped her up in his arms. Through a half-open door he could see a large canopied bed.

"The wine," she repeated foolishly.

He kicked the bedroom door shut behind them. "Later."

Suddenly there seemed to be a different quality to her impatience, but he couldn't make out what it was. As he stripped off her gown, tugged her petticoats and chemise into a froth of lace about her ankles, she hastily pulled off his clothes. She seemed almost . . . resigned. He knew that couldn't be it.

He lifted her onto the bed, running his hands over her creamy satin skin. His mouth explored her large, shapely breasts, licking and sucking at her nipples until they were hard spires. She tried to pull him over her, but he gently put her hands aside and let his kisses trail down across the gentle curve of her belly. As he nipped at the soft insides of her thighs, she whimpered.

"No!" Her head tossed from side to side on the pillow. "No!"

He smiled to himself. She no longer seemed resigned, that was for certain. She wailed as his mouth settled at the juncture of her thighs. He didn't stop until her mouth hung open in long, ragged breaths. Then he moved swiftly over her and thrust into her.

"Oh!" Her eyes widened, so intense that for a moment they seemed full of hatred.

Then her long, slender legs wrapped around him, and she moved against him violently. Despite her whispered urgings he held back. The woman deserved to be made love to completely. Her nails clawed at his back; he was sure they drew blood. Her head thrashed; her breath shuddered. When she came she wailed, then again, almost in despair, it seemed, when she realized he wasn't finished. She gave in to his motions once more. The pressure built in him, but he held back until her breath quickened again. Then he began to pound himself into her.

"God damn you, yes!" she sobbed. "Damn you to

hell, yes! Oh, God, yes!'' She threw her head back, and her throat corded with her scream as she came again.

This time there was no holding back for him. Breath rushed out of him in a hoarse cry. His entire body convulsed with pleasure.

He rolled over, pulling her on top of him. His fingers stroked her back lightly, running down to the rising swell of her buttocks. She put her hands on his chest and looked down on him. Her dark eyes were unreadable.

"I may get the wine now?" she asked.

He blinked in surprise. "All right."

She lifted herself off him and padded into the outer room. In a moment she was back with the tray. She placed it on the night table, and sat on the bed to hand him a glass. Her body was slick with sweat, her breasts gleaming in the dim light from the other room. She raised her glass. "To the Fallons."

A strange toast for the time and place, he thought, but echoed, "To the Fallons," and sipped. She barely touched her glass to her lips.

"You must drain it, James Fallon. I am not finished with you yet."

"That sounds interesting," he laughed, tipping up his glass. She filled it again.

"I have plans for you tonight." Her fingers trailed across his chest. "You have never dreamed of what will happen to you."

"What—" His hand shook, slopping wine onto the bed. "Sorry," he muttered. He tried to rise to a better position for drinking, but his head felt so woozy he had to sink back.

Lucille took his glass. "Are you all right?"

"I feel . . . funny." He reached for her; his hand flopped on the bed.

She walked to the bellpull and tugged. When she turned back there was an exultation on her face. "When that black bitch Sanité Dédé said I had to stay among the quadroons until it was time to go, I never thought it would turn out like this." He wondered what she was talking about. He knew Sanité Dédé, a middle-aged quadroon

who peddled sweetmeats in the Place d'Armes. He tried to
speak and couldn't. He was as weak as a child. Lucille
knelt beside the bed. Her hands ran over him possessively.
Her tousled hair was a leonine mane.

"Not like this at all," she crooned. "That bitch
thought she was putting me in my place. She said I must
learn my blackness. *Merde!* An eighth, that is all, but it is
black to her and the rest of the world. She would have had
me scrubbing floors in her house if she had thought I
would put up with it. But it could not have turned out
better."

The door opened, and the driver from the carriage appeared. Lucille stood, not bothering to cover her nakedness. The black driver ducked his head.

"Yes, *maitresse*," he rumbled.

"Load him into the carriage," she commanded.

The driver loomed over him. He tried to struggle, but
there was no strength left in him. Darkness closed in.

Consciousness returned slowly; and when it did James
wondered if he was dreaming. He lay on his back; above
him, in flickering light, he could make out the rough
beams of a shed. Air stirred, and he felt a chill. He was
naked. A black cat with a strange glitter in its eye stood on
the beam above his head. With a shock he realized it was
dead, stuffed, its eyes glass.

A dull thrumming began. He rolled his eyes in that direction. A black man, his naked skin daubed with ochre,
sat astride a drum lying on its side, his fingers brushing
across the taut hide. Behind him was a dirty brick wall.

And then Lucille stepped into his line of sight. She was
naked to the waist, her left breast covered by a yellow
handprint, her right by a red. A crudely drawn black snake
seemed to crawl up her belly from the skirt that hung low
on her hips, the hem just brushing her bare feet as they
danced a shuffle in the dust. Half of her face was red, the
other half yellow. Her hair was held back by a white strip
around her forehead and partially covered by a madras
cloth tied so that seven points rose from it like an intricate
crown.

The flickering light, he could now see, came from fires at either end of the long room. He, Lucille, and the drummer were the only three souls in it, but it seemed crowded with the presence of evil.

Lucille stooped and lifted a white rooster from a basket. It flapped wildly, but in eerie silence, as she held it aloft, moaning as her dance raised puffs of dust. "Hain! Lon! Hilay! Sabaoth! Helim! Jehovah! Yah! Tetragrammaton! Alpha and Omega, the beginning and the end, by the powers of the fire and the grave, by the holy names of power, I require your doom!"

With two quick steps she was by his side, the cock held by head and feet. She lifted it to her mouth. Dainty white teeth severed the cock's throat, blood spurting across her chin. Quickly she swung the bird like a censer, sprinkling hot drops the length of his body.

"Danbhalah Wédo, attend me!" she chanted. "Ogou, Ogou-fer, Ogou-Chango, attend me! Afrique Guinin Tocan Dahoumin, attend me!"

She swayed, feet once more picking up the rhythm of the never-ceasing drum, white teeth smiling through blood-stained lips. She bent sinuously, and when she straightened, a black snake writhed in her hands.

"In the name of Lucifer, of Beelzabub and Sathanas, I give this soul to my *maitre*, to Baron Samedi! Hear your servant, O Lord of Darkness, and accept her gift!"

The snake's questing tongue flickered as, almost gently, she laid it on him, its tail disappearing into his groin, its head on his chest. It could none of it be real, and yet the snake's scales against his flesh were too real for a dream.

From somewhere she produced a knife, and for the first time she spoke words he could understand.

"The snake is holy, James Fallon." Her tongue flickered; she hissed the words like a snake herself. Great passion burned in her eyes, but with a cold heat. "It is sacred to Baron Samedi, Lord of the Tombs. By its presence it will sanctify your death, and consecrate it. James Fallon. I want you to know this, that you have no importance except for your blood. You used me tonight, but now I will use you. With your blood I will make a *gris-gris* to destroy—"

The door of the long shed crashed open. "Stop!" some-one shouted. Men with pistols stood there. Lucille whirled, emitting a howl of rage.

James knew the voice. "Bowie!" he croaked.

"Christopher!" Lucille shouted. The drummer seized a machete and launched himself at the intruders. A pistol cracked; he fell.

"Damn you!" Lucille screamed. "Damn you all!" Sud-denly she hurled the knife and darted into the shadows. Someone grunted; a pistol shot ricocheted off brick near the fire.

James managed to raise one hand and fumble the snake off his chest. "Bowie!" he grunted.

Footsteps hurried closer, and then three men were help-ing him to sit up. Needles of pain ran along his arms and legs. He recognized Bowie, Henry Cameron, and pale-eyed Rob Macklin. Macklin was clutching his arm, blood running down over his fingers. The hilt of Lucille's knife protruded through them.

"You came alone?" James mumbled.

"Didn't have time to get anybody else," Bowie said. He studied Macklin's arm. "Henry said you were in danger, and we came running. This was the last place we thought to look. Grit your teeth, Rob." He braced a hand against Macklin's shoulder and jerked the knife free.

"Christ!" Macklin swore.

Henry pressed a coat around James' shoulders and help-ed him to his feet. "She gave you something. You got to walk it out of your blood."

"She kept talking about my blood," James muttered. "Where is this place, anyway?"

"The old brickyard on Dumaine Street," Bowie said.

"The brickyard!" James shook his head and wished he hadn't. "How did you think to come here? For that matter, how did you know I was in trouble, Henry?"

"This is where all the big voodoo ceremonies are held."

"But what made you think of voodoo?"

"About two weeks ago I went to fetch Marie from Sanité Dédé's place—least, I tried to fetch her. Anyway, this woman—"

"Lucille mentioned that peddlerwoman, too." Henry had gotten James to his feet; he was nudging him to try walking.

"That peddler woman," Henry said patiently, "is the voodoo queen of New Orleans. She say crawl, and half the blacks in this city, and some whites, too, drop on the ground. Anyway, I saw this Lucille, to Sanité Dédé's. They were having words, and it was plain she was a *mam'bo*, a priestess, herself. When I saw you going off with her . . . well, it ain't safe messing with no voodoo priestess. Too bad she get away. She cause more trouble now."

"All this voodoo mumbo-jumbo is so much hogwash," Macklin said. "That woman can't hurt you with her curses."

"I ain't worried about her curses," Henry said. "It's her knives concern me. All this come out, Sanité Dédé ain't going to sit still. She lose too much face if she don't do nothing to us. We'll all find *gris-gris* on our doorsteps and knives in our backs, and almost anybody in the city could put them there."

"Then it can't come out," James said. He pushed free of Henry and took a few tottering steps on his own.

"You mean go away and not say anything?" Macklin said. "How do I explain away a knife in my arm? How do you explain staggering around naked?"

"You got knifed in the Swamp," Bowie said. "We all went to Girod Street for a little excitement and got in the biggest to-do since Bill Sedley killed Juan Contrearas and his brother in Mother Colby's."

"Ain't good enough," Henry said. "I think I going to Texas with James."

"That's well and good," James said. Then, to push away the memory of what had happened, he added, "There is a serious difficulty here. My lack of pants. I don't want to have to explain coming home naked."

Laughing quietly, the others began to help him search.

XXI

On the evening of the twenty-third of September, 1822, leading two pack mules and River Wind behind their mounts, James and Henry crossed the Sabine River, leaving the United States. The air was dry, and still held the summer's heat. The mules were heavy laden, for James' sisters hadn't been the only ones with farewell gifts. Most had as much application to the life he expected in Texas as Barbara's lawn shirts, but one, at least, would be useful. Bowie had given him a knife, made by Jesse Cliffe, the Bowie plantation blacksmith. Up to the last minute he had tried to convince Bowie to come along, but Bowie just laughed his easy laugh and said Texas was too wild for him.

Their first night in Texas was spent in an abandoned cabin beside *El Camino Réal*, the Royal Road. Once it had been as fine a road as existed in the world; now it was a rutted, weed-grown track. Two days later they rode through the abandoned town of Nacogdoches, empty adobe buildings, their roofs fallen in, home only for scorpions and rattlesnakes. A stone mission sat on a knoll between two streams.

At Nacogdoches they struck crosscountry for San Felipe de Austin, the settlement Austin had founded. Canebreaks stretched for miles; brown and dying reeds rose twenty-five feet from ground covered with decayed old growth, tops arching to block the sky so that they rode through tunnels. In vast open stretches, drying grass stood chest-high to the horses. Stands of giant pecans and cottonwoods gave way to tangled thickets of chinquapin, elderberry, and catclaw. Deep, clear pools lay covered with lily pads, and sandy-bottomed streams teemed with fish. Everywhere were signs and tracks of game—deer and bear, turkey and rabbit. Squirrels chattered in the trees, and quail broke cover beneath the horses' hooves. When they crossed the Rio del Brazos de Dios and found San Felipe on its bluff by the river, they had not seen another human in two hundred miles.

James walked his horse down the single rambling dirt street of the town, River Wind on a lead tied to his saddle. Henry had the mules. The town consisted of twenty-five log cabins, scattered haphazardly. Men, most in buck-skins and fur caps, hurried everywhere, but there were few women to be seen. The men called greetings as they passed.

"I guess they don't see many strangers," Henry said as they drew rein in front of a cabin with a sign announcing Groce's Store. A pretty black woman sat on the end of the porch.

"Not surprising." James stepped down, looping his reins on the hitching rail. "You coming in?"

"I don't think so." Cameron smiled. "After staring at you across a campfire the past couple of weeks, I'm ready to talk to a girl again."

"You better be careful. A girl that pretty probably has a man around somewhere."

Henry laughed and hitched his horse and the pack mules. James went inside.

Inside there were a few crude shelves on the walls. Pots, pans, axes and scythes hung from the rafters, and the floor was covered with open sacks and crates. A plump man was pawing desultorily through a pile of coarse workshirts. Two more, with well-cut coats showing hard wear, looked up from their conversation.

One came forward, a smile on his broad face. "Can I help you?" He proffered a hand and James took it. His dark eyes had a twinkle that James liked.

"James Fallon, of Louisiana. I'm looking for Stephen Austin."

"Jared Groce. Alabama. I'm—"

"I'm in charge while Mr. Austin is away," the other well-dressed man broke in. He was short, with a receding chin and watery blue eyes. "I'm Josiah Bell."

"He's not here?"

"He's been gone since March," Groce said. Bell opened his mouth and shut it again. "What with the revolution, he had to get his grant confirmed by the new government. General Iturbide's proclaimed himself emperor."

"We're going to lose everything," the man looking through the shirts said sourly. "Why should they recognize a grant from the Spanish? Some families have left already, and I say they're the smart ones."

"Come, come, Harrell," Bell said soothingly. "It will all work out."

"That's right," Groce said. "They still can't get their own people to settle here in sufficient numbers. Spanish or Mexican, they need us."

Harrell sneered. "Maybe the rest of us would be as confident if we had forty thousand acres to look forward to. You—Fallon?—you don't get much around here unless you're one of Austin's cronies."

"Come, Harrell," Bell said, blinking furiously. "There's no call to talk that way." Harrell glared at each of them, then stalked out. "I better try to quiet him," Bell said, and hurried out after the other man.

"Damn fool," Groce muttered. "Austin allows extra land for men with needed skills, or who bring property into the colony. I came in with fifty wagons full of supplies. Harrell brought a pack of brats and no seed, but he's always ready to think he's been slighted."

"How's the land apportioned?" James asked. "I brought a good stud. I intend to breed horses."

"Six hundred and forty acres a man, three hundred and twenty more for a wife, and half that for each child. Then there's another eighty acres for each slave brought in. Most are trying to put in cotton or corn, but I wouldn't doubt your horses will be needed enough to let you buy some extra."

"I suppose I'd better go see Mr. Bell?"

"You'll have to wait till Austin gets back."

James frowned. "Mr. Bell said he was in charge."

Groce laughed bitterly. "That's what Austin intended, but Bell can't do a thing but flap and dither. All he's good for, anyway."

"When is Austin expected back?"

Groce hesitated before saying, "Any day."

It was clear to James the man had no idea when Austin would return. It might be months. "Well, I thank you, Mr. Groce. I'd better see about finding a place to stay."

"Just move into any empty cabin. There are several. We've had some quitters."

On the porch Henry was talking to the pretty girl. At James' footsteps on the porch she looked around. Her eyes went wide. Suddenly she leaped to her feet and disappeared down the alley beside the building.

"What's the matter?" Henry called after her. "Come on back! Where you going?"

"She seemed to be scared of me," James said. He walked over and looked down the alley, but the girl was nowhere in sight. "Sorry, Henry."

"I guess she's a little skittish. She got spirit, though. She's pregnant, and her husband's dead, but she ain't giving up."

"Don't worry. It's a small place. You'll see her again."

"I suppose. Pretty girl. Pretty name, too. Leonie."

"Come on," James laughed. "Let's go find a house."

Leonie didn't stop running until she was back at Mrs. Jensen's cabin. Mrs. Jensen looked up from her scrubboard.

"Where have you been, girl? Lollygagging around again, I'll wager."

"I'm sorry, ma'am." Leonie grabbed the broom from the hearth and began sweeping. It was work that brought her room and board, and she couldn't afford to be sent away. "I'll try to do better, ma'am."

Mrs. Jensen's smile was not unfriendly. "I know, girl. When I had my first, I went around staring at moonbeams, too."

Leonie kept her face averted as she swept. Leonie didn't want friendship with any white.

Working cleared her panic enough for her to think. That man had been a Fallon, though not one she'd ever seen before. He must be the "James" that nice Henry had spoken of, but a Fallon without doubt. She couldn't let him, or Henry, either, know she came from Charleston, or she'd find Robert Fallon and her mother there to take her back.

She had set out for the free states. In Alabama, though, her horse and cart had been stolen. More than once only fleetness of foot had kept her from being seized as a runaway—and sold for court costs when no one claimed her. A kindly-seeming old carter who offered her a ride had tried to sell her to a fancy house. It seemed that everyone who offered help had something else in mind. Several times she had come across people claiming to help runaways reach the north, white people as wary and suspicious as she. For their color she had not trusted them.

In New Orleans a smiling black woman wanted to put her in a nice house frequented only by clean white gentlemen. She had resisted too strongly. The patrol had taken an interest, thinking her a runaway, and she had taken to her heels again. But the city wasn't the same as the countryside. They followed her even when she managed to cross the river. In desperation she had hidden in an ox-drawn wagon moving down the road with a dozen others. Five days later, when she was caught on one of her nightly forays for food, she had discovered where the wagons were bound. Texas.

As she swept the cabin she found tears streaming down her face. She was so far from anyone who loved her, and so alone. So very alone.

Cordelia Applegate turned quickly from the mirror. She preferred to remember herself as she had been, not as age had made her. Still, she thought, there were satisfactions. Her *hacienda*, not far from the Rio San Jacinto, was cool and luxurious. The contents of her basement strongroom had provided the bribes that procured her thousands of acres from the Spanish and convinced the revolutionaries that her grant should be confirmed. When life as *patrona* palled, she traveled with a stylish retinue to Mexico City, where society was as flamboyant as in Paris or Vienna.

She sat down, reaching for her Tarot cards, and ran her eye over the table, noting with satisfaction that the maids had polished it well. Fear of her had prevailed over fear of the box of Tarot cards. She clicked the cards face down on the table, two in the center crossed by a third, four around them to form a cross. She could feel the power flowing in her hands. She spoke aloud. "What does the future bring for me?"

It was a daily ritual, that question. With breathless excitement she turned over the three cards in the center. A smile curled her mouth. The eight of swords inverted and the six of batons, crossed with the seven of swords. Good news; new plans. Swords and batons were male symbols. Quickly she turned up the other cards. The Star, a mixing of the past and present to influence the future. The Tower, an unexpected event. The Magician, guile and craft. The Chariot, vengeance.

She threw back her head and laughed. News would come that Robert Fallon was destroyed. It had to be. The cards did not lie. She would believe them ahead of her own judgment. But best to be sure.

Quickly she gathered the cards up, shuffled them, and began a new layout.

"What kind of man is he?" She turned the cards. The Emperor and the Magician, crossed with the King of Swords. A man who was active and determined, self-confident and aggressive. The three of batons. Enterprising. The Queen of batons. Charming. The Moon. Dangerous. Hercules. A man of accomplishment and strength.

She tapped the Moon with a fingernail. If she was victorious already, if that was the news, why was he still dangerous? Yet, the cards described Robert Fallon as she had last seen him perfectly.

Her questions at a single sitting were always limited to three, a number of power. She seldom used all three on one topic, but this was too important not to.

"What is yet required of me toward this man?"

The array was made and displayed. She stared at the cards for a long time. The Tower and the Hanged Man crossed by the Star. The mixing of past and present would require, or cause, sacrifice, change, and disruption. The Chariot, vengeance. The Hierophant inverted, ability to adapt. The World, earthly triumph. The Devil, downfall and doom. All the cards were of the Major Arcana, making the display very powerful.

It made no sense, not in answer to her question.

She had to find out what the cards really meant. She had to visit the old woman.

Distasteful as that need was, once she admitted it, she wasted no time. The cards went back in the box. Arranging a black lace shawl around her shoulders, she made her way outside. On the red-tiled veranda Ramirez was leaning indolently against one of the adobe columns. She couldn't help admiring the way his short black jacket fit his lean, hard body. He returned her look with hot, insolent eyes. The fool, she thought. If he showed no more care, anyone who saw would know he was more than her *jefe de vaqueros*.

"Hector, you've been making advances to my serving girls." She was disconcerted—far too disconcerted—to see his smile slip.

"But no, *Doña* Cordelia," he protested. "I have eyes, and hands, only for you."

"You forget yourself!"

He hung his head sullenly. "*Sí, Doña* Cordelia."

"There are others who would be *jefe de vaqueros*."

"*Clemencia, señora, por favor.*" The way his mouth twisted around the words showed how it pained him to say them. He saw himself as master of the *rancho* in all but name.

"See that you don't forget your place again."

She could feel his eyes following her as she crossed the flagstone courtyard, past the fountain and under the towering pecan trees. Humbling him fortified her for what was to come, as did the curtsies of scurrying maids, the tipped hats of the men. She was *la patrona*. Here she ruled.

A small door in the adobe wall surrounding the *hacienda* led to a rough dirt path that wound for almost a mile through the *chapparal* to a small hut of branches and mud, set in the middle of a dusty clearing. A brace of rabbits and three bunches of flowers, offerings from the people of her *rancho*, lay before the low opening of the hut. None knew she came there as well.

The old woman who dwelt inside was at least half the reason Cordelia was still in Texas. At first Cordelia had only sought a refuge from which to operate unseen against Lopes and Lafitte. Then she had found the old woman—Indian, Mexican, something else entirely, no one knew. No one knew her name, or her age, though her withered frame and wrinkles spoke of more years than Cordelia cared to contemplate. They knew her powers, though. The old woman rarely left her hut, would not think of leaving Texas. Cordelia was afraid to try forcing her to go, and afraid to leave her behind.

Grimacing, she stooped to enter. The hovel was lit only by a firepit in the middle of the dirt floor. Smoke exited through a hole in the roof. A pile of blankets against one wall served as a bed, and a single battered chest held all the old woman's possessions. The crone herself sat on a rickety wooden chair on the far side of the firepit. Bony wrists sticking from her dingy black sleeves ended in what seemed more claws than hands. Her face was weathered to the texture and color of shoe leather, but her black eyes were raven sharp. She didn't move when Cordelia entered.

Cordelia knelt and waited for the old woman to acknowledge her. Thank God none of the servants had the courage to enter unbidden.

"What is it you want, *moza?*" the old woman croaked finally.

Moza. Girl, as used to address a servant. "*Mi dueña,* I beg a sight."

"Something of this world." The old woman's voice was dry. "You are always concerned with this world, *moza.*

You will never enter the world of *los espiritos* until you
learn the unimportance of this world.''

"Forgive me, *mi dueña*. I know I am too concerned with
the material world, but I cannot purge my mind." She
hoped that sounded properly contrite. "I beg this favor of
a sight. This morning the cards told me of a man who will
affect my life, but they were not clear. I must know about
this man. I must."

The old woman made a gesture of dismissal. "Your
cards . . . toys for children. No matter, *moza*, I will give
you your sight."

Cordelia shuddered with relief. The old woman was not
always so accommodating. From inside her dress the crone
dug a leather pouch and carefully sprinkled powder on the
fire. It sparked and flared, and blue-gray smoke rose. The
old woman leaned forward to inhale deeply. Cordelia
inched back, holding her breath. Once she had been
allowed to breathe the smoke. Her retches had almost
turned her inside out, and she had crawled from the hut,
puking and weeping, pursued by the crone's laughter.

The old woman drew deeply on the fumes. When she
straightened, her eyes were glassy and unblinking. She
mumbled to herself, then began to speak in a hollow
voice.

"I see a man. He is proud and strong. The sea is in his
blood, but he does not follow the sea. He comes from the
east, but he will remain here. There is a bond between
your past and his. He must, of his own will, come under
your roof and remain there. His presence will bring wealth
and power. If he does not remain content under your roof,
you will know agony and despair. Doom will be yours, and
death unnatural. Beware the man who changes his name,
who dies, yet does not die." She trailed off into vague
mumblings.

Cordelia would get no more that day, nor any other.
The old woman would not give a second sight on the same
question. Worse was what she *had* been told. She was to
take Fallon into her home? It had to be Fallon. The sea.
The bond. She stumbled back to the *hacienda* in a daze.
Let Robert Fallon once come in arm's reach of her, and if

she did not kill him he would strangle her with his bare hands. But . . . agony . . . death . . . she would do anything to avoid that.

Just inside the *hacienda* wall a maid dropped a curtsey to her. "*Señora, Señorita* Gautier has come. She is in your *escritorio.*"

Lucille! Cordelia brushed by the girl. When she had finally tracked down the old Gautier woman—after being cheated of the family money, she would have hunted beyond the grave, if need be—she had long since forgotten that she had ever borne her quadroon husband a child. That Marianne Gautier had been a sister of the black arts only provided the means of her death; that she had begun training Lucille in them made the girl suddenly of interest. Lucille had been of use over the years, but for what she was, Cordelia could never acknowledge her, could never entirely forgive her.

Cordelia's study was hung with tapestries and paintings except on the wall dominated by the huge stone fireplace. A Turkey carpet covered the tile floor. Her desk was a long, massive table that faced the door. A silver candelabrum stood on each end of the table, between them a silver pen holder and inkwell, a crystal paperweight, and a dagger, hilt inlaid with silver and turquoise, that she liked to fondle.

Lucille was seated behind the table sipping a glass of wine. Her gray silk traveling dress was, as always, impeccable. Cordelia hated her youth; she stopped just inside the door, staring at the girl. After a moment Lucille tossed her head and rose with sinuous grace. Cordelia took her place.

For long moments she did not speak. She picked up the dagger, examining the turquoise, caressing the blade with her fingers. Finally she deigned to look at Lucille. The girl's head was up, flashing defiance at being treated like a servant. If it weren't for a hex doll of Lucille, carefully made when she was first found, Cordelia wasn't sure she could control her.

"I trust, Lucille, you've some explanation why I haven't heard from you for months? Robert Fallon is dead, isn't he?'' Her face tightened as the girl hesitated.

"Not exactly, *maitresse*."

"Not exactly? Either he's dead, or he's not."

"I believe he is still alive, *maitresse*. But it was not my fault. He bribed Felipe to keep an eye on me, and to get more money the fool betrayed me."

"So you failed."

"I was imprisoned, *maitresse*. I barely escaped, and I have been months working my way back here."

"And Robert Fallon is still alive." Cordelia's temples throbbed. She closed her eyes. She must not show weakness. Let the girl think it was anger.

"In New Orleans, *maitresse*, I met his son, James Fallon. Only he did not know his father was alive." She hesitated. "He, too, eluded me."

"What do you mean he didn't know he was alive?"

"He said his father died when he was a small child, and his mother remarried and moved to Louisiana. He is a bastard." Her tone left doubt if she spoke of his birth or his personality. "He was on his way to Texas . . . ." Her voice trailed off as Cordelia laughed.

"A bastard? Yes, the Fallon men run to bastards, both by birth and by actions. He—" Her eyes flew open, and she stared at Lucille so intently the girl took a step back. "Coming to Texas? This Fallon—whatever his name is—is coming to Texas?"

"Why, yes." Lucille paused. "If you wish to kill him, too—he is a Fallon, after all—I would like to help."

Cordelia heard nothing after the "yes." It was all so clear. The man tied to her past, the sea in his blood. The man who would give her vengeance and doom for the Fallons. Such a sweet way to get it. "He won't be hard to find. All the Americans are in that foolish colony Stephen Austin is starting. In the town of San Felipe," she sneered, "or in the settlement on the Rio Colorado."

Lucille put on a smile like a cat in the cream. "Then we will kill him?"

"Certainly not!" Cordelia said sharply.

"*Mon Dieu!* I do not understand."

"It has been foretold, in the cards, and by the old woman. Power, wealth, revenge, will all come if he remains content under my roof.'' She ignored Lucille's gasp. Surprise? Anger? ''Somehow I'll bring him here. He knows you tried to kill him? There's another hut not far from the old woman's. You'll stay there.''

Protest was plain on Lucille's face—she liked comfort and luxury as much as Cordelia—then abruptly it disappeared. ''Of course.''

Cordelia looked up sharply. ''You'll stay away from the old woman.'' Her skin crawled at the thought of Lucille learning the old woman's secrets, the secrets she had failed to learn.

''If you wish it.''

''I do. And remember, I have your hex doll. I will punish disobedience in this severely.'' The shiver that ran through the girl was satisfying.

''As you command, *maitresse*.''

She had to be content. If she pressed it too much, the girl might decide there was something worth risking Cordelia's anger. And she couldn't be sure the old woman couldn't teach Lucille how to render a hex doll powerless. ''Go fetch Hector Ramirez. He'll be useful in getting this Fallon here. James, you said?''

XXII

For over two months, into early December, James and Henry shared an abandoned cabin on the outskirts of San Felipe, waiting in vain for Austin's return. Despite the settlers' dire mutterings, James had bought forty mustang mares. They cost two dollars wild, four broken to saddle. The hairy little animals were only five feet tall at the shoulder—many settlers contemptuously called them sheep—but Thomas Martin had told him of their strength and endurance. He knew he could breed horses suited to the land.

Other than buy horses, there was little to do except hunt—a necessity with no crops in—play chess with Groce, and read. He never tired of the small library he had brought—primarily histories and the essays of Montesquieu and Montaigne—but the lending and borrowing of books was considered neighborly in the colony, so he fleshed his reading out with gleanings from others' selections. They ran heavily to Lord Byron and Sir Walter Scott.

With a sigh he set *Kenilworth*—only a year old and fresh from England—back on the rude shelf and tapped out his pipe. He was due to meet Groce for another game of chess.

The air outside was chill through his gloves and sheep-skin coat, the sky cloudless but gray. Henry sat on a split-log bench in front of the cabin with Leonie. She looked up at James, then turned away, her coat pulled tight over her very obvious pregnancy. Henry motioned James to step up the road and followed.

"I'm sorry about Leonie, James. I don't know why she can't get comfortable around you. She wouldn't even come in out of the cold with you there. I've told her everything about you, trying to get it into her head that you're not going to hurt her."

"It's all right, Henry. Looks to me as if she likes you all right." He looked back at the girl. She was watching them suspiciously, her breath frosting the air. "You getting serious about her?"

"She's a nice girl," Henry said vaguely. "Look, I think I'm going hunting. That deer you got is just about gone."

"Take care. Groce says some Karankawa have been sniffing around the settlement the last few days."

"Ain't no Indian going to get this child."

James laughed. "Well, you take care anyway."

He made his way up the frozen, rutted road into town, tipping his hat to the women he passed, stopping for a word with the men. His easy way had made friends quickly. Outside Groce's store a short, powerful man named St. George stopped him. Only the man's eyes showed between his fur cap and his turned-up collar.

"You hear, Fallon? Henderson left this morning. Traded all his holdings for one mule, packed up his family, and went back to Georgia."

That made ten families who'd gone since he'd arrived. He wondered if there'd be a settlement left for Austin to return to. "That's too bad. And not too smart. This is a bad time of year to travel."

St. George shook his head. "It looks damned bleak. Some say the Mexicans won't recognize Austin's grant. Some say Austin isn't even coming back."

"He'll come back," James said sharply. "If he has to walk all the way he'll come back."

"Maybe. You're a bachelor. I've a wife and four children to think about. Speaking of which, I'd better get on home. Be seeing you, Fallon."

Inside, Groce had the board set up on a crate, with a bottle of brandy and two glasses on another. A hearty fire crackled in the fireplace. "Evening," the bluff man said.

He held out his pouch. "Tobacco?"

"Thanks. Have you heard about Henderson?" He shed his outer garments and loaded his pipe, using tongs to light it with a coal from the fire.

Groce snorted. "I've heard. The faint hearts are filtering out."

"I suppose."

They settled in at the chess board. James pushed forward his king's pawn. "It makes no difference why they go, if not enough stay to keep the colony going."

"James, you haven't been here long enough to know what we're up against. The Indians—Karankawas, mainly, but even Apache and Comanche—don't see any difference between our stock and wild game. They've been raiding the Mexicans for years. What's different about us? And then there's our own kind. Some of those single men upriver and over on the Colorado came looking for quick money. And they're not particular. James, this is a hard land, and it takes a hard man to settle here. You burn in summer and freeze in winter. The crops failed this year. The weak ones will be driven out, and that's all there is to it."

"In New Orleans, Austin told me he wanted solid family men above all. Families are what makes the difference between settlers and adventurers."

"I'd like that, too, James, but it's for the future. Damn it, are we going to play chess or sit here talking all day?"

"We'll play."

Worry made him play poorly, though, and after losing three games he walked dourly back to his cabin, stopping to check the log corrals out back. River Wind seemed restive, pawing the ground, making short runs at the rails that separated him from the mares.

"Your turn will come, boy." As soon as Austin returned. He couldn't start breeding without being assured of grazing land.

He had an intimation of wrongness as he stepped into the cabin, then something crashed into his head. He staggered to his knees, fighting to rise. There was more than one man in the room; he couldn't be sure how many.

Another blow to his head, and he fell forward into unconsciousness.

When he awoke, he was on one of the crude beds built against the wall, and Henry Cameron was wiping his face with a damp cloth. He tried to sit up, but fell back groaning. His ribs were a mass of sharp pains. They must have worked him over with their boots once he was down.

The cabin had been ransacked. His books lay scattered on the floor, along with his tattered clothes. The chairs were sticks of wood; the water bucket had been smashed against the fireplace. His rifle was gone from the wall. He felt under the bed. The pouch of money he'd kept tied to the mattress lashing wasn't there. Cameron read his expression. "The mares are gone, too. And River Wind."

"Can you track them?"

"Ground's froze solid, James."

"Damn! We need help."

"Who? Josiah Bell? That man don't never do nothing."

"Groce. If there's anyone who might have an idea who did this, it's him."

"You need to get yourself looked at by a doctor," Henry said, but he helped him up and supported him to the store.

To James' surprise, an ornate closed coach and four stood out front, surrounded by mounted *vaqueros* bundled into heavy coats. Each man had a rifle, and they looked capable of using them.

When Henry helped him inside, Groce came running. "James! What happened?"

"I was jumped." He winced as Henry eased him down to sit on an upended crate. "Somebody hit me over the head and tore up the cabin. They got my guns, my money, and River Wind."

"River Wind?" The owner of the soft voice moved forward, and Groce stepped back deferentially. The woman's auburn hair was elaborately coiffed, her blue velvet gown looked Parisian, and her face bore a mask of powder and rouge. A woman refusing to let go of her youth, James decided, however far past it was.

"Mrs. Applegate, may I present James Fallon? James, Mrs. Cordelia Applegate. Mrs. Applegate owns one of the largest *ranchos* around here, about a day's travel to the east."

"Yes," she said. "I thought I might see how your colony is doing." She smiled. "It seems . . . sparse."

"It'll grow." James winced as Groce dabbed at his forehead with some stinging liquid on a cloth.

"You have the ardency of the young," she laughed.

"I have faith, Mrs. Applegate. This land will grow, but it'll take time, and work." She laughed again, and his ears grew hot.

"I think some of his ribs are busted," Henry said.

"Damn," Groce muttered. "Begging your pardon, Mrs. Applegate. James, you need a real doctor."

"You'll have to do," James replied.

Mrs. Applegate touched his shoulder lightly. "But why? One of the *vaqueros* at my *rancho* serves as our doctor. He knows all there is to know about setting bones, and poultices for your cuts. You'll come with me."

"I don't know," James said slowly. "It's kind of you, ma'am, but I should stay here to help find the men who stole River Wind. That's my stallion."

"James," Groce said, "you know there's not much chance of that. By tomorrow morning he'll be fifty miles from here, and likely getting further away every day. You'd best take Mrs. Applegate up on her offer. You'll get better care than anyone here will have time to give you."

"You see, Mr. Fallon? Everyone agrees with me. It's settled then." Mrs. Applegate smiled.

James still felt doubtful, but in short order the others had him bundled into her coach. The *vaqueros* packed his clothing and effects as if they had planned it beforehand.

Henry poked his head into the coach. "I'll come see you in a few days. I don't want to leave Leonie right now. You understand."

"Sure. You keep an eye out, though. The men who stole River Wind might still be around."

Cordelia Applegate smiled. "I doubt that, Mr. Fallon.

You heard Mr. Groce." She rapped on the roof of the coach. "Ramon, *adelante!*"

The trip took closer to a day and a half than a day, with a stop that night. He slept in blankets on the ground with the *vaqueros.* Cordelia slept in the coach. She was by turns coquettish, amused at his supposed youthful *naïveté*, and superciliously aloof. Which, if any, was the real woman he couldn't say. Her eyes devoured her *jefe de vaqueros*, though her words to the lean, dark man were imperious to the point of insult. The *jefe*, Hector Ramirez, seemed to accept her treatment sullenly, and his dark eyes smouldered jealously whenever he looked at James.

It was a relief when the coach with its escort of horsemen rolled through the arched gate of Cordelia's *hacienda* into a flagstone courtyard, surrounded on the other three sides by sprawling adobe buildings with red tile roofs, a frozen fountain in the center. *Peóns* in coarse white cotton darted out, shivering and hats in hand, to spirit away the luggage. Cordelia climbed down on Ramirez' arm, smiling and waving. Curtseying maids waited at the door with finger-bowls, damp towels, and hot spiced wine.

James clambered out of the coach with the aid of the handstraps above the door, wincing at the sudden wrench to his ribs as his weight came on his arms. Cordelia saw him, and her face darkened.

"Hector, why has he had to climb from the carriage by himself? He's injured! Fetch a litter. Quickly!"

"I don't—" James began, but two *peóns* came running with a litter, and others pressed him back on it. His ribs hurt too much to resist.

"Take him upstairs," Cordelia commanded. "Fetch José."

Four of the *peóns* raised the litter to their shoulders and carried him up to an airy room with a large bed. There they set the litter down and bent over him.

"*Basta!* I can get up by myself." The men stood doubtfully aside while he pulled himself up on the bed and relaxed with a sigh. Picking up the litter, they began to file out. "*Gracias, señores.*"

They looked back in surprise from the doorway. "*De*

nada, señor,'' one replied. *''Sois usted muy amable.''*

Cordelia appeared, staring at the *peóns.* "Why are you still here? *Fuera de qui!* There's work to be done!" As the men left, she swept around on James with a smile. A small gray-haired man in the short jacket of a *vaquero* stood respectfully behind her. "Mr. Fallon, James, this is José. He's good with injuries. Don't you worry, now. He'll have you on your feet in no time."

James managed something of a bow from the bed. *"Muchisimó gustó, señor. Dispense me,* but I regrettably did not hear your name."

The leather-faced man drew himself up with great dignity and bowed. *"El gusto is mío, señor.* I am José Escobar." He moved quickly to the bed, touching James' head with gentle fingers, then opened his shirt and began to feel along his empurpled ribs. "Tell me where there is sharp pain, *Señor* Fallon."

James hissed. "There, *Señor* Escobar. And there."

"I fear there are four, perhaps five, ribs broken, *señor.* I will prepare a poultice to draw the swelling, and bind them. The cuts on your head have been well cleaned. A simple bandage will do for them."

Cordelia cleared her throat. "This is your nurse, *Señor* Fallon. Yolanda."

An olive-skinned young girl giggled her way into the room, ducking her head shyly. Her dark eyes were anything but shy, though, and rounded breasts strained out of the top of her brightly colored blouse. José looked at the girl in surprise, glanced at Cordelia, and began to bandage James' head. James smiled, and the girl smiled back coquettishly.

"Mrs. Applegate," he said, "I think I'm going to enjoy my stay here."

Watching the girl, he didn't see her satisfied smile. "I'm sure that you will, Mr. Fallon. I'll see to it."

XXIII

Leonie shifted beneath her blankets, trying to ease the dull ache in the small of her back. It was New Year's Day; the baby was due in a month. She jumped when Mrs. Jensen put her head in.

"Leonie, it's that nice Henry Cameron. I told him it wasn't proper, you being in bed and all, but he insists, and I think maybe . . . . Will you see him?"

What had the woman in such a dither? "I'll see him."

Mrs. Jensen disappeared, and in a moment Henry came in, rubbing his hands and looking ill at ease. "*Feliz Año Nuevo,* Leonie."

"Happy New Year to you, too, Henry. I think your accent is improving. What are you in such a pother about?"

He took a deep breath, and spoke in a rush. "Leonie, will you marry me?"

She stared at him in surprise. She liked him. He was a gentle, kind man. But he wasn't Denmark. "Henry, I—"

"Don't answer too quick, girl. Think on it. I love you, and I'll be as good to you and the baby as I know how. A man can get a piece of land here, make something of himself. I aim to. And I'd like you to share it with me. We can share a life together."

Tears started in her eyes. Being alone was such a big part of her fear. "Henry, I like you, but I don't love you. If you can take me on that basis, I'd be proud to be your wife."

His smile was warming. "I love you," he said gently, "and I expect in time maybe you'll come to love me. I hope so."

Suddenly much of her fear was gone. "Henry, stay with me. Don't go away, not for anything."

"As much as I can, girl. I have to go see James some."

"You like him very much."

"I do. He's something else. Right now he's stove up fierce, but I think he's bedding half Mrs. Applegate's maids. Excuse me, Leonie. I shouldn't have said that."

She sniffed. "Sounds like a Fallon."

"You sound like you seen a lot of them," he laughed.

"No. No, of course not. You don't have to visit him very often, do you?"

His reply was hesitant. "I think he's got some trouble, Leonie. He might need me."

"You don't need any white man's trouble, Henry."

"He's my friend, Leonie. And I don't trust that Mrs. Applegate. When she don't think you're looking at her, she's got a look like she's up to something. That Ramirez slips around looking mean. I know they helped him out, but I don't trust them."

"Let it alone, Henry." She reached out, and he stepped close enough to give her his hand. "Please?"

"I can't," he said miserably. "Can't you understand that?"

"I do understand," she whispered, pressing the back of his hand to her cheek. It was he who didn't understand. This Fallon was like the others. He walked with a whirlwind, destroying those around him who couldn't ride it. But she wouldn't let him destroy Henry.

Cordelia frowned at Ramirez, next to her in the bed. She had broken him of thinking he could roll off her and go right to sleep without so much as a word, but she couldn't do anything about his snoring. She had even secreted a charm in his clothes. She wondered if he had gone to the old woman for a protection against charms, for rather than ceasing he had snored more vigorously since.

Steeling herself to the February cold, she got out of bed and hurriedly swathed herself in a green velvet robe and layers of shawls. Fur slippers protected her feet from the chill floor tiles. She wouldn't allow the maids in to see to a fire; they would know then that she was sleeping with her *jefe de vaqueros.*

Bonita, her personal maid, leaped to her feet as soon as she entered the sitting room next to her bedchamber. "Your *té* is ready, *Doña* Cordelia," she said, dropping a curtsey. She quickly filled a delicate cup from the ornate silver pot.

Cordelia took the cup and sat in her favorite chair without speaking. The maid moved behind her with a hairbrush and began brushing, careful not to pull any tangles. Cordelia sipped her tea thoughtfully. Hector was not her problem at the moment. It was Fallon. He had healed, and he was talking of returning to San Felipe. The old woman had refused her any help in the matter, saying it was of this world. However it was handled, she must do it herself.

"Bonita, is *Señor* Fallon awake yet?"

"I . . . I believe I heard him moving about, *señora.*"

She looked at the girl acidly. She had likely been in Fallon's bed already this morning. The maids seemed to dote on his blue eyes and handsome features. She wondered why that angered her; she refused to consider that it was because he had made no move toward her own bed.

"Help me dress, girl, then bring him to my *escritorio.* Tell him it is important I speak with him immediately."

Immediately, she had said, but even when he walked into the study she wasn't sure what she was going to say. "Please have a seat, Mr. Fallon."

"Thank you, ma'am." She couldn't avoid the annoying thought that he was being respectful, not flirtatious. "Bonita said it was important, ma'am."

"Yes." She ran a finger along her dagger, thinking furiously. "You intend to leave us soon? Aren't you enjoying your stay?" She looked up suddenly and caught him coloring. And well he might. She was only sure of Ramona and Yolanda, but she thought Bonita and perhaps one or two others had shared his bed as well. She ignored the fact that she had encouraged it, telling the maids they were to see to his *every* need.

"I'm grateful for your hospitality," he said, "but my

ribs are mended enough for me to ride, now. It's time for me to stop imposing.''

''Not at all.'' She cast about for something, anything to catch his fancy. ''Hector Ramirez believes he may be on the track of your horse.''

He bounded out of the chair. ''River Wind? He knows where River Wind is?''

''Not exactly. He's asked questions. I think, though, in time, your horse might be returned.'' Why not? She cared nothing for a horse. Keeping Fallon there was all.

''If he finds out anything, ma'am, please send word to San Felipe immediately.''

''I was hoping you'd remain here, Mr. Fallon.'' Why? There had to be a reason. ''I had hoped you might consent to . . . to run my *rancho* for me.'' Yes, that was good. She simpered. ''I am just a woman, you know, with no head for managing a large estate.''

''I thank you, Mrs. Applegate, but I want to make my own way.''

The fool! ''I had thought of making you a partner.'' The words were out before she realized. She had thought of no such thing. Letting go of a single unnecessary acre or a coin she didn't have to was almost physically painful for her.

Fallon seemed as startled as she. ''That's incredibly generous. Too much so for me to accept. Besides, you have a *jefe de vaqueros* already.''

She dismissed Ramirez with a gesture. ''A fit overseer, but not a man who understands building and increasing an estate. I believe that you do. You will be a manager, above him. As for the terms, don't think you won't work for what you get. If you agree to work for me for, say, five years, I will sign a paper stating that at the end of that period you are to receive one quarter of my estate.'' That was very good indeed. Much could happen in five years. ''I have no relatives, Mr. Fallon. No one to dispute what I do with my property.'' That would set him thinking that he might end up with it all. Good, if it made him stay.

''Five years is a long time,'' he said slowly. ''You understand I need to think it over.''

So far as the man knew, she thought incredulously, he was having wealth thrust at him. What could he possibly have to think over? "I understand perfectly. Do say you'll stay as my guest, at least until you give me an answer."

Even at that he hesitated. "Of course, Mrs. Applegate. I'll be pleased to."

After he was gone she sat behind the long table, fondling the turquoise-mounted dagger. On the surface he gave every appearance of being open and straightforward, but she couldn't read what was beneath. In her experience there was always another person beneath the surface, and another beneath that. Her inability to perceive the true man made him dangerous . . . . She would have to try to get another sight from the old woman.

James walked slowly across the courtyard, thinking about Cordelia Applegate. Her offer might be a reasonable one for a man of experience and mature years, but he was painfully aware that he wouldn't be twenty-one for some months yet. That brought up the possibility that she wanted something else. He knew he was a good-looking man, and he knew aging women sometimes did strange things. He had been approached more than once in New Orleans with clear, if obliquely worded, advances from wealthy widows. He'd managed to ignore those, and he certainly had no intention of ending up in Cordelia Applegate's bed.

On the other hand, he had no evidence of any such intention on her part. Embarrassment flooded him at the thought that he might be manufacturing all this out of whole cloth. She didn't seem to mind his bedding serving girls. In some ways she seemed to foster it, always making sure that the prettiest girls were set to clean his room and tend his clothes. Could it be she was actually encouraging them?

He threw back his head and laughed out loud, drawing looks from servants bustling about the courtyard. His imagination was getting fevered. He went on into the tackroom, where José Escobar was mending a bridle. He had come to like the diminutive *vaquero*, often spending an evening with him, sharing a pipe and talking.

José looked up as he walked in. "You are amused by something, *señor?*"

"A stray thought," James said. He needed to talk to someone about Cordelia's offer, and he respected José's opinions. He laid out the bare facts to the man.

"There is *bondad y maldad* in everything," José said when he finished.

"I certainly can't see any evil in Mrs. Applegate. I suppose most men would see her offer as a dream come true. What about you, José? Haven't you ever wanted to be master of thousands of acres?"

José shrugged. "Always I have followed *el patron* or *la patrona.* They gave orders, and I did not question if they were right or wrong. It was enough that they were who they were. To be master of anything more than my own manhood is beyond my dreams."

"A man can be whatever he wants to be," James said earnestly. "In San Felipe there are men with no fewer years than you, who intend to build, if not empires, at least tidy *ranchos.*"

"Among my people, *señor,* a man does not rise from nothing to become a master. I am content."

"If you ever change your mind, I'd be proud to have you join me. You are a man to ride the river with." José gestured in self-deprecation. James recognized his embarrassment at the compliment, and hurried on. "Mrs. Applegate says Ramirez is on the track of River Wind. I may have him back before much longer."

José grimaced.

"Should I accept Mrs. Applegate's offer?"

The old *vaquero* spoke with his face turned away. "Accept it, *señor.* In the long run it will be best. In the long run, all things are good."

XXIV

Lucille shivered despite her robe and tried to immerse herself in the volume of Byron. The dirt-floored cabin that was her prison—after three months she thought of it so— was cold, even now in March. Cordelia was supposed to see that someone came to cut wood, but even in the depth of winter she had often had to venture out to gather dead twigs and branches.

With a cry of rage she hurled the book across the sparsely furnished room. James Fallon was warm, living in luxury and with his fill of women—she heard things from the serving girls who brought her food—while she lived like an animal.

She went to the door and peered out. Less than half a mile away through the thick undergrowth of mesquite and catclaw lay the old woman's hovel. Fear of the hex doll in Cordelia's hands had kept her away for the months past, but now . . . . James Fallon had to be kept alive and used. She wouldn't argue with the cards, or the old woman's sight. If Fallon was to be at the *hacienda*, she had to hide. She accepted that. But she wasn't a servant. She wasn't an animal. She had a right to be treated properly.

Abruptly, before she could change her mind, she left the cabin. There was no real path through the *chapparal*; thorns caught at her dress. Twice she stumbled into briar patches, floundering out with painful red scratches. With startling suddenness, though, she pushed into the clearing around the old woman's hut. A thin reed of smoke rose from the smoke hole; otherwise the clearing was still. The only sound was her own breathing. No bird chirped; no leaf rustled.

"Come in, *moza!*"

She flinched at the call from the hut. The crone might have powers, but she had not let Sanité Dédé overawe her; she wouldn't allow it of a peasant witch woman. She stooped to enter the hut, but once inside her back straightened pridefully. The old woman, leather-skinned and wrinkled, sat in a wooden chair on the far side of the firepit.

"I am Lucille Gautier. I am not—"

"*Mis mozas* address me as '*mi dueña.*'"

The chill of the old woman's words arrested her. For the first time she felt the oddness of the hut, as if it weren't connected to the rest of the world. And there was an aura about the shabby old woman. Power radiated from her. Beside her Sanité Dédé was a worm, nothing.

"You still doubt." A claw of a hand gestured. "Let your breathing not disturb your thoughts."

Lucille opened her mouth, but no words came out. She couldn't breathe. Her frantic fingers tore at the neck of her dress, clutched her throat. Her face began to turn blue. Her eyes bulged. Her legs turned to water, and she crumpled. Her face scrubbed in the dirt as she tried to claw her way to the old woman. She had to make her understand. Silver flecks obscured her vision. Fringed shadows channeled her sight to pinpoints. She was dying. She couldn't! Not like this!

"*Puedes respirar, moza.*"

In her private darkness the old woman's words were faint, but as she heard, air rushed into her lungs. Blessed cooling air. She sucked at it as if at the sweetest wine. "Thank you," she managed. Ominous answering silence spurred her. "*Mi dueña!* I thank *mi dueña!*"

"Good, *moza.* You live in the world of things, but this small hut is the doorway to a much greater world, the world of *los espiritos.* The one who dyes her hair and paints her face to hide her years does not understand this. You must, *moza.* I have been waiting for you."

Waiting for her? Cautiously she raised herself to her

knees and sat back on her heels. "I want to learn, *mi dueña*. Will you teach me?"

"Perhaps, *moza*. I must examine you. *Quitese la ropa!*"

Lucille scrambled to her feet. As her clothes fell in a welter around her feet the cold raised bumps all over her skin, but for once she didn't mind.

The old woman came around the firepit. Her bony fingers poked and prodded and burrowed as if she were examining a horse. Before she was done, Lucille was flushed and breathing hard.

"Am I acceptable?"

The old woman took a pair of dingy pouches from the chest against the wall. "That must be still be seen, *moza*. Now, be quiet."

Carelessly she kicked Lucille's clothes aside. From one pouch she took dried snakeskins and laid them in a ring around Lucille's feet. On each foot was placed a snake skull, fangs lightly indenting her arches. Delving into the other bag she came out with full hands. She began a keening chant and opened her fists. Small bones, tiny animal skulls, something that might have been a dried finger, fell at Lucille's feet. The old woman rubbed her bony chin with one thin finger and studied the display.

"*Quizas, moza,*" she said finally. "Perhaps." The snakeskins and bones went back into the pouches. Lucille wet her lips and kept silent. "Kneel by the fire, *moza*."

Hesitantly, Lucille knelt. She understood nothing of what was happening, but somehow she knew this next was the crux. From under her dress the old woman took a small leather pouch and sprinkled powder on the fire. Multicolored sparks flew; blue-gray smoke billowed toward the smoke hole.

"Breathe the smoke, *moza*. Breathe deep."

Lucille rubbed her sweating palms. She leaned forward, inhaled deeply, choked and coughed. Nothing happened. She looked at the old woman questioningly.

"Breathe, *moza*."

Lucille put her face back into the smoke and breathed. And again. Again. She stared at the wall behind the old woman. At the detail in the swirls of mud plastered over woven branches. There were patterns in the mud, patterns that moved and changed.

One appeared to be a wagon. She could see the horses galloping, the wheels spinning. There were houses, mansions, women dancing in colorful gowns. Boats with towering masts and sails that billowed before the wind like clouds. Steamships with paddlewheels churning. Cannon roared. Men in a mission fought an army and died. Sound boomed in her ears, hollow, impossible to make out, but she thought she was speaking. Or perhaps screaming.

The images changed. Deserts burned, flames towering to the sky. Mountains melted and flowed like hot wax. Oceans boiled. The air was jelly, swirling in a thousand colors that had no means. Blood rained from the sky. Skulls talked, and dead men walked, and the earth opened and died.

She became aware of herself, slick with sweat, head on her knees, whimpering like a child. Her throat was sore. Her eyes throbbed. She had a memory of fear, and even the memory wrenched her stomach. The old woman watched calmly from her chair, sipping from a cracked cup.

"What . . . what happened, *mi dueña?* My head hurts."

"Never use the smoke unless it is needed, *moza,*" the crone said quietly. "It eats souls. You will come to need it, to want it more than food or drink. Some have died of thirst and hunger, content with breathing the smoke."

"There are people who like that?" Lucille asked incredulously, then the old woman's words penetrated. "Do you mean you will teach me, *mi dueña?*"

"Are you ready for it, *moza?* If you will learn, then you will know hunger and thirst, cold, heat, and pain. When you are stupid, you will suffer with your face in the dirt." Despite her words, her tone was not unkindly. "I cannot guarantee that you will learn, *moza,* but you will survive. I did, many years ago. If these things frighten you, leave. Come to me like the red-haired one, to ask for a sight, or a potion, or the telling of the bones. Well, *moza?*"

Lucille shivered under that raven gaze. She was frightened, more frightened than she had ever been before. "Teach me, *mi dueña*," she said.

"*Señor* Ramirez!" James strode toward the stable, where the *jefe* was mounting his horse. It was a crisp March morning, and soon James, too, would be riding out to join the *vaqueros*, but today he had a reason for lagging behind at the *hacienda*. "*Señor* Ramirez, *por favor*. I have been trying to speak to you for two days."

"I am busy," Ramirez replied sourly.

"I won't keep you a minute. Have you found out any more about River Wind?"

"I have more important things to do than look for your horse. Every day you badger me."

"Over a week ago I asked," James said levelly. "You mumbled at me vaguely, and said you had work to do."

Ramirez stared at him, jerking the reins. His horse danced a few steps sidewards. "Your horse will be found when it is found. If I were *patron*—" Abruptly the hawk-faced man dug his spurs into his mount's flanks.

James frowned as the *vaquero* galloped away. It was his opinion that Ramirez feared he would be supplanted in Cordelia's embraces.

As Ramirez galloped out of the courtyard, another rider entered. With surprised delight James recognized Henry Cameron. "Henry! How's the wife and little Denmark? Married life still agreeing with you?"

"It's agreeing." Henry stepped down and tossed his reins to a waiting stablehand. "Why don't you find yourself a wife, James? It'll agree with you, too."

"Too many pretty flowers," James laughed. "I can't pick just one." He hadn't thought of marriage since Helene said no. "Truth to tell, Henry, I just might. After today, maybe I'll take a trip back home and see if Helene St. Albin is ready to change her mind."

"Why would she, James? You still ain't got a mansion."

James nodded. "But I'll have one in five years. Mrs.

Applegate offered me a quarter of her land to manage her estate for that long. She wants a man to run things for her."

"And she come to you?" Henry asked drily. "I ain't noticed you got a whole lot of experience."

"That's why I took three weeks to decide. It's too good a chance to pass up, Henry. I'll never get another like it. And with River Wind gone, it's the best thing I can see."

"It's too damned good, James. Don't you wonder why she make an offer like that to somebody your age? I don't trust her. That woman got a twist in her."

"What do you mean?" James said hotly. Though he'd considered his youth himself, the reference still stung. "Do you know something, or are you just talking?"

Henry shook his head. "It's just . . . well, when she looks at you, it's like one of them quadroon gals back in New Orleans, got her man on a string like a puppy dog."

"Damn it, she's old enough to be my mother. This is a business arrangement. Nothing more."

"That ain't what I meant," Henry protested.

"I'm not wet behind the ears. I don't need you to lead me around by the hand."

"I just meant—"

"I know what I'm doing. I can take care of myself."

"Damn it, you're stubborn as a mule and twice as stupid!"

"Then why in hell do you bother with me! Why don't you pack up your suspicions and take them somewhere else!"

They stood toe to toe, both breathing hard. Their voices had risen; everyone in the courtyard was staring at them. Men had come out of the stable to watch.

"All right!" Henry said finally. He turned away and snatched his reins from the stablehand. "God damn it, all right!"

He swung into the saddle. James opened his mouth to call him back, and closed it without speaking. Pride stood in the way. Henry whirled his horse, then stopped to look at him, and for a moment he thought the other man might take the first step. Then Henry booted his horse in

the ribs, and he watched his friend gallop out of the courtyard.

He didn't need Henry. He could get along very well
without him. But, God, he'd miss him. Stiffening his re-
solve, he started for the main house to tell Cordelia she
had a manager.

XXV

Lucille shifted on her chair and winced at a stab of pain from her buttocks. Asking the old woman to let her use the smoke more often had earned her a whipping and a command to spend the rest of the day meditating. It meant a day learning nothing, and the learning was so slow as it was.

She was willing to endure it, though, the long hours kneeling naked, assisting the old woman in incomprehensible rituals, the fasts that shriveled her stomach, the sweat baths where the air was so hot she expected blisters to rise on her skin. She knew she was on the threshold of a world of power, a world Cordelia could never enter. When she had that, she'd not be content with a hovel. That power would command palaces.

She leaped to her feet as the cabin door crashed open. Hector Ramirez swaggered in out of the April day, bringing a scowl to her face. "What are you doing here?"

"I came to see you, *niña*. You want to be nice to me." He moved deeper into the room, unsteady on his feet. He was drunk.

"You had better return to the *hacienda*, Ramirez. *Señora* Applegate will not like you being here."

"Old *ramera*," he muttered. "What do you two play at?"

"I do not know what you mean. Go back—"

"You! Why do you hide here instead of using your rooms at the *hacienda*? Why is your name not to be mentioned to this Fallon? And Fallon himself. Why is he first

210

beaten, then treated like a king? Tell me these things."

The fool, she thought. He could expose everything. "You should talk to *Señora* Applegate. Go talk to her. She will explain everything."

"She tells me nothing," he said sullenly. "When I am master here, *la patrona grande* will do as she is told."

She couldn't stop herself from laughing. "You! You are master of nothing, *chulo.*"

"*Puta!*" Like a snake his hand darted to her chin. His breath smelled of brandy. "She needs me. Whatever it is she plans, I can destroy it with a word to that *cachorro bastardo* Fallon. I will marry the old *puerca*, and if she does not step quickly enough when I command, I will whip her fat *culo* until she screams for mercy." His tongue licked his thin lips. "You must be nice to me, *niña*, if you wish to retain your favored position."

She met his eyes coldly, and hissed, "*Quedese con vuestras manos puercos lejos de mi, marica!* Find yourself a plump boy!"

She didn't see his free hand move, but there was suddenly an explosion against the side of her head, and she found herself on the dirt floor. She sobbed in rage and pain. As she tried to push herself up, he grabbed the front of her dress and jerked. She was lifted from the floor, then cloth tore and she fell back, her round breasts spilling free.

"I will keep you," he added hoarsely. "The old one can warm her own bed."

"She will have your *cojones,*" she managed. "You will spend the rest of your miserable life in prison!"

"You will not go to the authorities," he laughed drunkenly. "Beating men. Stealing horses. What else? You do not want the authorities to look too closely."

When he bent to her again, she tried to claw him. An open-handed blow smashed her back to the ground. He tore at the remains of her dress, dragging her across the floor, rolling her this way and that despite her struggles until she lay naked except for her stockings. Tangling a hand in her hair, he lifted her up.

She screamed from the pain. "*Dieu! Au secours! Cochon*, I will kill you!"

He pushed her down on the table, his breath hot on the back of her neck as he fumbled with his clothes. She wept as her feet scrabbled at the dirt; she clawed helplessly at the table top. She'd cut his heart out, she thought as he entered her. If Cordelia didn't first, she'd kill him.

"I always love April," Cordelia said. "Don't you, Mr. Fallon? New leaves on the trees. Flowers. The world renewing itself."

James shifted uncomfortably in his chair. They were in her study, she behind the long table, and they were supposed to be going over the decisions he had made since beginning to manage the *rancho*, but she seemed bent on diverting the talk into other channels.

"Yes, ma'am. It's very pretty."

Amusement appeared on her face. "You're impatient to be at the work, aren't you? I wager I have some news that'll make you forget."

She paused, making him say, "Ma'am?"

"I shouldn't tease you. Your horse, Mr. Fallon. Ramirez is very close to finding him. Within the week, I should think."

James frowned. "He didn't say anything about River Wind when I saw him this morning." Ramirez had, in fact, been drunk and abusive.

"I'm afraid he's jealous of you, Mr. Fallon. Before you, he ran the *rancho* day to day. You took his place."

She eyed him with such open speculation he wondered if she was considering how else he might replace Ramirez. When she smiled, he was certain. It was a complication he had not believed in. He dug into the journal where he kept his notes.

"Mrs. Applegate, we do have to talk about your horse camp. You have only one, upriver. It would be much more efficient to have four smaller camps. Forage would be easier to find. Your herd is just too bunched up."

"Whatever you wish, Mr. Fallon."

"Very well." He made a note. "I've set up books to keep track of supplies sent to the outlying camps. Things have been sent places where they're of no use at all. Just last week, six sacks of oats were sent downriver. The ponies the cattlemen ride do quite well on corn and mesquite grass.''

"But think how the creatures must have enjoyed oats. A banquet.'' Her laugh was a little forced.

James smiled politely. He supposed that was something he'd have to get used to, smiling at her bad jokes. "I'll ask them how they liked the oats.''

"You . . . you're going downriver, Mr. Fallon?''

"I need to make a round of all the camps. I might as well start there. Are you all right, Mrs. Applegate?''

Her face had paled. She swayed in her chair. "I . . . I don't feel well.''

"I'll fetch Bonita," he said, getting to his feet. She stretched a hand toward him.

"Don't go, Mr. Fallon.''

"You need your maid. Don't be afraid.''

She laughed shakily. "Afraid?'' She took a deep breath, and a little of her color returned. "I meant, don't leave for the outlying camps until we finish this discussion. I should be well enough to continue by this afternoon.'' Her tone was suddenly anxious. "There's no hurry, is there?''

"No, ma'am.'' She must be sicker than she thought to get so upset. "It can wait a few days, until you're better. I'll get your maid.''

"I'd rather be alone.'' She closed her eyes and leaned back. "I just need to think,'' she said as he left.

He found Bonita and asked her to keep an eye on Mrs. Applegate, then headed for the stable. He wanted to talk to José. The old *vaquero* had a saddle on a high rail in the tackroom, repairing a girth.

"*Hola, señor,*'' he said without looking up. "You must forgive me if I continue to work. I have much to do.''

"I won't bother you long,'' James said. "What has Ramirez found out about my stallion?''

José's hands stopped on the leather, but he didn't turn around. He was silent for a moment. "I do not know, *señor.*''

"Mrs. Applegate said I might have the horse in a week. But when I saw Ramirez this morning, he never mentioned

River Wind. Could he be playing some sort of double game?''

''What *Doña* Cordelia says will happen has a way of happening, *señor.*'' The old man resumed work, more slowly than before. ''Things are better as they happened, no, *señor*? Soon you will have your stallion, and you are assured much good land for breeding your horses. If you had not been robbed, you would have only the stallion.''

''There's still the matter of fourteen hundred dollars.''

''But the land is worth more.'' José twisted around to look at him.

''I suppose. But, strange as it might sound, I'd rather be back with Henry, breeding River Wind in a log corral we'd built ourselves.'' He'd been a fool, he knew, to argue with a man who'd been his friend so long.

''I understand, *señor,*'' José said.

As if James' thought had been a signal, the tackroom door opened, and Henry Cameron stepped inside, his fur cap tilted at a jaunty angle, carrying his rifle in both hands. He looked behind him, then pushed the door almost closed, leaving a crack that he kept an eye on.

''Damn it, Henry,'' James said, ''I was just thinking about you. If you came to knock some sense into my head, start knocking. I deserve it. What I'm trying to say is, if you'll accept my apology, it's yours.''

''Hell, James, I seem to recollect saying a few damned fool things myself. You kick my butt, and I'll kick yours.''

''I think we call it square,'' James laughed. ''Why do you keep looking out the door? You'd think Indians were coming.''

''The Applegate woman don't know I'm here. I hope.'' He glanced at José again. ''You know what's south of here, José?''

''I know, *señor,*'' José replied soberly.

James looked from one to the other in bewilderment.

''I been slipping around,'' Henry said, ''visiting one camp and then another. Downriver from here I found a little one, a cabin where half a dozen cattle herders sleep. Only out back they got a corral and a shed. And River Wind.''

Six sacks of oats flitted through James' mind. "Ramirez! I thought he was up to something."

Henry shook his head. "That Applegate woman is who."

"That's insane!" James protested. "She has me beaten up, steals my horse, then brings me to her *rancho* and offers me a quarter of it if I manage it for her five years?"

"Them *vaqueros* didn't know me from Job's off ox. They talked to me, James. Right after they got the horse— that was maybe three, four days after you was attacked— she used to go down there in her coach to look at River Wind. They snickered and said some women get real taken with a pretty stud horse like him."

No wonder she'd taken ill when he talked about going downriver. No wonder she was so confident he'd get River Wind back. But it still didn't make any sense.

"Why, José?" he asked finally.

The old *vaquero* sighed heavily. "For *Doña* Cordelia, I do not know. For me, I have lived my life obeying orders. When you became my friend . . . ." He lifted his hands and let them fall. "For each thing you lost, there was a gain. You yourself admitted you are better off than if it had not happened."

"Except that somebody's playing with my life as though I was a rag doll. Henry, can you get River Wind away from those men?"

Cameron nodded. "Easy."

"Then you go get him, and meet me on the way to San Felipe. I'm going to go get my money back. José, I'm afraid I'll have to tie you up."

"As you wish, *señor*. But you may need help. I have a shotgun." James looked at him questioningly, and he went on. "I would rather have you as my *patron* than remain here. If you will have me."

"If you ride with me," James said, "it has to be as a friend. I don't want to be anybody's master." He held out his hand, and after a moment Escobar took it.

"If we're going in to get your money," Henry said, "we better go. Don't say it, James. I'm going, too. We might need every gun we got."

"It is true, *señor*. The *vaqueros* like you, but they will obey *Doña* Cordelia, or Ramirez."

There were enough Indians around for the stable to have its own rack of arms. James helped himself with a musket and a pair of pistols, powder flask and shot bag. He eased his knife, the gift from Bowie, and they started for the house.

In the courtyard two *peóns* swept with twig brooms. A few *vaqueros* lounged in the sunlight in front of the *barracón*, watching a maid hurrying by with a basket of laundry. The three men drew only incurious glances; in that country, all men carried guns.

Inside the house, though, Bonita took one look at them and turned to run. James grabbed her arm.

"Where is Mrs. Applegate? We won't hurt you, girl. Just tell me."

She looked at him, and swallowed. "She . . . is in her *escritorio*. But she does not wish to be disturbed. Why . . . why have you brought guns into—"

"You first," James said, and gave her a gentle shove toward the study. Whimpering softly, she led the way.

When he pushed open the study door, James wondered if he had stumbled into a nightmare. Ramirez, clothing disarrayed and scratches on both cheeks, had Cordelia pushed down onto the massive table, her skirts up around her waist and her hair down around her shoulders. She was kicking and punching at him; he seemed to ignore her blows, laughing and tugging at her clothes. When they became aware of the people at the door, they froze. James pushed Bonita towards them.

"What are you doing here?" Ramirez demanded, staggering to his feet. James realized the man was very drunk. The blood on his cheeks had dried. Apparently, Cordelia wasn't the first woman to suffer his attentions that day.

Cordelia scrambled to her feet, hands fluttering over her torn dress. "He tried to rape me!" she cried. "Shoot him, James! Kill him!"

With a growl Ramirez backhanded her to the floor. James stepped in and hooked a short left under the hawk-faced man's ribs. Ramirez' eyes bulged. Gagging, he sank to the floor, and vomited down his shirt front.

Cordelia gave him a look of sour satisfaction. A thin trickle of blood ran from the corner of her mouth. "You must kill him. My honor demands it."

"Shut up, Cordelia," James said. Her mouth fell open. "Henry found River Wind."

"It was Ramirez," she said hurriedly. "He babbled about it just now. He intended to keep the horse. I've no idea when he actually recovered—"

"It won't work, Cordelia. You had me beaten. You had the horse stolen, and my money. I want the money."

"That's madness." She laughed, unconvincingly. "I took you in, offered you a quarter of—"

"*Puta!*" Ramirez muttered from the floor. "*Ramera!* Take the horse. Give the horse back. When I am master . . . ."

"The money, Cordelia," James said levelly.

"I'll sign the land over to you now." She wet her lips. "This minute."

"My money."

"Half the estate. I'll give you half. Just stay here with me."

"My money, Cordelia. That's all I want."

"It's not what you think. I know I'm . . . old." The last word seemed wrenched from her depths. She shuddered and went on. "I can have the most beautiful women brought here for you. Young women."

"You aren't listening!" he shouted. "All I want is what's mine! And to have no more part of you!"

"What's yours." She made a sound half laughter, half weeping. "A pittance. I can make you rich. You want money? I'll show you money."

She started past him, but he stopped her. "You and Bonita help Ramirez. We're bringing him along."

She grimaced, but motioned the maid to help her get the befouled man to his feet. Staggering under his weight, they led the way, into the hall and down narrow stairs into the cellar.

The stone walls were almost hidden by barrels of flour and rice, sacks of beans and peas. The low ceiling, hung with strings of garlic, onions and peppers, was supported by squat stone columns. At the far wall of the room was an iron-bound wooden door, secured with a massive lock.

Cordelia produced a key from inside her dress. "You'll see," she panted. "Rich. I'll make you rich." The lock clicked.

James motioned the two women to support Ramirez through ahead of him, then followed.

"*Madre de Dios,*" José breathed.

It was a small, windowless room. Two oil lamps, already lit, sat on a table against the far wall, among leather and canvas bags, some lying open to spill forth gold coins. Four chests stood near the table, one open and filled with rings, brooches, loose gems, and coins. It looked like a pirate's cache.

"Campeche was just downriver from here," Henry said.

"I had nothing to do with Lafitte!" Cordelia snapped. "The man is vile! An animal!" She drew a deep, shuddering breath. "This is mine, James. Mine! I'll give half of it to you if you stay."

James picked up a sack and dumped coins on the table until he estimated there was about fifteen hundred dollars left inside it. "Mine," he said, stuffing the sack into his coat pocket. "Plus a mite of interest. And for my friends' troubles . . . ." He treated two more sacks the same way, tossing one to Henry, one to José. They caught the money, looking surprised, then tucked it away.

"Listen to me," Cordelia said intently. "You must stay. You have to!"

"Have to? José, will you go up and bring three saddled horses to the veranda?" Something caught his eye behind the chests. With a glad exclamation, he pulled out the rifle and pistols Thomas Martin had given him. "A fitting end, Cordelia."

She grabbed his arm. "For the love of God, you don't know what you're doing!" Spittle frothed at her mouth. "You must stay! The cards foretold it! The old woman had a vision! I'll give you anything you want!"

"You really are crazy," he said. Pushing Henry out ahead of him, he slammed the door in her face and locked it. He could still hear her muffled screaming and pounding. "Let's get out of here," he said, and Henry nodded quickly.

José led the horses up as they came onto the veranda. James laid the key in plain sight, where it would be found once the search for Cordelia started. A few *vaqueros* watched incuriously as they rode out of the courtyard.

"Won't be long," Henry said, "before somebody goes looking for her."

James nodded. "So let's go fetch River Wind and get the hell back to San Felipe."

The three men galloped steadily south, away from the *hacienda*.

XXVI

Cordelia shuffled the Tarot deck with shaking hands. The room was cool, even in the dry August heat, but sweat beaded her face. The months since Fallon's leaving had not been easy. She laughed bitterly, fighting tears. Not easy. Ramirez had had to be dealt with. Lucille had grown more forward, and the doom the old woman had predicted loomed in her mind. Ramirez had had so much blood in him. So much blood.

And then there was Fallon. Oh, God, Fallon. Her pleading notes had gone unanswered. Emissaries with generous offers had been turned away. Finally she had herself gone to San Felipe, to the wretched cabin he shared with the treacherous Escobar. The black man, Cameron, had been there with his wife and a squalling brat. Fallon had refused even to speak to her. Damn them!

Every spell at her command, every *gris-gris* and *juju* had been tried. Mysteriously, all had failed. The old woman had refused to aid her. It was Cordelia's problem, to be solved by Cordelia. Cordelia was too little concerned with the world of the spirits.

She snapped the cards down viciously.

"What does the future bring for me?"

As she turned the cards up her breath rattled in her throat. The eight of swords inverted and the six of batons, crossed with the seven of swords. The Star, the Tower, the Magician, and the Chariot. The same array as had answered her question the day she learned of James Fallon's existence. It was impossible. Such exact duplication did not happen.

Hesitantly she made the next array, asked the next question. "What kind of man is he?"

The Emperor and the Magician, crossed with the King of Swords. The three of batons, the Queen of batons, the Moon, and Hercules. She realized she was whimpering deep in her throat and couldn't stop.

She made the third array. "What . . . what is required of me toward this man?"

The Tower and the Hanged Man, crossed by the Star. The Chariot. The Hierophant inverted. The World. The Devil. Three times the same. Never before had this happened. It seemed a mocking of her. Could it be a punishment? Or a spirit coming back to taunt her? There had been so much blood in Ramirez.

At a tap on the door she hastily thrust the cards back into their box. "Who is it? What do you mean disturbing me?"

A plump maid entered. "*Dispense me, mi dueña*, but visitors have arrived."

"Visitors, girl? I am expecting no visitors. Who are they?"

"*Coronel* Solano, *Doña* Cordelia, and an Englishman. They are in the *sala de descanso*. I gave them wine."

Esteban Solano was one of her Mexico City acquaintances. "See that his men are taken care of, Rosita."

When she swept into the sitting room, Solano, his bulk straining a gold-braided blue uniform, kissed her hand with fleshy lips. "*Doña* Cordelia, how good it is to see you again."

"*Coronel*, what brings you so far from the gaiety of the city?"

"Hunting." The fat colonel gestured toward his companion. "My friend and I have hunted our way north. Jaguar. Bear. Wild boar. I forget myself. *Doña* Cordelia Applegate, may I present *Señor* Gerard Fourrier? My dear, are you all right?"

She stared at the other man. She knew him of old, tall, broad-shouldered, going to fat now, his sensually handsome face coarsened and thickened, but with the same obsidian eyes that reflected his hard core. A man linked to her past. A man whose family had followed the sea, but himself did not. "Gerard, you'll never know how glad I am to see you."

"The pleasure is mine, Cordelia," he said with a smile. "You are as lovely as I remember." He had always had a nimble, lying tongue, she thought wryly.

Solano was flabbergasted. "But . . . you know each other?"

"For a long time," Cordelia said. She wondered if Solano knew that Gerard had been a British officer, and a spy. Those were days she would just as soon forget, when she and Gerard had spied against the Americans at New Orleans, and Robert Fallon had beaten them at every turn. That was a lever to use on him, if he preferred that Solano not know.

"Yes," Gerard said smoothly. "We met for the first time in New Orleans. You remember, *coronel.* I told you about that. When I was operating against the *yanquis.*" He smiled at her. She bared her teeth in return.

"Of course," Solano said. "I remember now. Most amusing. You did not tell me you had been a spy, *Doña* Cordelia." His look told her that that bit of information was going to cost her money. But Gerard was the important one. Fallon could go to hell.

"Tell me, Gerard, what are you doing in Mexico?" she asked. He had always been one for the fleshpots of Europe, beautiful women and high-stakes gambling.

"The family business," he said in an offhand manner. "Our dealings with the government of Mexico are important to us. My family believes in Mexico." He made a short bow toward Solano, and the *coronel* returned it with a satisfied preen.

Had he actually turned into a dull man of business? His eye caught hers again, and she saw there was no fear of that. The old Gerard was still behind the mask. But the old Gerard would be much more difficult to handle than the innocent James Fallon.

"Gentlemen, excuse me for a moment." She hurried out before they had completed their murmurs of assent. In the hall she stopped a maid. "Fetch *Señorita* Gautier to my *escritorio* immediately. On the instant, or I'll peel your hide like a grape."

The girl scurried away as Cordelia darted into her study. The plan she was forming required Lucille's cooperation, and the way the girl had been acting of late, that meant she must be cowed first. When Lucille entered, Cordelia was behind the long table, toying with the dagger.

"Do you remember Casilda Manriquez, Lucille? In Mexico City?"

Lucille's eyes were wary. "The one with a *palacio* full of pretty girls she calls ladies' maids? What of her?"

"She has asked to have you pay her a nice long visit."

"No," Lucille said faintly.

"Then be aware that if you hinder my plans one iota, I'll pack you off to her before the day is out. With your hex doll. You'll dance nicely for her then, won't you?"

Lucille shivered. "I will do whatever you say."

Cordelia frowned. There'd been pure fear in her voice, but she had the strange feeling it was not fear of being giving to Casilda. Well, she would do what she was told. "The cards were wrong," she said abruptly. "James Fallon isn't the man."

"Then it is all right to kill him?" Lucille said eagerly.

"First things first." It *was* all right to kill him; she actually hadn't realized that until Lucille said it. How sweet it would be to avenge her humiliations at his hands. "First things first," she repeated. "The proper man is named Gerard Fourrier, and he is in the sitting room this moment."

"Fourrier," Lucille mused. "You spoke of him once. He was a spy? Why, he must be a shriveled old man by now."

"He's in his forties," Cordelia said sharply. Gerard was younger than she.

Lucille didn't seem to notice. "And will you offer him a quarter of your estate, too?"

"Half," Cordelia said. He wouldn't be satisfied with less, and worse, with him she would have to deliver. "And you, my dear."

"Me! I have slept with many men on your command,

Cordelia. I am tired of it!"

"Remember Casilda Manriques." Cordelia waited for her to wilt before going on. "You won't just sleep with him, you're going to marry him. Yes. We'll tell him you're my niece. Gerard always did have a weakness for dark-eyed girls with big tits."

"Marry!" Lucille wailed. "But he is old!"

"Gerard," Cordelia said quietly, "is t-, five years younger than me. The same age as Casilda." Lucille seemed to sink in on herself. Casilda made an excellent whip, Cordelia thought. Why hadn't she thought of her sooner? "I'm confident, my dear, in your ability to wind any man around your finger, even Gerard Fourrier. I'll leave the means to you, but I expect him to remain here when *Colonel* Solano leaves, and to ask for your hand soon after. Do I make myself clear?"

"Perfectly." Lucille's voice was bitter. "I will try to make him an excellent wife."

"Good, my dear. Shall we join the gentlemen?"

That night Gerard Fourrier lay in the moonlight, staring up at the ceiling in the room Cordelia had given him. She had come up in the world, he thought sourly. In New Orleans she had seemed nothing but an expensive whore, mistress to whoever had the money. Now she had the friendship of men high in the government. And wealth.

He tossed irritably. The bitch had gone up while he had gone down. Then he had been wealthy, a major in the British Army, mentioned more than once in dispatches. And with his father's death he had inherited more wealth. But he hadn't had Justin Fourrier's touch. Investments had gone sour. The number of ships flying the Fourrier flag had decreased. Even the market for smuggled slaves had dried up.

While that whore lived in luxury, he, the scion of an old and honored family, was reduced to personally hawking guns to greasy men in fancy uniforms who called themselves generals and colonels. Laughing at the bad jokes, complimenting their rotten marksmanship, letting them have first pick of the women.

There was a woman under that very roof he'd like to tumble. Cordelia's niece, Lucille. She'd inherited her aunt's tits, that was for sure. He wondered if she'd inherited anything else. As he remembered, Cordelia had been a blazing vixen once her clothes were off. If the girl was available, she was sweating under Solano's bulk right that minute. But if he knew Cordelia, the girl was a virgin. He'd never met a whore yet who wouldn't keep her daughter or niece a virgin to the grave if she could.

He lurched out of bed naked and dug a bottle of whiskey out of his baggage. It burned, sliding down his throat, but had no other effect. He tilted up the bottle again. Oblivion was his goal.

There was a soft rap at the door. Why were they bothering him, he wondered. He jerked it open, an angry retort ready on his lips.

In the dark he had an impression of dark, silken hair, of sweetly perfumed flesh. Lucille squeezed past him into his moonlit room. He had enough presence of mind to close the door. The long nightdress she wore was transparent over the curves of her body.

"Girl," he mumbled, "what do you want?" He followed her stare and realized for the first time he was naked. And erect. Well, damn her, let her look.

Her eyes dropped to the floor. Her breathing sounded frightened. "At dinner, I . . . . You are so different. The men who dine here, *Tia* Cordelia's friends, they are like the *coronel*. Coarse men. Once, when I was a little girl, I went to Mexico City, and I saw men like you. Men of culture."

By God, he thought, he'd been right. Cordelia kept the girl locked up in this desolated *hacienda*, away from the temptations of the city. She was a virgin!

"Why did you come to my room, girl?"

"Sometimes I hear the serving girls talk of what they do with the *vaqueros*." Her breath caught, and he was sure she blushed. "I know these things are wrong. The priests tell us so. But when I hear them, I feel so funny. Hot. My skin wants to jump off of me. You are not a mere *vaquero*, or a coarse fool like the *coronel*. I thought, if I came to you . . . ." She looked at him in supplication, and he thought he'd come on the spot.

"Child, you don't know what you do to a man." He took her arm—it was all he could do not to throw her down on the floor—and guided her back through the door. "This must be done slowly to be right, Lucille."

"But you are going. *Coronel* Solano said you are leaving tomorrow."

"The *coronel* is, but I'm not. You and I will have a lot of time together. But it must be our secret. You understand?"

"Our secret," she whispered, and darted down the hall.

He closed the door and fell against it laughing. Cordelia's niece. Rich Cordelia's virgin. Rich Cordelia's bigtitted, hot-tailed virgin. He hoisted the bottle in celebration. Things were looking up.

XXVII

James and José herded the last of the lean mustangs into
the corral behind their cabin. The unbroken mares milled,
some wheeling back as they quickly pushed the gate shut.
In a smaller corral a dozen yards away, River Wind scented
the new mares and reared, screaming and pawing at the
air. James decided he'd better add another row of rails to
his corral.

Henry came from the *chapparal* behind the corrals, rifle
in hand. They were taking no chances of another theft.
"He's getting impatient, James. When you going to let
him at them?"

"Not until Austin gets back. I want to have my claim
improved before I start worrying about foals."

"Damn, James, I clean forgot. He got back this morning. He wants to see you, too. Sent Josiah Bell down
here two, three hours ago. I told him you was out buying
horses, and he said you was to see Austin soon as you got
in."

"We've got our land!" James yelled. Whooping, he
galloped up the dusty road toward San Felipe.

James slowed in the rutted street outside Austin's cabin.
A dozen *vaqueros* from Cordelia's *rancho* sat their horses
there. They stared as he stepped down, but none spoke or
made a move.

As he started in, another man came out and paused to
stare at him. The man's hair was graying, but the black
eyes in his fleshy face were hard and unblinking.

"Do I know you, *señor*?" James asked.

The man turned on his heel, mounted a horse led forward by one of the *vaqueros*, and galloped away, the *vaqueros* trailing after. Wondering, James went inside.

The interior consisted of a hall with a room on either side. The room to the left was sparsely furnished, a rude table and chairs, rough plank shelves, a bunk built onto the log wall. Jared Groce and Josiah Bell were there, and so was Stephen Austin—a small, almost frail-appearing man whose triangular face was dominated by a high forehead and large brown eyes. Like the others, he wore buckskins.

James trotted forward with his hand extended. "Stephen! Damn, but it's good to see you again. How did things go in Mexico City?"

There was a wary look on Austin's face as he took James' hand. "James, what in hell have you been doing?"

Groce was studying him, his broad face baffled, and Bell's receding chin waggled with indignation. James realized that the stranger had come with some new ploy from Cordelia.

"Who was that man who just left?" he asked. "What's Cordelia Applegate up to now?"

"Name's Gerard Fourrier," Groce growled. "He seems to be pretty close to Mrs. Applegate."

"Murder!" Bell snapped. "There's no use your denying it. I haven't trusted you from the first."

"Easy," Groce said. "I trust Fallon. And I'm not believing anybody's unsupported word against him."

Austin sighed. "This is one hell of a mess to come back to, James. Mrs. Applegate claims you killed her *jefe de vaqueros*, Hector Ramirez. In a fight over her, it seems, though Fourrier never said it straight out."

"That's insane!" James said. He hadn't told the true story when he returned to San Felipe. It had sounded unbelievable, even to him. Now he wished he had.

"Everybody knows how hard she tried to get you back," Bell sneered. "There's a name for men who try to make their fortune that way."

"If I killed a man, why did they wait so long to make a charge?"

"According to Fourrier," Austin sighed, "she did

nothing because of 'a misguided sense of friendship.' Leering while he said it. I know it's crazy, but there it is."

James managed to keep his voice calm. "I killed nobody. Henry Cameron and José Escobar can testify to that."

Austin shook his head. "I believe them, and you, James, but who will a Mexican judge believe? Them, or a wealthy woman with friends high in Mexico City?"

"Are you going to arrest me?"

"Of course," Bell began, but Groce cut him off: "Bugger it!" Bell blinked at the big man and subsided.

Austin ran his hands through his hair. His face was twisted with pain. "We could stand by you, James. Morally, we should. God damn it, we should."

"We'll go to Governor Martinez," Groce said.

"My father," Austin said as if Groce hadn't spoken, "got this grant from the Spanish. He died before he could do anything with it, but on his deathbed I swore to him I'd carry on. Before I more than began, though, the revolution came. I went to Mexico City to salvage what I could. And all the while it seemed like it was going to hell. Iturbide proclaimed himself Emperor. Everything was confusion and flux. Five months of lobbying the Congress day and night, and when I almost had enough support, Iturbide dissolved the Congress. So I set out to convince him, personally, that Americans should be allowed to colonize Texas. Three months it took, but I got him to sign a colonization law. Then Negrete, Bravo, and Victoria overthrew him, and I had to start from scratch. But I got it. Despite all of them, I got it. They gave me more than I asked for. I can give a league, more than four thousand acres, to every colonist. Damn it, I can fill Texas with American colonists. My father's dream. And mine."

"Stephen," James said, "it sounds like you're ready to throw me to the wolves."

"You will be turned over to proper authorities," Bell said primly.

"Bell," Groce growled, "if you open your mouth again, I'll call you out. James didn't kill anybody. I know that as well as if I were with him every minute."

Bell drew himself up. "If you think I'm afraid—"

"Damn it!" Austin cried. He sounded on the point of tears. "Damn it, James, I know you didn't kill this Ramirez. But it doesn't matter. Don't you understand that? If it goes to a trial, you'll be convicted, and the entire colony may come tumbling right after you."

"I won't go to prison for something I didn't do, Stephen."

"I know," Austin said wearily. "But you can't stay here. You understand that, don't you? I can't risk the colony for one man. Not even a friend."

James nodded slowly. The nightmare had him by the coattail again. "I'll be gone by morning."

"Thank you. I'd have hated to order you out. But I'd have done it, James. For the colony. You understand I can't do anything if Cordelia Applegate takes this to a higher authority. Your best bet is to be back in the United States before she realizes I haven't arrested you."

"I won't be chased out," James said grimly. "Not by her."

"What will you do?" Groce wanted to know. "Where will you go?"

James looked at Bell silently. The man would tell everything he knew as soon as he got the chance. The others understood immediately. Bell's face swelled and grew red.

"Whatever you do," Austin said, "my prayers go with you. I wish it didn't have to be this way."

"I know, Stephen. Goodbye, and good luck. Goodbye, Jared."

As he turned for the door, Bell started to follow, but Groce pushed the smaller man down into a chair. "I think we'll play some chess, Bell. And I won't take no for an answer."

James rode back to the cabin slowly, with no idea of where to go or what to do. It seemed that any plan he made was fated to be wrecked from the start. When he got down off his horse José and Henry came out to meet him. Leonie watched warily from the door, her dress opened enough for young Denmark to nurse.

"You are troubled, *señor?*" José said.

Tersely he explained what had happened. The two men seemed stunned when he finished. Finally, Leonie spoke.

"Did you kill that man?"

"Hush up, girl," Cameron said. "I was there. Remember?" She subsided sulkily.

"What do we do now, *señor?*" Escobar smiled at James' look. "I will ride with you a time longer."

"Me, too," Cameron said. "I ain't staying no place that don't want you."

James smiled in spite of himself. Suddenly things didn't seem so bleak. "I'm not going to the States. That's what I'll let folks think, though, in case Cordelia tries to find me."

"Then where, *señor?*"

"West. Maybe all the way to San Antonio. Cordelia will never think to look there."

Cameron shook his head. "The authorities in Bexar won't be too happy to see us, us not having any kind of papers."

"We'll take care of that when we come to it," James said. "Let's start packing. I don't want to spend an hour more here than I have to."

XXVIII

San Antonio de Bexar lay in a bend of the San Antonio River, a small adobe town, but a metropolis compared to San Felipe. It had two plazas, thronging with sauntering *vaqueros, peóns* in varicolored *serapes*, and women whose skirts were a rainbow. Between the low, flat-roofed houses facing the plazas towered the steeple of San Fernando Church, the tallest structure in the town. Indeed, in the flat country around the San Antonio, dense with mesquite thickets to the south and west, it was taller than anything until one reached the rolling hills north of town.

James studied the two men across the table from him in the Governor's long, low *palacio*. One was Antonio Martinez, Governor of Texas, the other Erasmo Sequin, *alcalde* of San Antonio. He had just finished telling them a version of his situation and asking for permission to settle.

Martinez shook his narrow, balding head. "By your own admission, *señor*, you are in Mexico without proper papers. By rights I should arrest you."

"*Su Excelencia,*" James said, "I have no wish to break the laws of Mexico. As I said, I am a horse breeder. There is little market for my horses in the Austin colony. In San Antonio, I might be able to take advantage of the trade routes."

"As a plan," Seguin said, "it has merit." He was a short man, and stout, but with an enormous dignity that made him seem more suited to high office that the governor himself.

"No," Martinez said, "the law is quite clear. Do not

think I do not sympathize. I supported *Señor* Austin's petition for a grant. But under the Colonization Law, those who are not citizens of Mexico must be residents in good standing of a recognized colony. For the moment, the only such colony is that of *Señor* Austin. If you wish to remain in Mexico, I must urge you to return there."

"But perhaps something temporary could be—"

"I am sorry," Martinez said. "There is no provision for anything 'temporary.' You may remain for a few days of rest—but then you must leave. And now, if you will forgive me, I am expecting guests. *Buenas tardes, señor.*"

"*Buena suerte, Señor* Fallon," Sequin said.

As James left the Governor's Palace, a coach drew to a halt at the foot of the steps. One of the accompanying *vaqueros* dismounted to open the coach door, and an elderly, distinguished-appearing man stepped out, his clothing the same as the *vaqueros'*, but of finer cut. He handed a young woman from the coach. James found himself staring.

She was a dark, slender woman, her ivory lace *mantilla* surrounding an oval face that seemed filled by liquid brown eyes. The distinguished man—her father rather than her husband, James found himself hoping—took her arm and came up the steps.

James made his best bow. "*Buenas tardes, señor, señorita.*" He thought the girl flickered an eye in his direction, but the man didn't pause. They disappeared into the Governor's Palace.

God, the girl had been beautiful. James approached the *vaqueros*. "Pardon me, *señores*. Could you tell me the name of the gentleman who just went inside?"

The men regarded him with blank eyes; then one said arrogantly, "*Don* Tomás Ibarra y Velasquez."

"And the *señorita*?"

The first man who had spoken pushed his horse forward. His was the flat, dark face of the Indio, a jagged scar on his left cheek. A silver-mounted quirt dangled from his wrist. "Who are you to ask these questions?"

"I'm James Christopher Fallon. And your name, *Señor*?"

"I am Diego Almada, *yanqui. Jefe de vaqueros* to *Don* Tomás. *Don* Tomás knows you *norteamericanos* for the greedy *langostas* that you are."

James had no hope of remaining in San Antonio if he got into a fight in front of the Governor's Palace. Without a word he unhitched his horse and mounted. His ears burned with Almada's laughter as he rode away.

His way led across the split-log bridge east of town, past the ruins of an old mission to a stand of cottonwoods by an irrigation ditch. The others were gathered around a fire where a coffee pot and a kettle of stew bubbled.

"What word?" Cameron said quietly. José looked up from stirring the stew without speaking.

"Can we stay?" Leonie asked.

She was frightened, and the two men, if not frightened, were at least worried. If San Antonio refused them, there was nothing left but to return to the United States.

"Martinez, the governor, likes to quote law," he said. "But the *alcalde*, Seguin, seems reasonable. I'll go back to see him in the morning."

Their faces fell.

José filled a tin cup with coffee and passed it to him. "Is there truly a chance, *señor?*"

"There's always a chance, José." Suddenly he had to change the subject. There wasn't any chance at all. He was just going through the motions. "I saw a girl in town."

"A girl!" Henry hooted. "Another pretty flower, James?"

"Prettiest girl I ever saw in my life."

"It is a wondrous thing to be young," José said, failing to conceal a smile.

"A roving eye," Henry laughed, "and no cares."

Abruptly it wasn't funny to James any more. He had to find a way. He had to.

The next morning James rode into San Antonio with José, to the *alcalde*'s adobe house, with its red-tiled roof. Over a low wall he could see a courtyard with fig trees and oleanders. He tossed his reins to José and got down to rap at the door.

A plump, dark maid opened the door a crack. "*Sí, señor?*"

"I wish to see the *alcalde*."

"*Don* Erasmo has gone to Laredo. He left before first light." The door shut firmly.

"That finishes it," James told José. "No telling when he'll be back, and Martinez said I could stay only a few days."

"You will find a way, *señor*."

They were all counting on him, he thought as he mounted. He hoped he was up to it.

"I'll do my best, José." Suddenly he pointed to *vaqueros* forming around a coach in front of the Governor's Palace. Men were coming down the steps, as well. And a girl. "That's her, José. Now tell me if she isn't enough to turn a man's head. *Doña* Drusilla Ibarra y Velasquez."

"Velasquez, *señor?* I believe I know . . . yes, I know that man."

James waited, wondering, while José rode to the steps and doffed his hat to Drusilla's father. The two men talked, then José waved for James to come forward. The *vaqueros* parted to let him through, Almada moving aside with obvious reluctance. James removed his hat and said nothing. Drusilla stood demurely behind her father.

"*Don* Tomás," Escobar said, "may I present my friend, *Señor* James Christopher Fallon?"

James bowed in the saddle. "I am honored, *Don* Tomás."

Velasquez regarded him thoughtfully. "I do not generally like *norteamericanos, Señor* Fallon, but the fact that José Escobar names you his friend speaks well for you."

"He honors me with his friendship."

"I have known José for twice as many years as you have lived. He has told me you are a breeder of horses, *Señor* Fallon."

"I intend to be so, sir. My *yeguada*, River Wind, is part Arab and part Spanish Barb. By crossing him with mustang mares I hope to produce a mount larger and faster than the mustang, but with the wild horses' stamina."

"That could prove interesting, *Señor* Fallon. Others have crossbred with the mustangs, but never with such good bloodstock. Still, I understand that you have some difficulties."

"I hope to remedy them, sir."

"A man who does not quail in the face of adversity. I like that, *señor*." He glanced at José, then nodded as if confirming a thought. "I offer you the hospitality of my *hacienda* until your way is clear. It is a long journey; we leave for the north within the hour."

James could barely contain his grin. As *Don* Tomás' guest he'd hear no official talk of his leaving in a few days, or even weeks. "Thank you, sir. Thank you very much. We'll be ready to ride."

Velasquez offered his hand to his daughter. "Come, Drusilla." He helped her into the coach, the *vaqueros* formed behind it, and the procession rolled away.

"He didn't introduce me to Drusilla," he mused.

Escobar looked troubled. "*Señor*, he respects your perseverance, and he knows me, but still . . . ."

"I'm just another *yanqui* adventurer?"

"I am sorry."

James shook his head. He had no time for opium dreams about some girl. "Come on, José. We have packing to do." He dug in his spurs with unusual vehemence.

Lucille turned from her dressing table mirror as Cordelia entered her room. Irritably she drew her peignoir over her breasts. "What do you want, dear 'aunt'? I do not have much time. Gerard will be up here any minute demanding his husbandly rights."

"Don't get above yourself." Cordelia's voice was soft, but there was a razor edge underneath. "Gerard may think you're my niece, but to me you're still just an octoroon servant girl. Your part is done with marrying Fourrier, and you'd better remember it."

Lucille knotted her fists in the lace of her peignoir. "Why have you come to me? *Zut!* You have been avoiding me since the wedding." Wedding, she thought.

An itinerant Franciscan and two *vaqueros* for witnesses. The papers had been signed for her dowry: half of Cordelia's estate, one-third now, one-third in five years, one-third in ten. Cordelia had signed as reluctantly as if the ink were her blood. Gerard had been so eager he hadn't complained, though, and she had been amused by the whole thing. Until she found out how much a young bride rejuvenated him.

Cordelia tossed a note on the dressing table. "I thought you might be interested in this. It's from that clerk in the Governor's Palace. About time he had something of interest to report for what I pay him."

Lucille read, frowning.

Senora,
   A *Norteamericano* calling himself James Christopher Fallon and claiming to be a breeder of horses has lately come to San Antonio. After but two days in the city, however, he insinuated himself into the company of *Don* Tomás Ibarra y Velasquez and has gone north with him to his *rancho*. It is obvious that he is up to some nefarious purpose, of which I will dutifully inform you as soon as I discover it.

It was unsigned.

"Cowardly fool," Cordelia snorted. "He wouldn't know a nefarious purpose if one bit him. He doesn't know if he's more afraid of being found out by Martinez or losing my money."

"We have him," Lucille crooned. "We can tell the authorities right where to find him."

"Fool! You're as big a fool as that clerk. Don't you recognize that name? Tomás Ibarra y Velasquez is a personal friend of Pedro Negrete. Does that name mean anything to you?"

"He is one of the Regency, in Mexico City. What does that matter?"

"What good to have him thrown in jail if Velasquez just has him released again? And he will, if he's taken Fallon under his protection."

Lucille's voice rose shakily. "You are not going to let him go? Forget about him? *Merde!* I will not have it! He must die!'' She was so angry she didn't notice Cordelia's stare until the other woman spoke.

"Sometimes, Lucille, I think you hate the Fallons as much as I do. I wonder why. Someday I'll find out what really happened in Charleston. And in New Orleans.''

Lucille turned away. "I told you what happened." She picked up her brush, then put it down again. Her hand was shaking. She didn't want Cordelia to see that.

"Perhaps. In any case, I won't let James Fallon go, nor any Fallon. But I'll handle him in my own way and in my own time.''

"Of course, Cordelia.''

"And I want to keep Gerard happy. I haven't been able to get anything out of the old woman about how long we need him. You understand?''

"I understand," Lucille sighed. She began to run the brush violently through her hair. Cordelia could take her time about Fallon if she wanted. She intended to settle with him. Soon.

XXIX

As James reached the *hacienda* the orange sun sat low on the horizon, filling the courtyard with long shadows. Through the fall and winter he, Henry, and José had ridden with the Velasquez *vaqueros*. Now, in April 1824, they were helping with the branding. He turned his horse over to a *peón* and made his way to the main house. To his surprise, Drusilla opened the door.

She put a hand to her throat and said, "*Señor* Fallon," as if she hadn't expected to see him. For the few seconds before she took her eyes from his face he felt as if he were drowning in them.

His ears burned. "Manuel said your father wanted to see me, *Doña* Drusilla."

"Come in. I will tell him you are here." She disappeared before he could say another word, leaving him standing there.

And what could he say, he thought. He couldn't repay *Don* Tomás's kindness by paying court to his daughter. Not when his future was as substantial as winter cobwebs.

He felt eyes on him, and looked up. It was *Don* Tomás's other daughter, Elena, twelve years old, and with eyes as big as her sister's. Those brown eyes regarded him soberly.

"Is it really true," Elena asked, "that you have sisters who are twins? And that one of them has my name?"

"Their names are Eleanor and Elaine. I suppose that's close enough to Elena. But how did you know about them?"

"Drusilla told me. I should like very much to be twins. I

239

should be able to go twice as many places and see twice as many things.''

He chuckled. "From what I understand, your father thinks you do more than enough by yourself.''

"Fathers," she said in a long-suffering voice, "are like that.'' She brightened. "I have watched you, *Señor* Fallon, and studied you at length. I think it is time to tell you that I find you quite suitable.''

"I thank you, *Doña* Elena. I find you quite suitable, too.''

"That is good. When I am old enough, I shall marry you.''

Drusilla returned in time to hear her sister's last remark. "Elena! A lady does not say such things. Return to your room at once. Play with your dolls.''

"I am not playing with dolls this evening,'' Elena replied levelly. "I am doing my embroidery. Which I do better than you, Drusilla.'' She drew herself up and made a regal exit, spoiled at the last minute by sticking her tongue out at her sister.

"You must forgive her, *Señor* Fallon,'' Drusilla said. "Except when we are in Mexico City she is too much alone. She needs children her own age. Why, I often catch her playing with the *peón* children. In the dirt.''

"It hasn't seemed to hurt her so far.''

"Of course.'' Suddenly she seemed to realize she had been looking him in the eye. She dropped her eyes to the floor and smoothed her skirt nervously with her hands. "*Mi papá* will see you now, *Señor* Fallon.''

He twisted his hat in his hands, searching for something more to say, but in the end there was nothing to do but go into the study.

Don Tomás stood in front of a massive stone fireplace, the marble mantel carved with a coat of arms. Beams as thick as a man's body crossed the vaulted ceiling. The furniture was heavy, the chairs upholstered in dark leather. It was the room of a man of culture, but a man who knew his way in rough lands as well. A polished rack on the wall held rifles and shotguns that showed the patina of use, flanked by deer antlers and the head of a jaguar. A bear-

skin rug, complete with snarling head, lay on the floor
with the Turkey carpets.

"*Señor* Fallon," Velasquez said. "Brandy?"

"Thank you, sir." He waited while the other man filled
two glasses.

"You are comfortable in the bunkhouse, *Señor* Fallon?"

"Quite comfortable, *Don* José."

"What do you think of the spring calves?"

"A fine crop, sir. You've lost a few to pumas and
coyotes, but not many. I'm surprised you don't have theft
by the Comanches, though. It's not far to their country."

"The Comanche will sometimes kill a cow, *Señor*
Fallon, but they despise it as food. They, and the Apache
as well, prefer mule."

"Mule!"

The old man chuckled. "Mule. They will steal horses to
ride, and mules to eat, but if they kill a cow, they leave it
to rot."

They sipped their brandy. *Don* Tomás led the conversation from Indians to Mexican politics to the future of the
Austin colony. After a time he brought out dark Cuban
cigars. James wondered when *Don* Tomás would come to
the point.

"Your horses," *Don* Tomás said finally. "You have
begun breeding?"

"No, sir." This was odd. *Don* Tomás followed every detail of the *rancho* closely; he surely knew. "That would be
an imposition on your hospitality."

Don Tomás nodded. "You are a man of sensibilities,
Señor Fallon. Many of your countrymen would have gone
ahead, using my land to raise their foals. I now give you
my permission to do so."

"That would be asking too much, *Don* Tomás."

"Nonsense. You truly wish to remain in Mexico? You
must have connections, or friends with connections, or
money for *los sobornos* to officials. And it would be good
if your horse breeding were begun, not merely a dream."

"I'll take you up on your offer, sir. But for each mare of
mine, you must allow me to offer River Wind to cover a

mate of yours. Otherwise, I cannot except your generosity.''

"A man of sensibilities," *Don* Tomás murmured. "Tell me, *Señor* Fallon. Do you play the game of chess?"

"Yes, sir."

"We must find time to play. Very well. As you accept my generosity, I accept yours. And now you must pardon me. As my years advance, the hours weigh more heavily, and earlier."

"Of course, sir." Making his goodbyes, he slipped out of the study. He'd never dreamed *Don* Tomás would make the offer. And that mention of friends with connections . . . . He left the house with a spring in his step.

The sound of the door opening behind him stopped him on the edge of the veranda. The glow of the half moon, sitting high in a black velvet sky, lit the courtyard beyond the yellow light from the windows of the *hacienda* and bunkhouse. Drusilla came out, drawing her shawl around her shoulders. For a moment she looked uncertain.

"Oh! *Señor* Fallon. Good evening."

"Good evening, *Doña* Drusilla."

"Tell me, is New Orleans as grand as Mexico City?"

"I've never been to Mexico City."

She sighed. "I am no good at this. When my father takes me to Mexico City, the ladies tell me I must make conversation with the gentlemen, but it is so long between visits, and there is no one to practice with here."

"Is that what I am?" he said softly. "Practice? Your *peón* to play in the dirt with?" The instant the words were out he wanted to call them back, but all he could do was watch her stiffen.

"That was most unkindly said, *Señor* Fallon."

"I'm sorry. I didn't mean it. I can't imagine you as anything but lovely and perfect in every way, Drusilla."

Her eyes grew even larger. Without another word she dashed back into the *hacienda*, the big door slamming shut behind her.

"Damn," he muttered. It was the first time he'd managed to exchange more than two words with her, and all he'd done was frighten her. His joy was gone as he started for the bunkhouse.

Diego Almada suddenly appeared in front of him, fingering the knife hilt sticking out of his sash, looking at the ground. "She is not for you, *yanqui*."

"Get out of my way, Almada. I'm tired."

"Leave this place if you know what is good for you, *yanqui*. *Doña* Drusilla is not for you, nor any like you."

Didn't Almada think he knew that? "It's late," James said, and pushed past the other man.

"She is not for you, *yanqui*," Almada called after him. "She is not for you!"

James entered the bunkhouse without answering.

The next day was like every April day in that part of Texas, warm but not hot, beneath a cloudless, pale blue sky. A light wind ruffled the clumps of mesquite grass that dotted the prairie, the stand of tall cottonwoods along the meandering creek.

A calf darted into the open. James cut his steeldust gelding sharply, and his *riata* settled about the calf's neck. Quickly he looped the braided rawhide rope around the horn of his high-pommeled Spanish saddle. The *riata* jerked tight and the calf ran off its feet. Just as quickly it was back up, bawling.

"You are becoming adept, *señor*," José called. "A true *vaquero*."

"No flattery, José," he yelled back. He had seen what the *vaqueros* could do with their *riatas*, some a hundred feet long, picking objects from the ground at a dead gallop, snaring a running horse at almost the full length of the rope.

He led the calf to the clearing in the grass where the branding fire burned. One *vaquero* threw the calf down, while another snatched an iron from the fire. Three more calves were being branded, one brought in by Henry, and knots of those already marked bawled in the surrounding grass. A large kettle of beef and peppers was simmering for the midday meal.

"Where's Almada?" James called to no one in particular. He had been around the fire all morning, watching as if they were his calves.

"He rode out just before you came in," Henry answered. "Maybe he decided to do some of the work." The *vaqueros* around the fire laughed.

James did not. There was enough bad blood between him and Almada already. It'd be a wonder if they didn't come to blows sooner or later. He turned from the fire and rode out again.

As he rounded a small mesquite thicket, a calf broke for the tall grass ahead of him. Gathering *riata* in hand, he dug in his spurs. A cloud of smoke blossomed from the thicket. A fist hit him in the chest. He heard the boom as he was falling, and realized he'd been shot. He hit the ground like a sack of meal. There wasn't any pain, but his chest was numb. Breath wouldn't come.

Footsteps rustled toward him in the tall grass. He clawed feebly at the double-barreled pistol in his sash. A hand rolled him over, and he was staring up at the sweating face of Diego Almada.

"You should have gone, *yanqui*." The *vaquero* pulled out his knife. "You should have gone."

Straining, James managed to tip up the pistol and pull the trigger. The fifty-caliber ball took Almada in the throat. The gun dropped from James' hand as the *vaqueros* galloped up, Cameron and Escobar with them.

One of the *vaqueros* dismounted and went to Almada. After a moment he called, "*El jefe* is dead."

"*Madre de Dios!*" José said. "What has happened?

"Ambush," James said, and passed out.

He came to briefly, swaying in a litter slung between two horses. When next he regained consciousness he was in a bed, surrounded by long faces. José Escobar was cutting his shirt away. Henry and *Don* Tomás stood at the foot of the bed.

"Don't look so glum," he croaked. "I'm not dead yet."

José poured a powder that burned like fire onto his chest. Do not talk, *señor*."

"I have been told what happened, *Señor* Fallon," *Don* Tomás said. "Almada had gold in his pockets, more than he could ever have obtained honestly. Do you have enemies, *señor*?''

James struggled for breath. "All men have enemies."
Cordelia, he thought.

"I said, do not talk," José said. "The bullet is still in
your chest, *señor*. I am a fit *medico* for broken legs and
horse colic, but this bullet must be cut from you."

"Get on with it," James said. His chest burned with
every labored breath.

José pressed a brandy bottle to James' lips. "Drink as
much as you can." James gulped at the fiery liquid until
his head swam. José took away the bottle and pushed a
piece of leather between his teeth. "Bite, *señor*." The old
vaquero held up a knife, pouring the last of the bottle over
the gleaming blade.

James gritted his teeth as José bent over him. The fire in
his chest flared higher, and a scream bubbled up to be
stopped by the gag. The bubble burst into blackness.

Awareness returned to him in a darkened room, the curtains drawn. His head ached. Every breath came like lead.
But he was alive. He felt like laughing over that. He
couldn't tell if it were day or night, or how much time had
passed. Thick bandages swaddled him, and a sheet covered
him to the waist. A shape sat in a chair against the wall.

"What . . . what day is it?" he asked. "How long?"

The shape started. "You are awake!" It was Drusilla.
"*Gracias a Dios!* How long? It has been three days."

The urge to laugh returned. He started coughing, and
then Drusilla was wiping his face with a cool damp cloth.
"Thank you, *Doña* Drusilla. I am honored by my nurse."

Her voice was so soft he almost missed her words. "You
called me Drusilla before."

"Drusilla. Thank you, Drusilla."

She stroked the cloth gently across his forehead. "You
must sleep. It will heal you, James."

He wanted to say something more, but he suddenly
found that he really was tired. Sleep clouded his brain.
The last thing he noticed was Drusilla, smoothing his hair.

XXX

A mid-September breeze ruffled James' hair as he stood on a balcony overlooking the *hacienda* courtyard. Below him, women crossed the flagstones beneath the morning sun with bundles of wash. Two *vaqueros* worked on harnesses in front of the stable. The sky was cloudless, and in the distance he could see dust raised by the vaqueros with the horse herd.

He was healed enough to be riding with the *vaqueros* again, with Henry and José. During the summer of his convalescence, though, his status had changed in subtle ways. There had been long afternoons of chess and conversation with *Don* Tomás.

Drusilla stepped onto the balcony behind him. "*Mi papá* wishes to see you in his study," she said coldly.

"Thank you," he said. "I—" She turned and left as if he hadn't spoken.

He cursed inwardly. While he had been confined to his bed, she had sat every day reading to him from the Spanish poets, but since he had regained his feet she had grown more and more distant. The plain and simple of it was that he loved her, and he had begun to dream of what might be. Her coldness cut him like a knife.

Muttering to himself, he made his way to *Don* Tomás' study, entering without knocking. The older man looked up from his book.

"You want to see me, sir?"

"Yes, *señor*. Brandy? A cigar? Sit down."

"No, thank you, sir. And I'd rather stand."

Don Tomás blinked and set his book aside. "Very well. What I wish to ask you, *Señor* Fallon, is your intentions toward my daughter."

"I love her," James said stiffly.

The other man nodded gravely. "There are many men in Mexico City, *Señor* Fallon, who would like very much to marry my daughter. Men of family, men of wealth, men of position and power. Some of them I would welcome; others I would not allow beneath my roof."

"I understand, sir. In the morning I will be—"

"There is, however, a difficulty," *Don* Tomás said as if James had not spoken. "I am, perhaps, an untypical father. There are many sorts of men I would not allow my daughter to marry. A thief, a drunkard, a man who would be cruel to her." He made a gesture of distaste. "But I also would never force her to marry against her will."

"I don't understand, sir," James said.

Don Tomás grunted. "Young men are slower of wit than when I was young. Do you not know that the man must speak his heart first? That a woman may grow angry waiting?"

"Sir, do you mean . . . ." It didn't seem possible.

"I do indeed mean. Drusilla loves you, you young fool. I do not like seeing her worry herself sick because you do not speak."

James realized he was grinning ear to ear. "*Don* Tomás, I ask the honor of your daughter's hand in marriage."

The older man nodded. "Very good, *señor*. You declare yourself. I was beginning to feel as if I were hawking my daughter."

"Then . . . I have your permission, sir?"

"First things first, *señor*. What are your plans should I allow you to court Drusilla?"

"Why, I'll marry her and start raising horses."

"You are sure of her answer," *Don* Tomás murmured. "Drusilla may make you suffer for your delay. I will tell you, *señor*, that I would be more at ease if my daughter's eye had fallen on one of *la raza*, but I would rather have her happy with a *yanqui* than in misery with a grandee of Castile."

"Then I may ask Drusilla to marry me?"

"Unless we have had this conversation for our own amusement," *Don* Tomás said drily. "If she says yes, I will approve the marriage. *Padre* Miquel Muldoon is expected here soon. He will perform the marriage in the cathedral at San Antonio. Then you and I will travel to Mexico City."

"Mexico City, sir? Why?"

"If you wish to remain in Mexico—and if you marry Drusilla, I certainly hope you will—you must become a citizen. For that, there are men we must see in Mexico City."

"I hadn't considered that, sir."

"The country is still in turmoil from the deposing of Iturbide. As a foreigner, you could be ordered from Mexico at any time. I am a selfish man, *señor*. I wish to see my grandchildren."

If changing citizenship would bring him Drusilla . . . . "I'm agreeable, sir. Mexico City, then."

"Very well. But are you not forgetting something?"

"Forgetting, sir?"

"Drusilla, my son. She has yet to be asked."

James grinned broadly. "If you'll pardon me, *Don* Tomás, I'll take care of that right now."

He found Drusilla in her sitting room, concentrating on an embroidery hoop. He watched her for a moment without letting her know he was there. Her dark slenderness was so beautiful. "Drusilla," he said finally, "I love you."

She leaped, yelped, and began sucking her finger. "I stuck myself," she said accusingly. "To sneak up behind me and say such a thing . . . ."

"I'm sorry. But I do love you. Your father—"

She sprang to her feet, face halfway between rage and horror. "What did my father tell you?"

"All he said was—"

"He had no right, no right. Oh, I should have known. The way he has been looking at me. Neither of you has a right! Leave me! I never wish to see you again!"

"Listen to me!" His shout seemed to set her back on her heels, but she still regarded him with angry eyes. "What

your father told me was that I could ask for your hand. I
want to marry you.''

"That is all he said?'' she asked cautiously.

"What else could there be?'' He moved closer. She let
him take her hand, a smile playing about her lips. "Once
again, Drusilla. I love you. I know I haven't spoken of it
before, but I couldn't keep it in any longer.''

She traced his mouth and cheek lightly with her fingers.
"You were so silent,'' she whispered. "I love you also, *mi
corazón.*''

He pulled her to him; her mouth flowered under his,
her slender body trembled against him. "Will you marry
me?'' he breathed. "I'll beg if I must.''

Her smile was joyous. "Oh, yes, *querido.* I will. I will.''

Three days later *Padre* Muldoon arrived. That evening,
with the aid of the easy-going priest and a donation to the
church, James became a Catholic. With Henry and José
standing up for him, they were married in the Cathedral of
San Fernando. Their honeymoon was spent on the road to
Mexico City, more than a thousand miles away.

XXXI

Mexico City, by its very gaudiness, outstripped New Orleans. Magnificent cathedrals and palatial mansions vied with fetid hovels. Broad avenues led to huge paved plazas past giant open-air markets, where the produce of the surrounding country was hawked by people who were every possible combination of black, Indian and Mexican.

In the Plaza de Liberacion and the Parque de Almeda officers, politicians and wealthy businessmen paraded in clothing decorated with silver embroidery, silver buttons, silver bells, silver spikes and drops. Many bedecked their saddles and their carriage horses with silver as well. The city lived on silver, and when the sun struck just right the many buildings of white stone seemed built of it, as well.

After two weeks in the city, James wished never to see another bureaucrat's crowded anteroom. This one had a high arched ceiling, its white plaster worked in arabesques and acanthus leaves. Waiting men, James among them, sat shoulder to shoulder on hard benches. Despite *Don* Tomás' assurances that each day brought them a little closer, he couldn't see that anything had changed. One *burocrata* after another listened, smiled politely, and sent him on to another.

The door to the inner office opened; James got to his feet along with a score of others. All surged toward the man who came out, a stout man in black intricately embroidered with silver. Everyone began to speak at once.

"*Señor* Cabral," James called. "*Señor* Cabral, I have an appointment to see you. I'm James Fallon. *Don* Tomás—"

"No time," Cabral shouted, waving his arms. He forced his way through the crowd. "No time."

"*Señor* Cabral," James said, "*Don* Tomás Ibarra y Velasquez arranged—"

Cabral glanced at him, frowning, still moving toward the door. "*Sí.* I remember. You are *Señor* James Fallon. The press of business . . . you must come back tomorrow . . . or next week might be better. Yes, next week." The bureaucrat slipped out of the anteroom, shutting the door in the faces of the clamoring men.

James stared at the door, cursed, and rushed into the hall after Cabral. Outside the door he crashed into a broad man, taller and heavier than he. He had an impression of a heavy chin, small eyes, and bushy sidewhiskers.

"Your pardon, *señor.* I—"

"Watch where you're going," the other man grumbled. "You almost knocked me down."

"I was attempting to apologize," James said stiffly.

After a moment, the other nodded and stuck out a large, square hand. "Accepted. I'm Haden Edwards."

"James Fallon. If you're here to see *Señor* Cabral, I'm afraid he just left."

"Left!" Edwards seemed to puff even bigger. "Why, that bastard! That fat little . . . I'll wring his neck!"

"If I might suggest keeping your voice down, Mr. Edwards. I haven't been here long, but I do know almost everyone is quick to take offense, especially at *norteamericanos.*"

"Uh? Oh, of course. I suppose you're right." Edwards glared at the few clerks scurrying through the hall. "I've been being shunted from one greasy bastard of an official to another since April."

James shook his head. Seven months. "I hope my business doesn't take as long."

"It will, Fallon. It will." Edwards drew himself up angrily—he seemed to do everything angrily—and made a stiff bow. "If you'll excuse me, I have things to attend to."

"Certainly," James began, but the big man was already striding away. Whatever Edwards wanted, he thought, he'd have difficulty with a people to whom courtesy and proper form were everything. He hurried out into what passed for a November chill in Mexico City, and headed for the small *palacio Don* Tomás had rented.

"You are back early, *mi corazón*," Drusilla greeted him as soon as he was inside.

"It was thinking of you that drew me back," he said. He swung her in a circle, kissing her while she clung to him breathlessly.

For a minute she returned his kiss, then pulled her head back and beat at his shoulders. "Put me down, my husband. Remember where we are. What if one of the servants should come in?"

"I'd send them back out again," he said, but set her on her feet.

She smoothed her dress with both hands. "You must forgive me, James. I am barely used to the maids knowing what it is we do each night." She colored slightly. "I am sure if I were truly a lady I would not . . . not make so much noise."

"You mean," he laughed, "when you moan and scream and claw my back and wrap your legs around me?"

Scarlet suffused her face. "James! Someone might hear!"

"Let them hear. Oh, very well. I'll be good."

"You will never be good. You are a wicked, wicked man. I think that is part of why I love you."

"Why don't we go to our room and discuss my wickedness?" he grinned.

"I will thank you, my husband, to stop making me blush," she said primly, but there was a twinkle in her big, round eyes.

Dispense me, señor." It was José's voice. James turned; Henry and the small Mexican had come into the back of the hall. José continued. "We did not mean to interrupt."

"One of the stablehands told us you was back," Henry added. "How did things go?"

James sighed. "Cabral didn't even talk to me except to say come back next week. How about a drink?"

"I will go check on the cook," Drusilla said. "Do not worry, James. My father will set everything right."

The men followed James into the study, where he poured brandy for them.

"She has a sight of confidence in her papa," Henry said, taking a stance in front of the fireplace.

José sipped his brandy. "*Don* Tomás is a man of much importance, much influence."

"I don't know how much good it's doing," James said. "A few bureaucrats sweat when they hear his name, but they do no more than the ones who don't sweat. He's been fuming, I can tell you."

"There is perhaps a reason, *señor*," José said. "Not two hours ago we saw *Señora* Applegate."

Henry nodded. "Rode right by us in her carriage, over to the Plaza de Santo Domingo."

James felt the hairs on the back of his neck lift. Cordelia Applegate frightened him, and he wasn't ashamed to admit it. "She mentioned vacations in Mexico City. It could just be coincidence." He didn't believe it himself. "Does she have enough influence to counter *Don* Tomás?"

"She has influence, *señor*. How much, I am not certain. But she has money. Money can buy influence."

"I thought part of the reason for kicking Iturbide out was getting rid of corruption," Henry said.

Escobar shrugged. "Some things are ingrained, *señor*. It will take years to get rid of *soborno*, and of those who take bribes."

"From all the talk I been hearing," Henry said, "I figured that constitution the Congress got out this year was supposed to make this a Republic, like the United States. You find a few fools holding office in the States, but I don't reckon there's many of them are crooked."

"Whatever the Congress intended," James said, "I doubt it was to make Mexico like the United States. This constitution is just a law, really. They can change it, or repeal it, any time they want. There's no trial by jury, no *habeas corpus*, nor right to peaceable assembly or petition for redress of grievances. And the President, once they decide who he's going to be, can declare himself dictator whenever he wants."

"Not exactly, James," *Don* Tomás said as he came into the room. "He must have a good reason. Mexico is still unsettled."

"Brandy, sir?" James said. "Good reason or not, it's hardly what we in the United States consider a proper constitution, setting out people's rights and the limits of government powers. This gives no rights to the people and unlimited power to the government."

"Thank you." Velasquez accepted the glass. "But you are no longer a citizen of the United States. As of this morning, you are a citizen of Mexico."

"You did it!" James whooped. "But how?"

"I found Pedro Negrete, at last. You have an honor, James. Your papers of citizenship are signed by a member of the Regency."

"Then we can return to Texas."

"Not yet," *Don* Tomás said. "If you are to raise horses properly, you must have land of your own. My acres of suitable forage are crowded already. For this we must go to the true power in Mexico at the moment, the army." He frowned abruptly. "The trouble we have had seems to be caused by rumors of what happened between you and *Señora* Applegate. There are many versions, none favorable to you."

James had told *Don* Tomás everything before the wedding. "Henry and José saw her today," he said.

Don Tomás nodded. "That explains much. But I do not think her influence, or her bribes, will reach into the army. Tonight we are going to Colonel Antonio Lopez de Santa Anna. He is giving a ball tonight. If you say that you hope to sell horses to the army, your grant is all but assured."

"A colonel, sir? He has that much say?"

"He does indeed. If he were not only thirty years of age he might be one of the Regency. He was a leader of the revolution against the Spanish, and he also helped remove Iturbide when he became an oppressor." It was plain from Velasquez' voice that he admired the man greatly.

"I'd better tell Drusilla then. Women take longer to get

ready for these things.''

Don Tomás put a hand on his arm. "I am afraid this affair will be no place for a wife. You understand?''

James looked at him a moment. "I'm not sure that's the sort of thing for a newlywed husband.''

"James," *Don* Tomás said irritably, "of course you will not avail yourself of the, ah, entertainments, but if you want this grant of land, you will attend.''

James nodded slowly.

XXXII

Colonel Santa Anna's carriage drive wound for miles, it seemed, through a landscaped garden full of towering trees. At last white marble colonnades and balconies gleamed in the moonlight, and a golden dome thrust into the night. Liveried servants rushed to open the carriage door, and James and *Don* Tomás climbed marble steps over a red carpet. Both wore short, embroidered jackets and silver ornaments.

The vaulted entry hall was painted with cherubs and clouds. On the broad main stairs an eight-piece band of strings and horns played; more music drifted through tall double doors standing open on either side of the hall.

"*Don* Tomás!" A man in a high-collared, gold-braided-and-epauleted blue uniform came forward with his hand outstretched. "Welcome, my old friend." He was darkly handsome with a high forehead and deepset brown eyes.

"*Coronel* Santa Anna," *Don* Tomás replied warmly. "It is good to see you again. May I present my *yerno*, *Señor* James Christopher Fallon."

Santa Anna regarded him with surprise for a bare instant before offering his hand. "Welcome, *señor*. If you come with *Don* Tomás, you come well recommended. You are visiting our country?"

"As of today, *coronel*, I'm a citizen of Mexico."

"*Un ciudadano*. Tell me, *Señor* Fallon, why is it that you come here? I mean all of you *norteamericanos*, those with *Señor* Stephen Austin, as well."

256

"A new land to grow with," James said promptly. "My grandfather left Ireland, *coronel,* for the same reason, as did the fathers and grandfathers of many of us."

"We must talk more later," Santa Anna said. "For now, *Don* Tomás, *Señor* Fallon, join the party and enjoy." With a short bow he moved away to greet new arrivals.

"*Bueno,*" *Don* Tomás said quietly. "*Muy bueno.*"

"If you say so, sir," James said.

"Let yourself be guided by me," the older man said. "Now let us do as the *coronel* suggested."

They strolled into one of the ballrooms. The high ceiling was painted in much the same style as that of the entry hall, with three huge crystal chandeliers providing candlelight. Elaborate crystal sconces gave more light along the paneled walls. At the far end of the room an orchestra played on a raised platform; in the center, scores of men and women moved in the intricate patterns of a dance. There were as many colors of satin and velvet, silk and damask, as there were women. The men rivaled them in brilliance, their broadly flared trousers slashed with a rainbow of colors, their short black jackets set off by scarlet sashes and lavish silver ornaments. Knots of people stood around the edges of the dance floor, the buzz of conversation competing with the music.

"What is there about this that Drusilla couldn't come?" James asked. "It looks like any ball to me."

Don Tomás pointed to a cluster of slender young men and fat old ones near the orchestra. "Those are *maricas. Sodomitas.*" His face twisted distastefully. "They have not yet drunk enough to begin fondling one another publicly."

"Good God! You're not saying this Santa Anna likes boys!"

"No, no, no. He likes women. Young ones, preferably, and as many as he can obtain. But he also likes . . . wickedness. Regard that stout woman, the one in red satin, with a mustache. You see her? That is Casilda Manriquez. The two young girls following her are her lovers. The horse-faced man who just passed us is *Don* Enrique de Vallejo, who spends his idle hours seducing married women. That skinny woman in front of us is *Doña* Sylvana Torres de Navarra, an ancient house she besmirches with a taste for boys, none over sixteen years of age. The rest are little better. They are willing prey, if not hunters.''

James stared at *Doña* Sylvana as she danced by, with a man of adult years, he was relieved to note. He thought of himself as cosmopolitan and worldly—what man could grow up in New Orleans otherwise?—but at the moment he felt very callow.

"Sir, we aren't expected to . . . well, join in?"

The older man chuckled. "The thought disturbs you?"

"I prefer one woman and myself, alone. If that's provincial . . . ."

Don Tomás looked at him with an expression James could not read. It looked like amusement, but of course could not be. He said, "I, too, am more old-fashioned, if not so entirely virtuous. If you are approached, simply put them off. They will seek easier game. Now, if you will mingle, I will seek to closet myself with *Coronel* Santa Anna. Be ready for a summons at any moment. And do not fear, James.''

James wondered if he spoke of the land, or the guests. He took a drink from a liveried servant and found a place against the wall.

The dancing went through several sets—and he through several drinks—and he began to think *Don* Tomás had been exaggerating. Even as the conviction settled on him, bringing an uncomfortable mixture of relief and disappointment, he realized the nature of the evening was changing. Several couples were no longer dancing, only clinging together and swaying to the music as they kissed. On a gilded bench near him, a man forced his hand into a woman's bodice. She laughed shrilly.

Two women climbed onto the dais with the orchestra and, as the music quickened, danced the flamenco, tossing their skirts high. They were naked beneath.

A pretty brunette walked up to James, hair mussed, rouge smeared, and naked from the waist up. In one hand she held a wine glass, the other arm curved casually across her chest, more supporting her breasts than hiding them.

She sipped her wine and regarded him through heavy-lidded eyes.

"*Como se llama usted, señor?*" she said in a sultry alto.

"James Fallon," he replied, and tried to avoid admiring what she had on view. He reminded himself sternly of Drusilla, but it didn't work.

"Ah, you are English? A *yanqui?*" Her English was heavily accented.

"Yes. That is, no. I'm a Mexican citizen now."

"How interesting. Your eyes are such a beautiful blue."

He shifted uncomfortably. "Thank you, *señorita*. My wife thinks so, too." Perhaps she would take the hint. Her nipples were a wonderful pink.

"*Señora,*" she corrected. "*Señora* Isobel de las Piedras." She ran her eyes over him like a caress. "With each promotion my husband has grown fatter. Now that he is a *commandante*, he is quite fat. I prefer men with hard bodies, men with the vigor of youth." Her small pink tongue licked delicately at her lips.

He realized his face was reddening. Even tavern girls weren't this forward. The idle thought came that *Don* Tomás probably wouldn't send for him for some time, and there were no doubt plenty of unoccupied bedrooms. He managed to put that thought aside. But a little harmless flirtation . . . . "I prefer soft bodies, *Señora* de las Piedras."

"Isobel." She dropped her protective arm and moved closer, until her erect nipples were brushing his coat. "How nice it is that each of us has what the other prefers." She frowned, and it took him a moment to realize why. A liveried servant was tugging at his sleeve.

"*Señor? Señor* Fallon? *Coronel* Santa Anna wishes to see you, *señor*. If you will follow me?"

"Yes, of course. If you will excuse me, *Señora*—Isobel?"

"For a short time only." She smiled, showing her tongue again. He swallowed hard.

Hastily he followed the servant. At the door he looked back. She was already making her way to where a dozen people stood watching two women, naked but for stockings and jewelry, tearing at each other's hair on the floor.

Santa Anna's study was huge and heavily ornamented. A fireplace large enough for a ten-foot log stood at either end of the room. Portraits covered the walls, while this time the ceiling held men in ancient Greek armor mounted on winged horses. *Don* Tomás and the colonel sat in the middle of the room on chairs gilded in the French style, sipping brandy.

"Pour yourself a glass and join us, *Señor* Fallon," Santa Anna said as James entered. "Or perhaps you prefer opium?"

James blinked, but *Don* Tomás' face didn't change. "Thank you, *coronel*, but I'll take brandy." He poured a glass. As he sat, Santa Anna spoke again.

"I trust we did not take you from some charming lady."

"The ladies were certainly charming, *coronel*, but I am a newly married man."

"A faithful husband!" Santa Anna laughed, then cut off with a seated bow to *Don* Tomás. "*Dispense me.* Of course he is faithful, and to be commended for it."

Don Tomás nodded. "*Lo concedo, coronel.*"

"Tell me, *Señor* Fallon," the colonel went on. "Have you yet been to the Plaza de San Pablo, to watch the *corrida de toros?*"

"I have." One visit had been enough. Despite thick padding two horses had been badly gored. The riders had been in no danger that he could see. If they wanted to make a fight of it, let the men fight on foot.

"And what did you think of it?"

"It was . . . interesting, *coronel.*"

Santa Anna smiled broadly. "It is the soul of Mexico incarnate. Many *yanquis* do not understand this. It is good that you do. This is a hard land, but we embrace the hardness and the violence of it. That is what makes us great."

"I'm sure." There didn't seem to be much else to say.

"I met *yanquis* in battle once, eleven years ago, when that pig who called himself a priest, Hidalgo, was in rebellion. They were the scum of the earth, freebooters who had followed the pirate Lafitte, ruffians from the Neutral Ground. I was a cadet under General Arredondo.

We met them at San Antonio de Bexar. There were more than eight hundred of the *yanquis*, nearly two thousand others, *Indios* and *peóns*. We were a bare two thousand. We formed in a 'U' and pulled them in. Our fire was murderous. First *los Indios* ran, and then the *peóns*. Finally the *yanquis* tried, but we cut them down. I do not think one hundred escaped. They did not know the fire and iron that is in the Mexican soul, the fire and iron shown by *la corrida de toros*. They paid the price of their ignorance, the price of rebellion. And the town that had sheltered them. Three hundred twenty seven traitors General Arredondo had put to the sword.''

James swallowed, uncertain of what to say, or why the story had been told. *Don* Tomás seemed to be studying his drink. ''There are always excesses, *coronel*, in battle.''

''Excesses? There were no excesses, *Señor* Fallon. What is it that you want here in Mexico?''

''To raise a family, build a home, and breed horses, *coronel*.''

''Breed horses. This stallion of yours, is he as magnificent as *Don* Tomás says?''

''Magnificent is the word. Part Arab, part Barb, and as fast as his name.''

''Bring him to Mexico City. A man could make a fortune racing a horse such as you describe.''

''Money made racing horses goes as fast as it comes. I want to build something for the future.'' He wondered why *Don* Tomás was so silent.

''I have heard, *Señor* Fallon, that you have had trouble with a lady of Texas. *Señora* Cordelia Applegate?'' The colonel's smile was unreadable.

''*Señora* Applegate,'' James said carefully, ''is a strange woman.''

''She is,'' Santa Anna agreed. ''Yes, *Señor* Fallon, I know the lady. She says you are a murderer.''

''I killed no one. Except a man she paid to kill me.'' *Don* Tomás made an unobtrusive gesture, and he swallowed the rest of his angry reply.

Santa Anna was watching James carefully. At last he nodded. ''I prefer to trust my old friend. You will need a great deal of land for these horses, no?''

"A league should be more than enough, *coronel.*"

Santa Anna made a gesture of dismissal. "A league. A trifle. It is land good for little, this Texas. Still, it would be good to have friends there, when there are so many who cannot be trusted.''

What in hell, James wondered, was the man talking about now? "I hope you consider me a friend, *coronel.*"

The colonel rose abruptly. James and *Don Tomás* scrambled to their feet. "*Señor* Fallon, you may expect word tomorrow. Now, perhaps you would like to return downstairs? The festivities should be progressing nicely.''

Don Tomás spoke at last. "I think we had better be going, *coronel,* if you will forgive us.''

Santa Anna nodded. "Until tomorrow then, *señores.*"

James waited until the carriage was leaving the *palacio* grounds. "What was all that about wanting me for a friend? His opinion of *yanquis* is plain.''

Don Tomás sighed. "Like the politics of my country, *el coronel* has as many layers as an onion. In truth he does not like *norteamericanos,* nor does he trust the colony of *Señor* Austin. He opposed the grant to Austin. He believes that by giving you his favor he will gain your loyalty, that you will keep him informed of what happens in the Austin colony in order to retain that favor.''

"Be damned to him, then! I'm no man's spy. Let him keep his favors. I'll get my land some other way.''

"*No te se un menso!*" the older man snapped. "If you insult Santa Anna now, you will not get one *vara* of land if you remain the rest of your life.''

"Then how did Austin get his? You said Santa Anna opposed him.''

"He began by not insulting the most powerful man in the army. And how long did he remain here? A year? More?'' *Don* Tomás shook his head. "Could you put up with a year of running from one bureaucrat to another? You are young, and hot of blood. In six months, in three, you would challenge one of them. My daughter has no need of *un esposo* who is dead or sought for murder. That is why I arranged this meeting, though I believed beforehand

Santa Anna would expect some such bargain.''

"You believed . . . .'' He ground his teeth to stifle angry words. "I won't do it. I won't spy on my friends.''

"A bargain made on one side is no bargain. Listen to me, my young friend. You will be given raw land, wilderness, not a *rancho*. Whatever you have, rude cabin or *hacienda*, you will build. Deer and mustangs will see your crops as forage. Puma, wolf, and bear will savage your horses. Indians will try to kill you. You will earn every stone of it with your sweat and your blood.''

Before James could reply, he was thrown forward by the carriage stopping suddenly. The horses screamed, harness jangling as they reared, and a shot rang out. The driver cried out once and was silent.

"*Bandidos!*'' *Don* Tomás hissed. Quickly he produced pistols from a compartment beneath his seat, handing two to James. "You to the left, I to the right.''

James checked the primings, kicked open the carriage door and dove out. Then he was tucking his shoulder under to roll across the pavement and come up in the shadows against a building front. The horses stamped and snorted. The driver's arm hung over the side of his perch.

A pistol cracked on the far side of the coach. At the same instant men appeared on his side of the equipage, running at him out of the darkness. Pistols flashed in their hands. A ball spat past his cheek; another tugged at his coat. He steadied his pistol and squeezed the trigger. One of the men shouted and fell; he fired again, and another went down, but then they were on him. A knife flashed, and pain burned down his side. He twisted aside; his fist crunched into a man's face.

Suddenly there were riders among them, horses rearing. Guns barked. A man with an upraised knife collapsed against James. Another screamed and fell. The rest melted into the night.

James pushed aside the body. Now that the confusion was over, he could see there were only two horses.

"What the hell's going on here?'' Haden Edwards growled. A man like enough to be his brother glowered from the other horse.

"Bandits." James ran to the other side of the coach. *Don* Tomás lay propped against the carriage step, a bleeding slash across his forehead, an ugly wet patch on his coat. He made a feeble effort to rise as James knelt beside him. "Rest easy, sir." He gently pulled open the other's coat. There were no bubbles around the wound; the lung hadn't been punctured. He tore his shirt and wadded it against the wound, binding it with his sash.

"How's the old man?" Haden asked. The two men had ridden around the coach.

"What's been going on here?" the other asked. Neither dismounted.

"We were set on by bandits." James lifted *Don Tomás* and laid him in the carriage. "He'll be all right. You'll be all right, sir." The old man nodded. James scrambled up to the driver's perch and saw that the driver was dead.

"Damn it, Fallon," Haden shouted, "we hear all the shouting and shooting, and instead of minding our own business we come and pull you out of trouble. The least we deserve is an explanation. I never heard of bandits attacking carriages in the city."

"Edwards, I'll thank you later; right now I have to get *Don* Tomás to help." He whipped up the horses, and the carriage lurched into the night.

XXXIII

At the house servants raced to fetch a doctor, maids rushed around with bandages and hot water. James kept vigil outside *Don* Tomás' room with Henry and José, pacing the carpet in silence. Drusilla had collapsed in tears and the doctor gave her laudanum to make her sleep. As light began to peek through the hall windows, the doctor finally came out of the bedroom, rolling down his shirt sleeves. His plump face was damp with sweat.

James hurried to meet him. "How is he?"

"He will live, *señor,* but he will need time to heal. A younger man might be up and around in a few days, but *Don* Tomás has seen sixty years." He shrugged into his coat, held by a maid. "*La venda* must be changed every day. I have left *laúdano* in case he feels pain.

"Is he conscious? Can I talk to him?"

"So long as he is not overtaxed, *señor.*" The stout doctor hid a yawn behind his hand. "I am going to bed, *señor.* I suggest you do the same. You need the rest also."

James saw the doctor out and returned to Henry and José. "You two go on," he said.

"And you, *señor?*" José said.

Henry nodded. "You need rest worse than us. What did that doctor say about that slash you took?"

"He put a plaster on it," James said. "I can't sleep. You—"

One of the maids touched his arm. "*Señor*, there is a man to see you. *Un norteamericano.*"

"One of the Edwardses?" James asked. "I know I owe

265

them my life, but after the way they wanted to stand around talking last night, it's hard to feel gratitude."

"What them Edwardses do best is talk," Henry said.

"His name is not Edwards, *señor*," the maid said. "He said he was *Señor* John Lafflin."

"Lafflin? I don't know any Lafflin. I'd better see what he wants. Where is he?"

"In the *vestibulo, señor*."

Lafflin was a dark-eyed man with a full black beard, an athlete gone to fat with advancing years. He stared at James, coming down the stairs, as if seeing a ghost. "By damn, you are the spitting image of . . . . Forgive a strange question, but you are the son of Robert Fallon? I heard your name in the city, and it is hardly of the most common."

"Robert Fallon was my father," James said. "You knew him?"

Lafflin spoke slowly. "You speak as if he were dead."

"When I was an infant. Barbary pirates. Forgive me, Mr. Lafflin. I'm forgetting my manners. Won't you step into my study?" Lafflin nodded mutely and followed him. "Brandy? Wine? Perhaps coffee or tea, considering the hour."

"Brandy. I know . . . knew your father, yes. In New Orleans. Many years ago."

James abruptly realized he was taking the man at face value. With Cordelia in the city, after the incident last night—had that been her doing?—he should be more suspicious. "Mr. Lafflin, there aren't many foreigners in Mexico City."

"I have business interests on the coast." Lafflin chuckled. "Shipping, by damn."

"Is that how you knew my father?"

"Not exactly. We spied on the French before the United States bought Louisiana. I tell you true, I do not think they would have bought it if not for your father and me. By damn, that is true."

He'd never heard that story before, but it fit with the kind of man his mother had told him of. Still . . . . "Have you ever heard of Cordelia Applegate, Mr.

Lafflin?''

Lafflin half rose from his chair. ''Where you hear that name?''

''So you know the lady.''

''Lady! That *chienne* was no lady the best day she live. That *putain!*'' He spat. ''She try to kill your father. She try to kill me. And she did kill one very good friend of us both. Esteban Lopes.''

''Lopes? In New Orleans? I remember his death, a few years back now. There was something odd about it, but no one talked of it much.''

''They believe it was voodoo,'' Lafflin snorted. ''But it was Cordelia. And Esteban was not the first man she has killed. How do you know her? It is important you tell me. Believe me when I say she will try to do you harm for your father's sake.''

''I met her soon after I arrived in Texas.'' He hesitated. ''She accused me of murder.''

''It sounds like her, this trying to kill a man and blacken his name at the same time. Where is she in Texas?''

''She has a *rancho* near the San Jacinto, below the forks.'' James decided against mentioning that she was in the city. If Lafflin was her man, his knowledge of that was best kept to himself.

''Campeche,'' Lafflin muttered. ''By damn, just the place for her! Just the place nobody think to look.''

''Lafitte's place? I asked her once if she was part of that. She denied it.''

''No, she is no friend of Jean Lafitte, by damn. But you don't believe her about nothing else. Not if you want to stay alive.''

''I won't.'' James frowned, full of questions. ''Why did she hate my father enough to try to kill him? You did say that, didn't you?''

''She was always on the other side from your *papa,* and she always lose. A woman like her, she don't like to lose, maybe more so because he shared her bed. I tell you, that woman is a viper.''

He could agree on that, James thought. There were still more questions, but he didn't trust this man who called himself Lafflin. Perhaps he could find out something in a roundabout way. "Tell me about my father, Mr. Lafflin. I'm afraid I don't remember him at all."

Lafflin threw his arms wide and laughed expansively. "By *le bon Dieu*, he is a man. I am sorry. I mean 'was.' I am proud to have a man like him for a friend . . . ."

For over an hour Lafflin talked, and James found that though his suspicion didn't fade, he believed the picture of Robert Fallon that Lafflin drew. Or perhaps, he thought, he simply wanted to. Lafflin's Robert Fallon was a man to be admired, a lusty adventurer, a courageous sea captain, a man with dreams. It was the last, the drive to build, that impressed James most. It seemed as if he shared something with the father he couldn't remember.

Lafflin interspersed his stories of Robert Fallon with many attempts to find out about James. James was careful to tell him no more than Cordelia already knew: that he had grown up on Thomas Martin's sugar plantation in Louisiana, that he'd always dreamed of Texas, that he'd spent an interlude at Cordelia's *rancho* after his arrival at San Felipe de Austin. He let slip that he was married—he had no idea whether Cordelia knew that—but he concealed Drusilla's maiden name, leaving the impression she was just a girl he had met in San Antonio.

As Lafflin left, a Mexican Army lieutenant came to the door.

"*Señor* Fallon? *Señor* James Fallon?" His dragoon's boots were brightly polished, fawn trousers spotless, high-collared blue coat immaculate, gold braid gleaming. A staff officer, James thought.

"I'm James Fallon."

The lieutenant inclined his head an eighth of an inch. "*Teniente* Jorge Serra, on the staff of *Coronel* Antonio Lopez de Santa Anna. I am instructed to deliver this to you." He thrust an oilskin packet into James' hands, made another miniscule inclination of his head and stalked down the steps to mount his horse.

James fumbled the door closed, staring at the packet in his hands. He felt like a boy on Christmas. But there was always the chance it was something other than what he expected. Hurriedly he found a knife and ripped the packet open. Four layers of oilskin surrounded a parchment document. Laboriously he worked his way through the ornate script, so elaborately scrolled and curlicued as to be almost unreadable.

Almost, but not quite. With a sudden grunt he dropped into the closest chair. In the name of the Republic of Mexico, before God and the Holy Mother Church, James Christopher Fallon was granted one hundred leagues of land in the state of Texas. There had to be a mistake. A hundred leagues! Over four hundred and sixty thousand acres. A clerk's error. A mistake adding zeros where none were intended.

He started to thrust the grant back into its oilskin covering and something in the covering rustled. He pulled out a note, so badly scrawled he could barely read it.

Horses need a great deal of land. Mexico needs loyal men.
Santa Anna

The signature was little more than an S and an A, with something else scribbled there, but he knew it could be no other. There was no mistake, then.

Slowly he made his way up to *Don* Tomás' room and put his head in. The curtains were drawn, a single candle lighting the dim room. A maid sat in one corner, black shawl drawn over her dark hair, swift fingers telling her beads. Her black eyes swiveled to James, but she made no sound except for the clicking of the beads.

Don Tomás was awake, his face drawn and sunken. He turned his head on the pillow. "James, my son. Come in." His voice was faint. James hesitated. The old man caught sight of the packet in his hands. "The grant! Tell me of it."

There was nothing to do but go in and shut the door. "I've been given a hundred leagues, sir." There was a pause in the clicking of the beads. "And a note from *Coronel* Santa Anna. He says Mexico needs loyal men."

"So much," *Don* Tomás murmured. "I had not expected so much."

"Neither did I. Good God! There'll be a scandal if this

gets out. Even governments don't give that much land to one man.''

"Governments are the only ones who can, my son. *A caballo dado no se le mira el colmillo.*"

"You can talk about gift horses. I'm the one who's being bribed! And for a bribe this size, Santa Anna is going to be damned sure I carry out my side.''

"A bargain made on one side—"

"I know, sir, but—"

"James, do you intend to commit an act of rebellion?"

"No, sir, but—"

"Do you believe that Stephen Austin intends such?"

"Of course not. He's an honorable man."

"Then accept the land, man. Do you not see there is no side of *el coronel*'s bargain for you to carry out? Accept the land.'' His chest heaved with the effort of saying so much.

James had to agree that there really wasn't anything for him to spy on. And what couldn't he do with that much land? His father had had dreams. He could carry them out. His enthusiasm faded. "It's still so damned much, though. There are whole parishes in Louisiana that aren't as big.''

"There is land, and there is land. Where is this land located? In the fertile country near the Austin grant?''

He unfolded the parchment and pored over it. "I am not certain of all the landmarks, sir, but it seems to be on the Rio Trinidad, well to the north.''

"Comanche country. And the Apache not so far to the west. Not of the best land, either, though for horses it might do. Remember what I said of your earning the land, James.''

"I remember.'' Blood and sweat. That would make the land his, if he could avoid another price. But . . . a hundred leagues. He turned to the woman, still telling her beads. "Consuela, fetch *Señor* Cameron and *Señor* Escobar. Quickly. I will watch *Don* Tomás.''

The dark woman darted a glance at *Don* Tomás, then scuttled from the room. "What do you intend?'' the old man asked.

"I am not sure, sir.'' But an idea was forming. He read

over the grant again; there was nothing to prevent it.
Henry and José came into the room, stifling yawns and still
pulling their clothes into place.

"What's the matter, James?" Henry said. "I just got to
sleep."

José shot a look at *Don* Tomás. His relief that the other
man still lived was apparent.

"I got my land grant this morning," James said. "I'm
splitting half of it between the two of you."

Don Tomás laughed. *"Un hombre de moda!"*

"I don't know about José," Henry said, "but half
sounds like too much to me. You going to need plenty of
land for them horses. You let me have ten acres or so, if
you can spare it. It's more than I had in Louisiana." Escobar murmured assent.

"I think I can spare it," James said. "I'm keeping fifty
leagues for myself." *Don* Tomás laughed again.

"Just the same, *señor*," José began, and stopped, his
eyes going wide.

Henry gasped for breath. "You're crazy, James! No
man gives away land like that."

"I am. Damn it, I'm keeping enough for ten of the
biggest plantations in Louisiana. The two of you have
sweated with those horses with me every foot of the way.
You've worked your butts off, and you haven't had more
than a few dollars from me."

"You had to save what you had," Henry protested.
"Wasn't like you had a lot."

"Well, I still don't have much. Except for land. I figure
it's as if we were partners. Well, it's time for the partnership to pay off. You're taking this land if I have to hold
the both of you down to make you."

Cameron shivered. "Twenty-five leagues. What's that?
Better than a hundred thousand acres. I'll bet there ain't
never been a black man owned that much land in this
whole country."

"There's one now," James said. "What about you,
José?"

The wizened little man looked troubled. "All of my
life, *señor*, I have taken orders, often from men I knew

were fools. Then there was you, who are not a fool, but you said you were not my *patrón*. You tell me that I am my own man. This is a strange thing to me, who has always followed *el patrón*. Still, I do as you say because there must be someone to give the orders, and because—I will admit it, *señor*—this thing of being my own man is frightening. I am ashamed of this, but it is true. As time passes I discovered that I truly am my own man, and that *Señor* Cameron is his own man. And I find that I am no longer frightened of being my own man. I will accept this land, *señor*, with the deepest of gratitude.''

Don Tomás nodded approvingly on the pillow. ''*Bien dicho, mi amigo.*''

''I'll be damned,'' Henry muttered. He was looking at José as if seeing him for the first time. ''You been there, too.''

''Then it's settled,'' James said. ''We'll draw the papers up today, and as soon as *Don* Tomás can travel, we'll go see what kind of land we have.''

''We should leave immediately,'' *Don* Tomás said. ''I do not like to run away, but we have what we came for. To remain now is just to give the men last night another chance at us.''

''You think it was Cordelia, too?'' James said.

''*Claro!*'' the old man replied. ''*Bandidos* do not rob within the very city.''

Haden Edwards had said as much, James thought, grimacing. He didn't like being in the man's debt. ''We'll have to wait a few days. The doctor said—''

''*El médico!*'' the man on the bed snorted. ''He is an old woman, but I am not. I will heal faster if I am returning home.''

''He speaks the truth,'' José said. ''I know him.''

And, James knew, he spoke the truth about Cordelia having another chance at them. ''Then, *Don* Tomás, I suggest we leave this afternoon. As soon as we can pack.''

''But we will have only a few hours travel before we must stop,'' *Don* Tomás protested. ''Long travel begins in the morning.''

"Yes, sir. And if Cordelia is behind this, she won't expect us to leave now. She might not even know we're gone until tomorrow, and she'll waste time then making sure we haven't just changed houses. We'll be back at your *hacienda* before she can catch us."

The old man's face twisted. "Running away! *Maldito sea!* We could try conclusions with her here and now."

"How, sir?" James said. "We don't have a scrap of proof. And I can't challenge her."

"And she might even rake up those old charges against you," *Don* Tomás growled. "For a moment I thought I was twenty again, ready to let hot blood rule my—"

Drusilla burst into the room without knocking, her normally soft eyes cold, her face frozen. The four men looked at her in surprise.

"*Mi hija,*" *Don* Tomás said, "is something wrong?"

"I must speak to my husband, *papá.*" She didn't look at James. "Alone."

James blinked. He hadn't been married long, but he knew enough of women to recognize trouble. But about what? "If you will excuse me, *Don* Tomás. José, Henry, will you see to preparations? I'll be along in a few minutes."

They murmured assent, avoiding looking at Drusilla. They recognized trouble, too, James thought. He turned to Drusilla; she walked out of the room, her back stiff. He shrugged and followed.

In her sitting room he put his hands on her shoulders, but she shrugged them off. "Who is Isobel de las Piedras?"

He stared at her in amazement and no little relief. So she thought there was another woman. "I don't know," he said truthfully.

Scorn twisted her mouth. "You forget your *amantes* so easily." She thrust a note at him.

He opened it—the seal was already broken—and read the feminine hand.

Querido, A man who so admired my breasts should not

find it difficult to find the rest of me. My husband is in Vera Cruz for a month. We shall have time for the enjoyment of breasts, and other things.

Isobel de las Piedras

The woman at Santa Anna's *palacio!* The events of the night had driven her out of his mind.

"So," Drusilla snapped, "you remember the *puta!* And her *tetas!*"

"Drusilla!"

"Do not school me for my language, my husband. Instead learn to school your face."

Denying it now was worse than useless. But, he thought, the best defense . . . . "I remember her. Now. With your father being shot last night, minor details of the ball slipped my mind."

"Minor details!" she shouted, but he could see she was beginning to doubt her own charges.

"There was a woman there, a *Señora* de las Piedras. And she did wear a low-cut dress." He did indeed have to school his face when he said that. "I talked with her for perhaps two minutes. I'm shocked at you, doubting me this way."

"But the note."

"And I'm shocked at you for opening something clearly addressed to me."

"In a woman's hand," she said, but she was clearly on the defensive.

"To think after only a few months of marriage you trust me so little." He turned his back, carefully watching her in the mirror.

She chewed at her lip, frowning, then sighed and put a hand on his arm. "Do not be angry with me. It is just that I am jealous."

He put his arms around her, stroking her hair. "You have nothing to be jealous about." Silently he thanked God he hadn't given in to temptation. If he had, he would never have been able to carry this off. "It's you I love."

"And I you, *querido.*" She turned up her face, and he kissed her passionately. He began undoing the laces of her dress. "Your wound," she protested.

"A scratch." He tugged the top of her dress down, slipped the straps of her silk chemise off her smooth shoulders and pulled it down to reveal satin-sheened olive breasts, each just more than enough to fill his hand. He laved her brown nipples with his tongue till they were stiff.

Her breath caught. "The bed."

"Bother the bed." He finished stripping her, fumbling off his own clothes at the same time.

Her cheeks flushed as she looked around the sitting room. "The servants, my husband. Someone might come in."

"Bother the servants, too."

He pressed her down on the carpet, his hands and lips trailing over her slender body, stroking her soft thighs, licking across her drum-taut belly, flicking her quivering breasts. Her protests faded to gasps, and when he parted her thighs and thrust into her, she wrapped her legs around him, head tossing wildly from side to side, matching him thrust for thrust.

"*Mi querido!*" she cried. "*Mi corazón! Ah, precioso! Mi amante dominante!*"

Abruptly her eyes went wide and staring. Her teeth sank into his chest, stifling her cries as she spasmed against him, and he could hold back no longer.

After, she lay in the crook of his arm, smiling as she traced the mark she had left on his chest. He smoothed her dark hair back from her forehead.

"I hope we have made a baby, my husband."

"Before we even have a house of our own?" She colored slightly under his gaze.

"I want your baby. A baby would . . . ."

He knew the rest of the sentence. A baby would bind him tighter to her, perhaps keep him away from other women. He wanted to tell her he was bound to her as tightly as if there were chains on both of them, but to say it would be to acknowledge the other part. Instead, he said, "We're leaving for home this afternoon."

"So soon? Then your business here is complete?"

He nodded. "The grant was delivered this morning."

"Good," she murmured. "There will be fewer distractions at the *hacienda.*''

He sighed. How long before she forgot Isobel de las Piedras? Or would she ever?

Shyly her hands began to creep over his body, and to his surprise he realized he wasn't as tired as he thought he was. "Let's go into the bedroom," he said. "After all, a servant might come in."

Laughing gleefully, she led the way.

XXXIV

The December evening chill seeping through the study windows suited Cordelia's mood well. Her return from Mexico City had been something less than triumphant.

"Well?" Lucille said. "Did you send for me just to make me sit here all night?" She sat stiffly in one of the high-backed chairs, one foot tapping the floor nervously.

"It is time we talked about what happened in Mexico City." Cordelia suppressed a smile as the foot began tapping faster. If Lucille had been responsible for the fiasco, she had probably thought herself in the clear until now.

"You mean the way your fancy plans went wrong?" Lucille said sweetly. "Let me see. Right now James Fallon is supposed to be in prison in Mexico City, is he not?"

"A little more time, and—" Cordelia kept her anger in check. "*Coronel* Santa Anna was one of the first I told about Fallon. How was I to suppose he'd procure a grant for him? In the middle of the night!"

"Perhaps *el coronel* has plans."

"Don't try to change the subject. Did you arrange the attack on Fallon?"

Lucille's face was unreadable. "I thought you did. When you found out about the grant."

"Fool! I didn't know about that until the next day. What about Gerard?"

"Him? He spent all his time in the bordellos. Besides, he says he is not interested in this . . . bastard . . . Fallon."

"Perhaps," Cordelia said drily. Believing half what

Gerard said might be believing too much. "If you're taking care of Gerard as I've told you, why was he in the bordellos so much? Don't tell me he's no longer attracted, because I won't believe it."

The younger woman shifted irritably. "He is satisfied. Has he said he is not?"

"No." There was something in Lucille's tone, something that would bear investigation. "Go easy with him. We may still need him. The old woman refused again yesterday to give me a sight on him, and the cards are ambiguous."

"I know," Lucille muttered.

"So. You've been trying your hand at the cards, have you?"

"I do not have your touch with the Tarot."

"Don't be evasive. What did you learn?"

"Nothing. I told you I do not have your touch."

Cordelia nodded, reluctantly. Whether Gerard was still necessary was less important than other things. Fallon was more dangerous than she had thought. This alliance—whatever it was—with Santa Anna proved that. He had to be disposed of quickly.

"Lucille, I want to see you first thing in the morning." She frowned at the girl's blank face. *Could* she have instigated the attack on Fallon? Did Lucille dare go that much against her? And what in hell was going on between her and Gerard? More problems to solve. "We have plans to make. Be there when I wake. And stop that damned foot tapping!"

She swept out of the room angrily. She was surrounded by fools who couldn't see beyond their noses. Tomorrow she was going to set Gerard and Lucille straight about a few things.

"Damn," she muttered as she entered her dark room. Not a single lamp lit. Gerard and Lucille weren't the only ones. Bonita would have her rump blistered.

She fumbled her way toward the bell pull on the wall. Suddenly a light bloomed behind her. She spun, a startled scream dying in her throat as she saw the man standing in the shadows by her bed, a cocked pistol in his hand. A pool of light spilled onto the floor from a shielded lantern sitting on her bedtable. Marring the finish, she thought irrationally.

"Who—" He lifted the gun, and she moderated her tone. "Who are you?"

He stepped into the light, a dark, stout man with a full beard. His clothes were unrelieved black, dull and dirtied. "By damn, woman, you might say I am from hell. You don't recognize me?"

The voice sounded faintly familiar. "If you leave now, I'll let you go free. Don't you realize if I shout there will be thirty *vaqueros* here in minutes?"

"You shout, Cordelia, and in minutes you would be dead. And do not think anyone saw me enter. Some of the old skills still remain."

"Do you want money? I have a little." If she could lull him, get him to where she could signal someone . . . .

His laugh was soft and mocking. "By damn, you are a cool one. You have a little money, eh? You took a lot of money from me."

She had taken money from many men, one way or another, but she was sure she had never seen this man before. "Damn it, who are you?"

"You still do not remember? New Orleans? Campeche?"

Blood drained from her face. She felt suddenly faint. "You can't be," she whispered. Her memory could not find Lafitte in this bearded man going to fat. It had to be a trick. "I can give you money. Lots of it."

"I do not want your money." He moved. She stood rooted, like a bird watching a snake. "A bullet is too good for you. Too clean, by damn." Suddenly the gun thudded to the carpet, and his hands were around her throat.

Her paralysis disappeared with her breath. She clawed at his wrists, kicking and struggling. "Your treasure," she managed, and it sounded like a caw to her. "Cellar."

"And I can carry it away in my hands?" he rasped. "I don't want money."

The air was going red before her eyes. Her throat cracking under his thumbs echoed in her ears. She tried to scream, to beg, but there was no air. The sea, the past, the bond—the cards! Then there was only the blackness closing in.

Lucille yawned as she walked down the hall. Cordelia would be mad at her—but she had been too sleepy to rise earlier. She'd lain awake for hours worrying about Cordelia's suspicions of her. Damn it, Cordelia always had to have convoluted plans. Couldn't she see that some things were best taken care of simply?

She tapped on Cordelia's door; there was no answer. She frowned. Cordelia never overslept. She knocked again, and again there was no call to enter. Suddenly hesitant, she opened the door and went in.

Cordelia lay on the bed, on the coverlet, still in the dress she'd worn the night before. Lucille froze. Bulging eyes stared at her out of a swollen, discolored face. Abruptly Lucille found herself across the room, back against the door, trembling.

She clenched her teeth to stop them chattering. For all of her wishing, Cordelia dead was almost an impossibility in her mind. Who could possibly . . . Gerard! That sent a sobering chill through her.

Ignoring the body on the bed, she rifled the room. However Cordelia had died, she had to recover the hex doll. If Gerard got his hands on it . . . . She turned out every drawer and cabinet, tore dresses from the wardrobe, rooted under the bed, panting frantically. She sat back on her heels; the hex doll wasn't there. She cast a baleful look at Cordelia's corpse. If the hex doll had been kept somewhere else, she'd never find it. But at least no one else would, either. That was cold comfort, at best, but better than nothing.

She rose, smoothed her dress and left without a backward glance at the body. If Gerard had killed Cordelia—and she could see no other possibility—he had grown too dangerous to live. She returned to her room for a small pocket pistol. Gerard had killed Cordelia, and she, discovering it, had killed him in self-defense. A believable story.

She walked into the study, where Gerard was seated

behind Cordelia's desk going through her papers, and raised the pistol.

He smiled as she cocked it. "I wouldn't, Lucille. Remember the doll."

The gun wavered for an instant, then steadied on his face. "It is useless to you. You do not know how to use it."

"True." He shuffled the papers back into order and came unconcernedly around the desk. "But there's someone in Jamaica who does. And if anything happens to me, unpleasant things are going to happen to that doll. I relieved Cordelia of it the day we got back from Mexico City. Did you know she kept it under the bed? You'd better put that gun up. She'll be down soon, and we're supposed to present her with a picture of domestic tranquility, remember?"

"What game do you play, Gerard? Cordelia is dead, and you killed her." Such a stunned look passed over his face that her conviction wavered.

He took a deep breath before answering. "You know I didn't. I told you she had to be handled carefully if we were to get what we wanted. Damn you, didn't you stop to think that a murder would be investigated? I didn't hear a shot. What did you do, stab her?"

"She was . . . strangled." She shook herself. She mustn't allow him to interject doubts. "*Salaud!* I will not let you confuse me. You killed her! It had to be you."

"Why? This throws my plans on the garbage heap."

"The doll. She found out you stole the doll, and—"

"That doll left here two days ago by a fast rider who'll put it on a ship for Jamaica. With instructions. Don't forget that. And stop wasting time trying to shift blame. We have a lot of rethinking to do."

"But, if you did not, then who?"

He frowned at her thoughtfully. "I almost believe you didn't do it. Fallon? I wouldn't have thought it, but, God knows, it's what I'd have done in his place."

Carefully she laid the gun on the table. She was sure Gerard had done it, but if he wanted to put the murder off on Fallon, she would accept that. Publicly. "I think it is time to settle with James Fallon once and for all. We will send a half-dozen *vaqueros* to take care of him. An ambush on the Velasquez *rancho*.''

"Useless effort." He sat back down behind the desk. There was a proprietorial air about him as he surveyed the room. "Worse than useless. It would probably draw attention to us here. We have to conceal Cordelia's murder, you realize."

"Conceal it! She is dead! How do we conceal that?"

"Not the death. The manner of it. Murder will bring government officials. Her finances will become a matter of record." He smiled conspiratorially. "You say she was strangled? A seizure, then. We'll bury her tomorrow, because of contagion. That will keep anyone from wanting to look too close. Then an itinerant Franciscan to mumble over her grave, and it's done. *All* of her money is ours."

As much as she hated to admit it, he was right. "But what of Fallon? I want him dead. And his father."

He threw back his head and laughed. "So bloodthirsty, my dear. You must learn to control it. I want Robert Fallon, too. I've wanted him for years before you knew he existed. For years I've waited until I could do it properly. With Cordelia's money, I can destroy him. When he's beggared, in the gutter, I'll let him know who did it, and why. And then I'll kill him."

"You and Cordelia," she muttered. "What about James? Or do you intend to play games with him, too?"

"No games. But you'll have to leave him alone until I calculate the ramifications of killing him."

"Ramifications! *Oh, la vache!* We are partners, yes? I give you Robert Fallon. You give me James Fallon."

"Partners?" He shifted a few of the papers on the desk, not looking at her. "I think, in view of the doll, we have to rethink our partnership. We'll still work together, but from now on, let's think of me as the senior partner. And I'm afraid I'll have to restrict your, ah, activities a trifle."

She put a hand to her throat and swallowed. "What do you mean?"

"Nothing too onerous, my dear. I want heirs, and I don't want some other man's bastards."

"*Batard!*"

"I don't intend to make you desperate enough to put a knife in my back, despite what will happen to you if you do." She grimaced; he would hold the doll over her head just as Cordelia had done. "As much as possible," he went on, "I'll confine myself to other women. I've already noted two or three girls among the *peóns* who might be presentable once they're cleaned up."

She stifled her anger. He thought he had won, but she was not about to lose everything now. Gerard would find that out. And so would Fallon.

"Happy New Year." James called to Elena, as he trotted down the stairs to the *hacienda*'s entry hall. "Have you seen Henry, or José?"

"*Feliz Año Nuevo,*" the young girl replied. She spread the skirt of her white ruffled dress and spun. "Do you like it? Conchita made it especially for today."

"*Lindo,* Elena. *Hermoso.* You are as beautiful as ever." She smiled and preened under his compliments. "Have you seen them?"

"*Señor* Cameron is with *papá,* in his study. I have not seen *Señor* Escobar. Would you sit with me, James? *Papá* gave me two volumes of Cervantes and a translation of Lord Byron for *Navidad.* I will read to you, or you can read to me."

"I'm sorry, Elenita, but I have to see Henry and your father."

"I like your present ever so much." She lifted her wrist to display a bracelet of woven silver wire. "*Papá* gave me very many books. An old thing called *La Perfecta Casada,* full of musty maxims. I could be a perfect wife without a dusty book, do you not think so?"

"I think your *papá* gave you those books to improve your mind," he laughed, and made his escape into the study.

Don Tomás and Henry had their heads together over a map of northern Mexico, from the Neutral Ground, the land disputed with the United States, east of the Sabine River, to the Rio Pecos in the west. Along the northern edge ran the Rio Colorado del Norte, called the Red River by *norteamericanos*, while the Rio Bravo del Norte, called the Rio Grande by some, meandered up from the south. The map covered the entire table top.

"Come," *Don* Tomás said when he entered. "*Señor* Cameron and I are discussing the best routes for you to use in surveying your grant in the spring." Logs the size of a big man's leg burned in the fireplace.

James traced a path with his finger. "I thought we'd go north, and east, then cross the Brazos far enough south to clear the Cross Timbers, then north again."

"I figured so, too," Henry said. "Until *Don* Tomás started talking."

"The last is all right," the old man said, "but you must begin by going east." He tapped the mountains north of the *hacienda*. "San Saba. Apache country. There were once silver mines there, but the Apache killed everyone."

"But surely if we stay out of the mountains . . . ."

"The Apache does not limit himself to the mountains," *Don* Tomás said. "You will want a large, well-armed party —and a very good reason—to venture into their lands."

"The *vaqueros*," James said, "tell me there are wild cattle and horses between the mountains and the Brazos. I want to make use of them, the cattle as well as the horses."

"Wild horses are bad enough," Henry said, "but I seen wild cattle back in the bayous, and they're quicker than a cat and meaner than a snake. If we got to fight Apaches, too . . . ."

Don Tomás nodded. "You may have to, if you intend to capture from those herds."

"If I'm going to keep Santa Anna from calling in his bargain, I'd better be able to deliver horses to the Mexican Army like I said. And that'll take more mustang mares than I can afford to buy. The cattle will provide us with beef, and later maybe I can sell some. In Mexico, or the United States. If the land will support horses, it'll support cattle."

"Perhaps," *Don* Tomás said. "But first you must capture them."

They straightened from the map as the door banged

open. Drusilla hurried into the room, José close on her heels. Escobar was dusty, as if he'd just finished a hard ride.

"Cordelia Applegate is dead," she burst out.

José nodded. "It is true. I was with the *vaqueros* when a rider from San Antonio mentioned it in passing. I rode straight here."

Don Tomás made the sign of the cross. "*Que en paz descanse.*"

"God forgive me," James said. "I'm glad she's dead."

"Amen," Henry breathed. "There's a whole batch of trouble went to the grave with that woman."

James nodded. "No more looking at every shadow wondering if there's a man in it with a gun. I can't think of better news."

"I . . . I have other news," Drusilla said. He looked at her questioningly, and she colored again, redder than before. "Alone, my husband. In the hall?"

He looked at the others—they seemed as mystified as he —and followed her into the entry hall. She plucked at her dress and stared at the floor.

"Drusilla, is something wrong?"

"No, my husband. It is just . . ." She looked up at him, her face still red, and whispered, "I am with child, my husband."

He let out a whoop and swung her in a circle. The others came crowding out of the study. "I'm going to be a father," he shouted.

He ignored their congratulations, kissing his wife despite her faint protests. A child on the way and the shadow of Cordelia Applegate lifted, all in one day. If he believed in omens, he'd believe the future was assured. Damn it, he thought, it was.

XXXV

Lucille stumbled on the narrow path from the *hacienda* to the old woman's hut. Cursing, she pulled her shawl tighter around her head and went on. In the four months since Cordelia's death she had kept away from the old woman. If she went, sooner or later she must tell her of Cordelia's death, and not the story of a seizure, either. She hated knowing she didn't dare lie to the old woman. But would the old woman believe she wasn't lying? Would the old woman think she had helped Gerard murder Cordelia? After all, Cordelia had been an apprentice of sorts, too.

Her pale green silk dress snagged on mesquite thorns; she ripped it loose without stopping. For weeks she had agonized about this. It had become clear that Gerard's "calculation of ramifications" was going nowhere. Absorbed in making bribes to insure Cordelia's money was theirs—she kept a close eye on him to make certain it was theirs, not his—he could not care less about James Fallon. And as the *vaqueros* had shown a disgusting haste to take orders from a man again, this visit had become imperative.

She hesitated before the low entrance to the hovel, but the old woman's cracked voice came immediately. "Come in, *moza*."

Lucille sighed and ducked through the doorway, kneeling across the firepit from the old woman in her rickety chair. The battered teapot bubbled on the fire. "*Mi dueña*, I come to ask a favor."

"After so long, *moza*, you are not even going to tell me of her death?" The old woman's black eyes regarded her

286

over the rim of her chipped cup.

"Someone has told you already."

"No one has told me, *moza*. No one tells me things, because they expect me to know already." She chuckled drily. "And I do."

"You know how she died, *mi duena?*"

"Strangled by a man from her past. But that is a thing of this world, and of no matter."

Lucille breathed a small sigh of relief. So Gerard had done it. And the old woman didn't think she was involved. "*Mi dueña*, I have come for a favor."

"So you said, *moza*."

"You . . . you are well thought of by the Comanche, is it not so?"

For a moment she thought she had surprised the woman across from her. The cup stopped halfway to her mouth. She leaned forward to stare at Lucille.

"That is a strange question, *moza*. *Los Indios* know I am part of the world of the spirits. Before the *vaqueros* came and the *hacienda* was built, Comanche, Karankawa and others left gifts at my door. Even now, some come in the night."

"Then you could get a message to the Comanche? Offer them payment? Horses. I will give them one hundred horses."

"*Por qué?*"

"To kill a man, mi *dueña*. He—"

The old woman snorted. "Of this world, *moza*. Always you think of this world. If you wish this man dead, then kill him, but do not bother me with it."

"I must, *mi dueña*. He has been given a grant in the Comanche lands. I have no other way to reach him."

"In the Comanche lands," the old woman mused. "A brave man. Or a fool. Why do you not let the Comanche take care of him in their own time?"

"He will have armed men with him, *mi dueña*. The attack must be large enough that there are no survivors."

The old woman nodded slowly. "And what is to be *mi pago, moza?* I have no use for horses."

Nor any use for gold, Lucille thought. She could not

imagine what the old woman would want. "I will pay whatever you wish, *mi dueña*."

"*Su hija*," the old woman said, and took a sip of tea.

Lucille blinked. "I do not have a daughter."

"You will, *moza*. *Su marido* will put children in your belly, and the first daughter born is to be given to me. From the day she is born, she is mine, *moza*."

"*Si, mi dueña*," Lucille whispered. It wasn't mother love that shook her. It was the realization that Gerard and the old woman were both going to use her as a brood mare. Once again the Fallons were costing her. She realized the old woman was speaking. "I am sorry, *mi dueña?*"

"I said," the old woman repeated with asperity, "this will take some time, *moza*."

"Time? But why?"

"*Idiota!* I do not just walk out of my hut and speak to the Comanche. And when they have sent a man to talk to me, he must be handled properly."

"You are afraid of them?" Lucille said disbelievingly. The old woman's answering cackle made her skin crawl.

"Oh, they would not harm me, *moza*. But they are a proud people. If they think themselves insulted, they may come here, burn the *hacienda*. I cannot have that, *moza*. You have yet a daughter to give me."

Lucille wet her lips. "How long, *mi dueña?*"

"As long as I think necessary, *moza*. Now leave me." She buried her face in the cup, and Lucille knew she wouldn't get another word.

Back at the *hacienda* she found Gerard closeted in the study with a man she recognized vaguely. His broad face seemed broader for piggish brown eyes, his heavy chin heavier for bushy side whiskers. He wore black broadcloth, looking, she thought, like a Boston banker searching for a mortgage to foreclose.

"Ah, my dear," Gerard said without rising from behind the long table. "Haden, this is my wife, Lucille. Lucille, Haden Edwards. Mr. Edwards has just been given three hundred thousand acres around Nacogdoches."

"Mrs. Fourrier." Edwards bent over her hand, kissing it

too long. She extricated it from his grip as he straightened.

"*Félicitations*, Mr. Edwards. What do you intend to do with your grant?"

"Make money," he laughed, a head-back bray that ended with a cough. "Your pardon, ma'am. I intend to do the same as Stephen Austin and all the rest that're sitting in Mexico City, scrabbling for what I already have. There are thousands in the United States who want land in Texas. The papers are full of it, the new land of milk and honey. Plant a crowbar and it'll sprout ten-penny nails. That's the sort of thing they're printing. And when those thousands come pouring into Texas—Austin's getting a trickle by comparison, now—I'll be ready to sell them their own piece of the promised land."

"And what," she began, but Gerard cut her off. "If you'll excuse us, my dear. We have business to discuss."

Lucille bristled. They meant men's business, and none of hers. She opened her mouth and then shut it again.

"Gentlemen." She dropped a perfect curtsey and swept out of the room. Damn them, they'd learn not to treat her as an imbecile just because she was a woman.

XXXVI

Along the stream, lined with tall cottonwoods, sycamore, elm and oak, a slight breeze palliated the June heat. Leonie sat in the dappled shade watching Denmark, two years old now, wave his chubby hands at a pool of sunlight by the stream. It wasn't deep, but she didn't look away from him for long.

One thing she did look at was the work going on atop a long, low hill, crested with plum and pecan trees, half a mile away. The men Fallon had hired in San Antonio were building cabins and stables, skidding trees from far upstream. She curled a lip whenever she saw them, *peóns* in dirty white cotton walking beside the horses dragging the logs. It was just like a Fallon to make them cut so far away when there were trees ready to hand.

At the sound of a horse downstream she snatched Denmark to her, then breathed a sigh of relief when she saw Henry. "Are you trying to scare me to death, Henry? I thought you were an Indian."

He swung his horse in close to her. His rifle was held across his saddle. "Damn it, woman, I could've been. Didn't I tell you to stay on the hill?" Sweat rolled down his face from under his shapeless hat.

"Don't take that tone with me, Henry Cameron. It's hot up there. Fallon's wife keeps moaning about the heat and throwing up. And every time I turn around there's another *vaquero* with a rifle."

He made an exasperated sound that raised her hackles. "You think they carrying them rifles for show? I saw

Comanche sign myself yesterday, not three miles from here. You going to run all the way back to the hill carrying Denmark if they show up?"

"Why do we have to stay here, anyway? You have your own land, and no more than you deserve, either."

"I swear to the Lord God Almighty, woman, you got a serpent's tongue. What did James ever do to you?"

He was a Fallon, she thought, but she couldn't explain that to Henry. "I don't like you being under his thumb. You ought to be building your own place, not his."

"You want us scattered over hell and half of creation so the Comanche can pick us off? Now you collect that child and get up the hill."

"Henry, it's hot up there."

He leaned over to break off a willow switch. "You want me to make your seat hot, too? If I have to whip the devil out of your fanny to save the hair on your head, I will. Now, get!"

With as much dignity as she could muster she cradled Denmark in her arms and started for the hill. Halfway there she looked back. Henry was cantering to the south, where a rider was fast approaching. Slowing, she stooped to pick a handful of wildflowers. He was stubborn, but sooner or later she'd teach him she had a mind of her own.

At the base of the hill, James dipped a kerchief in the spring bubbling up among rocks and mopped his forehead. A rivulet ran off from the spring through grass dotted with purple patches of moradilla and quilted with firewheel, butterfly weed, and black-eyed susans to join the stream, which in turn flowed north into the Rio Trinidad. He could see Leonie picking some of the wildflowers. Men skidding logs passed him on their way up the hill, gouging furrows in the earth.

"*Arbuelos buenos, señor*," one of them called, thumbing over his shoulder toward the stream. "*E muy cerca*."

"They're closer," James agreed. "But work is good for the soul." Some laughed, and he spurred up the hill before any of the rest could voice another complaint. Some of them would have cut the plum trees atop the hill for the cabins. They wouldn't understand that he didn't want to look at stumps from his front step.

A *vaquero* with a rifle under his arm tipped his hat as James passed. There were others around the hill. He knew if the Comanche came calling he'd wish he had ten times as many.

Men were swarming over each of the three cabins, lifting logs into place, hammering in the wooden pegs they were using in place of too-expensive nails. A sawpit was already working at the north end of hills. He swung to the ground in front of the tent next to what would be the largest cabin, four rooms with a hall down the middle and sawn plank floors. All sides of the tent had been propped up. He ducked inside. Consuela, Drusilla's maid, knelt by the cot where Drusilla lay, fanning her slowly. Drusilla was in her seventh month, and not faring well with the heat.

"*Querida*, is there anything I can get for you?" He managed a smile, and she answered it with a weak one of her own.

"No, my darling. I am fine."

A shimmer of sweat covered her face. Hardly fine, he thought. She couldn't walk fifty yards without resting. He had been against her coming before the baby was born, but without actually arguing she had ignored all his objections. Short of physically putting her off the wagon, he hadn't known how to stop her.

"*Pobrecita.*" Consuela glowered at James. "*Mi doñacita* should be in the *hacienda* of her *papá.*"

"You should," he said. "*Don* Tomás certainly would like to see the baby as soon as it's born."

"Not it," Drusilla said. "He or she. I think she." She swallowed and closed her eyes. "Forgive me, my husband," she said faintly, "but I am tired.

He motioned the plump maid to follow him outside. She did so with a bad grace. "Isn't there anything you can do to keep her cool?"

"There is cool water from the spring, *señor*, but it does not remain cool very long, and to bring it I must leave her. Without the fan, it is very hot. Perhaps if the tent could be moved to the stream. There are breezes there.''

''There may also be Comanche,'' he said drily.

Her breath caught, and she clutched her crucifix. ''*Mi doñacita* should be safe at home.''

''This is her home now,'' he growled, wondering how he could get Drusilla to her father for the rest of her pregnancy. ''You there,'' he called to one of the men working on the cabin. ''What's your name?''

The man lowered the end of the log he had been lifting and stepped forward with a doubtful smile. His yellow teeth were spaced with numerous blackened stumps. He doffed his hat and bowed. ''Pepino, *señor*. I am called Pepino.''

''Get two buckets,'' James told him, ''and start fetching water from the spring to this tent. You make sure there's a bucket of the coldest spring water you can get up the hill in this tent all the time. Understand?''

''*Sí, señor*. It will be as you say.'' He ducked his head and scurried away.

''Shouldn't you be fanning?'' he said to Consuela. She gave a small cry and darted back into the tent. And he had work as well, he thought. The logs were coming more slowly from upriver. Stone had to be gathered from the river for a spring house. Meat was getting low, but thank God game was plentiful. A *barracón* to be built for the men. A stable. As he swung into the saddle, still enumerating things to be done, Henry galloped up the hill with a man he'd never seen before. Not a Mexican.

''News,'' Henry said as they reached him. ''News and a letter from Austin. This here's Michael Cullen.''

Cullen's face was red from the sun beneath the broad brim of his hat. He ran a curious eye over the work on the hilltop as he dug the letter from under his coat. ''Mr. Austin, he said to say it was urgent. Said that when he give it to me. Looks like you got a fine place here.''

''Thanks,'' James said. He was in no hurry to break the seal. The only urgent matter that connected Austin and him was the charges Cordelia had brought.

''Got a President in Mexico City,'' Henry said. ''Cullen here says the Regency is broke up.''

Cullen nodded. "That's right. Guadalupe Victoria. Him that was one of the Regency."

"Any word about the grants being affected?"

"Not yet, Mr. Fallon. Mr. Austin's been writing letters trying to find out."

It was one of the worst things about the Mexican government: this President could change everything the Regency had done, revoke every decree and land grant, and do it overnight. The only restraint in the system seemed to be the fear of rebellion if he went too far.

"Got a new President in the States, too," Henry said. James ripped open the seal. "Jackson?"

"Adams."

"Yes, sir," Cullen said. "Seems Henry Clay threw his support to Adams. Understand there's a big uproar about it."

James nodded distractedly as he unfolded the letter.

Dear James,
  I hope I may still address you that way after the way we parted. You may not know that Cordelia Applegate is dead. I think I may safely say that seems to put the quietus to any charges against you. I understand that your circumstances are very good at present, and I wish you good fortune.
  I write because the situation in Nacogdoches can be disastrous for all of us *norteamericanos*, especially now that Guadalupe Victoria is President. He is appointing a commission under General Teran to study the "problem" of Texas. You know Haden Edwards, or have at least met him, which is more than I can say. Come with the bearer of this to meet me in Nacogdoches. We may yet keep ourselves from being expelled from Mexico.

                                        Stephen F. Austin

"What's happening in Nacogdoches?" James asked. "And what does Haden Edwards have to do with it?"

"There's a ruckus for sure," Cullen said. "Didn't you know Edwards got a grant over Nacogdoches way? Well, anyway, he's saying everybody who's already settled on the grant—and there's a sight of them—has to prove they got title. Some's Mexicans, and Mr. Austin says that's likely to cause trouble.''

"That it is. If Edwards kicks a Mexican off his land, title or no, there'd be hell to pay for every *yanqui* in Texas. I'll come, Mr. Cullen. When are we supposed to meet Mr. Austin?''

"Him and Jared Groce left the same time I did. They might already be there.''

"There's no time to waste, then. Henry, would you find José? I want him to come with me. You'll be in charge till I get back.''

Henry shook his head. "James, he's a good man, but he's an old man. If it comes to rough and tumble you'll want a strong right arm beside you.''

"If it comes to rough and tumble. I'll need more than a strong right arm. No, Henry, José can talk to the Mexicans, get their side of what's going on. Besides, Leonie won't be too happy if you go off. She's been looking daggers at me ever since we got here as it is.''

"Fool woman," Henry muttered. "What about yourself?'' He jerked his head toward the tent.

"You go get José. Mr. Cullen, I'm sure you can find some coffee over at the cook fire.''

James ducked into the tent. Drusilla turned her head away as he came in. Consuela shot an angry glance at him and waved her fan more vigorously, muttering under her breath.

"I see you heard," he said. "Drusilla, it's only—''

"You are leaving me," she said, still not looking at him. Her voice was tight and biting. "You bring me here to the middle of nowhere, and now—''

"I brought you! The only way I could have stopped you would have been to lock you in your room.'' Consuela moved as if to shield Drusilla with her body.

"I am surprised that you did not," Drusilla snapped. "A man who could leave his wife, and her with child, in the middle of a wilderness, should find no difficulty in imprisoning her.''

"Imprison!" He took a deep breath. "If you were

listening, you must realize—''

"I do not listen to the conversations of others, my husband.''

"—that trouble is breaking loose in Nacogdoches.''

"I do not care about Nacogdoches.''

"That trouble," he continued grimly, "could cost us this land.''

She was silent. He thought she lifted one eyelid enough to look at him. "I want you here when our child is born.''

"I'll be here, Drusilla. At most I'll be gone ten days.''

"Why cannot someone else do this thing, whatever it is?''

"There isn't anyone else. At least, Austin doesn't think so.'' He bent to kiss her, but she turned her head so his lips brushed her ear. "*Querida*, I must go.''

She didn't answer, and after a time he went outside. José and Cullen were waiting, mounted and with a horse saddled for him. Henry was afoot. "Henry," he said, "do you think this is as important as Austin makes out? He's not making a mountain out of a mole hill?''

"I don't reckon he's the kind for that.''

"That's what I think, too, but not what I want to hear. With Drusilla having a baby . . . .''

"James, you want that baby to have a place to sleep, I expect you better go on to Nacogdoches.''

"I suppose you're right,'' he sighed. He swung into the saddle. "Let's ride.'' As they started down the hill he thought he heard Drusilla call his name. He didn't turn back.

XXXVII

Nacogdoches had changed since James had last seen it, soon after crossing the Sabine into Texas for the first time. The old stone mission was still there on the low knoll between two streams, but the buildings of the town were no longer in ruin. Those that hadn't been repaired had been torn down, and new structures erected in their place. The town swarmed with a hodgepodge of Mexicans and *yanquis*, settlers in homespun, *vaqueros* in short jackets and sashes, smugglers, trappers, hunters, gamblers, would-be planters, and everyone else who thought there was a dollar to be had in Texas. Streets where coyotes had hunted fieldmice in sagebrush were now rutted with wagon traffic. Raucous music floated from half-a-dozen bars, and here were twice as many bartenders doing business with a plank set across two barrels.

"Austin said to meet him at Adolphus Sterne's store," Cullen told James. "Sterne's about the only man in Nacogdoches Mr. Austin even halfway trusts."

"Honest man?"

Cullen shrugged. "Honest as you'll find in Nacogdoches."

James was chewing on that when a tall *vaquero* with a birthmark like a dark bruise on his cheek came out of a saloon and called, *"Hola,* José!"

"Hola, Esteban! A friend I have not seen in a long time, *señor,"* he added to James, and turned his horse aside.

José leaned out of the saddle with a laugh, but the tall *vaquero* shot a dark look at James and Cullen before beginning to speak. All the others in front of the saloon were Mexican as well, and the sounds of a guitar drifted from the dark interior. Three doors down, someone was playing *The Old Oaken Bucket* loudly on an out-of-tune piano. The men there all seemed to be *yanquis*.

"Maybe we shouldn't stand around here," Cullen said. "Mr. Austin said I was to be careful not to act like I was on one side or the other, Mr. Fallon."

"So Austin's going to put himself in the middle."

"I wouldn't know, Mr. Fallon."

James wished Austin had sent someone who knew a little more. Cullen's store of information had apparently been exhausted before they left the ranch.

José walked his horse back and spoke quietly to James. "My friend, Esteban Morales, would like to speak to you."

"The man you were talking to? Surely." When he looked toward the saloon, though, the tall *vaquero* wasn't there. "Where did he go?"

"He does not wish to be seen speaking to you, *señor*. I tried to tell him that you are not an *empresario*, but he and the others think of you so."

"He doesn't want to be seen talking to an *empresario*?"

"In many eyes, *señor*, such a one must be an ally of the *Señores* Edwards."

"Then where do I talk to him?"

"I will take you to him, *señor*."

"Wait a minute, Mr. Fallon," Cullen said. "Mr. Austin said I was to bring you to him soon as we got here."

"I'll find him," James said. "Adolphus Sterne's store." Once he knew more of what was going on.

The way led out of town, through a thicket of post oak, chinquapin and catclaw, to a ruined adobe farmhouse. Part of the roof had collapsed, and a sweetgum grew through the hole. Morales was inside, peering through out to see if they had been followed.

"There is much ill feeling against the *empresarios*," he said. "And against those who are friendly with them."

"I'm not an *empresario*," James said.

Morales looked at him sharply. "Because you keep the land for yourself? What right do you have to it? You are not Mexican."

"What did you Mexicans do with it? You let it lie fallow. I've sweated for it." He clamped his mouth shut, too late.

"You see!" Morales said to José. "He is the same as the others."

"Talk to him, Esteban," José said. "He is a good man. Perhaps he can help."

Morales barked a laugh. "Why should I believe any *yanqui* is good?"

"You believe what you want to," James said. "But aren't there *yanquis* having trouble with the Edwardses too?"

"Small trouble, *señor*. Trouble soon mended. It is for the *mexicanos* that the trouble is great, and our land stolen."

"Tell me about these troubles," James said. "*Señor* Austin has asked me here to help with putting an end to them."

Morales looked at José doubtfully, then began. "Soon after the *Señores* Edwards came to Nacogdoches, they posted *los avisos* about the town. Everyone must come to them with documents proving that the land on which they live belongs to them. Many have no paper, and they are told they must buy their own land from the *Señores* Edwards. Their own land, *señor*."

"But I understood Edwards was given a grant by the Congress. And, if you'll forgive me, when I passed through this town three years ago there was no one here."

"Many in Nacogdoches supported the rebellion of *Padre* Hidalgo against *los espanoles*. For this the town was ordered abandoned, and everyone was forbidden to return. Now the Congress has said we may come back to the land our fathers owned, but we return to find the *Señores* Edwards."

"I'll do what I can, *Señor* Morales." From the little he remembered of Haden Edwards, he wasn't sure what that would be.

Sterne's store was a one-story adobe building with a two-story wooden false front. Inside, a counter rimmed the room, the large open space in the middle filled with piled blankets and sacks of sundries.

"James!" The broad-faced man vaulted over the counter and grabbed his hand. It was Jared Groce. "Damn it all to hell, James, but it's good to see you! I heard you were north of here about a hundred and fifty miles. How are you?"

"Fine, Jared. Got a horse ranch started. How are things for you?"

"Put my own cotton through my own gins this year, James. Say, I heard you married a Mexican girl. That true?"

James nodded. "Her name's Drusilla. We're expecting a baby in a couple of months now."

"Well, I'll be! What brings you to Nacogdoches at a time like that?"

"Austin sent for me. Didn't he tell you?"

"Not about you." Groce's face darkened suddenly. "Did Cullen bring you? Damn him. I asked what he was doing here, and he mumbled something about Austin and ducked out. Keeping secrets from me."

"I think Austin told him to, Jared. He didn't tell me more than enough to get me to come."

"He's being close-mouthed about this, James. That's for sure."

"I wish I was sure of more," James said. He reminded himself that he trusted Austin, and at the same time remembered he hadn't seen him in three years. "What do you think about this business of Edwards taking Mexicans' land?"

"It is not precisely so," said a small man in a store-keeper's apron. James hadn't noticed his approach. He was balding on top, with spectacles and plump cheeks, and a warm smile. He spoke with a German accent.

"Forgetting my manners," Groce said. "James, this is Adolphus Sterne. Adolphus, James Fallon."

They shook hands, and James said, "What isn't precise about it?"

"You see, Mr. Fallon," Sterne said, "until recently Nacogdoches had been *verlassen*, abandoned, for a decade. But of course, you know that. Now people are returning, no few drawn by the rumors that a grant would be made here to an *empresario*."

"But what about people who owned land here before the town was abandoned? Aren't many of them returning?"

"Some, Mr. Fallon. Some. But without *die Dokumente*, who is to tell who has a valid claim? Even with papers . . . ." He took off his glasses and wiped them with a corner of his apron. "Do you know what it takes to get a valid deed from the Congress? Three men who will swear that the land was in your family. *Nichts mehr.* There are men in this city with valid deeds from the Congress, no member of whose family was ever north of the Rio Bravo del Norte."

"Then you think Edwards is right?"

"I will tell you, Mr. Fallon. When I came to this town, this building was a ruin. It had no roof. It was full of *Schädlinge.* The first day I killed a rattlesnake right where we stand with a hoe. I cleaned this building. I repaired it. I built the floor, and the shelves, and the false front. Now at night I do not sleep. I worry. I would not be the first to have property claimed after it was built up."

"You're an Edwards man," James said.

Sterne spread his hands. "I try to keep an open mind, but I want to keep what I have built. Yes, I am an Edwards man." A man in buckskins came in and began pawing through the blankets. "You will forgive me, *bitte?* I have a customer."

James waited till Sterne was busy with the man in buckskins, then drew Groce further away. "You never did say what you thought, Jared. Do you support Edwards?"

"Edwards is an ass, James. But the Mexicans don't like us, you know. *Yanquis*, I mean."

"I haven't noticed any special dislike."

"Then you haven't met the right Mexicans. Most—the Congress, for instance—don't like what we're doing in Texas."

"Come on," James laughed. "If the Congress wanted us out, they'd revoke our grants in a minute."

"They want it both ways," Groce said seriously. "In three years we've brought more settlers into Texas than the Mexicans ever had here, or the Spanish before them. We've done more with the land than they ever did, too. That's all well and good, but once they see what can be done with the land, they remember we aren't Mexican. Why do you think they combined Texas and Coahuila, and only gave Texas one seat in the State Legislature? To make sure *yanquis* didn't get any sort of control."

"It's their country, Jaréd."

"Ours, too, James. Or don't you think that horse ranch is yours? What are you going to do if, after you build it all, they revoke your grant and give it to a Mexican?"

"I took out Mexican citizenship," James said, a trace doubtfully.

"That didn't change your blood. You're not one of *la raza*, and you'd better remember it."

"What I'm going to remember is that unless we get things straightened out here, we may all get chased out of Texas. Now, where can I get a room?"

"Quincannon's," Groce said promptly. "That's where Austin and I are staying. Seventy-five cents a day with meals, fifty cents without. It's better without. Beef and beans, or jackrabbit and beans, is about it."

"Where is Austin, anyway?"

"He's trying to chase down Ben Edwards, Haden's brother. With Haden gone, he's the only one who can slow things down. If he wants to."

"Gone! Where's he gone?"

"You didn't know? He's back in the States. Something about investors for the colony."

"Christ!" The only reason for his being there was Austin's belief that he could talk to Haden Edwards. When he saw Austin, it would be to say goodbye before going home to Drusilla.

Quincannon's Clean Rooms and Board was about what he expected, a two-story adobe with the sign painted on the front. There was a menu painted by the door, and he noticed that Groce was right. Beans and more beans. He and José were offered a tiny room with two pallets on the floor and a window with one remaining sheet of oiled paper. They were lucky to get that, the clerk said, considering the crowding in town. Leaving their saddlebags and bedrolls in the room, they split up, José to percolate among the *mexicanos,* James among the *yanquis.*

James worked his way from one saloon where *norteamericanos* predominated to another. They were a decidedly mixed bag. Farmers and tradesmen who'd come with their families and belongings, ready for the glorious new life described in the Eastern papers. Smugglers and river toughs drawn by the rumors of wealth to be had for the taking. Gamblers come to prey on the rest.

Some had bought certificates in the States, purporting to be good for land in Texas. The fine print revealed they merely promised the right to buy land, and then from *empresarios* no one had heard of. Others had bought land from Mexicans, and had the deeds to prove it, but there was no way to tell whether the Mexicans had had the right to sell it. At least half had bought land from the Edwards brothers, or were signed up to, and tempers were running high. He saw half a dozen fist-fights over land, and once knives were drawn. Others in the crowd managed to soothe the combatants down, but James could see it was only a matter of time. Knives, then guns, then the Mexican Army.

He returned to Quincannon's to find José with much the same story. The Mexicans were a mixture of sharpers and honest folk some of whom had bought land from the sharpers. A few had bought land from Edwards, land they claimed was already theirs, but for the rest only a distrust of *yanquis* kept them from joining with the *norteamericanos* who were complaining about Edwards.

It was late when a boy knocked on their doors and summoned *Señor* Fallon downstairs. Austin was standing outside in the night, leaning against the hitching rail. The town was only slightly less quiet than it had been in daylight. There were fewer people on the streets, but the increase in noise from the saloons more than made up for it.

"Reminds me of Girod Street," Austin said. "Cigar?"

"Thanks. Nothing's as bad as the Swamp." He paused

to bite the end off his cigar and puff it alight from Austin's. "I haven't seen any ears bitten off, or eyes gouged."

"The violence is there, James. Waiting to break out." Austin's fur cap was pulled low on his forehead. He wore fringed buckskins.

"How do you intend to stop it, Stephen? I'm assuming you do."

"I don't know, James."

"Christ, I don't even know which side you're on. I thought it was obvious, at first, but from what I've been hearing since I got here I don't know who's in the right."

Austin grimaced at his cigar. "These things are beginning to taste like rope. I'm smoking too many." He tossed it into the street, trailing sparks. "I'm not on any side, James. Or maybe I'm on everyone's side."

"Straddling a fence is a good way to get a sore crotch, Stephen. You have to come down on one side or the other."

"Which side are you on? Or are you just going to go back to your ranch and put your head in the sand?"

James puffed his cigar before replying. "I don't have to take sides. There's nothing I can do either way."

"And I can?" Austin laughed. "One side won't listen to me because I'm an *empresario*, and the other . . . . James, Haden has some right on his side—a little—but he seems of a mind to run roughshod over everybody. And Ben is a hothead. Siding with them is tantamount to setting a torch to Texas. Hell, siding with anyone will set Texas on fire."

"What's left?"

"Compromise."

"You don't need me for that. You're the lawyer."

"So you're going home?"

"Damn it, Stephen, Drusilla's expecting."

"I heard you'd married. Congratulations. You might even have time to see your baby walk before Mexican troops show up to tell you to leave."

"Damn you, Austin!" He flicked his cigar into the

darkness. "I'll stay. But only for a few days. I intend to be there when my baby is born."

"Thank you, James. A few days will do it. Just until Haden gets back."

XXXVIII

The days Austin had spoken of stretched into weeks.
More than once James was prepared to leave, but always
Austin managed to talk him out of it.

In front of Quincannon's he saw José, and hitched his
horse. "Any word, José?"

"Juan returned less than an hour ago, *señor*."

"A letter?" he asked hopefully. José shook his head.
"He said *Doña* Drusilla is in good health, though."

James nodded disconsolately. He'd written to Drusilla,
explaining. He'd written every week, the time it took a
messenger on a fast horse to carry the letter to the *rancho*
and return. And except for reports on Drusilla's health
from the messenger, there had been no word.

"Be of good heart, *señor*. With her time drawing near,
a woman's temper is uncertain at best. I mean . . . ."

"I know what you mean, old friend." He noticed two
men in buckskin and homespun lounging against the wall
a short distance away. "What are Walters and Lloyd doing
around here?" They were Edwards men, but not settlers.
James wasn't sure what they did, except follow Ben Edwards around.

"They were asking for you earlier, *señor*."

"For me?" He didn't like either man. Walters had a
face like a weasel and a nose that was always red at the tip.
Lloyd sucked his teeth, and a sour smell hung around him
in a cloud.

Apparently aware he'd seen them, they approached diffidently, crushing their hats in their hands. It was an un-

306

usual attitude for them.

"Mr. Fallon." Walters wore a toothy grin that slipped from time to time. "Mr. Fallon, me and Lloyd was wondering." Lloyd tried a grin as well.

"About what, Walters?"

Walters avoided looking at José. "You know the Mexes pretty good, don't you?"

"Get on with it."

"Well, sir, they wouldn't cause no trouble, would they? I mean, take the law in their own hands, so to speak?"

"Have you done something you're worried about, Walters?"

"Oh, no, sir. Nothing like that. I guess me and Lloyd's got to go. Come on, Lloyd." Lloyd mumbled something around his teeth, and the two hurried off.

James turned to José. "Do you have any idea what that's about?"

"I have heard nothing, *señor*. Perhaps if I ask a few questions."

"Do that. I'll see if Austin's heard anything."

James started looking for Austin in the saloons. Austin wasn't a drinker—if anything he led an ascetic life—but the saloons were the center of political talk in Nacogdoches, and if anything would draw Austin, it was politics. He didn't find Austin, but in the last one, a place called the Boston Saloon and Coffee House, he found Gerard Fourrier, sitting alone at a table with a bottle, listening to the talk around him with a sly smile.

He started to duck back out, but Fourrier looked at the door at just that moment. His smile deepened. "Ah, Fallon. Come, man. Sit. Sit. Don't think I hold anything against you. That was all Cordelia."

He couldn't help wondering why the man was in Nacogdoches. "I can only stay long enough for one drink."

"Just to signify that bygones are bygones." Fourrier called for another glass and filled it while James was taking a seat. His coat of navy superfine, pale fawn trousers, and curly brimmed beaver hat were more suited to New Orleans than Texas. "You have a place on the Trinidad, isn't that right? Just a few hundred miles north of us."

James felt a chill. This man knowing where Drusilla was, was disquieting. "You married Cordelia's niece, I heard."

"Yes. Lucille. Lovely girl."

"What brings you to Nacogdoches? I was a little surprised to see you so far north."

"Business," Fourrier said vaguely. "You're quite involved in the local situation?"

"A little. What sort of business?" He knew it was a rude question.

Fourrier frowned before answering. "I'm looking for investments."

"What sort of investments?"

Fourrier tossed back his drink and rose. "I must meet someone." With a tip of his hat, he was gone.

James finished his own drink angrily and followed. Whatever Fourrier was up to, it couldn't be important enough for him to waste time on. As he left the saloon he saw Austin, four houses down and headed the other way.

"Stephen!" Austin looked back and waved, but kept walking. James trotted after the smaller man until he caught up. "Stephen, I think there's some trouble afoot. Will you stop a minute?"

"There might well be," Austin said without slowing. "I just found out Haden Edwards is back."

"Walters and Lloyd approached me a little while ago. They're afraid the Mexicans might get up in arms about something. They wouldn't say what."

"It couldn't be Edwards. He only returned last night. Oh, damn!" he said as they rounded a corner. Ahead was the stone house the Edwards brothers shared, fronting on the plaza next to the old church. The plaza held two dozen mounted men. A score of horses with empty saddles indicated more men were inside.

The mounted men parted for them silently. They were divided about half-and-half, *yanquis* and *mexicanos*. James recognized several—they avoided his eye, now—all of whom were among those he considered honest.

"Did you mark them?" Austin said quietly when they reached the door.

James nodded. "No gamblers, no smugglers, no sharpers."

"Honest folk, James. And hell to pay, I fear." He knocked on the door. A black-bearded man with a work-hardened face jerked it open. James knew him, Cap Wainwright, a farmer from Virginia who had bought land from a Mexican before Edwards arrived.

"You two come to testify for him," Wainwright growled, "or against him?"

Austin crowded forward, and James stuck right behind him, so that Wainwright was obliged to let them in or physically bar them. He stepped aside reluctantly.

"Is Edwards on trial then, Cap?" James said. He tried to make it sound like a joke, but Wainwright's face tightened.

"That he is." He jerked his head toward the door at the end of the hall. "The two of you had best come on in, now you're here."

The parlor was crowded, the walls lined with men gripping rifles and muskets, three others—the leaders, James assumed—standing out in the floor. Only Haden Edwards was seated, lounging back in a wingchair, one leg over the other, puffing a cigar a trifle too casually and a touch too fast.

Wainwright took his place with three leaders, two *mexicanos* and a *yanqui*. Only then did it come to James that Wainwright was one of them. Two from each camp.

"You'll forgive me," Edwards said, "for not rising. These people seem nervous if I make sudden moves. Are the two of you also, ah, guests?" He flicked his cigar ash at Wainwright with a curl of his lip. His hand shook slightly.

"We're not prisoners," Austin said, more confidently than James thought he had a right to. "We came to help. What are the charges? *Senor* Wainwright mentioned a trial."

"They have no damned right," Edwards began, but one of the Mexicans cut him off.

"The charges are simple, *Señor* Austin." Pedro Marin was short, plump, and burned almost black by the sun. A farmer, he had left when Arredondo ordered Nacogdoches abandoned, and returned before Edwards. "*Señor* Edwards has stolen land from the men who own it, and he will steal more if he is not stopped."

"I've stolen nothing!" Edwards shouted. "I have a grant!"

"Gently," Austin said as Marin, Wainwright, and the other two rounded on Edwards. "Gently, *señores*, and we will work this out. Compromise can solve many things."

"When things are worked out, *señor*," Marin said, "It is always *Señor* Edwards who wins. It is we who were here before him who lose."

"But surely," Austin began.

"No, *señor*," Marin said. "Too many times have men found their land in the hands of *Señor* Edwards' *colonos*, who refuse to give it back even when the deeds are shown. Too many times men have been told that they must present papers to *Señor* Edwards to prove that the land they live on is theirs. And if they have no papers he has said he will take the land."

"That's what we must settle, *Señor* Marin," Austin said calmly. "There are many claims and counterclaims, and you know as well as I that some on both sides are false. This is a matter that must be solved by compromise."

Marin shook his head. "It is too late, *señor*. Yesterday the land owned by Esteban Morales was sold by the brother of this man to one of his *colonos*. When Morales refused to give up his land, he was beaten by *Señor* Edwards' *asesinos*. If friends had not found him, he would have died."

The men around the walls growled angrily. Scuffling feet and the firming of grips on weapons told James they were within seconds of hauling Edwards to the nearest tall tree.

"Why don't you take things into your own hands?" he said. Austin gave him a startled look. Edwards' mouth dropped open. "You can just take Edwards out and hang him. You say he deserves it."

"For the love of God, James!" Austin said in consternation. He pressed on.

"No need for a trial, or even a *magistrado*. Of course,

you'll each of you have to keep a close eye on the others."

"What do you mean, *señor*?" Carlos Sarmento asked. A tall, mustachioed *vaquero*, he had come to Nacogdoches to reclaim his father's land. That his was a valid claim was evidenced to James by the facts that the land was not the best available, it had not been improved by one of Edwards' colonists, and Sarmento had resisted all efforts to buy it.

"I mean you'll know what each other has done," James said. "Even if you give it the trappings of law, you don't have the authority. You'll be the lawbreakers, then. Which of you will talk of it while drunk? Talk about how he helped hang Haden Edwards, and wasn't it a good day's work? Which of you will begin to worry and go to the authorities, turning in the rest in exchange for clemency? So watch each other. And watch your own backs, too. If somebody thinks you're about to talk . . . ." He made a motion like driving a knife home.

"We never mentioned no hanging," Peter Skelton muttered. He was a leather-skinned Georgia blacksmith whose shoulders seemed about to burst the seams of his coat. He had brought his wife and six children to Texas.

James looked at Austin, and the smaller man stepped right in. "Of course no one did. You're all law-abiding men. If anyone here attempted anything illegal, I'm sure that he would be promptly reported to the authorities."

The four leaders had lost much of their belligerence. Those against the wall looked at each other suspiciously.

"But what are we to do then, *Señor*?" Marin asked. "We cannot carry him to Saltillo for trial. It is too far."

"First you must decide whether there's reason for a trial," Austin said.

Wainwright bristled, beard shaking angrily. "Reason! He's stealing land, ain't he? He had Morales beat, didn't he?"

"Did he?" Austin said. "*Señor* Morales was attacked yesterday, you say. Haden Edwards didn't return to Nacogdoches until last night."

"It was his men," Wainwright said stolidly.

"But he couldn't have given the order."

"That's right," Edwards spoke up suddenly. "All this happened while I was on my way back from the States. You can't blame me for what men do while I'm not here."

"They are in your hire," Sarmento said ominously. Wainwright and Skelton moved closer to Edwards.

"He could've come back sooner than you think," the blacksmith rumbled.

"Then prove it," Austin said. Edwards' eyes, small in his broad face, shifted uneasily. Austin went on. "Find someone who saw him. Not someone who just wants to see him in prison, someone who actually saw him. You think he sent those men to Morales' *rancho?* Find proof. Did Morales recognize any of his attackers? Find them."

"Cuevas," Marin said. "Limón . . . ." He looked at Skelton.

"Oakes and Dunning," the big man said.

Marin nodded. "You have heard *Señor* Austin. Ask questions. Find . . . .," he hesitated again, obviously reluctant. "Find the truth." The four men they had named filed out.

"We know some names," Skelton said, "and we're looking. Hogan, Lloyd, Dickson, Altman, and Walters. We'll find them," he finished grimly.

"No unnecessary violence," Austin cautioned. "That would weaken your case." There was some grumbling from the men around the wall, but Marin and the other leaders nodded. "Mr. Edwards," Austin went on, "I'm sure you'll help as much as you're able."

"Help?" Edwards said.

"These men acted without your orders; you'll want to see them brought to justice."

Edwards answered in a sour voice. "Naturally."

"All this don't pluck no chickens," Wainwright said. "He's still trying to take everybody's land."

"Damn you," Edwards said, "I have a grant! The land is—"

"Edwards," James broke in, "why don't you be quiet and let Austin try to keep you from a lynching?"

Edwards glared about the room and subsided.

"What do you suggest, *Señor* Austin?" Marin asked.

"Submit the matter to the *jefe politico* in San Antonio, *Don* José Saucedo."

"Submit—" Edwards shouted.

"That will take months!" Marin cried.

"Shut up!" James bellowed. The entire room hushed; they all stared at him. "*Señor* Marin, you think you're in the right. Mr. Edwards, you think you are. Why not submit it to San Antonio? *Don* José has no axe to grind. Would any of you rather have the army in here?"

Austin quickly spoke into the silence. "*Señor* Marin, there are paper and pen in the writing desk. Perhaps you and the other gentlemen and you, Mr. Edwards, could set down your grievances.

Marin, muttering, removed to the far end of the room with pen and paper. Edwards glowered in his chair, making no move toward the desk. James bent closer to the broad man's ears.

"Edwards, Austin has stopped them hanging you. Don't think they won't change their minds, though, if you start dragging your heels."

"The grant is mine," Edwards growled, "but every Mexican with three friends claims part of it. You think I'll get a fair hearing before Saucedo? He's Mexican."

"You don't have much choice, unless you want to let your brother avenge you. And that doesn't appeal to me, because these men might just take it into their heads to hang Austin and me, too."

Edwards drew in a deep breath. "Damn their souls to hell. All right, Fallon. All right, damn you."

As Edwards took his seat at the writing desk, scowling, James drew Austin to a far corner of the room.

"Stephen, do you think this will work?"

Austin shrugged. "It buys peace a while longer, in any case. There is right on both sides, remember."

"I don't like Edwards, even if he did save my life. I do like Morales, and Marin and Skelton and a lot of the rest."

"So you'd side with them against Edwards? That would put your land at risk, too! You may find yourself ordered out of Mexico."

"I can't match your dispassion, Stephen. When I like people, I want to be on their side."

"Damn you, James!" Suddenly Austin's eyes were burning. His words were low but forceful. "I have a colony. Hundreds of people who depend on me. I can't put all that on the table and gamble. I won't. It might not be glorious, but compromise is the only way we can live in Mexico. The only way, James."

James grimaced. Edwards was still writing. The discussion around Marin had risen in volume. Could a man live his entire life through compromise? "Let's get a drink, Stephen. I think it's going to be a long day."

A long day proved to be an understatement. Wainwright and the others demanded to see Edwards' letter to Saucedo; when he refused, they were ready to take it from him. Austin managed to persuade everyone into allowing him to read both petitions aloud. That almost put everything back in the fire. As should have been expected, the two documents were wildly different. Edwards began shouting that the others were sending a pack of lies to Saucedo; Wainwright, among others, was ready to forget all about petitions and hang Edwards immediately. Marin, one of the more reasonable men there, wanted to burn Edwards' petition and hold him under guard until their appeal brought an answer. Once more, Austin achieved agreement: both documents would go to Saucedo, and Edwards would be allowed to choose his own messenger.

As evening approached, a crowd of Edwards' supporters began to gather across the plaza. James watched them for a time from a window, holding the curtain aside. Farmers and storekeepers, the honest folk who had bought land from Edwards, or wanted to. The smugglers and riffraff, perhaps sensing the possibility of violence, weren't in evidence. It was good that Ben Edwards hadn't shown up. That hothead would be a match in dry tinder. The crowd continued to grow, though, until it numbered over a hundred.

"God damn it," Wainwright said. It was less than an hour till full night, the street already dusky with shadows.

"If they bottle us up in here tonight, we'll be ducks down a well."

Marin nodded disconsolately. "I fear you are right, *señor*. But what are we to do with *Señor* Edwards? I do not relish trying to take him away through that crowd."

"Why take him anywhere?" Austin asked.

"You think we're fools?" Wainwright snapped. "We let him go, we ain't never going to get our hands on him again."

"Why should you need to, Mr. Wainwright? Both messengers have been away for hours. This matter will be settled by *Don* José Saucedo."

"But—" Wainwright sputtered.

James chuckled. The sound was so unexpected that everyone turned to stare at him. "You afraid he'll run off, Wainwright? So what? If he stays, the *jefe político* will decide between you, as *Señor* Austin says. If he goes, you win by default."

"I'm staying," Edwards said heavily. "No rag-tag bob-tail bunch of—"

"Easy," Austin said. "Gentlemen, as *Señor* Fallon has succinctly pointed out, you have no need to take *Señor* Edwards with you. As *Señor* Marin has suggested, you would scarcely get him away without bloodshed. Is it worth it, for no reason?"

Marin, Skelton, Sarmento and Wainwright conferred. Finally Marin turned to Edwards.

"*Señor* Edwards, we will leave you here. Do not think this means we are forgetting our charges against you. We intend to see you punished, for the beating given to Esteban Morales and for the theft of land. You will hear from us, *señor*." He bowed to Austin and James. "*Buenas noches, señores. Hasta la vista.*"

When they were gone, Edwards surged out of his chair with a bitter, nervous laugh. "Damn them. Arrest me, will they? I'll show them."

"It's all up to the authorities now," Austin cautioned.

There was a knock on the door. Edwards sidled to the window, lifting the edge of the curtain slightly. With another laugh he dropped it. "Friends. *My* friends. Stay and have a drink with us."

A full day of Edwards was already more than James could take. "Sorry. It's been a long day, and I'm tired."

"I, too," Austin added.

Edwards opened the door, quickly absorbed with the adulation of the men who crowded in. James and Austin slipped out quietly. It was a gray twilight, pierced by light from windows along the street. Laughter floated from the house they'd just left, and someone struck up a fiddle.

"Did you hear them?" James said disgustedly. "And him? They think he faced down Marin and the rest. They think he's a damned hero, and he's letting them."

Austin sighed. "Sometimes I think that when the histories are written of the settling of Texas, it's men like Edwards who'll be given all the credit. You and I will be lucky to merit a footnote."

"You want to be in the histories?"

For a moment Austin seemed to stand taller. "Only a fool sets out to be in the history books, James. But only a fool refuses the chance if it comes."

"I think you'll make more than a footnote, Stephen."

Austin laughed and shook his head. "Let's go have a friendly drink, James."

Together they headed down the street, away from the sounds of revelry.

XXXIX

"I'm going home," James said three days later. He and Austin were in the Boston Restaurant and Coffee House, at a table with a good view of the street.

"I wonder if they actually serve catfish stew in Boston." Austin sipped his coffee.

"Stephen, I'm going. Drusilla's going to have her baby any day. I shouldn't have left her alone this long."

"You're needed, James. You've already proved that. Now smoke your cigar, drink your coffee, and—"

"I damn well am not needed. The petitions are safely off to San Antonio, Edwards has stopped his land dealings altogether, and Marin and the rest are staying out of town."

The restaurant's lone waiter made his disjointed way to their table with a large tin coffee pot and refilled their cups. Austin waited until he had shambled away.

"You think they'll stay quiet, James?"

"I want to go home, Stephen."

"As soon as Edwards starts thinking about how they made him back down—that's the way he'll see it—he'll be dealing in land with a vengeance. Ben's already been mouthing off about ragamuffin squatters who should be driven out of Texas without further ado."

"I haven't seen my wife in six weeks, Stephen. She's going to have a baby."

"And what about Marin and Skelton and Wainwright?" Austin went on. "Especially Wainwright? They're still after the men who beat Morales, and if they

317

find them, and they say they got orders from the Edwardses, we'll have a small war on our hands." He laughed bitterly. "If I wasn't an educated man, sometimes I'd believe there was an evil genius manipulating events to produce chaos."

The words triggered James' thoughts. Evil. Manipulating. Cordelia Applegate. Gerard Fourrier. He couldn't see Fourrier as Austin's evil genius, but still . . . . "Stephen, what do you know about Fourrier? He's in Nacogdoches, you know."

"He has widespread business interests, or so I understand. Travels a good bit. Now, even if they don't catch Lloyd or one of the others—"

"No, what do you know about Fourrier?"

"James, I never met the man above half-a-dozen times. Why are you so interested in him?"

"I don't trust him. And I don't like the coincidence of him being here now. What kind of business could he have here? Except for the Edwardses, the only ones who think to make big money are the gamblers, and most of them won't." His chair creaked as he leaned back. "Just foolishness, I guess. I want to go home."

"Even if I believed in an evil genius, James, it wouldn't be him. I don't like the man, but he's respectable. I talked with him once about the problems of *yanquis* in Mexico, and he showed a good grasp. He's well thought of in Mexico City. Bell and others in San Felipe respect him, too. I don't know all his business interests, but those I do know are extensive. Cattle, horses, a freight line, shipping along the coast."

"Land?"

Austin shook his head. "Not that I've heard. Do you think he's involved with Edwards?"

It was James' turn to shake his head. He wasn't sure himself what he meant. "It doesn't matter, Stephen. I'm going home."

"James—" Austin broke off as José Escobar trotted in, beating dust from his clothes as he hurried to their table. He spoke swiftly.

"*Señores*, Lloyd, Walters and some of the others named

by Esteban Morales have been taken. They are on their way here under guard. I passed them only a short distance away."

"Have they implicated Edwards?" Austin asked.

James interrupted him. "Wait a minute, Stephen. There's something else, isn't there?"

Escobar's face was drawn. "*Señor* Wainwright says they will be tried."

"And I don't suppose he means to take them to Saltillo," James said.

"No, *señor*. He says they will be tried in Nacogdoches. And hung."

"What about Marin?" Austin said. "Skelton? Where are they?"

"With the others, *Señor* Austin. They do not approve, but *Señor* Wainwright has swayed many."

In the street a number of mounted men clattered past, most clutching rifles. Through their dust James caught sight of Lloyd, his face twitching with fear.

Austin scraped back his chair. "We'd better see what we can do."

"One last time," James said.

The three men headed down the street after the horsemen.

Gerard watched Haden pacing back and forth and wondered, not for the first time, if he had made a mistake in backing the man. Edwards had a cigar in one hand and a whiskey in the other, and he replaced both as needed.

"I don't understand you," Edwards growled. "Why shouldn't Saucedo decide in my favor? I'm the *empresario*, the grant holder."

"You aren't Mexican," Gerard said quietly.

Edwards mulled that over. "Damn Mexicans," the broad-faced man muttered. "Damn them all." He spun to face Gerard. "Why in hell do you want me to hold off on the land? I ought to be selling every acre I can. Damn it, if those bastards are going to throw me out, I'll God damned well take every dollar with me I can."

"If you go."

Edwards sank slowly into a chair, his eyes on Gerard's face. "All right, Fourrier. Say what's on your mind."

"Yes." Ben Edwards strode into the room. "I'd like to hear why we're letting Austin and Fallon talk us around like schoolgirls, and why we're letting a bunch of damned Mexes and poor white trash strut around like they owned everything in sight."

Gerard scowled. Ben was a foolish swaggerer, hunting for a chance to wave a sword. Once more he reconsidered his plans. But no one else was in place, as the Edwardses were, and God alone knew when another chance would come along.

"I'm still working out a number of things," he lied. "If you listen to me, though, you'll end up with more than you dream of."

Haden opened his mouth, but Ben cut him off. "Why should we listen to you? All you've done so far is sit on your ass and tell us to go along with Austin and wait. My maiden Aunt Agatha could match that."

Once his usefulness was past, Gerard thought, Ben should meet with a fatal accident. "If you start selling land again, Marin and the rest will almost certainly start fighting you. The army will come in. If you manage to get back across the Sabine without being arrested, you'll take a thousand dollars with you. Two thousand."

"And if we wait," Haden began, then, as his brother started to speak, "Shut up, Ben. If we wait, Fourrier, what do we get? I thought we'd get rich in Texas, but if we have to settle for a few thousand, that's better than sitting by and letting the Mexes take everything."

"Is it better than hundreds of thousands of dollars?" Gerard asked slyly, and watched greed light their eyes. The fools couldn't see further than a gold piece.

"How?" the elder Edwards said simply.

"That you'll have to leave to me. If you lack the courage to gamble a paltry few thousand for the chance at hundreds of thousands, now's the time to throw in your cards and run." Protest formed on their faces.

"Run!" Ben exclaimed. "I never ran from anything in my life."

Gerard hid a smile. It had been an excellent choice of words.

Haden said carefully, "I'd still like to know what these plans of yours are."

"For the time being, you'll have to settle for what I've told you already. When it's time for you to know more, I'll send word by a man named Nat Coffee."

"Coffee," Ben mused. "I've heard that name somewhere."

"He works for me at times," Gerard said. "What you must do now is delay, conciliate."

"Damn it," Ben began.

"I said conciliate," Gerard snapped. "Unless you'd rather settle for a pittance and hope you get out before you're arrested."

There was a long silence. Then Haden nodded. "We'll stay."

Gerard was careful to control his sigh of relief. "Then, as I said, the first thing is to conciliate. Let Austin be your guide on that. He knows how to get on with the Mexicans. Next, you must get as many solid citizens supporting you as possible. Men like Sterne and—"

There was a clatter of feet in the hall, and the door burst open. A beefy man stood in the doorway, wringing his hat in his hands.

"Hogan," Ben exploded, "what in hell do you mean breaking in like that? You're supposed to be laying low."

"They got 'em," Hogan said. "Got 'em all. Lloyd and the rest. I was out to the necessary was the only reason they didn't get me."

"Who has them?" Haden asked.

"Who the hell you think?" Ben said. He was checking the loads in a pair of pistols. "Marin, Skelton, that lot." Hogan nodded wordlessly.

"Are you forgetting so quickly?" Gerard said.

Ben went on with the pistols, but Haden licked his lips and nodded. "Ben, put those up. Hogan, get out of here."

"But Mr. Edwards," Hogan protested, "they brung 'em in. They holding some kind of trial right now."

"Get out," Haden said. Hogan hesitated, then hurried out, moving faster as he went. "Ben, put those guns away. We're doing this Fourrier's way. And since we are, Fourrier, what are we going to do about this trial? If Lloyd and those other scum think they're going to hang, they'll try to take me with them."

Gerard was pleased to see one of them, at least, beginning to think. "We act like gentlemen who are completely innocent. We get our hats and go see the trail of these malefactors."

Everyone was gathering to watch the trial; those who couldn't crowd inside the adobe-and-stone town hall filled the street outside. An ugly muttering started as Fourrier and the Edwardses pushed through, but mixed with it were shouts of, "You show 'em, Mr. Edwards!" "Damned squatters!" "Show 'em who's running things, Mr. Edwards!"

Inside, Marin, Skelton, Wainwright, and Sarmento sat behind a long table at the head of the room. Lloyd and the other three were on a bench in front of them, under the eyes of a dozen armed men. Fourrier was relieved to see Austin addressing the so-called court. Austin was the one man who might be able to calm the situation.

" . . . We have heard *Señor* Morales say that these men are responsible for his injuries." Austin gestured to where Morales sat, his face still puffy with yellowing bruises, one arm in a sling. "But remember that what you propose is equally illegal under the laws of Mexico."

"Let's find places near the back," Gerard said.

Ben looked around the crowded room nervously. "Won't do any good. If they turn ugly, we'll never get out."

Gerard said nothing. He found a place on a bench against the back wall and settled down to see if Austin could save his plans.

James turned to check the crowd's reaction to Austin's speech—according to Marin, the crowd would be the jury —and frowned when he saw Fourrier and the Edwardses at the back of the room. Of course, the Edwardses had a right to be there, but the mood of the crowd was uncertain. Fourrier wasn't seated with Haden and Ben, but James still had the feeling they were together.

"Let me remind you in conclusion," Austin addressed the room, "that even if you decide these men are guilty, assault is not a capital crime in any civilized country. Remember that that is what you want Texas to be, a civilized land where you can safely live and raise your families. Do nothing to taint that dream, gentlemen." He bowed and sat down beside James. A murmur of discussion rolled through the room.

"What do you think, James?" Austin asked quietly.

James shrugged. "I'm no lawyer, Stephen. You sounded convincing to me, but who can tell?"

"Damn," Austin muttered.

At the table Marin pounded with a block of wood until the noise in the room sank to foot shuffling and throat clearing. "I see that the *Señores* Edwards have come to witness our trial." Heads turned to look for them, and muttering rose again. Marin pounded harder. "Quiet! Quiet! This is a trial, *señores*, not a *cantina*. Now. Perhaps the *Señores* Edwards wish to say something to this court."

Haden and Ben looked at each other—and at Fourrier, James noted. Then Haden rose, holding his lapels like a man about to orate. "First of all, I must say that I believe these men to be innocent." An angry rumble rolled across the room. Ignoring it, he bowed slightly in the direction of Morales. "It is difficult to expect a man who has taken a savage beating to recognize the men responsible. If you believe there is in fact reason for a trial, they should be carried to Saltillo and put before the proper authorities."

"More than six hundred miles!" someone shouted.

Edwards took no notice. "Beyond that," he continued, "I am here only as an honest citizen, to see justice done." He made a short bow to the room and sat down.

There was a long moment of silence. James was surprised. No denunciation of what they were doing? Almost no defense of the men being tried? The prisoners looked disconcerted, and Walters' weasel face was beginning to look cornered, dangerous. Fourrier wore a small, satisfied smile.

Austin clutched James' sleeve. "Speak to the court. Quickly, before one of those fools names Edwards. Look at Walters. He's ready to break."

"I don't feel right," James said. "If Edwards did give the orders—"

"Damn your sensibilities, James!"

James looked to the back of the room. Fourrier was watching them with evident satisfaction. "You talk to them. You're the lawyer."

"It wouldn't have the effect. Quickly, man."

Reluctantly, James stood. Marin looked at him in surprise, and rapped his improvised gavel. "You wish to speak, *Señor* Fallon?"

"I do, *Señor* Marin."

"We going to listen to everybody in Texas?" Wainwright burst out. He scraped his chair back and rose, shaking his fist. "Let's get on with what we come here for. Hanging."

There was a roar of approval. Marin pounded furiously. "We are a court, *señores*," he shouted. "Not a mob. Sit down, *Señor* Wainwright. We will listen to *Señor* Fallon."

While the room settled down once more, James looked at Fourrier, leaning forward intently, and Walters, eyes darting for a way to escape, then brought his eyes back to the men at the table.

"We've heard a lot of talk," he said. "Most have told us these men are worthless animals. A few have said they are sterling citizens, and this is all a mistake." There was an ugly mutter at that. He ignored it. "Stephen Austin asked you to be civilized. Well, I don't know how civilized Texas is, and I believe these men are guilty as hell." He glanced at Fourrier. He was pleased to see the man's satisfaction had slipped. "The question is, what do we do about it?"

"Hang them!" Wainwright shouted.

"That's one way," James said quickly. "Maybe they even deserve it. But we'd better think of the consequences before we do. We don't have a shred of legal authority, and sooner or later we'll be called to account." The only sound in the room was their breathing. He had their attention now. "If we act in some accordance with Mexican law, we'll be all right. Maybe. If we don't, we'll be considered as much criminals as Walters and the rest. Maybe we can keep the authorities from finding out who did the hanging. Maybe. But even if we do, Nacogdoches will be marked. A trouble spot. A nest of criminals. General Arredondo ordered this town abandoned more than a decade ago. How many of you doubt President Victoria will do the same? Some things the government might overlook, but not this. Not hanging." He waited, then. The noise level rose, everyone loudly discussing what he'd said. He couldn't tell whether Austin or Fourrier was looking more satisfied. If only Stephen weren't so obviously right about the effect of hanging these men . . . .

Skelton asked the question James had been waiting for. "Damn it, Fallon, what in hell are we supposed to do with them? We can't just turn them loose." A roar of agreement punctuated his sentence.

"You could always take them to Saltillo, the way the law calls for," he said casually, knowing they could not. The trip would take a month, let alone time waiting to testify, and none there could afford so long away from families and farms.

"You know we cannot, señor," Marin said.

"Then exile them. Chase them out of Texas, with a promise of hanging if they return. That way, at least, you can tell the authorities you made every effort to handle the situation without violence."

"This makes sense, señor." Wainwright opened his mouth, but Marin rapped the block of wood. "Enough of talk, Señor Wainwright. Will you sit down, Señor Fallon?" He looked up and down the table as James resumed his place next to Austin. "Do we ask for a verdict? I say, yes."

"Aye," said Skelton. Sarmento echoed, "Sí."

Wainwright eyed the room doubtfully, then nodded with obvious reluctance. "All right. I don't suppose it matters much what I say, anyway."

Austin whispered. "Pray God not."

"So!" Marin took a deep breath and met James' eye. They nodded at each other. "Who finds these men *culpable?*"

The room erupted, men clambering to their feet. "Guilty!" *"Culpable!"* "Guilty!" Wainwright leaped up, screaming, "Hang 'em!" Lloyd, Walters, and the other accused seemed to shrink in their chairs. The guards standing over them were shouting as loud as the rest.

"Now, *señores*, we must decide on a sentence." Someone muttered, and someone else coughed, but otherwise there was silence. Marin looked at the other judges, and they nodded, although Wainwright did so angrily. "I will ask for a show of hands, *señores*. All those in favor of hanging."

Wainwright jumped to his feet again. "Hang 'em! Hang 'em!" Half a dozen men yelled their agreement, but when they realized how few they were, they fell silent, leaving Wainwright alone. "Hang 'em! Damn you, don't you figure they deserve to hang? It ain't their fault Morales ain't dead!"

Silence answered him.

Skelton sat back and wiped his face with a kerchief. Marin heaved a sigh and hurried to get his next words out. "Exile. How many for exile?"

For a moment no one moved. Then grudgingly a hand went up, and another, until two thirds of the men had their arms up. None looked pleased. Some stared at their feet; all avoided their neighbors' eyes. The Edwardses had slipped out as the vote began. Fourrier was still there, though, his face unreadable.

"Let the prisoners face the bench," Marin said. Under the watchful eyes of the guards the six men rose. Marin looked at the other judges; Sarmento and Skelton nodded, although Wainwright shook his head. Marin faced the prisoners. "You have been found guilty. You deserve death." Walters opened his mouth. Lloyd poked him in the side, and he shut it again. "Despite this," Marin continued, "you will live. You will live, but you will never again foul Mexico with your presence. You will leave

Nacogdoches today, and if you are ever found again in Mexico, we will hang you. Now, *mis amigos*, let us escort these animals out of town.''

Walters and the others were inundated by the crowd, disappearing under a roaring rush. They appeared again, lifted overhead, struggling uselessly, and were borne toward the door.

''Wainwright was right about one thing,'' James said to Austin. ''They'd just as soon have killed Morales.''

''We'd better make sure they get out of town safely,'' Austin replied. ''Tempers are running pretty high.''

''You aren't listening, Stephen. Well, you go. I'm going home.''

''James—''

''My wife needs me, Stephen.'' They had followed the pack outside. The prisoners were being loaded on horses with much shouting. James turned away from them, up the street.

''Damn it, James!'' Austin called after him. Behind Austin, Marin and the others had mounted, clustered around the prisoners. He hesitated, staring at James, then turned and hurried for his horse.

James kept on walking. Behind him, they pounded out of town. Let Austin look after Texas. It was too devious for him. He was going to look after his family. He smiled, and his step quickened.

XXXX

Five days after leaving Nacogdoches James and José rode
up on the *rancho*. The cabins were finished, and so were
the *barracón* and the log-and-sod barn. Above the main
cabin a watch tower poked through the plum and pecan
trees. Henry came pounding to meet them, leading a rush
of *vaqueros*.

"James! Damn, it's good to see you back. José, you old
chicken thief, you been whooping it up in Nacogdoches?
Whiskey, women, and cards, eh?"

"Not exactly, *señor*," José grinned.

James eyed the cabin. There was no sign of Drusilla.
"How's Drusilla? The baby showing any signs of coming?"

Henry slapped his forehead. "My God, 'course you
wouldn't know. You been a daddy a week, now."

James gave a whoop, leaped down and ran inside.
"Drusilla! *Querida*, I'm home!"

She was in the big front room they called the parlor.
Consuela had a swaddled bundle in her arms, and Drusilla
was fastening the front of her dress. She didn't rise, and
her face and voice were cool. "I see that you are, my husband. You may take Amelinda, Consuela."

James grabbed the maid's arm. "Let me see." He
twitched the blanket aside, grinning. Large brown eyes
peered back at him out of a chubby face. "A pretty
name."

"My mother's name," Drusilla said. "You were not
here. I had to choose without you."

The maid sniffed loudly, replaced the blanket, and marched out. Drusilla rose and stood before the long stone fireplace.

"I said it was a pretty name," he said quietly. She didn't speak. "Drusilla, there were reasons I had to stay—"

"Reasons!" she spat. *"Madre de Dios!"*

"There was trouble, Drusilla. I had to—"

"Ah, trouble. I begged you not to go, but you went. You promised to return in two weeks, but you did not."

"I wrote you every week. I explained—"

"You explained!"

"Damn it, woman," he shouted, "let me get a word in edgeways."

"Now you raise your voice to me. You go off on *la aventure grande* with your friend *Señor* Austin, break your promise, and now you shout at me."

He took a deep breath. It was hard to argue when the other side had some justice. "Drusilla, if Nacogdoches had gone wrong, we might have lost everything."

"And this *calamidad* has been avoided?"

"For the time." He felt a twinge, then, at leaving Austin. It was far from certain that anything had been settled.

She raised one eyebrow. "For the time only? And yet you leave to return home?"

"I'd put off my promise to you too long," he replied, and cursed the moment the words were out.

She simply nodded. *"Es asi.* But you are too late. Perhaps now you will return to your friends and your very important business in Nacogdoches?"

"No." He drew her into his arms. She was rigid, her eyes expressionless. *"Querida,* let's not argue. I'm sorry about staying away so long. I didn't mean to worry you. I won't let it happen again." He tried to kiss her, but she turned her head.

"I am *fatigado,* my husband."

His arms fell away. She stood stiffly with her head still turned, not looking at him. After a moment he went out. The *vaqueros* were dispersing. Henry and José looked up

from their conversation when he stepped onto the porch.
Leonie watched from her cabin door, young Denmark
straddling her hip.

"Does either of you have a bottle?" James asked.

They glanced at each other, then nodded understand-
ingly. Without a word, the three of them headed for José's
cabin.

James continued to live in the big cabin, but he slept on
a pallet in front of the parlor fireplace. When Drusilla
didn't have headaches, she had the vapors, or delicately-
referred-to female complaints. Sometimes he wondered
why he remained.

Amelinda was one reason. Aside from the wonder of
knowing he had a baby girl, he enjoyed holding her chubby infant in his arms, trying to bring a smile to her
usually serious mien. Not even Consuela remaining nearby, watching him as if she suspected he might harm the
child, could detract from the pleasure of the baby's gur-
gling.

Drusilla never tried to keep the baby from him, but she
always left the room when he took his daughter into his
chair. At first he made efforts to break through her silence
and coldness, but she ignored his overtures. Slowly his attempts stopped. Conversation between them dwindled to
the minimum necessary for occupying the same house. Except for the time he spent with Amelinda, he began to
spend as few waking hours as possible in the cabin. He ate
with the men and threw himself into work.

That was the second reason he remained. The *rancho*
was his dream, and he couldn't abandon it. A spring
house had to be built, a cistern dug on the hill and lined
with stone, corrals erected for the mares, and the new foals
and yearlings. One day he envisioned herds roaming his
acres, but that was for the future, when he had more
horses, and the men needed to work them. There were already cattle grazing his grass. At great effort he and the
men gathered three hundred head, slab-sided, needle-
horned, wild as buffalo and mean as pumas. Calves were
removed as soon as they could be weaned in the hopes they

would grow gentler away from their wild parents. Hay had to be made, the last sweet mesquite grass of fall, dried as it stood. Wolves, coyotes, the occasional bear or puma had to be kept from the stock. Hunting for the table. Clearing waterholes. Into the saddle long before the sun rose, climbing wearily down hours into the night. James lost himself in it.

Gerard Fourrier bowed pleasantly to a couple in slightly worn finery as they danced past. The *hacienda* reverberated to the music of guitars and violins. Bell, he thought the man's name was, and his fat wife. Not the sort of people he would normally ask to a Christmas ball. Only Jared Groce and Stephen Austin, among those present, were his sort. But the entire affair had been arranged to assure Austin's presence. He bowed and smiled his way into the hall, and went to the study. There he found Austin with a knot of men in front of the fireplace, drinks in hand, refugees from wives and dancing.

"Wonderful get-together, Mr. Fourrier," Jared Groce said as the circle widened to make a place for him. The broad-faced man wore a scarlet Mexican sash with his dark gray broadcloth coat.

"I thank you, Mr. Groce. My pleasure to have you. If you'll forgive me, I came to take Mr. Austin away for a few minutes. Business, you understand." There was a murmur of sympathetic understanding.

Austin wore the shabbiest coat there, and his face reminded Fourrier of an ascetic Renaissance monk. No one who didn't know would take him for the *empresario* of a successful colony. Fourrier himself was in a short Mexican jacket and black *banda*, as always of the finest cut possible.

Austin followed him out to the rear of the entry hall with a slightly puzzled expression.

"You spoke of business, Mr. Fourrier?" Austin said quietly. "I don't believe we have any."

Fourrier opened the door leading back to the servants' quarters. The undecorated hall on the other side was empty. "In a way we have, Mr. Austin. Nacogdoches." Austin's face was unreadable, but he fancied he knew what was going on behind that prominent forehead.

"If you'll forgive a blunt question, Mr. Fourrier, what exactly is your connection with Nacogdoches? More specifically, with the Edwards brothers?"

"So far as the general public is concerned, Mr. Austin, there is no connection."

"And so far as the general public is not concerned?"

Fourrier smiled ruefully. "Strictly between the two of us, I'm one of their principal backers. I trust that will go no further."

In truth, Fourrier had put not one penny more into the Edwards' land deals than he had to. But he needed Austin's belief, and his silence, for safety.

"Very well, Mr. Fourrier," Austin said at last. "But I find it strange that you want to hide your involvement."

"Come, Mr. Austin. It's no secret that Haden Edwards and his brother may get all of us thrown out of Mexico. Hardly the sort of thing one wants to be known for."

"In Nacogdoches, you didn't seem concerned."

Fourrier shook his head sadly. "Haden's a foolish man in some ways, Mr. Austin, but occasionally he will listen to me. When he's opposed publicly, though, he seems to take great delight in digging his heels in."

"Doesn't sound like an ideal partner," Austin said drily.

"At the time, you were the only other *empresario* in Texas, and you weren't looking for investors."

"What is it you want, Mr. Fourrier?"

"The one man beside myself who Haden will listen to seems to be you. I'd like you to continue your interest." He hid his satisfaction at Austin's surprise. The man was almost hooked.

"I'd do that in any case."

"I'm sure you would, Mr. Austin. But there's one other thing. You know many men in the Mexican government. If you could speak to them, urge them to go slowly, it would gain us time to talk sense into the Edwardses."

"I've written to my friends already. Have you?"

Fourrier nodded. He had, in carefully worded terms. "Then we'll do our best, between us. You on the outside, and I on the inside.''

''Why are you doing this, Mr. Fourrier? If you'll forgive me, you don't strike me as an altruistic man.''

''No,'' Fourrier laughed. ''Pure greed. If Edwards gets us all thrown out, I'll lose a great deal.'' He saw that he had worded it properly. Distaste mixed with belief on Austin's face.

''Very well, Mr. Fourrier. And now, if you'll excuse me . . . .'' He bowed stiffly and went back into the front hall.

Fourrier watched him go with mixed feelings. It had all worked out as he wanted, but it galled him to know he had lost the respect of one of the few men in Texas he considered of his own class.

''What are you planning now, Gerard?''

He jumped in spite of himself. Lucille stood behind him, eyeing him speculatively. ''How long have you been listening? And what are you doing back there anyway? You should be out with our guests.''

Her sensuous mouth twisted. ''Bumpkins and *canaille*. I wondered why you invited such. Now I know. It was to have this *tête-à-tête* with Austin, was it not? What is it you are plotting?''

''You still haven't told me why you were back there, Lucille.''

Her eyes shifted. ''I told you. I was—''

A *vaquero* stepped into the passage behind her, hat in hand, eyed her uncertainly, and bowed to Gerard. ''*Dispense me, por favor, Don* Gerard.''

''You'd better see to our guests, Lucille,'' Gerard said. She made a sarcastically deep curtsey to him and swept away. He waited until she was well out of earshot before speaking. ''What is it, Pedro?''

''The man Coffee is in the stable, *Don* Gerard.''

Fourrier grunted. Coffee had been delivering a shipment of guns to Sterne's store in Nacogdoches. It was important none of his guests saw the man. He pushed angrily past the *vaquero*.

A light snowfall had powdered the courtyard; Gerard made black footprints across it. Music from the house followed him. He opened the stable door.

"Coffee! Where in hell are you?" The darkness smelled of dry hay and horse manure.

"Here." The fat man stepped out of a stall ten feet away. His buckskins were stained and patched. "Wait a minute. I'll light a lamp."

"Don't. I don't want anyone coming out here and seeing you. Why aren't you delivering those muskets to Adolphus Sterne?"

"Don't worry. The Jew'll get the guns." Coffee stepped closer. Starlight picked out a flattened nose and scars above piggy eyes that belied the softness of his round face.

"You were supposed to see to it yourself. Where are the guns?"

"In bales of drygoods, on their way to Nacogdoches. Pretty good, eh?" Coffee leered, revealing three missing teeth on the right side. "I knew you wanted me, so I come as quick as I could."

Fourrier sighed. The man was bone stupid, but he did have uses. "When I tell you to do something, Coffee, you do it exactly the way I tell you. Understand?"

"Sure. But you said I was supposed to get here—"

"Oh, shut up!" He took a deep breath. "I believe you know some of the Cherokee chiefs."

"Yeah. Bowl, and Big Mush, and a couple small ones."

"Good." He had known the names before he asked the question. "I'll give you a letter to deliver to Haden Edwards. Don't mention it to anyone else, and deliver it sealed."

"Can't read anyways," Coffee laughed.

"Deliver it sealed." It would only identify Coffee as the man he and Edwards had spoken of, but it was still a connection between them. Edwards had instructions to burn all their correspondence. "Then you'll guide Ben Edwards north and introduce him to Bowl and the rest."

Coffee scratched his neck. "What's all this about, eh? You figuring on selling guns to them Cherokee?"

"Are you satisfied with my gold, Coffee?" he asked quietly. "Or would you rather go back to smuggling on your own?"

"I ain't never got caught," Coffee said defensively.

"And you never made a tenth of what I'm paying you."
The fat man shrugged. "I'm satisfied. Never said I weren't."

"Then take your money and do what you're told. Without unnecessary questions."

"Yes, sir," Coffee mumbled. "You got a fire in there? Maybe a little rum? It's cold as a witch's tit out here."

"Burrow in the straw. You appeared when you won't supposed to; you have to live with the consequences." Coffee began to protest, but Fourrier turned his back and shut the stable door.

It was all prepared. If everything fell apart, Austin and those 'friends' in Saltillo would testify that he had been a moderating force. But if his plans succeeded, he would make tracks across Texas as plain as his footprints in the snowy courtyard. It had been a wise decision to remain in Mexico. A land waiting to be shaped in his image. And he would shape it.

Whistling tunelessly, he started back to the *hacienda*.

XXXXI

James rode toward the hill thinking of all the work to be done. The last snow was three weeks gone from the ground, thank God, but twenty-three calves and nine foals had died during the winter, and they would be lucky not to double those losses before spring was on them good. He still wore his heavy wool coat and wool mittens with the trigger finger separate.

He noticed the man in the watchtower peering toward the creek, behind him, and looked over his shoulder. A mass of Comanche burst from the trees, screaming and waving lances as they galloped for the cabins.

The watchman began to beat the piece of sheet iron that served as an alarm.

Jerking his rifle from the saddle scabbard, James dug his heels into his horse and bent low over the saddle. Behind him the cries of the Indians came closer. Ahead he could see men rushing to their prearranged positions, shutters slamming shut on the cabins, muskets appearing at loopholes. Smoke blossomed from the watchtower, followed an instant later by the hollow boom of a musket. And then he was up the hill and among the cabins. Gunfire crackled in the crisp air.

Grabbing the pistol holsters from in front of his saddle, he dropped to the ground in front of his cabin. He prayed Drusilla was safely inside.

A squat Comanche, bare-chested, face daubed with black and topped by a fur cap, couched a long lance and kicked his horse forward at him. He threw his rifle to his

336

shoulder and fired the right-hand barrel. The Indian jerked on his saddle pad but came on. James threw himself aside, tucked a shoulder under and rolled to his feet. A second Comanche, his chest covered with red hand-prints, was almost on him. A fifty-caliber ball from the left-hand barrel rolled him over his horse's rump.

James dropped the rifle as the Indian was falling, pulled one of his pistols, and whirled to face the first Comanche, who was pulling his horse around for another try. Blood flowed down his chest from James' first barrel. A shot from the cabin plucked his fur cap off; he kicked his horse forward again. Even as James raised his pistol, he knew he wouldn't make it. Suddenly the Comanche stiffened, more blood pouring from a second hole in his chest, and toppled from his horse. Henry stepped around the corner of the cabin.

"Thanks!" James called, darting for the cabin door. "Drusilla!"

Henry grabbed his arm. "No! They're after the horses. The west corral."

A quick look around showed only the two dead Comanche. The attack on the cabins had been a feint. "How many men outside?"

"Maybe six," Henry said.

James raised his voice. "Everyone inside, stay inside! Keep your eyes open! Everyone outside, follow me!" He set out in a shambling run, awkwardly reloading his rifle as he went. Half a dozen *vaqueros*, showing wounds, fell in behind him and Henry.

Around the corral a score of Comanche were tearing at the split rails. James silently thanked God River Wind was in the barn. He led his men down the hill at a dead run. One of the Comanche spotted them and yelled.

"Spread out and lie down!" James ordered. "Down! And hold your fire!" The Comanche whirled toward them as they fanned out and dropped. James checked his priming. Some warriors held lances. Arrows arched up from others. A *vaquero* named Higuera grunted and clutched his thigh, now sporting a feathered shaft, then twisted back to his rifle, his dark face contorted with pain. The

Comanche were two hundred yards away, then a hundred, the ground drumming beneath their hooves. "Fire!" James shouted, and squeezed the trigger.

The other guns cracked in a ragged salvo. Four horses were abruptly riderless. "Fire!" he shouted again, and again a volley rang out. Three more Comanche dropped to the prairie.

Then the Comanche were among the men on the ground. James rolled aside from a lance thrust and pistoled the rider as he went by. Another left his horse in a low dive, slashing at him with a knife. The blade dug into his arm; he succeeded in grabbing the wiry Comanche's wrist. The Indian clawed at him with his free hand. The Comanche's smelled of stale sweat, grease and horse. They kneed at each other; the Comanche sank his teeth into James' shoulder.

James fumbled at his belt for the knife Bowie had given him so many years before. As he pulled it free, the other man grabbed his wrist. They lay locked chest to chest, feet scrabbling for leverage. The Comanche's black, hate-filled eyes stared into his. Inch by inch the Indian forced the blade closer to James' throat. The point dug in; he felt blood running down his chest. With his last ounce of strength he forced himself up, put his weight behind his blade, felt it socket home in the Comanche's ribs. The dark eyes took on a surprised look and faded to filmy sightlessness.

Breathing hard, James rolled off the dead man, hunting for his pistols. But the Comanche were retreating. They had suffered; every survivor had at least one wound. Higuera plucked weakly at the lance that pinned him to the hard prairie, then breath rattled out of him and he lay staring at the sky.

"They'll try again," Henry panted. Blood ran down his face from a gash across his forehead. His coat had been torn off, and another slash darkened his shirt. "They want them horses." He turned at a scream from atop the hill. Gunfire sounded again from the crest. A column of smoke rose from the trees.

James took up a staggering run. He found he had the

knife in one hand, a pistol in the other. He didn't know if it was loaded. There was no time to check. He was sure that scream was Drusilla's. His throat was choked as he ran.

At last he reached the top of the hill. The roof of José's cabin was aflame. A pair of Comanche darted from in front of the barn and scrambled onto their horses. A volley from the men following James dropped one; the other galloped down the hill.

James barely noticed. Two Indian ponies stood riderless in front of his cabin, and the door was wide open.

"Drusilla!" he screamed as he ran inside. Alfredo Clemente, a lanky *vaquero*, sat in the hall, clutching his belly with both hands. Blood leaked through his fingers. He looked up weakly as James came in shouting, "Drusilla!"

A comanche appeared at the far end of the hall. James fired from the waist, the heavy ball taking the Indian in the face. Before the man hit the floor, another came screaming out of the parlor, chest smeared with someone else's blood, knife in hand. There were scratches down his cheeks, as if he had been clawed.

"Drusilla!" James screamed again, and pulled the trigger. Nothing happened. He used the empty pistol to beat aside the Comanche's thrust, slashed at him, screaming with rage.

The Indian dodged aside, but James followed him, roaring, hacking without any thought of defense. Drusilla was dead, and this man had killed her. He took a cut across the chest, another down his ribs, but then one of his enraged swings caught the Comanche's throat, half severing his head. He caught the man by the hair as he fell, slamming him against the wall, driving his blade again and again into the dirty chest.

Arms surrounded him, pulled him away. He struggled until his head cleared enough to see it was Henry. "He's dead, James. He's dead."

James drew a shuddering breath. "So's Drusilla."

Shrugging free of a shocked Henry, he walked slowly into the parlor. She was there, lying face down, legs ex-

posed by her torn dress. Tears ran unheeded down his
cheeks as he dropped to his knees beside her. Almost hesitantly he picked her up. She had been lying across Amelinda; the baby still lived. Drusilla's eyes opened.

"You're alive," he gasped. Sobs welled up in him, and
he couldn't stop them.

"He wanted—" she said quaveringly. "He tried to—"
She buried her face against his chest, weeping.

"You're alive." He rocked back and forth, hugging
her. "Thank God. You're alive."

"I saw you go," she murmured into his shirt. "I wanted
to help you, so I went outside, and they . . . I am sorry,
my husband."

"It doesn't matter, *querida*. You're alive. That's all
that matters." She sighed and settled deeper into his
arms. For a moment he was content merely to stroke her
hair. Then he gently disengaged. "I have to go, *querida*."
Henry cleared his throat behind him, and he looked over
his shoulder. "Henry, you'd better go look after Leonie.
Then we'll get ready in case they come again."

"Leonie's all right," Henry said. "She's outside. And I
don't think they be coming back. They cleaned out the
west corral and run off to the north. Killed the foals."

"Damn! Who's hurt?"

Henry's face turned grim. "Higuera's dead. I don't
know about Clemente. José's looking after him and
Consuela now. Most everybody got some cuts. You ought
to get him to look at you, too."

Drusilla saw that James was bleeding. She pushed herself up and began calmly ripping strips from her already
demolished dress to bind his wounds. "What happened to
Consuela, *Señor* Cameron?"

Henry avoided her gaze. "Well, ma'am, she . . . I
mean, that Comanche . . . that is, he had his way with
her."

"*Pobrecita.* I must go to her, James. Your
wounds . . . ." She suddenly hugged him tightly. "Forgive me, *mi querida*, but your wounds are not so serious as
hers."

He caught her hand as she stood. "Drusilla, I don't

want to lose you. Not again.''

She smiled and caressed his cheek. "You will never lose me, *mi corazon.*"

His heart lifted. He got to his feet with renewed energy. "Come on, Henry. We have a lot to do."

By evening there were two graves on the south end of the hill. Clemente had lingered two hours before joining Higuera. Consuela was in her bed, with Drusilla, and to James' surprise, Leonie, in attendance. There was no question of trying to retrieve the stolen horses. Only José and the others who had been inside were in any shape to make a pursuit. José's cabin had burned to the ground, but he had been in the barn. They repaired the corral and marked trees to rebuild José's cabin. James was thankful they hadn't tried for the corral on the creekside as well.

As the sun touched the horizon—suitably blood red, James thought—the alarm was sounded again. Everyone hurried to barricade themselves, guns in hand, but the men who rode in from the south weren't Indians. James went outside as Jared Groce dismounted in front of the cabin. There were twenty men with him, all armed.

Groce eyed the still smouldering ruins of José's cabin. "Had some trouble, James?" He wore a broad-brimmed hat and a Mexican sash with his fringed buckskin coat.

"Comanche. Killed two men and ran off about a hundred head of horses. But what are you doing up here? Haden Edwards isn't acting up again, is he?"

"Not exactly. This is what we call a ranging company. We have Indian troubles down our way, too." Drusilla came out of the cabin; he swept off his hat in a courtly bow. "*Señora* Fallon. You are as beautiful as ever."

Drusilla's face and dress were smudged with soot and dirt, but she dropped a perfect curtsey. "*Gracias, Señor* Groce. Will you come inside? I fear we are somewhat disarranged, but I can offer you wine. Or perhaps hot tea? And perhaps something for your men?"

"I thank you, ma'am," Groce said. "And for my men. As for me, I must talk to your husband first. Company, dismount!"

"Come on down to the cistern," James told Groce as

the men climbed down. "We can have a drink of cool water while we talk." He led the way, drew up a bucket and offered Groce the ladle. "This ranging company of yours looks like a small army."

Groce drank and handed the ladle back. "Don't even suggest it. Governor Blanco's nervous enough about them as it is. We have to have them, but Austin insists we keep it as informal as possible."

"Jared, you're not after Indians this far north of San Felipe. So what is it you want to talk about?"

"Austin wants you to come down to San Felipe."

"After this?" James' gesture included the burned-out cabin.

Groce nodded. "I understand. I suppose Austin will, too."

"He has to. And if Edwards isn't acting up—"

"I said he isn't exactly acting up. Saucedo rejected his petition. Found in favor of Morales and ordered Edwards to favor the claims of citizens of Mexico over those of colonists."

James whistled between his teeth. "And how is Edwards taking that?"

"Not well. Austin finally got him to agree to appeal to *Don* Victor Blanco, though."

"Stephen thinks the governor'll overrule Saucedo? Haden Edwards will wake up Mexican first."

"James, he's playing for time. He needs you to help talk sense into Edwards. When Blanco upholds Saucedo, Edwards had better be ready to live with it, or all hell is going to break loose."

"Austin could get him to petition President Victoria."

Groce snorted. "You know better than that. Guadalupe Victoria won't take kindly to somebody trying to go over a governor's head. That's if Edwards would hold still for it."

"What else can he do?" James shook his head. "Stephen can handle this without me. My wife and baby almost died today, Jared. Now come on up to the house. Drusilla will appreciate the company."

Groce stayed for two days, trying to convince James to ride south, but James always changed the subject to chess, or the latest news of the Greek revolution against the Turks, or the use of the ranging companies. In the end Groce left, taking his company back south.

Life at the *rancho* returned as much as possible to normal. James rode sweeps with Henry watching for Indian sign, but they found nothing. In a month James felt confident enough to take José and four *vaqueros* west of Crossed Timbers after mustangs to replace what the Comanche had taken. Late in the spring he took Drusilla and Amelinda to *Don* Tomás' *rancho*. The old man spent long hours playing with his granddaughter. James found, to Drusilla's amusement, that at fourteen, Elena was twice as flirtatious as she had been. She stayed constantly in his company, embroidered two shirts for him, and gave him a sash of scarlet silk on the day they left. *Don* Tomás commanded him to visit again soon, and bring him more grandchildren.

The summer was a busy time, adding to the cabins, buying horses from the Cherokee to the east, selling his first thirty two-year-olds to the Mexican Army. Occasional visitors brought news of the outside world. General Teran had proposed stationing garrisons across Texas. The Creek Indians had finally agreed to give up their lands in Georgia. An ominous rumor circulated that Governor Blanco not only intended to reject Haden Edwards' petition, but to revoke his grant. Austin sent an urgent message for James to come to San Felipe. James refused, but as he looked at the little community of the *rancho*, he couldn't help feeling a chill despite the August sun.

"The Comanche are angry, *moza*," the old woman said. "Bear Paw wants his horses."

Lucille knelt naked in the dust of the hovel, her skin shiny with sweat in the August heat. Feathers of smoke rose, some failing to find their way through the smokehole, adding to the gloom. The old woman sat in her battered chair, drinking from her cracked cup. The leathery face was impassive.

Lucille made her tone soft. "*Mi dueña*, Bear Paw has not done what we agreed. James Fallon still lives. Bear Paw has not earned the horses.''

"You concern yourself too much with this, *moza*. You do not progress as I thought you would. Perhaps you are not as suited as I thought you were.''

Lucille licked lips suddenly dry. For all the times the old woman had chastened her about concern with 'this world,' she had never considered that it might endanger her apprenticeship. She couldn't lose that. But she couldn't lose Fallon, either. "I try very hard, *mi dueña*. It is just that so long as James Fallon lives, it is very hard for me. Thoughts of him distract me when I should be concentrating on the world of the spirits. Perhaps you could persuade Bear Paw to try again. You could give him charms for his men, to ward off bullets.''

"No! This affair is yours, *moza*. If you wish to change Bear Paw's mind, you must find the means yourself. But he lost men, and he says there are more *vaqueros* and more guns at the *rancho*, now. Changing his mind will not be easy. Go, *moza*. Your talk tires me.''

Lucille struggled into her clothes, barely noticing the smudges of dirt and smoke on her pale green silk dress. What more could she offer Bear Paw? There was a limit to how many horses she could give without Gerard discovering what she was doing. And he would stop her if he thought it would interfere with his own plans. What could they be?

"Remember your debts, *moza*," the old woman said as she turned to go.

She looked back, frowning. "Debts?"

"I have passed your messages to Bear Paw, *moza*. What else happens is no concern of mine. When the man Fourrier puts a girl child in your belly, she is mine.''

"Of course.'' She shuddered at the thought of making her body misshapen with Gerard's child. The old woman's raven eyes seemed amused at her reaction.

"And then there is the Comanche, *moza*.''

"Bear Paw? He will get his horses when James Fallon is dead.''

"No, no, no.'' The crone cackled shrilly. "In his eyes he has carried out his part of the bargain. If you do not carry out yours, he will leave nothing but ashes and bone where your fine *hacienda* now stands.''

Lucille swallowed. ''Bear Paw will get his horses. But he must kill Fallon.'' The old woman shrugged and sipped her tea. Muttering to herself, Lucille left.

She pulled her shawl over her head to shield her from the sun and hurried through the *chapparal*. Damn that fool Indian, she thought. There had to be some way to get him to face Fallon's guns. Suddenly she stopped dead. Gerard was expecting Coffee. Coffee, who was both stupid and venal. Coffee, who smuggled the guns Gerard didn't think she knew about. A few hundred dollars to Coffee, and a hundred muskets would put courage into Bear Paw. Smiling, she continued toward the *hacienda*.

XLII

Montaigne, James reflected, was the only reading a man really needed. He was enjoying a pipe and a read in front of the fire after a long day in the saddle. It was New Year's Eve, the last night of 1826, and tomorrow they would do as they had done Christmas, and work only half a day. Unless the snow ceased threatening and fell. In that case, the day would be spent seeing to the cattle and horses.

"You may take a day of rest, my husband," Drusilla said from where she stood by the fireplace with a pot lid in one hand, "but Leonie, Consuela, and I will work as always." He looked up from his book in surprise, and she laughed. "It is a gift given to women, *querida*, to read their husbands' minds."

"You'd better watch you don't get burned for a witch," he muttered, settling in his chair and looking for his place.

"Will you fetch me a pail of water, James? If this meal is to be ready tomorrow, we must work tonight."

With a sigh he marked his place and set the book down. As he left the room Consuela came in, shrinking aside to let him pass. It had taken her a month to get out of bed after the Comanche attack and the rape. Since then she had not looked a man in the eyes. He shrugged into his heavy wool coat, wrapped a muffler around his neck and got his rifle and a wooden pail.

Outside, his breath was icy white mist. The sky was cloudless black velvet, the stars thousands of sharp pinpricks of

346

light. He took a step and stopped. A horse was coming slowly up the hill, hooves thudding on frozen ground. The *vaqueros* would be in the bunkhouse, their horses in the corral behind the barn. He used the corner of his coat to muffle the sound of thumbing the hammers back.

A hoarse shout drifted up the hill. "Hello the house!" He could make out the rider, now, hunched in the saddle. "Hello the house!"

Suddenly he recognized the voice. "Jared?" He dropped the pail and hurried forward to catch Groce as he slid from his horse.

"James?" Beneath his hat Groce's face was drawn with exhaustion. "James, it's damned cold out here."

James half carried him inside. After one look Drusilla bustled for blankets and a hot brick for his feet, while James poured them each a whiskey. "Jared, what in hell are you doing here? You must have left San Felipe before Christmas, for God's sake."

Groce downed his drink and held out his glass for another. "You haven't heard? It's been . . . God, two weeks, now. Hell's broke loose in Texas."

James met Drusilla's eyes. Her face was pale. "Edwards?" he asked.

Groce nodded. "Blanco refused his petition. Haden and his brother have been ordered out of Mexico."

"I heard rumors." He couldn't look at Drusilla again. They were going to lose everything. "What about the rest of us?"

"Safe, for the moment."

"If we're safe," James said, "why did you spend Christmas in the saddle?"

"Two weeks ago that fool Ben proclaimed independence."

"Independence!" James shouted. Drusilla covered her mouth with her hands.

"That's right. The Republic of Fredonia, they call it. God alone knows what they're claiming. All of Texas, maybe. Anyway, once Ben made his move, Haden supported him."

James began to pace in front of the fireplace. "They're

insane. The Mexicans will send an army for sure. And not a damned lot of farmers, either. These—Fredonians, did you say?—will be cut to pieces. Unless . . . . They expect Austin's people to join them, don't they? And maybe reinforcements from the States?"

Groce nodded. "And more than a few say we should. All this title business has scared them. They think if we all throw in, we can beat the Mexicans."

"Oh, James," Drusilla said. "You cannot . . . you must not . . . ." Consuela had produced a rosary and was telling her beads, muttering her prayers.

"I won't," James replied. "And I assume Austin isn't of that mind. But how can we keep from being thrown out no matter what we do?"

"Austin thinks by demonstrating quickly that we support the legal government. He sent riders off to Saltillo and Mexico City as soon as he heard, reporting what had happened and offering support."

"That doesn't explain why you rode all this way, Jared. And at Christmas."

"We need you," Groce replied slowly. "I know you don't like leaving for long, but if we're lucky it'll only be a few weeks. And the Comanche don't start raiding until spring."

He had to go, James thought. This time the danger was hellishly real. If Edwards wasn't stopped quickly, if Mexican soldiers were killed, the Mexican Army wouldn't wait for orders from Mexico City to clear *yanquis* out of Texas. "Drusilla, I . . ."

"I know, my husband," she said quietly. "I will prepare a blanket roll and food for your journey."

He managed a smile. "More mind reading, *querida?*"

"Of a sort, James," she said. "This is the proper thing for you to do. No matter what happens, it will count well with the authorities that you have tried to aid the government."

"You are a witch," he said in surprise.

She laughed, but said seriously, "I can understand the situation as well as you, my husband. Let me go. Consu-

ela." Consuela scurried out after her, still telling her
beads.

"If we leave first thing in the morning," James said to
Groce, "we can be in San Felipe in—"

"No, Austin wants you to go to Nacogdoches. Marin
and Skelton know you, and they'll be at the head of any
move against the Edwardses. You see . . . ."

James rode into Nacogdoches on the third of January.
He had ridden hard to get there, stopping to rest his horse
but not to sleep. He could see a sentry, muffled in a heavy
coat and fur hat, carrying a musket on the wall of the stone
mission on the knoll. A red flag, lettered in white,
whipped in the stiff breeze above the mission. REPUBLIC OF
FREDONIA, it said. He turned his horse toward Sterne's
store.

The balding little storekeeper was on a stool behind the
counter, totting up his ledger. He looked up when James
came in, but instead of a welcoming smile a thoughtful
look appeared on his face. "*Nun wohl, Herr* Fallon, I did
not expect to see you here. You have perhaps come to join
with *Herr* Edwards?" The store was empty except for the
two of them.

"I came to find out what's happening. I've heard
rumors. Seems to be hurting your business, whatever it
is."

Sterne shut the ledger and pushed his spectacles up his
nose. "I do not think you have come because of rumors.
You are not a man to chase *das Gerücht*."

"I've heard a little more than rumors," he admitted.
"Are you still one of Edwards' supporters?"

"*Ach!* You see me in such *Glücksjägerei?* I am a simple
storekeeper. You would like a cup of tea?"

"That'd be fine." Sterne made his way into the back of
the store and returned in a few minutes with a tray and
teapot. As Sterne poured, James said, "I remember you
were in favor of Edwards' land policies."

"*Nicht genau.*" He made a sweeping gesture that included the entire store. "In the years since I came from

Köln, this is what I have built. I do not wish to have it taken from me. Your tea."

"Thank you. So you're just standing to one side and watching?"

"I do a little something from time to time. Is your tea hot enough? I have only molasses for sweetening."

"Molasses is fine. Mr. Sterne, do they really believe they can beat the Mexican Army? They can't have more than a hundred men, perhaps two."

The front door burst open and Ben Edwards stormed in. "Don't say any more, Sterne! He could be a spy!" He wore a bright red sash across his chest, and a cavalry saber belted outside his thick coat. With mittens and a broad-brimmed hat pulled low, it made a strange uniform.

His brother followed him in, trailed by two more bundled men, these carrying muskets. They wore cross belts and cartridge boxes over their coats. Haden seemed to be the only one not playing soldier. "If you want to know what we're doing, Fallon," he said, "ask us."

James looked at Sterne. The storekeeper shrugged. "The times, they are *schwere*. I thought it best to send for them." He shrugged again and avoided looking at James.

"What do you want here?" Ben demanded in a loud voice.

James kept his own voice level. "I came to find out what you're doing."

"You admit it! Damn it, Haden, I told you he was a spy."

"You expect men to join you without some idea of what they're joining?" James asked.

Ben's face reddened. "I'm no fool, Fallon. It's common knowledge you're soft on Mexes. Why, you even—"

"Shut up, Ben!" Haden broke in. "Nagle, Franklin, wait outside." The two men grumbled and shuffled out, letting in a blast of cold air. Ben opened his mouth, but Haden cut him off again. "I said be quiet, Ben. Fallon, will you be seeing Austin?"

"I might," James said cautiously. "I don't know."

Haden hesitated, then nodded. "Good enough. Tell

him he has to come in with us. Convince him."

"You need him, do you?"

"I'm expecting more men from the States any day. But if Austin joins, we'll control all of Texas. Or all that matters. And we can take the rest if we want it."

"Seems to me the Mexican Army might have something to say about that," James said drily.

Haden made a contemptuous gesture. "They can be beaten. Look at Augustus Magee, Samuel Kemper, and James Long. Only circumstances failed them."

"But they failed, in the end," James said.

"Damn it, Haden," Ben burst out, "we don't need that sanctimonious bastard Austin. Or Fallon either. Once the Indians move, we'll have more than enough to face any army the Mexicans put in the field."

"Indians?" James asked sharply.

Haden was looking daggers at his brother. "The Cherokee," he said reluctantly. "If the Mexes send an army, they'll join us. We've begun, Fallon. We have our own country now, free of Mexican control and interference. The Republic of Fredonia."

"I saw the flag," James said. "You keep saying we, Haden. Just who do you mean?"

Haden's face went blank. "Why, us. The people of Nacogdoches and the surrounding countryside. Who did you think?"

"I just thought Gerard Fourrier might have helped you."

"Fourrier? Doesn't he have a *rancho* down on the San Jacinto? What made you think he was involved in this?"

"I saw him up here last year. During the trial."

"I've spoken to him, of course. Listen, Fallon, the important point now is for you to convince Austin to join us. Remember, you owe me. I saved your life."

"I remember." He was certain Edwards was lying about Fourrier. But who was or was not involved at this point seemed unimportant alongside the possibility of war. "I'll carry your message, but I can't guarantee his reply."

"That'll have to do, I suppose," Haden muttered. Then his shoulders went back, and he straightened almost to attention. "You tell Austin if we don't do it now, we will have it to do later. Come on, Ben." The brothers marched out of the store, slamming the door behind them.

James looked at Sterne. The storekeeper grimaced. "I do what I must do. I work hard, and some Mexican *Hinterer* can take all I own merely by saying it is his. This is proper?"

"Mr. Sterne, how do I get in touch with Pedro Marin or Peter Skelton?"

"The tea is getting cold," Sterne said distractedly. "How would I know such things, *Herr* Fallon? I will freshen the tea."

James caught his arm as he turned away with the tray. "Mr. Sterne, it seems to me a man as doubtful of the Edwardses as you would keep in touch with the other camp."

"I . . . . Ride east out of town, *Herr* Fallon. Perhaps you will find what you seek. I really must freshen the tea." He hurried into the back as if afraid to be in James' presence any longer.

In the street, one of the men who had been with the Edwardses stood across from the store, his muffler wrapped around the lower half of his face. When James came out he set out in a shambling run for the mission. James turned his collar up against the wind and rode out of town to the west.

Out of sight of the mission he turned east. A mile east of Nacogdoches two armed men, one *yanqui* and one *mexicano*, rode out of the trees. They lacked the pseudo-military look of Haden Edwards' men, but they handled their muskets competently.

"You coming from Nacogdoches?" the *norteamericano* asked. He and the other man kept well apart. The Mexican's eyes searched James' backtrail.

"I am." James made certain his rifle pointed at neither man. "I'm looking for Pedro Marin or Peter Skelton. My name is James Fallon."

The two men looked at each other, then turned their

horses, motioning James to ride between them.

For two hours they rode, while the sun sank, changing directions often. The short Texas twilight was beginning as they rode into a camp where half-a-dozen small fires burned. Instantly they were surrounded by armed men.

"He wants to see Marin and Skelton," the *yanqui* said. There was a small commotion as three men pushed their way through. Marin, Skelton, and Wainwright.

"If you have come to join us," Marin said, "you are welcome, *Señor* Fallon. Join us at the fire."

As James climbed down, someone took his horse, and someone else shouted for sentries to return to their posts. There were seventy or eighty men in the camp, James thought.

"Stephen Austin asked me to find you," he said once he, Marin and the other two had squatted at one of the small fires, lit their pipes and poured tin cups of coffee.

Wainwright spat into the fire. "Austin!"

"What does he want?" Skelton asked around his pipe.

James looked at the other fires, at the men huddled around them. "Austin says you should go slow, try for a peaceful solution."

"God damn him!" Wainwright burst out. "Mr. high-and-mighty-by-God Austin always says wait. He wouldn't wait if it was his land."

Skelton waved him to silence with a big hand. "Way you said that, Mr. Fallon, that ain't your thought on it."

"Maybe not." James shook his head. "Maybe I'm crazy. What did you intend to do?"

"Fight him," Wainwright barked. "Chase him out of that damned mission, out of Texas."

"Do not be a fool," Marin said wearily. "He may have only a hundred men in the mission, but we are fewer than eighty. To attack the mission would be *suicidio*."

"Damn it," Wainwright began, but James broke in.

"It looked like they weren't too well prepared in Nacogdoches. Do you know what sort of supplies he has in the mission?"

"Not much," Skelton said. "We've kept an eye on

what they've taken inside. Couple of days' worth, maybe. They forage all the time, but this time of year there ain't much about in the way of crops.''

"They are expecting men," Marin added. "I have heard rumors that Edwards has recruited men in the United States.''

James tapped out his pipe and stuck it in his coat pocket. "Well, they haven't arrived yet. If you take the town, the mission becomes untenable.''

"Well, I'll be woolly damned," Wainwright said.

Skelton shook his head. "I don't understand.''

"If you take the town," James explained, "the men in the mission can't forage. In two days, or three, or five, their food will be gone, and they'll be forced to negotiate.''

"What is to stop them from attacking us?" Marin asked.

"What if they do? The numbers are nearly equal. Fortify a few houses. They don't have any cannon, do they?''

"No," Skelton said. "But there're still those men from the States. I heard them rumors, too. Maybe five, six hundred of them. They could show up tomorrow.''

"Or not for a month," James said. "Damn it, you can always retreat. You'll be no worse off than now, and you'll be able to show the government you tried to stop him.''

Wainwright laughed suddenly, an ugly sound. "I notice you ain't including yourself in none of this. Sounds to me like maybe you're sending us into some kind of trap in Nacogdoches.''

"I'll ride in with you," James said. "If there's a trap, it'll be easy enough to shoot me. Damn it, Wainwright, you were ready to attack a stone fort. The rest of you, are you willing to take a chance to beat Edwards?''

"What'll you be doing once we move?" Skelton asked.

"I'll ride to Austin. You'll need all the help you can get with Saltillo and Mexico City, and he's the man who can handle that." He held his breath while they exchanged looks.

Finally Marin said, "I will go into Nacogdoches with

you, *Señor Fallon.*"

"And me," Skelton said. Wainwright nodded sourly.

"In the morning, then," James said.

XLIII

James made the hundred and fifty miles to San Felipe in four days. Austin himself answered his knock.

"James! Come in, man. Come in out of the cold. What news from Nacogdoches?"

James was grateful when the door cut off the sharp wind. "We hold the town, Stephen. Edwards is bottled up in the old mission. Hell, by this time he may have surrendered. If you still have good connections in Saltillo, this whole mess may turn out all right after all."

"We hold . . . . What are you talking about, James?" Austin ran his fingers through his hair. "If there's been bloodshed, God knows what will happen."

"No bloodshed, Stephen. Marin and the rest rode in without a shot being fired. Edwards won't start anything unless he's a bigger fool than I think he is. Listen, Stephen, I think Gerard Fourrier is part and parcel with the Edwardses. I put it to Haden, and he came as near nothing denying he knew him, when they were in each other's pockets last year. If you want to avoid trouble with the Mexicans, it's Fourrier you have to worry about."

"Come into the parlor, James," Austin said.

James followed him out of the hall, and stopped dead. Gerard Fourrier sat in front of the fireplace, a red flannel muffler around his neck and a hot toddy in his hand.

"Mr. Fallon," Fourrier said, making a small bow where he sat. "Forgive me for not rising. I have a congestion. My doctor says it might turn into an inflammation of the lungs if I'm not careful."

"I'm surprised," James said, "that you're here in this weather, Mr. Fourrier, and you ill."

Fourrier smiled condescendingly. "Considering the circumstances, Mr. Fallon, I could hardly be elsewhere."

James looked at Austin wonderingly.

"You were right in a way, James," Austin said. "Mr. Fourrier was an investor with Edwards. He's been trying to work from within, to keep Edwards from blowing up in our faces."

"Needless to say," Fourrier added, "I don't want my involvement known. It would be an embarrassment to say the least."

"To say the least," James said. It was plausible, but he didn't believe a word. He wondered if his dislike of Fourrier was getting in the way of sense. "In any case, Edwards is done, now."

Fourrier's smile froze. "What do you mean?"

"You might as well explain it from the beginning," Austin said. "Sit down, and I'll get you a brandy."

James warily took a chair facing Fourrier. He couldn't see how anything he had to say might help him or hurt Marin and the others. "Four days back, about eighty men moved into Nacogdoches. Edwards was in the mission . . . ."

When James awoke the next morning, Austin was already gone from the other bed in the room. Soon after he finished detailing the situation in Nacogdoches the night before, Fourrier had retired to his bed across the hall. He had plead his illness and James was willing to bet if he hadn't been sick beforehand, he certainly was then.

With Fourrier gone he and Austin had talked into the night, avoiding the current trouble, discussing their plans for the future instead. His had all been for the *rancho*, for Drusilla and Amelinda and children to come. Austin's had been for Texas. He saw it settled by families from the United States, thousands of them living and working side by side with the Mexicans. He saw it filled with farms and cities, and sometimes his fervor was so strong he made James see it too.

With a sigh he got up and dressed. All of their plans depended on Nacogdoches, now.

He found Austin in the parlor, writing at his desk. "Fourrier still abed, Stephen?"

"He beat you up," Austin said without looking up. From the inkstains on his fingers he had been up and writing some time himself. "He's out around town somewhere."

"What about his congestion?"

"He wanted to talk to some of the colonists. If you don't mind, James, I'm rather busy right now."

What was Fourrier up to? James went outside. The morning was brisk, with a chill breeze from the river, but nowhere near as cold as the day before. San Felipe had grown, with over two hundred people living in the town proper. The houses were mainly unhewn logs with clapboard roofs, and there were two general stores. A new blacksmith shop bore a sign proclaiming it Noah Smithwick's. Wagons from the outlying holdings still rutted the single street, but now children rolled hoops and ran with dogs between the wagons.

As James turned up the street a young man on a lathered horse reined in in front of the cabin. "Mr. Fallon?"

"Yes?" He took a second look at the skinny, sallow-skinned youth, and recognized Philip Essen, one of Skelton's followers, a boy not more than seventeen. "Oh, yes, Philip. What word from Nacogdoches? You must have left right after me."

"More'n a day, Mr. Fallon, but I rode hard. All hell's broke loose, Mr. Fallon." Essen's chin quivered.

"What happened?" James said. "Tell me, Philip."

"Tell both of us," Austin said. He was pulling a heavy coat over his buckskins.

Essen blinked and took a deep breath. "It were Mr. Wainwright, sir. He got to talking how we could set fire to the mission gate to force them out. *Señor* Marin and Mr. Skelton said no, but Mr. Wainwright he got some men together, and they tried it."

"Damn fools," James muttered.

"Yes, sir. They got pinned down by musket fire from

the mission, and everybody rushed out to help them, and the men in the mission came out, and, and . . . . Marin's dead, Mr. Fallon. And Mr. Wainwright. And a couple more, too. And Mr. Skelton's got a musket ball in him. We got chased out, Mr. Fallon. That's what Mr. Skelton sent me down here to tell you." He fumbled with his reins.

"Go inside, boy," Austin said gently. "Sit in front of the fire, and I'll get you something to drink."

James stood staring at nothing as Essen climbed down and brushed past him. He hadn't counseled them the way Austin asked. He had had grandiose plans for beating Edwards at his own game.

"James? James!"

He turned to look at Austin. "My fault, Stephen. Those men are dead because of me."

"Perhaps. And perhaps they'd have attacked the mission the way Wainwright wanted anyway. It's something you have to learn to live with if you're the man who gives the orders, or if you advance one course of action over another. Learn to live with it, or go to bed and stay there the rest of your life. Damn, it looks as if we have more visitors."

Four Mexican lancers trotted up the street led by a lieutenant, attracting stares. They stopped in front of the cabin, and the lieutenant touched his broad-brimmed flat hat, looking questioningly from one to the other. "*Señor* Austin?"

"I'm Austin," Stephen said. "This is *Señor* James Fallon."

"I am *Teniente* Alphonso Gutierrez. I present the compliments of my commanding officer, *Coronel* Matco Ahumado. He has marched from Saltillo in response to your report of a revolt in the settlement of Nacogdoches, and will be here in three days' time."

"Please present my compliments to *Coronel* Ahumada," Austin said. "The colony of San Felipe welcomes him, and offers him such aide and supplies as we can. Inform the *coronel* that I will gather the men of the colony, and in token of our oath to the government of

Mexico, will march with him to put down the revolt. And now, *teniente*, will you enjoy the hospitality of my home?''

"I thank you, *señor*." He touched his hat again, and dismounted his men.

"James, will you join us?" Austin said.

"You'll have to excuse me, Stephen. I want to write Drusilla." Marin. Wainwright. Skelton wounded. When this was over, he would confine himself to his *rancho* and his family. Austin could have politics and Texas.

Four days later Gerard Fourrier made his way down the street in San Felipe, tipping his beaver hat as Colonel Ahumada rode past with some of his officers. Ahumada, slimly aristocratic, with thin *mustachios*, inclined his head slightly.

The sparse greeting suited Fourrier well. He had studied the townspeople's reactions to the troops before deciding on his own. The colonists were correct, but wary of having so many soldiers in their midst. The Mexicans were correct, but suspicious of the foreigners. No matter what happened, Fourrier intended to come out of it well thought of by both sides.

He turned in at Smithwick's blacksmith shop, nodding to the burly smith, who was pumping the bellows with one hand while the other held tongs with their end in glowing coals. "Good morning, Mr. Smithwick."

"Morning, Mr. Fourrier. Your friend's here, in the back. Didn't let any Mexicans see him."

He'd told Smithwick that Coffee—he used another name, of course—had once had a run-in with Mexican customs, and was still afraid he might be arrested. Smithwick had fallen in instantly.

The back was a storeroom, filled with sacks of coal and bar stock. Coffee sat on a spare anvil, picking his yellow teeth with a straw. "Can't say much for your meeting place," he grunted.

"Perhaps you'd rather be arrested? If you must sound like a fool, keep your mouth shut except to answer questions. What word from Nacogdoches?"

"Sarmento showed up to take over the squatters." Coffee gave an oily laugh. "But since they tangled with Edwards, they ain't much to worry about. I figure some of 'em probably slip away every night. By the time these Mex soldiers get up there, there won't be enough of 'em to be no help."

"Damn it, what about the men from across the Sabine? That's what I want to know."

Coffee shifted uncomfortably. "No word."

"What do you mean, 'no word'?"

"I sent off a man like you said, and Edwards did, too. They're supposed to be gathering. Leastways, that's what I hear."

Not for the first time, Fourrier cursed Ben Edwards for jumping the gun. The first overt move wasn't to have been made until five hundred men recruited in the United States arrived in Nacogdoches, complete with a pair of cannon, and that hadn't been planned for more than a month yet. He congratulated himself for his caution in keeping a foot in both camps. "You get back up to Nacogdoches. If those men haven't arrived, get across the Sabine and bring back as many as have gathered."

"Ain't going to be too many yet."

"Even a hundred might make the difference. Well?"

"It's cold out there," Coffee protested. "I was intending to get something hot to eat, and a night in a real bed."

"You get your ass in the saddle," Fourrier said, and his voice made Coffee start to his feet.

The fat trader turned to leave by the back way, looking over his shoulder at Fourrier. "You ain't heard about no Injun trouble, have you?"

"It's not Indians you have to worry about, Coffee. Get going."

"I just heard rumors," Coffee muttered. He scrubbed at his nose and shuffled out.

Fourrier nodded absently to Smithwick as he left the shop, not hearing the man's goodbye. Time was running out. In two more days Ahumada would march north. If he tried to talk the colonel into waiting longer, resting his men for the action ahead, it would expose him too much, and to little point. The hundred and fifty miles to Nacogdoches would take ten or twelve days for the infantry. In two weeks, then, they would be confronting Edwards. He added the time for Coffee to reach Nacogdoches to the time needed to reach the Sabine and return, and didn't like the answer.

Standing in the street, Fourrier bared his teeth in something halfway between a grimace and a smile. They thought they'd won, Austin, Fallon, and the rest. They would learn differently. If not this time, then the next.

January fifteenth dawned clear and cold. The sun seemed pale and distant, and men gathered in the main street of San Felipe were heavily bundled. The Mexican troops heading the column, a company of lancers, had covered their colorful blue and red uniforms with long coats, and the infantry, resting on their muskets, were tucking bare hands under ankle-length overcoats. Behind them were the colonists, three hundred of them, mounted and most armed with rifles. Their clothing, including some coats of bearskin or even buffalo hide, made no pretence at being uniforms, but they had one thing the Regulars didn't: Two four-pound cannon, their carriages hitched to wagon horses.

Colonel Ahumada reined in beside Austin, Groce, and James, looking at the cannon instead of them. "You are well prepared here in San Felipe, *Señor* Austin."

"We have had some trouble with Indians, *coronel*," Austin said.

Ahumada gave Austin a sharp look. "You will keep your men in good order, *Señor* Austin, and be attentive to my orders." He pulled his horse around and trotted back to the head of the column.

"He's touchy this morning," Groce chuckled.

Austin nodded sadly. "He gets that way every time he sees the cannon."

"We'll be damned glad of those guns if any of those rumors are true," James said.

"I heard a thousand men crossed the Sabine a week

ago," Groce said. "If so, Nacogdoches will be a close-run thing."

"It's not Nacogdoches that worries him," Austin said. "It's after. He sees in us the nucleus of another rebel army. He'll report to the governor that the colonists who support the government are potentially as big a threat as the rebels he was sent to put down."

James pointed to a closed coach and four making its way toward them past the column. "I still think he's behind much of our troubles."

"I know you don't like the man," Austin said, "but he's not the devil you seem to think him." The carriage halted alongside them, and Gerard Fourrier lifted a leather curtain.

"Mr. Austin," Fourrier said pleasantly. "Mr. Groce. Mr. Fallon." He was dressed in a bearskin coat and fur hat, the red flannel muffler wrapped high on his throat. "I regret not being able to accompany you, gentlemen, but the doctor tells me I must return home if I'm to avoid an inflammation of the lungs." He put a hand to his mouth to stifle a cough. James thought he looked in the prime of health.

"I hope you're better soon," Austin said.

Ahumada galloped up and drew his horse to a skidding halt. "You are leaving us now, *Señor* Fourrier? I trust you will feel better soon." He sounded, if not friendly, at least civil.

"Thank you, *Coronel* Ahumada. I wish you good fortune in the campaign ahead."

"Hardly a campaign, *Señor* Fourrier. The dispersal of brigands." He spun his horse to face the rest of them, his face and voice becoming cold. "We march soon. Stand ready."

As the colonel galloped once more up the column, James said, "A damned unpleasant man."

"Simply a Mexican officer," Fourrier said. "Good day, gentlemen." He rapped on the roof of the coach, and the driver whipped up the horses.

Groce stared after it sourly. "Sometimes I think that

man could play every hand in a poker game and cheat on all of them.''

At the head of the column Colonel Ahumada swept his arm forward, and the march began.

XLIV

The trees did little to cut the wind. Leonie pulled her shawl tighter and trudged on up the hill with her bucket of water. Denmark, almost five now, frolicked behind her, pretending the stick he carried was a rifle.

"Momma," he called, "can I get a real gun for my birthday?"

"You don't need a gun," she said. She waved to Drusilla, standing in the door of her cabin with Amelinda in her arms. Drusilla freed an arm to wave back. It was strange, Leonie thought. She hadn't wanted to like Drusilla, or any white, but some time during the long hours of sitting with Consuela she had realized she did.

"But momma," Denmark said, "what if Indians come? Bad Indians. I can shoot them if I have a gun."

"There haven't been any Indians around here since last year, Denmark." Henry appeared at the barn with a piece of harness. "There's your daddy, Denmark." The boy raced up the hill, waving his chubby arms. Henry waved back, laughing. Not for the first time she wondered if it was right to let Denmark grow up thinking Henry was his real father. But even Henry didn't know the truth, and Denmark was just too young to keep a secret from him. Later, she decided, as she always did. When he was older.

Up at the barn Henry had swung Denmark up in the air. Suddenly he stopped, staring down the hill. He began to wave wildly for her to come on, shouting words that the wind whipped away. She didn't need to hear the words. Indians. She started to run; an instant later the alarm on the tower rang out. A quick glance over her shoulder showed scores of Comanche bursting from the trees along the creek. She pulled her skirt and long coat up as much as she could, and ran even faster.

Henry handed Denmark to one of the *vaqueros* hurrying into the barn and came running down to her. "Go back!" she panted. "I'll make it!"

"Hush up, woman," he growled, and swept her up into his arms. Then he was running back up the hill, covering ground faster than she had despite her added weight.

She shut her eyes, pressing her face to his chest, and muttered a prayer, though she had long ago decided God was white. Muskets cracked; the Comanche screams came nearer. Abruptly Henry stumbled, then caught himself and ran on. She looked up at him. His face was strained.

"Henry?"

"Fine, woman," he gasped, and they were stumbling into the barn. Immediately two *vaqueros* pushed the doors shut and barred them.

"Henry," she began, but he put her down.

"No time, Leonie. Keep our muskets loaded."

He turned away. She stifled a scream. The back of his coat was bloody, and had a hole just above the waist. He grabbed up a rifle, though, and ran to a loophole in the wall. Other loopholes were already manned by *vaqueros*, firing at yelling Indians outside.

"They have muskets!" one of the *vaqueros* shouted. Suddenly he staggered back from the loophole, his face streaming blood, and crumpled.

Henry bent over him briefly before replacing him at the loophole. "Load, Leonie," he called. Thrusting his gun through the loophole, he tracked a target and fired.

Now, Leonie thought. She should tell Denmark now. If they were going to die he had a right to know his father had been a great man.

"Leonie! The muskets!"

Tears streaming down her face, she crawled across the straw-covered floor to where the muskets stood in a rack. She wanted to live. She wanted her child to live. Fumbling a musket out of the rack, she began to load.

From the crest of a low hill James studied the mission above Nacogdoches through a spyglass. The red-and-white flag was gone, and no one moved on the walls. He shifted his glass to the town. The streets were almost empty. No barricades up; no armed men in sight. Groce and some of the other colonists rode up.

"See anything, James?" Groce asked.

"Looks like they're gone."

"Gone!"

James handed over his glass. "Look for yourself."

Groce studied the town and the mission, then returned the glass. "We'd better report back. Ahumada doesn't like us being out of sight."

The force under Ahumada was waiting a few miles to the south of the colonists. The colonel had wanted the two cannon turned over to him, but Austin managed to convince him to leave them with him. Austin was with Ahumada when James and Groce rode up.

"Stephen," James said, "Edwards may have pulled out."

Austin opened his mouth, but Ahumada cut him off. "Make your report to me. *Señor* Austin does not command here. This claim of the mission being abandoned. What support have you for it?"

Austin caught his eye. He swallowed his angry retort, contenting himself with, "I said what I saw, *coronel.*"

"Town's practically empty," Groce added. "Nobody on the mission walls. No sign of defenses in the town or anywhere else."

"So." Ahumada rubbed his chin. "This town would be a good trap. If I were to march my men, expecting nothing, and there were, say, men in the buildings with muskets . . . . Perhaps I should use your cannon to bombard the town first, *Señor* Austin."

"*Coronel,*" Austin said, "there may well be women and children in the town."

Ahumada made a brushing gesture. "Fortunes of war. There are always casualties among the innocent. If there are truly any such."

"I don't think there's anybody else, *coronel*," James said. "I didn't see a single musket. Not a sign of anyone who even looked like he was under arms." Groce chimed in with confirmation.

Ahumada glanced at them, then looked away. "I will take the cannon close, for maximum effect. They must, of course, be under my direct command for the actual fighting. You, *Señor* Austin, will form your *colonos*, on foot, in the first rank. My regulars will form the second, so that I may apply them at the point of battle where they are most needed."

"So they can shoot us in the back," James muttered to Groce, "if we try to go over to Edwards."

Ahumada looked at him suspiciously, stroking his mustachios, but continued speaking to Austin. "Prepare your men to move, *Señor* Austin. Ah, here comes *Teniente* Gutierrez. Your report, *teniente*."

Gutierrez saluted smartly, sitting his saddle at attention. Half a dozen lancers followed him to a halt. "At your orders, *mi coronel*, I proceeded to investigate the mission above the town. It is empty, with signs of having been abandoned in haste. The town, as well, seems to be bare of armed men, though, as you commanded, I did not enter."

"Very well," Ahumada said. "I will take your party into the city to ascertain the direction in which the brigands have fled. After that we will pursue them, and cut them down."

Ahumada allowed Austin to accompany them, and when James and Groce attached themselves to Austin, Ahumada said nothing.

The town was practically empty. Almost everyone had fled in fear of either Edwards or the army. A lone dog ran in the streets. The lancers soon routed out a plump man, shaking in his boots, to answer Ahumada's questions. Edwards was retreating toward the Sabine River, expecting to be met by a thousand armed men with cannon from the United States. Before leaving he had boasted he would destroy the soldiers sent against him and return to punish everyone who had opposed him. Glowering, Ahumada ordered pursuit.

The chase after Edwards hardly deserved the name, in James' mind. The Sabine was forty-seven miles from Nacogdoches. Ahumada, though, seemed to believe in the thousand men, and moved cautiously, covering no more than eight miles a day. Edwards retreated slowly ahead of them; as James read the tracks, well under a hundred men were with Edwards. Other colonists, hunters and trappers, said the same. Ahumada ignored them all. It was all he would do to allow James and Groce to scout ahead. His lancers were kept in reserve for the attack he was sure Edwards would launch any hour.

James reined in at the bank of the Sabine River, and Groce stopped beside him, studying the tracks leading into the water. There were four other colonists behind them.

"They crossed over," he said. James nodded. There was no sign of men on the far bank. Certainly not the reinforcements Edwards was supposed to be meeting. "James, you think we should check the other side?"

"If he's joining a thousand men over there, we'd better know about it."

James and Groce swam their horses across, leaving the other men behind. It was strange, James thought, entering the United States. One side of the river was little different from the other, but there was something odd about it. Slowly he realized he was a stranger on this side of the river now. He had cast his lot with Texas more deeply than he had known.

Fifteen minutes later they found the remains of a fire, the ashes no more than an hour old. The tracks that left branched out in all directions.

"The reinforcements never showed up," James said.

Groce nodded. "So this is how it ends. At least there won't be any fighting. There's that."

"Let's get back across the river, Jared. I want to let Ahumada know it's over, and go home to my wife." With a laugh he swung back into the saddle and galloped for the river.

Ahumada's column was still ten miles from the river on

the Texas side. As James dismounted, he was surprised to see José speaking to Austin, who hurried over as they dismounted.

"Jared, please make your report to *Coronel* Ahumada. I have to talk to James alone." Groce raised an eyebrow, then nodded and went over to the colonel. Austin waited until everyone was out of earshot. "James, I . . . damn it, I'd rather be dead than tell you what I have to tell you."

"What . . . ." Suddenly José's presence took on meaning. "Drusilla? Amelinda?"

"They're dead, James. I'm sorry. Damn it, I'm sorry."

James rocked back and forth on his heels, keening deep in his throat. Suddenly he stepped away from Austin and vomited. "What happened?" he said hoarsely when he was empty.

"It was the Comanche, *señor*," José said. He had approached without James seeing, and stood shifting awkwardly from foot to foot. "They came—I do not know, a hundred, two hundred. They had muskets. They . . . they burned your cabin, *señor*."

James' stomach heaved, but there was nothing left to come up. Oh, merciful God in heaven. Burned! No, not a merciful God. Not a just God. Not a . . . . He had to function. He had to, or he'd go crazy. "Who . . . who else was hurt, José?"

"Pepino Celestine, Jorge Gonzales, and Antonio Nieto were killed," José said. "Henry and Benito Faria were wounded, but they will live."

"I'm going, Stephen. I have to go."

"I understand," Austin said. "José, go with him. Look after him."

"*Sí, Señor* Austin."

Ahumada came striding over as James climbed back into the saddle. "*Señor* Fallon, please accept my heartfelt condolences in—"

James didn't hear. He dug in his spurs, and his horse bounded forward.

The sun stood overhead when they rode up on the hill. They had covered two hundred miles in twenty-four hours, a killing pace for the horses. James saw the *vaqueros* coming out to meet him, Henry and Leonie and Denmark coming out of their cabin. He rode straight to the cemetery at the south end of the hill and reined in his horse.

There were five new graves, one so small. His eyes blurred so he couldn't read the wooden markers. He had done damned poorly by her. When she was having her baby and needed him, he had gone off to save men he didn't like from a fate they deserved. And now he had left her for even less, to fight men who drifted away like smoke. He had left her to die alone. Her and Amelinda. He couldn't make himself think about Amelinda. He couldn't make himself look at the charred ruins of their cabin.

He spoke without looking around. "José? Henry?"

"I'm here, James." "And I, señor."

He looked up then, at the prairie stretching west from the hill to the horizon. In a month the wildflowers would come. She had liked wildflowers. "You two take care of things around here."

"Take care of things, señor?"

In time he would have built her a castle on that hill. A castle to keep her safe.

"James," Henry said, "you ought to lie down. Get some sleep."

"When the wildflowers come, put some . . . ." He turned his horse toward the horizon and kicked it into a walk. He rode on without looking back. His eyes were on the horizon, but all he could see were flames.

Gerard Fourrier fed the papers into his study fireplace, frowning as he did. Every word that might connect him with the Republic of Fredonia was going in. At least he had gotten out of that fiasco with his skirts clean. Everyone thought he had been on their side.

"What are you burning, Gerard?"

He tossed the last paper in and turned, dusting his hands. "Old business, my dear." And damned expensive business, for no gain. "What have you been doing with yourself?"

"Nothing. Embroidery. Instructing the cook. *Mon dieu*, Gerard, you are the one who goes about making business. I sit at home."

"You don't know when you have the best of it," he said sourly. One of the *vaqueros* came bursting into the room. He rounded on the man savagely. "What in hell do you mean coming in here like that, Alvarado? Well, what is it you want?"

"The horse camp, *Don* Gerard. Comanches. They took two hundred horses."

"*Two* hundred?" Lucille said.

"What's so significant about the number?" Fourrier growled. "The damned savages ride where they please and take what they please. Something should be done about them."

"And yet, sometimes they have their uses, *n'est-ce pas?*" She had a satisfied smile. He didn't like not knowing the reason for it. "I heard today that James Fallon's *rancho* was burned out by Comanches. The entire family killed."

"As always, Lucille, you've heard wrongly. Fallon's wife and daughter were killed, but he wasn't. He was with Austin and Ahumada pursuing Haden Edwards."

Her face went pale with rage. *"Salaud!"*

"Who, my dear? Fallon, for not being there to be killed? Be sensible, Lucille."

"Of course." She calmed herself quickly.

He wondered at the entire outburst. Could she have had something to do with the attack on Fallon's holding? Preposterous! There were losses to recoup—the two hundred horses certainly didn't help there—and no time for idle speculation.

"Come along," he told Alvarado. "I'll see what other damage they did." Perhaps there was something useful in the Comanche. Some way to turn their depredations to profit. It might repay study. But whatever happened— Comanches, Fallon, or anyone else—he would still put his name on this land.

XLV

James Fallon rode north. It was the quickest route away from Texas, away from the memories he couldn't live with. At the Great Salt Lake he found a small trading post, and a party setting off in Jedediah Smith's footsteps, across the Mojave Desert to San Diego in California. He joined them. Further from Texas. Those the Kiowa and Apache didn't kill, those who survived the desert, found the Mexicans of California hospitable, and somewhat in awe of these *yanquis* who would not stop for mountain or desert. But there were too many aged, dignified men who could have been *Don* Tomás. Too many pretty women who, seen for an instant, glimpsed from a certain angle, looked like Drusilla. Too many chubby, dark-eyed baby girls.

He went north, up the coast, to the Pacific Northwest, the Oregon country. The British had forced John Jacob Astor out nearly fifteen years before, but there were still American trappers there. For almost ten years Great Britain and the United States had occupied it together. Americans weren't liked, though, and the British took advantage of having their Navy to call on. He headed east with a dozen trappers to the Great Western Mountains. Some called them the Great Rockies.

A man could lose himself in a winter of beaver trapping. The days were long and hard, filled with snow and wolves and empty traps. Blackfeet and Crow tried to kill them. There was no time or energy for thinking of Texas.

In the spring there was rendezvous, a gathering at Bear

Lake of every trapper in the Rockies who could ride, walk, or crawl. For two weeks they sold furs to the fur company representatives, drank and danced and celebrated living through another winter. Some of them asked James to come to St. Louis with them, where they intended to outfit a trip to find one of those valleys everyone talked about, where the Indians were friendly, the snows came late, and the beaver were knee-high to a horse. But something seemed to be pulling him. He drifted south.

He wasn't going back to Texas, he told himself. He was simply drifting, leaving the last place he had been before he had been there long enough to form memories. Memories were something to avoid. Memories brought pain. There were memories in Texas.

In May of 1828 he rode into San Antonio de Bexar.

San Antonio had changed little. The two plazas flanking the church of San Fernando were still filled with a gaily colored mixture of *peóns* displaying vegetables and baskets, marketing women, strolling *vaqueros,* and Indians down from the hills. The music of guitars drifted on the air, from wandering musicians and from *cantinas.*

No one gave him a second look. The feather on his fur cap and the length of his hair marked him for a trapper, but his buckskins were relatively clean, he was clean-shaven, and San Antonio was used to the rough *yanqui* trappers. He dismounted in front of a *cantina* and went in.

"Whiskey," he said. The *cantinero* waited. He laid a coin on the bar. The *cantinero* brought out a bottle and glass. He tossed down the first glass and poured another. He should get back on his horse and ride north.

"James? James Fallon?"

He turned his head and frowned at the tall, sandy-haired man who had addressed him. His clothes were Eastern, a black frock coat, pale gray trousers, snowy lawn shirt and well-polished boots. "Bowie. What are you doing in Texas, Jim?"

"Why, all your talk finally got to me. I've been out here a couple of months. Damn it, man, you look rough as ten miles of bad road." Bowie's face sobered. "I heard what happened, James. I'm sorry as hell. I wish—''

"Let's sit down," James said. He went to a table near the back and waited for Bowie to join him. "What's the news from the States, Jim?'' He filled his glass and pushed the bottle across to Bowie.

"Well, your mama and your step-pa are fine. They were kind of broke up about . . . ." Bowie cleared his throat and looked away. "Elaine and Eleanor said I was to give you their love if I ran into you. They're prettier than ever. Barbara got married just before Christmas. Charles Devereaux. You know him. Thomas Devereaux's son.''

News of his family reminded him too much of the family he had lost. "Adams still President?''

"What? Oh, yes.'' He seemed to understand James' need. "Maybe he won't be much longer, though.''

"Andy Jackson going to run again?''

"Of course. Most folks figure Adams to win, though. Except, the Congress is considering a tariff that has everybody up in arms, North and South. The South's hottest about it. Calhoun says it's an attempt to make agricultural states colonies of industrial states, and the South won't stand for it. He could be right. Anyway, if it passes, there may be enough people mad at Adams for Jackson to win.''

Tariffs. Elections. It was hard for James to believe there were people who tied up their entire lives in such things. "Do you know I haven't seen a newspaper in—it must be a year, now. Can't say that I missed it.''

"You haven't missed much,'' Bowie agreed. "Same things as always. The Russians are at war with the Persians. The Turks captured Athens. There's a civil war just started in Brazil. Hell, you haven't missed a thing.''

"You never said why you came, Jim. It's hard to picture you settling down as a rancher. Or a farmer.''

"God save me from that,'' Bowie laughed. "I'm no farmer. No. Does the name San Saba mean anything to you, James?''

"The San Saba silver mines? There are easier ways to commit suicide.''

Bowie leaned forward excitedly. "When Louis de St. Denis found them back in 1714, he took a fortune out.''

"The Lipans killéd St. Denis, Jim. His wife took the fortune out, if there was one. All anybody knows for sure is that she went to Spain and supposedly lived in luxury. Supposedly."

"You know a good bit about them," Bowie said.

"Everybody in Texas does. Finding them might be hard; staying alive is harder."

"Come with me, James. I'm going to find them. You were a pretty good scrapper, even as a boy. Now you look hard as nails and mean as a puma."

"I'm not interested in silver, Jim. In the morning I'm leaving Texas, and I'm not coming back."

"You could go a lot further with a muleload of silver."

"I'll go further with my scalp on my head."

Bowie pulled a pocket watch from under his coat and frowned. "Damn! I have an appointment to see the *jefe politico*, James. Why don't we have dinner afterwards? We'll make a night of it. Show these folks what New Orleans drinkers can do."

"We'll start here. In a couple of hours?"

They split outside the *cantina*. Bowie hurried toward the old Governor's Palace, while James strolled the plazas. The town was poorer than it had been. More of the clothing was worn; more of the *peóns* were in patches. Prosperity had drained out of San Antonio with the moving of the capital to Saltillo. But there was still pride and dignity. The worn clothing was neat and clean. The *peóns* still joked and laughed, the strolling *vaqueros* still smiled, and the music was still merry. A few were still wealthy, lace-shawled women followed by maids with baskets for their purchases, and there was no envy or hatred visible among the poor.

Suddenly he stopped, rooted to the spot. There was a girl, perhaps sixteen, haggling over peppers, an ivory lace shawl drawn over her raven hair, dark eyes large in her oval face, her complexion olive satin. She was beautiful, and she looked so much like Drusilla he knew she must be Elena. Her maid, waiting patiently behind her, noticed his stare and touched the arm of a large, bearded *vaquero*.

The last thing James wanted was a meeting with Elena

or *Don* Tomás. He turned away into the crowd. Before he had gone a dozen places, a hand grabbed his arm. He turned to face the bearded *vaquero*. He looked vaguely familiar.

"*Dispense me, señor,*" the *vaquero* said in a deep bass, "but—"

"I don't know you," James said angrily. He put a hand to the knife in his belt. "Back off!" The *vaquero* took a quick step back, reaching for his own knife. The crowd around them buzzed and opened a space. James began to back away. If he could lose himself in the plaza . . . .

The people behind the big *vaquero* parted to let Elena through. "Felipe, put up that knife!" she snapped. "And you, *señor*—" Her eyes widened. "James? Blessed Mary, it is you! You have returned." She grabbed his hand in both of hers. "Felipe, it is *Señor* Fallon. He has come back to us."

"*Señor* Fallon?" Felipe rumbled wonderingly. "*Madre di Dios*, it is. Forgive me, *señor.* I did not recognize you." The crowd buzzed louder now that the *yanqui* had been recognized.

James spoke haltingly. "Elena, I . . . it's been a long time. Too long. It's best you go back to your shopping and forget you saw me."

"Never," she said fiercely. "I will never let you go again."

He suppressed a smile that caught him unawares. "You're getting to be a grownup lady, Elenita."

"You will think of me as a child," she said tight-lipped. Suddenly she put a hand to her mouth. "Oh, I have forgotten. It has been so long. There are letters for you. I have kept them as they came, carried them against your return. You must come with me, and I will give them to you."

Letters. Word from his mother and stepfather, no doubt, and his sisters. He hadn't realized how much he wanted to hear from them. But getting them would mean meeting *Don* Tomás. "Will you send them to me? I'll be at the Cantina Lopez for tonight."

"You must come for them yourself, James. *Papá* and I

are staying in the house of *Don* Juan Verimende. I wish
papá was here to see you. But he and *Don* Juan have gone
to Saltillo, and they will not be back for another week at
least.''

"I might as well go get them right now.'' She looked so
much like Drusilla, he thought.

"Of course,'' she said quietly. "Felipe, Conchita, come
along.''

The Verimende *hacienda* was a mansion by San Antonio
standards. Broad, spacious verandas looked out on a flagstone courtyard with fig trees and oleanders and a burbling
fountain. *Señorita* Ursula Verimende was a petite blonde
with merry blue eyes, perhaps a year older than Elena.

"So,'' she said when James had been led to a sitting
room, "you are the *Señor* James Fallon of whom Elena is
always . . . .'' She caught Elena's eye and spread her
hands. "I fear, *Señor* Fallon, that I talk too much. I am
sure that you and Elenita have enough to talk of without
me about.'' The smile she gave Elena as she left held considerable mischief.

Elena scowled after her, changing it to a smile when she
realized James was watching. "I will fetch your letters,
James. Would you like something to drink? I can ring for
coffee, or tea. Or perhaps wine?''

"Nothing, thank you.''

She hesitated for a moment, then hurried out, and
James was left alone. Was it right, he wondered, to be
here? Bowie, Elena, the letters were all ties to the past,
roots reestablishing themselves. He would have to pull
them loose again when he went, this time without the
anesthetic of numbness.

"Here they are.'' She trotted back into the room, and
stopped with a small laugh, holding out a bundle of letters
tied with a yellow ribbon. "I thought . . . I feared that
you might go.''

"I won't go without saying goodbye, Elena.''

"Of course not. Here.'' She thrust the bundle into his
hands. "I will leave you to read them. You . . . you will
say goodbye before you go?''

"Don't go,'' he said. "I would enjoy the company.''

Her face lit with a smile that twisted his heart. She obviously still bore her childhood love for him, and she looked so much like Drusilla that . . . . She still was a child, he reminded himself. He would be gone in the morning.

He sat across from her and untied the ribbon, thumbing through the letters. They bore the stamps and seals of their travel through the United States and Mexico, endorsements by post offices, ship captains and express riders. Three were from his mother and stepfather, two from Barbara—the last bearing the name Mrs. Charles Devereaux—and four each from the twins. One bore the postmark "Charleston, South Carolina," and the name Robert Fallon.

He shivered with the feel of feet walking on his grave. Elena half rose from her chair. "James, what is the matter? Are you all right?"

"I don't know," he said, turning the letter over and over. "I don't know," he repeated, and broke the seal.

My Dear Son,

His hand shook, and for a moment the page blurred. He took a deep breath and read on.

I know no other way to do this than to plunge in. I am your father. I can only plead with you to hear my case and find it in your heart to understand.

Before you were born, I sailed for France for what I thought at the time were good reasons. I promised your mother I would return before you were born, and I earnestly tried to do so. Unfortunately, my ship fell prey to Barbary pirates. I was given up by the world for dead, and in truth I was not far from it. For two years I lived in chains, a slave in a North African quarry.

When at last I managed to escape and return to Charleston I found that your mother, believing me dead, had married again and left Charleston with her new husband and you. I have never found it in my heart to blame her. She was a young woman with a baby and, she thought, no husband. The man she married was a good man. I wished them, and still do wish them, all the best that life can bring.

And yet, I could not simply abandon you, my son. Even if your mother had another life, a life I could not enter, I had to find you. For years I have tried, without success. Then, when I was on the point of despair, a friend of mine, John Lafflin, wrote that he had met my younger image in Mexico City, and that that man was named James Fallon. He told me of the life you are building for yourself in Mexico, of the young woman you have married. I am glad that you have found happiness, my son.

We Fallons are often driven men, driven to build, driven to follow our dreams, often at the cost of those we love. So it was with your grandfather; so it has been with me. If you share this Fallon legacy, I ask you to temper it, as I have never been able to. Build, follow your dreams, but hold hard to those you love, and to those who love you. That last duty, to those who love you, is sometimes the easiest to forget. In such cases the right thing to do is often that which is hardest.

But enough of advice from a man you have never seen and may never wish to see. What further contact exists between us I must leave to you. Long ago I forfeited any right to do otherwise. But know this, James. Over the years I have gathered some measure of wealth. Should you ever have need, it is yours to call on. My love, my son, is yours always.

Robert Fallon

His father was right. His dreams possessed him as firmly as any Fallon ever could have been. But he didn't want to be possessed. He wanted to forget, to run. To hide. Maybe his father was right about something else, too. *Don* Tomás, Elena, Henry, José, all people who loved him. *The right thing to do for people who loved you was often the hardest.*

"How are Henry and José? And Leonie? Do you know?"

"They visit *papá* often. Leonie has just had a baby boy, Peter. *Señor* Cameron is so proud of him. They want you back, too. Whenever they speak of the future, of their plans, they speak of you."

"I have to write some letters," he said. "To my mother and stepfather. To my sisters." He fingered the open letter. "To my father."

"*Su papá!* I saw the name, but I thought only that he was a relation."

"My father. It's a long story, Elena. I'll tell you some time. Is there someone who can carry a message to the Governor's Palace? I need to tell a man there I'm staying."

Elena leaped to her feet, her face lit with that glowing smile. "You are truly staying? Oh, James, I am so happy."

He laughed, and reached out to flick the tip of her nose with one finger. "Be careful, little Elena, or you will break my heart when you marry."

The right thing to do was the hardest. If he was driven, by dreams or by nightmares, he would nevertheless remain in Texas, and do his duty by those who loved him.

BOOK THREE

Texas, South Carolina, and Washington
1832-1833

XLVI
Texas, 1832

"Are you going?"

James didn't pause in slipping on his buckskin jacket as Isobel de las Piedras sat up in bed, letting the sheet fall to reveal rosy-tipped breasts. He had rented the room in Hillyard's Tavern two days earlier, when he arrived in Nacogdoches to sell horses. He stuffed his father's latest letter into his pocket. "I have business, Isobel."

She stretched langorously. "I knew how wonderful you would be when I met you at *General* Santa Anna's *palacio*. How many years ago that was!"

James didn't want to remember. Drusilla had been alive then. Isobel's husband now commanded the garrison in Nacogdoches. If he hadn't been drunk, James would never have brought her to his room. He drank too much in recent years. And gambled too much, wenched too much, and ranched too little.

"We'd better let it go at this, Isobel."

"My husband would not like knowing that his wife is being bedded by a *yanqui*," she said. "There are not many suitable men in this benighted place."

Blackmail? He changed the subject. "Your husband will have trouble enough with the *yanquis* if he doesn't stop stirring up trouble between them and the Indians."

"There is no proof," she said chidingly. "Besides, he does not like it here in the wilderness. But I am afraid José is still a royalist at heart, and even *Presidente* Bustamente would not give him a command closer to Mexico City." She giggled. "*El presidente* does not like *yanquis*, either."

Bustamente certainly didn't like *yanquis,* James thought sourly. Two years before he'd signed what most Texans called Bustamente's Law, usually spitting for punctuation. New immigrants were forbidden to settle in any Mexican state bordering their country of origin. Colonization grants not already fulfilled were canceled. Only Austin's and Green DeWitt's grants had been fulfilled; hundreds of settlers were still wondering if their land titles had been destroyed along with the grants. Passports were required for all foreigners, including colonists; customs duties had been raised, making even necessities almost too expensive to afford; and worst of all, *presidarios,* convict troops, had been garrisoned throughout Texas.

"I have to go," he said.

"I will see you tomorrow," she called as he shut the door. It was not a question.

Bowie was waiting in the common room, stylish in short, embroidered jacket and flared trousers slashed at the cuff with gold. He had married Ursula Veremendi the year before and become a solid citizen, opening a cotton mill in Saltillo. There was a bottle and two glasses on his table.

"I was going up to your room," he said as James sat down, "but the *cantinero* said you had a woman up there. Anybody I know?"

James shook his head. "Any particular reason you're looking for me?"

"I got word this morning." Bowie leaned across the table and lowered his voice. "Santa Anna's taken the field against Bustamente."

"Again," James muttered. Pedraza had been elected president of Mexico in '28. In '29 Guerrero overthrew him, and in '30 Bustamente overthrew Guerrero. Now Santa Anna, with his opium and orgies, was taking a turn. "I'm beginning to think Branch Archer is right. We're just a bone for the winner to toss to his dogs."

"I tell you, you'd better watch that talk. Sooner or later somebody's going to think you're advocating rebellion. Have a drink and calm down."

"Would that be so bad, Jim?"

Bowie froze in the act of reaching for the bottle. "A lot

of people are trying to make lives, James. You want to see ranches burned, men hung, women and children going hungry? If we keep calm and petition, the way the Mexicans do, everything can be cleared up. Compromise, James. Compromise."

"You're beginning to sound like Austin."

"And you're beginning to sound like William Barrett by-God Travis."

"At least Buck Travis is doing something."

"Yes," Bowie said heatedly. "Taking the law into his own hands."

A month earlier four *presidarios* had tried to rape a settler's wife near Anahuac. She managed to drive them off, and two weeks later Travis and others had caught three of them, tarred and feathered them, and left them at the gates of the fort at Anahuac. The commander, a renegade Kentuckian named John Bradburn, was said to be in a rage.

"I'm heading for Saltillo," Bowie went on. "Why don't you come with me? Forget all this trouble awhile."

"Sorry, Jim. I brought in some horses. I have to stay until they're sold. Maybe I can come down after."

After Bowie was gone, he sat and thought. He was spending too little time with his friends. He'd ridden with the ranging companies so much that Henry and José had finally set up their own places. On half the acreage, they produced twice as much as he. The one thing he seemed able to concentrate on was the troubles.

He dug out the latest letter from his father and found the passage he wanted.

> You ask for an explanation of our problems here with the Federal government. They are at once complex and simple. The 1828 tariff has proven a stranglehold on the South. Southerners are forced to buy inferior goods in the north at prices much higher than we could buy from Europe if the tariff did not exist. The Nullifiers believe there is no other course but open defiance of Washington. They preach that any state has the right to nullify within its borders Federal laws of which it disapproves. We Unionists believe no less in the evils of the tariff, but it is our con-

tention that every step within the law must be taken before anything else is contemplated. If the Nullifiers win the legislative elections this fall, as I fear they may, they will get their nullification law, and the matter may, in the end, be settled by bayonets. In the troubles you write of, in Texas, remember that moving outside the law must remain a last act of desperation.

"We are desperate," he murmured, sticking the letter back in his pocket. Deciding against another drink, he went out to check on his horses. The rutted street bustled with freight wagons and horsemen. Settlers in homespun coats shopped with their wives, bonneted against the May sun. There were law offices, and two doctors had shingles out. Some stores sold newspapers, not only the *Texas Gazette* and the *Telegraph and Texas Register*, but papers from New Orleans, St. Louis and Nashville. He waved to Adolphus Sterne, sweeping the boardwalk in front of his store. The storekeeper had been allowed to remain in Texas after the Edwards affair, on his oath never to take part in political activity again. And some said because his military judges had been, like him, Masons.

At Alderman's Livery Stable, Jack Alderman himself had a foot up on the bottom rail, watching James' fifty two-year-olds. His long face was fringed with a beard, but he wore no mustache.

"Pretty horses, Mr. Fallon. How much you asking again?"

Smiling, James joined him. Alderman knew the price as well as he. "Eighty dollars a head. No land." Texas was currency poor; land was accepted for many debts. Not by James Fallon, though.

"Lot of money," Alderman said mournfully.

"A bargain. Anybody else would ask a hundred. You hear about Santa Anna? Seems he's taken to the field against Bustamente."

"Old news, Mr. Fallon." Alderman didn't take his eyes off the horses. "Latest thing I heard is about Buck Travis being arrested. Listen, I might be able to go fifty apiece for—"

"Arrested?"

"Bradburn had him and Patrick Jack arrested right in their law office by a squad of soldiers. Let's see . . . must've been four, maybe five days ago. I could maybe go fifty-five—"

"Trot out my gelding, Mr. Alderman." He didn't know Travis or Jack very well—they were relative newcomers, not in Texas more than a year—but suddenly it seemed important to go to Anahuac.

Alderman stared at him. "Are you selling horses or not? I might be able to scrape together sixty, but that's as—"

"The horses have to wait," James said. Alderman muttered his way into the stable. "Be sure my canteens are full."

He was pacing, waiting for his horse, when he saw a coach that should have been five hundred miles from Nacogdoches. He was so surprised he didn't move until it had drawn to a stop in front of the stable, and Elena climbed out.

"What on earth are you doing here?" he said. "Where's your father?"

"With *Coronel* de las Piedras," she answered in her warm alto. "I begged him to let me see what has become of Nacogdoches. It has grown so much, has it not?" Her big, dark eyes looked at him through long lashes. "Of course, I thought I might see you, as well."

She still looked like Drusilla, he thought, but taller. And definitely fuller breasted. He reminded himself sternly that he had given her dolls on Christmases past, but he couldn't avoid the thought that she was twenty, now. And no child.

"Tell *Don* Tomás I'm sorry I missed him."

Her face fell. "You are leaving? But surely you can stay a day or two longer."

"I'm sorry." Alderman came out with his horse, rifle and canteens on the saddle.

"José visited *papá* last month," she said suddenly. "I am so glad he married Rosita. Three babies she has given him in three years, and they love each other greatly." She looked him straight in the eye. "Rosita was twenty when she married José."

"Rosita's a good woman," he mumbled, and scrambled into the saddle. "Remember to give my apologies to your father." He was glad to be heading for Anahuac, glad to be leaving Elena before he forgot she was Drusilla's sister.

James studied the stone fort at Anahuac from a stand of trees. Except for a lone sentry in a tower by the gate, no one was to be seen. A single thread of smoke rose peacefully from somewhere inside.

Quickly he rode back to where Frank Johnson, the rotund rancher who had been elected colonel, waited with a hundred and fifty mounted men, recruited from the area over the past two weeks. William Jack, whose brother was one of the prisoners in the fort, was one of them. Their clothing was a mixture of homespun and buckskin, but their rifles were well cared for.

"It's quiet," James said. "Maybe too quiet. Could be a trap."

Johnson nodded. "I want to get those men out, but there's no point in giving Bradburn a hundred and fifty new prisoners."

"Word is," Jack said quietly, "he's fixing to send them all down to the military prison in San Juan de Ulloa." He was a lanky man of fifty, who'd been a judge before coming to Texas. "And you've all heard about the hard treatment they've been receiving." His failure to mention his brother was pointed. Everyone there had heard that Patrick Jack and Travis were the two who'd been most often singled out for torture. Bradburn's proclamations had as much admitted lack of food and water. Hot irons and worse had been hinted at.

"I said I'd get them out, William," Johnson said. "Fallon, unless you're certain it's a trap, I'm going in. We wait too long, and he will ship them off."

"Then let's leave half the men back, so they can cover us. And don't anybody go inside the fort."

Johnson nodded agreement. "Franklin, you tell off half the boys and keep them back about three hundred yards." A short man with a bushy mustache moved his horse through the pack, touching a man here and there. "I suppose," Johnson went on, "the rest of us better get on with it." William Jack nodded fiercely.

James rode on one side of Johnson, Jack on the other, the three out in front as they approached the fort gate. In the tower, the sentry shouted something down into the fort. They reined in, less than fifty feet from the gate. Franklin and the others were where they were supposed to be, a long rifle shot back. The gate swung open.

Inside, Travis and Jack were spreadeagled on the ground, pinioned, and *Coronel* John Bradburn stood over them, a pistol in each hand. A dozen *presidarios* formed a semicircle behind him.

"How nice," Bradburn called. "You've come to pay me a visit." He was tall, and his bushy side whiskers made his square jaw even broader.

Johnson ignored the men on the ground. "We demand that all prisoners illegally held by you be released immediately."

"With public apologies," William Jack shouted. James gripped his rifle tightly.

"You demand?" Abruptly Bradburn cocked his pistols, pointing them at the men on the ground. "You'll withdraw immediately, or I'll shoot these men on the spot. You're rabble and traitors, and you're lucky I don't arrest all of you."

"Attack!" Travis shouted from the ground. A redhaired six-footer, his usually florid face was scarlet with anger. "I'd rather die than give in! Attack, damn you!"

"That can be easily arranged," Bradburn laughed. "Well, gentlemen? Do you want to grant Mr. Travis' request for a quick death?"

William Jack started forward, but Johnson grabbed his arm. "We'll pull back, Bradburn. But you haven't heard the last of us." Bradburn's laughter could be heard as the gate swung shut.

Dispiritedly, James and the others returned to their camp in the woods. Bradburn had them so long as he was willing to kill his prisoners. Depression seemed to settle among the men. Johnson, though, set up round-the-clock watches on the fort, and a system of regular patrols around the entire vicinity of Anahuac. Three days after the fiasco at the fort gate, one of the patrols captured a six-man scouting party.

The respectable *teniente* commanding the party refused even to talk to his captors. The other five under guard with him were *presidarios* of the worse sort. Shifty-eyed, their uniforms slovenly, they looked like the convicts they had been before the army got them.

"Why should Bradburn trade our people for this lot?" James asked. "Aside from the lieutenant, I can't see they're much loss to him." He accepted a tin cup of coffee from William Jack. The three of them were squatting around a fire not far from the prisoners.

"He only has a hundred and twenty men," Jack said. "Even these are a loss."

"Whatever they are," Johnson said, "they're all we have. We'll try a trade. Now, who puts it to Bradburn?"

"Me," Jack said quickly.

"You might like company," James said. Jack extended his hand, and he gripped it.

"You two, then," Johnson said. He looked at them in embarrassment. "You see . . . ."

"Better not to risk any more," James said.

"They'd just crowd us," Jack added.

At two that afternoon they rode up to the gate. The sentry had spotted them coming, and Bradburn was in the tower.

"My answer's still the same," he called down.

"You missing anything, Bradburn?" James called. "Like a lieutenant and five of your scum?"

Bradburn turned to confer with someone behind him. When he turned back his face was dark. "It seems there is a patrol overdue. I warn you, if one of those men is harmed, I'll have you all in chains."

"They're all right," James said.

Jack added, "For the moment."

"If you want them back," James went on, "we'll be glad to make a trade. Your men for the seventeen Texans in your cells."

"Done," Bradburn said quickly. James blinked. "My

terms are these. Withdraw all of your patrols six miles from the fort and release my men. When they return to the fort, I'll release my prisoners.''

"You must be crazy," James laughed.

Bradburn looked as if he might jump from the tower at him, then got a grip on himself. "Those are my terms. You have my word as a gentleman on them. Signal your acceptance by a red flag at the edge of the trees. If I see nothing by noon tomorrow, I'll assume you've decided to kill your prisoners, and act accordingly." He disappeared.

"Bradburn!" James shouted. "Bradburn!" The sentry stared down blankly. "Damn," James muttered. Jack was suddenly looking his age.

When James put the proposal to the others, they stood without speaking. The loudest sound in the clearing was the buzzing of insects. Finally someone said, "He ain't going to turn them loose, no matter what."

"He surely isn't unless we turn ours loose," James said. "Whether he will even then, I don't know. He gave his word as a gentleman, for what that's worth. You men know him better than I do."

Johnson snorted. "My horse is more of a gentleman than John Bradburn."

"You'd better know one more thing," James said. "He said if we don't accept, he'll act as if we've killed our prisoners." Their faces showed they understood.

Johnson mopped his forehead. "Up to now, you've all done what I said. Well, you elected me colonel, but we're not an army. I know what I think, but this decision is too important. I'm calling for a show of hands. Everybody in favor of sending Bradburn back his men?"

One by one hands went up, until every man in the clearing had his hand raised.

Jack cleared his throat. "Thank you," he said quietly. "Unless somebody has a good reason to delay, I'll make the signal to Bradburn." One of the men found a red flannel shirt in his saddlebags, and Jack rode out with it fastened to a stick. The Mexicans huddled together under the watchful eyes of the settlers.

When Jack returned, reporting that his wave had been

answered from the fort, they moved the required six miles before nightfall, choosing a hill with good visibility. At dawn the Mexicans were given their horses. They galloped away as if afraid they'd be shot.

"If they keep flogging those horses," James said drily, "they'll be at the fort in less than half an hour."

"Then our people will be here that much quicker," Johnson said, but he didn't sound hopeful. He posted lookouts in the trees to watch for treachery.

James sat chewing on a blade of grass, rifle across his knees. "Do you ever think," he said as Johnson dropped down next to him, "about breaking away? Texas, that is?"

"You mean . . . independence?" James nodded, and Johnson frowned. "That'd take rebellion, Fallon."

"What do you think you're doing right now?" He hurried on before Johnson could protest. "It's as much as become a Mexican custom, Frank."

"If we get rid of the bad apples like Bradburn," Johnson said stubbornly, "Santa Anna will straighten things out in Mexico City. You'll see. It'll be like it was."

"I don't remember it was that good," James said. He could see that Johnson was worrying at it, though, and that was enough for the moment. He tipped his hat over his eyes. His grandfather, he knew, had helped start the American Revolution. But how had he gone about it?

The morning sun seemed to sit still in the cloudless sky. By ten o'clock, men were beginning to look for Travis and the others. At eleven, they said maybe lieutenant and his men had been slow getting back to the fort. Noon came, and a few wondered laughingly if Bradburn had set his prisoners free barefooted. By one, nobody had any hope left.

"Rider coming!" came a shout from one of the lookouts.

They scrambled to their feet. A lone rider was passing. When he saw them, he reined in, then came on at a gallop. James recognized him. It was Arthur Price, a sandy-haired storekeeper from Anahuac.

"Been looking for you everywhere," Price said as men surrounded his horse. "We didn't know where you were, so we just rode in all directions, hoping."

"Did Bradburn free Travis and the others?" Johnson asked.

"Bradburn didn't turn anybody loose," the storekeeper said. "About ten o'clock, though, he rode into town. He ransacked everything of Travis' and the rest, and some of your places, too. Took away all the gunpowder and muskets and food he could find. Then he read a proclamation. Said you'd broken some kind of agreement, so he wasn't bound by it. Said you're all rebels and traitors, and he's confiscating all your property."

"Lying bastard!" Jack muttered. An angry murmur from the others echoed him.

"We'll need more men," James said.

Johnson nodded. "We'll move over to Turtle Bayou. That's far enough away Bradburn isn't likely to try anything, but anybody who wants to join will be able to find us. Price, will you spread the word in town?"

"I'll spread it," the storekeeper said. "I'll be coming to join myself. Bradburn isn't going to stop until he's taken everything we own."

XLVII
Texas, 1832

James lay on the grassy bank, watching the turtles that gave the bayou its name basking on half-sunken logs in the late June sun. They'd have called it a stream in Louisiana, he thought, but hardly a bayou. Behind him, up the bank, Johnson and a score of others were arguing about a statement of grievances they intended to publish.

"Then it's agreed," Johnson said. "We condemn Bustamente for tyrannical and unlawful conduct, and declare our adherence to the laws of Mexico and the Constitution of 1824."

James smiled grimly.

"What about Santa Anna?" somebody else said. "He's in favor of the constitution. Shouldn't we declare for him, as well?"

Another argument blew up, and James left. According to the resolutions, they were in arms against a colonel of the Mexican Army, but they were still loyal subjects of Mexico. It wasn't what James wanted by a long shot.

Along the bayou stretched cooking fires for the men who had answered Johnson's call—James estimated over four hundred ranchers and farmers, mounted and armed. The nucleus of a real army if he could get Johnson to see it.

He caught sight of John Austin—no relation to Stephen —a tall, swarthy coasting captain he'd been drinking with the previous night. Austin was squatting by a fire, stirring a pot of stew. James dropped down next to him.

"Afternoon, Fallon." The coaster tasted his stew and grimaced. "Good thing Taylor White's been supplying us, or we'd all be starving." Most of the men had brought supplies for only a day or two, and the game in the area had quickly been exhausted. "I hear he's not charging for it, neither."

"Taylor's a good man," James said. "Austin, I'd like you to tell Johnson what you told me about those cannon in Brazoria."

Austin dropped the spoon in the stew and stood. "Might as well. I'm no damned cook, that's for sure."

Johnson and the others were seated on the ground in a shady clearing, Johnson with a camp desk on his lap.

"What about duties?" Jack was saying as they walked up. "Bradburn collects twice the rate from most of us, and lets his friends go through free." He broke off when he saw James. "You decided to join us after all?"

"I want you to hear something," James said. "Captain Austin, will you tell these men what you told me?"

"Well," Austin began hesitantly, "you know some coasters do a little smuggling." A chuckle ran through the assembly. Since Bustamente had raised the tariffs, almost everyone smuggled. "Anyhow, there's this fellow, I don't think I ought to say his name, decided he might have to fight off Mexican revenue cutters. He bought himself a pair of six-pounders for his sloop. He's got them down to Brazoria right now."

"Cannon," Johnson said thoughtfully. "Can you get these cannon, Captain Austin?"

Austin nodded. "I expect I can."

"Is anybody opposed?" Johnson asked the others. "If so, speak up."

"Hell no, nobody's opposed," Jack said, and a few men laughed. Some of the others looked grim, as if the implications of bringing in cannon might be occurring to them. But at least, James thought, no one was speaking in opposition.

"All right," Johnson said finally. "Captain Austin, how soon?"

"As soon as I get my schooner to Brazoria and back," Austin said. As they were walking away, he added to James, "If Ugartechea doesn't try to stop me, anyway. The fort at Velasco covers the approaches to Brazoria.''

"You think he'll be able to stop you?''

Austin grinned. "I hear you think Texas should be independent. You're not alone, you know. Ugartechea won't stop me."

Two days later the force moved to Liberty, upriver from Anahuac, and camped outside the town. Men poured in until they numbered close to eight hundred. When the cannon came, they would move on the stone walls of Bradburn's fort.

The last day of June, a Saturday, dawned hot, the few clouds in the sky dissipating quickly under a merciless sun. Rude brush shelters and pieces of canvas sheltered the small army. James was attempting to shave, using a broken triangle of mirror propped on the ground, when one of the patrols came galloping in from the north. Wiping his face, James hurried after them to Johnson's tent, a square of canvas supported on poles and sagging in the middle.

"It's Piedras, all right," Lucius McCoy, the sallow Tennessean who commanded the patrol was saying. A crowd was gathering around the tent to listen. "I've seen him in Nacogdoches. He should be about two hours away by now, with maybe two hundred and fifty men, maybe thirty lancers, the rest infantry. He's got a cannon, too."

That last brought mutters from the crowd. Everyone was tired of waiting for cannon of their own.

"Get everybody mounted," Johnson ordered, and the men scattered for their horses.

"We're attacking?" James said. "If we catch him on the march—"

"We'll talk," Johnson said. "I just want to make sure he listens."

The Texans were impressive as they rode in a column of fours. Their ranks weren't straight, but the musket or rifle each man carried made up for it. When they came in sight of the Mexican force, Johnson signaled the column to halt, and motioned James and William Jack to ride forward with him.

At the appearance of the Texan column, the Mexicans had been thrown into confusion. Officers galloped up and

down the column, beating men with the flats of their
sabers to hurry them into formation facing the Texans.
The lancers took a position on the left flank, lance points
gleaming in the sun.

As the three drew closer, a lone lieutenant rode out
rigidly to meet them. He never looked past them to the
Texans, half a mile back. "I am instructed by *Coronel* de
las Piedras to demand an explanation for this unlawful
gathering under—"

Johnson cut him off. "Convey our compliments to the
coronel, teniente. I'm Frank Johnson, and this is James
Fallon, and William Jack. We wish to talk to the *coronel*
on a matter of some importance. So there'll be no mis-
understanding our intentions, our advance guard will
remain where they are."

The lieutenant's eyes drifted to the Texas column and
widened. James hid a smile. "I will convey your message."
The lieutenant wheeled his horse and galloped back to his
own lines. They could see Piedras gesticulating at him.

"I don't think he likes your message, Frank," James
said.

Jack laughed. "Especially that bit about advance
guard."

In five minutes the lieutenant was back. "I will take you
to *Coronel* de las Piedras. You are warned that any hostile
move on the part of your . . . of the others will be con-
strued as an act of rebellion."

As if, James thought, the gathering of armed men
wasn't in itself rebellion under Mexican law. Johnson
seemed to accept it, though, and they followed the lieutenant to where Piedras sat his horse behind the lines.

The colonel was making an obvious effort to ignore the
eight hundred armed Texans his men faced. The skin of
his round face was tight to the point of bursting, and his
neck lapped over his high gold-braided uniform collar.
"You say you wish to speak to me," he said in a high
voice.

"First, *coronel*," Johnson said, "you must understand
that we are loyal to the Mexican government. We wish to
adhere to all points of Mexican law."

Piedras grunted. "That is what you wish to tell me?"

"We wish to present to you our grievances with John Bradburn."

"Grievances?"

"He's violated our rights, *coronel*, time and again. He declared martial law and seized property without cause. He has . . . ."

As Johnson droned on, James studied the Mexican soldiers. Like Bradburn's men, they were for the most part *presidarios*, their uniforms barely presentable, their muskets showing rust spots. Even so, if they maintained discipline, they'd be difficult to defeat, especially backed by a cannon and lancers who were definitely not conscripts. It would be clumsy, though.

" . . . these charges," Johnson was finishing up, "will be upheld by an impartial investigation. If Bradburn and the *presidarios* are removed, we will submit ourselves to any properly constituted civil authority."

"I have heard rumors," Piedras mused. "Very well, I will investigate your charges. If they are well founded, you may rest assured that *Coronel* Bradburn and the presidarios will be removed."

"I thank you, *coronel*. To show good faith, we'll see there are no large gatherings of men in the town or near the fort until after your decision has been reached." Johnson and Piedras made short bows to each other, and the three Texans rode away from the Mexicans.

James said, "Once he's with Bradburn in the fort, we'll have a real fight on our hands. He'll be wary today, but by tomorrow he'll be thinking he's fooled us. We can hit him before he reaches Anahuac—"

"No!" Johnson broke in. "I gave my word. This can be settled peacefully. You'll see."

The Texans withdrew, and the Mexicans reached the fort without an attack. The Texans made camp to wait. James retired to Schiller's Tavern in Anahuac in disgust.

Two days later James was seated in the common room, drinking alone, when Buck Travis walked in. James stared at him as if at an apparition. "I'll be damned," he said softly. "The bastard did let you go."

"I'm glad you can contain your joy," Travis said as he sat down across the table. He was usually full of energy, but now he was pale. He poured a glass of James' whiskey without asking and downed it.

"I'm happy to see you," James said. "I just didn't think Piedras would really let you go."

"Let us all go. The *presidarios* are marching north with him, and Bradburn is being sent back to Mexico City under arrest. I understand he's terrified the settlers'll hang him if they get their hands on him."

"This doesn't sound like Piedras, Buck. He hates *yanquis*."

Travis barked a laugh and took another drink. "It wasn't love moved him, James. The man's convinced Johnson has thousands of men. How he thinks that, I'll never know."

Laughing, James explained about 'the advance guard,' and Travis joined in.

The smile slowly faded from Travis' face. "It's not really finished, you know. Piedras just backed down because he's scared. Whoever's sent in to replace Bradburn will be up to his old tricks in no time, and Piedras will be up to his. The only way anything will be solved is . . . ." He trailed off, but James finished for him.

"Independence?"

The two men shared a look of understanding, then Frank Johnson came in.

"William Jack's looking for you," he told Travis. "Seems he and his brother want to do a little serious drinking with you. You see, Fallon? We did it peacefully."

"There'll be another time," Travis said darkly.

Johnson grimaced. "There already has been. That damned fool we sent for the cannon, John Austin. Colonel Ugartechea wouldn't let him pass the fort—the idiot made no secret he had cannon on board—so he raised the damned countryside. They took Velasco three days ago. Word just got here this morning. Seven Texans dead, and thirty-five Mexicans."

"Austin still has his men together?" James asked.

Johnson shook his head.

"They let Ugartechea and his men march for Matamoros, then dispersed. Thank God."

"I think I'd better get back to Nacogdoches, Frank," James said. He grinned at Travis. "Until the next time?"

"Until the next time," Travis grinned back.

"Take the child. I wish a bath drawn," Lucille told the maid as she handed her Selena, just a year old. Hurrying up to her dressing room, she stripped hastily. Since she had begun taking the baby to the hovel for the weekly ritual she had felt a dirtiness that had nothing to do with the heavy July heat. And the baths didn't seem to help.

Critically she examined her breasts in the mirror. They were still presentable, if not, at thirty, so high as they had been at twenty. The worst had been that the old woman insisted on her nursing Selena. She had gotten a wet nurse, of course, for Guillaume, almost three now.

She snatched up a black lace negligee as the door opened, thinking it was her bath being brought up. Gerard closed the door behind him, smirking at her.

"Don't cover all that loveliness on my account, my dear."

She belted the negligee viciously. "What do you want, Gerard? I am expecting my bath."

"To talk to you, of course."

"*Zut!* You disappear for weeks, and now you return to talk? I suppose you have been involved in the turmoil we hear of," she sneered. "Another Haden Edwards?"

"Actually," he said, "I did go up to Nacogdoches before I came home. Piedras has already created a crisis up there with his dealings with the Comanche. No, my dear, this is much better than Edwards, and with less risk."

"You have an aversion to risks, do you not?" she said drily. "Where have you been, then?"

"Preparing a surprise for old friends. Did you know James Fallon is in Nacogdoches? I think he's bedding Piedras' wife, but I'm not sure."

"You know I no longer follow his activities." She grimaced at his bray of laughter.

"If he didn't have such irregular habits, he'd be dead a dozen times over. Don't take me for a fool, Lucille."

He took off his coat and began undoing his shirt. He had developed quite a disgusting paunch, she thought. If he didn't control that hex doll . . . . "You say that Fallon is Isobel de las Piedras' lover? I know her."

He was stripping off his trousers. "I don't want you disturbing that situation." Naked, he padded toward her.

"Gerard, it is hot, and I am sweaty."

The door opened, and Luz, her maid, stopped in confusion with one foot in the room. "Your bath, *mi dueña*," she said uncertainly.

"Come back in half an hour," Gerard growled. "I'll be through by then."

Face flaming, Lucille let him pull her into the bedroom by her wrist. She would concentrate on Fallon. Locking herself into a corner of her mind, she would ignore the man grunting atop her. Perhaps Isobel, willing or not, could be a key.

"Bets, gentlemen," the faro dealer said, and James put ten dollars on the queen. There were four other men at the table in Crawford's, a Nacogdoches gambling den, and they put their money down around the green felt layout. The dealer slipped two cards from the box. Four of spades and jack of diamonds. A man who'd bet on the first card groaned as his bet was raked in. The others waited for the next deal.

"Any more bets?" the dealer asked. The smoke-filled room was busy, a dozen tables split evenly between monte and poker, a roulette wheel and a wheel of fortune. All were crowded by anxious gamblers. The second card out was the queen of hearts. James shifted the twenty dollars to the ace.

"Didn't expect to see you bucking the tiger," Henry Cameron said. He had become beefier in the last few years, but it wasn't fat.

"Something to do," James said. The ace of spades was the first card; the dealer took his bet. He put a ten-dollar gold piece on the tray. "Sit down." He lost again.

"Why don't we find a table some place else? Can't talk while you're gambling."

"Might as well. I'm losing anyway." He took a hundred dollars from the table in front of him—he'd started with two—and followed Henry to one of the few tables that wasn't given over to gambling. "Whiskey," he told a passing waiter. "What are you doing in Nacogdoches, Henry?"

"Ortiz, your foreman, says you haven't been back to the ranch since May. That's damned near three months, James. I thought I'd see if something was the matter."

The waiter brought a bottle and two glasses, and James poured, studying Henry. "You ever think about politics?"

Henry shook his head. "Politics ain't for black folks. You mixed up in them goings on down south?"

"A little." It was a mistake to involve Henry, he thought. Leonie's fourth was less than a year old. Hostages to fortune, he seemed to remember reading. "I'm fine, Henry. You can go home with a clean conscience."

"You look drug through a knothole," Henry said. "I seen Elena over to San Antonio. That girl's in love with you, James. You could do a lot worse."

He felt a rise of irritation. "She's just a child, Henry."

"That is no child," Henry said emphatically. "She's old enough to be having babies of her own."

He readied an acid retort, but before he could deliver it the door to the gambling den burst open and a squad of soldiers burst in. The room went silent except for the clatter of the wheel of fortune, still spinning from its last turn. James recognized the sergeant in command, Pedro Marcos. Piedras loved his contempt of *yanquis*.

He looked around for a handy window and whispered to Henry, "If anything happens, hit the floor and stay there till it's over."

Marcos, tall and broad across the shoulders, surveyed the room, a smile appearing on his dark face when he sighted James. "So, *Señor* Fallon, you are not so hard to find. In the name of the Republic of Mexico, I arrest you—"

James leaped from his chair and dove through the

window. Glass showered around him into the alley behind Crawford's. A musket ball spat splinters from the window frame, and then he was on his feet and running. More muskets cracked. He heard feet pounding after him. A lone man, by the sound.

He pulled his knife, ducked around a corner and crouched. The feet pounded closer. A shape whirled around the corner, and he grappled it, knife raised— and stopped. It was Henry.

"What in hell are you doing here?" he whispered angrily. "I told you not to get involved."

"I am involved," Henry whispered back. "One of those soldiers was headed for the window for a good shot, so I kicked him in the *cojones*. Got out that window about half a second ahead of musket ball my own self."

"Damn it all to hell. Your wife'll kill both of us. Follow me, and keep quiet."

By dark alleys they reached Alderman's Livery Stable, and entered the back way. In the shadows he fumbled for his saddle.

"Fallon?" somebody whispered. "Is that you?" James drew his knife again and remained silent. "It's Hollins," the voice went on.

James sighed with relief. "It's me, Hollins. Marcos just tried to arrest me. Piedras must be getting suspicious. I'm moving out to the camp."

"You been messing around with the colonel's wife, Fallon?"

Something about the tone made James pause. "What do you mean?"

"Man we got spying on Piedras says a note came maybe three hours ago now. He didn't see who delivered it, but he says Piedras went right through the roof. Had a big argument with his wife, then beat the hell out of her. Says you could hear her yelling all through the mission. Then Piedras put out orders for your arrest. We been looking for you since we found out."

"Still wenching, James?" Henry chuckled.

"Who's that?"

"A friend," James said, frowning. Isobel had kept their

affair going by hinting that she'd tell her husband he'd
made advances if he didn't. He couldn't stay in Nacogdoches without bedding her, and he had to admit it
hadn't been a chore. "Hollins, you didn't come into town
just to save my hide."

"We're moving," Hollins said. "Me and Simpkins and
Ford are passing the word."

"James," Henry said, "you ready to tell me what's
going on?"

"While we ride," James said.

The camp was a few miles east of town, a scattering of
men the last time James had been there, a constellation of
fires under the trees, now. He had explained the situation
as best he could on the ride from town; Henry had ridden
the last mile in thoughtful silence, not speaking until they
were drinking coffee beside one of the fires.

"You really expect to make Piedras declare for Santa
Anna, James?"

"That's what most everyone here is after," James said.

"But you're after something different, aren't you? I
know you a long time, James. You're holding back."

James nodded. "Independence for Texas. And I'm not
the only one."

"Jesus Christ! Then why all this about Santa Anna?"

"Because most people aren't ready to think about independence. But the way I see it, the Mexican government
won't care who we're supporting. All they'll see is *yanquis*
with guns, a rebel army ready and waiting. If the revolution doesn't start on our side, they'll force it after this.
You ready to go back to Leonie now?"

"I expect I'll stay awhile," Henry said. "Let me have
some more of that coffee."

Early the next morning a delegation rode into Nacogdoches to present the Texans' demands to Piedras: declare
for Santa Anna and the Constitution of 1824, or abandon
Nacogdoches. Isaac Burton, Philip Sublette and Henry
Augustin returned about ten o'clock with Piedras' refusal.
James Bullock, a lanky rancher from the San Augustine
settlement, had been elected colonel that morning before
the delegation set out. In half an hour he had them mov-

ing toward Nacogdoches.

When they reached the town, about three hundred strong, sweat was pouring down James' face from the noon sun. The streets were empty. The column moved into the town square, heading for the mission on the knoll, where the Mexican tricolor flew boldly. Abruptly there was a clatter of hooves, and Mexican cavalry charged from side streets, firing their short musketoons. Horses reared, screaming, and men shouted.

James fired into the mass, then dropped to the ground and fired his second barrel. He thought he saw a soldier go down. Henry was beside him, kneeling and reloading. Other Texans fired, some from horseback, some from the ground. The Mexicans wheeled and disappeared back up the side streets, leaving half a dozen of their number on the ground.

Abruptly musketry rattled from the west end of the square. "They're in the stone house!" James shouted. He remembered when it had been Haden Edwards' headquarters.

"And the church!" another man screamed.

"Dismount!" Bullock called. "Into the buildings! For your lives!"

James joined the rush for the buildings along the south side of the square, Henry at his heels, found a place at a window and began to reload.

"What do we do now?" Henry yelled, poking his musket through another window and firing.

"You're doing it," James said. "You're doing it."

Throughout the day the fire kept up, the Texans peppering the church and the stone house, the Mexicans returning fire desultorily. By nightfall James knew they were in for a stalemate unless one side or the other broke. The soldiers had made one sortie, about two in the afternoon, but the Texans had beaten it back with withering fire. Bodies still lay in the square. After that Piedras had contented himself with increasingly scattered return of the Texans' fire. Conserving powder, James thought. The Texans had slackened their fire to save powder as well, but they still managed to keep up a continuous fusillade.

From midnight on there was nothing at all from the soldiers' positions. When a cautious party investigated at daybreak, the church and the stone house were empty except for dead and wounded.

James ran out into the square with several hundred other weary men, all those who hadn't fallen asleep from sheer exhaustion. He'd left Henry sleeping. He was surprised to see Bowie.

"When did you arrive, Jim?"

"Couple of hours ago," Bowie replied. The Texans swirled around the two of them, arguing over what to do next. "As soon as the word of Anahuac and Velasco got to Saltillo, I came back."

"I didn't think you approved."

"There's not much choice now, is there, James?" Bowie looked at him sharply. "They keep talking about Santa Anna. Don't any of them know what they're into?"

"They'll find out," James replied.

"Quiet!" Bullock shouted, forcing his way through the crowd. "Let me have some quiet!" Slowly silence fell. "That's better. It looks like Piedras has pulled out to the west, probably trying to reach San Antonio. He's left his wounded behind, but most of his men are afoot, so he won't be moving too fast. We could catch him and finish this, only most of you are so tired you'd fall out of the saddle in an hour."

"Might as well do this right," Bowie sighed. "Colonel," he called, "I'm not tired, and I'll bet I can find fifty more who aren't either." There was immediately an uproar of men clamoring to volunteer. Bullock fired a musket in the air to restore quiet.

When the shouting had died, he called out, "Jim Bowie has said he'll take fifty men after Piedras. I reckon it's up to him to pick them. Mr. Bowie, you've got yourself a job to do."

Bowie picked his men quickly, and in half an hour they were riding west. In less than two hours, pushing hard, they reached the Angelina. Cottonwoods bordered the ford, and an abandoned house looked down from a nearby brush-covered hill. It was the closest ford to Nacogdoches, the one Piedras would certainly head for, but a quick check showed that no large body of men had crossed recently. They crossed over and hid themselves among the cottonwoods on the far side.

An hour later Piedras' column appeared. Twenty cavalry were in the lead, Sergeant Marcos at their head. The rest of the cavalry brought up the rear, no doubt in fear of pursuit. The infantry, dusty and staggering as they marched, showed the strains of being under fire all night and marching hard all morning.

Marcos rode into the water. Bowie shouted, "Fire!" and the Texans opened up.

Marcos and half the advance guard fell, the water around them whipped to froth. The survivors fell back toward the column in panic. Scrambling out of formation, the infantry ran for the house on the hill. The cavalry galloped through them to get there first, jumping off their horses and fighting each other to get inside. Piedras and Major Medina, his second in command, tried to force them back into some semblance of order, but the infantry had reached the house and were going to ground around it.

"Let's hit them while they're off balance," James said, and Bowie rose to his feet.

"Follow me!" Bowie shouted. Screaming like ten thousand devils, the Texans splashed across the river.

At the base of the hill James found cover behind a bush and fired up at the house. The Texans fired, reloaded and fired again until they sounded like ten times their number.

The return musketry was sporadic, and after a few minutes Bowie called for cease fire. He crawled over to James. "I think we have him. Do you have a clean handkerchief?" James produced one, and Bowie tied it to the end of his musket. He waved it in the air, then stood up cautiously when the fire from the hilltop stopped. "You coming, James?"

They walked up the hill side by side, James conscious of what a good target he made if Piedras did indeed know about Isobel. Twenty feet from the old house they stopped. The soldiers lying on the ground looked at them with frightened eyes. They probably thought the entire force had followed them, James realized. He hoped Bowie realized it, too.

After a few minutes Piedras and Medina appeared from inside. The usually dapper Medina was haggard, his uniform tunic half undone. Piedras' face swelled when he saw James. He knew.

"You have come to surrender?" Piedras said.

"Let's not beat around the bush, *coronel*," Bowie replied. "Your men are worn out, you're short on ammunition, and you're trapped on this hill with no water except what you have in your canteens. We can sit at the bottom sniping till your tongues swell up. You're the one who has to surrender. And state your allegiance to the 1824 constitution. Your men will be well treated, their hurts will be tended, and they'll be escorted to San Antonio."

"I will never," Piedras said stiffly, "surrender to any force that numbers among it that man." He indicated James with his chin.

Bowie looked at James. He muttered, "A personal matter."

Medina took advantage of the lull. "*Mi coronel*, I urge you to accept this offer. The men are indeed exhausted. Our powder and water are almost gone. Further resistance can only result in a massacre. *Mi coronel*, you cannot ask it of them."

"*Mayor* Medina," Piedras said, glaring at James until his eyes seemed ready to burst, "I hereby relinquish command of the Nacogdoches garrison to you." With that he turned on his heel and marched back into the house.

Medina heaved a sigh of obvious relief. "*Señores*, I now declare my complete allegiance and adherence to the Constitution of 1824. And I surrender my command to you. Lay down your arms!" he called. "Lay down your arms and stand up!" One by one the soldiers rose, leaving their muskets on the ground, shuffling their feet uncertainly. "And now, *señores*, if we could get water? We intended to replenish our canteens at the river."

"Certainly," Bowie said. He called down the hill, then

turned back to Medina. "Major, if you'll be so kind as to lead your men down, single file."

Medina made a short bow that included both James and Bowie, then motioned his men to follow down the hill. The soldiers fell in hesitantly, looking uncertainly to James and Bowie as they passed.

"We've done it," James said.

"We've done it, all right," Bowie said. "I wonder what Texas will say when they find out we've given them a war."

"We've given them a nation, if they can take it."

XLVIII
Charleston, 1832

Rain-laden winds blustered off the harbor, hammering at the house on East Bay Street. Soon Robert Fallon would have to leave the crackling fire in his study, and go out to meet with Langdon Cheves and James Pettigru. For the moment he could forget his own troubles by reading of James'.

And so (the letter concluded) we are to hold a convention in San Felipe in October. Stephen Austin still believes in negotiation and compromise, and has announced he means to use the convention to frame a petition for redress of grievances to Mexico City. It is entirely possible General Santa Anna will occupy the Presidential Palace by that time, and many feel he would look favorably on such a petition. The events of the past six months, however, have split Texas into a Peace Party—Austin's— and a War Party, of whom William Wharton seems to have emerged as the foremost spokesman. I am on my way to the convention, with William Barrett Travis, James Bowie and others, in support of the War Party and Independence. We must have it, or the Mexicans, when they are finished with their revolutions, will surely drive us from our lands, from Texas. I know you preach moderation, but a time comes when you must fight. It has come for us. From what you have told me of your situation, I pray it has not come for you.

> Your Son,
> James Fallon

He folded the letter with a sigh. It was the fifth of Oc-

tober today. Their convention would meet soon if it
hadn't already. His son was committed to starting a war;
he was committed to stopping one. And now that Jackson
had replaced Calhoun as Vice-President on his ticket with
this Martin Van Buren for the upcoming election, war
seemed even closer. The entire South saw Calhoun's re-
moval as a slap in the face. If only he could be as sure of his
course as young James seemed of his.

The tall clock against the wall chimed ten. He hastily
put the letter away in his desk; the meeting was for ten-
thirty. In the hall Albert was waiting with his caped overcoat and hat. The butler's hair showed gray at the temples,
but he still cut a swathe among the ladies of the city's free
black society.

As Robert shrugged into the overcoat, he found a brace
of pocket pistols in the capacious side pockets. He took one
out and raised an eyebrow. "Are things that bad, then?"

Alfred shrugged. "Who can tell, sir? The mobs are
worse by the day." He hesitated. "I had Josephus put a
shotgun under the driver's perch."

Robert nodded sadly. "Thank you, Alfred. Please tell
Mrs. Fallon I'll be home for dinner."

"You can tell her yourself," Moira said, coming down
the sweeping stairs. Alfred discretely withdrew. "Another
political meeting, Robert?"

"Another, I'm afraid."

She wore her forty years with queenly elegance, he
thought, raven hair untouched by gray, face smooth as it
had been at twenty. She was one of those women who grew
more beautiful with the years. Conscious of his own age—
sixty-one, he reminded himself grimly—he straightened
his shoulders. One day, he feared, she'd realize she was
married to an old man. He refused to admit that age had
only made him look more the corsair and the splashes of
gray at his temples more distinguished, or that almost as
many women eyed him now as had twenty years before.

"I thought," she said, straightening his lapel unneces-
sarily, "that I'd invite John Lafflin and his bride for
supper next week. But I'm not sure I want to remind you
how attractive men your age are to young women."

He grinned, wondering if she'd read his mind. She was wont to do that. "John's gone to St. Louis on business. He won't be back till Christmas." Lafitte had managed to carry off his disguise—to the world he was six years dead in Yucatán—going into business with Glenn Mortimore and, just that year, marrying Mortimore's young daughter, Emma. The thought of supper invitations sparked something in the back of his head, and when he remembered what it was, he knew Moira wouldn't be pleased. "Last week I asked Edward to come to supper tonight. With the elections coming up, and all the troubles, it slipped my mind."

"For one night, Robert, I can stand him."

From the way her jaw tightened it wasn't as simple as that, but he wisely let the matter lie. Edward was twenty-four now, in his own apartments two years, and much as Robert hated to admit it, life had been more peaceful since he moved out. Abruptly he remembered the time.

"I have to rush, dear. I'll see you at dinner."

"Don't forget," she called after him as he hurried out, "Elizabeth is going to Charlotte's poetry reading tonight."

The rain pelted against him like birdshot as he hurried down the walk to where a heavily cloaked Josephus held the coach door. Purple-gray thunderheads were building up out to sea.

As the coach rattled over cobblestones he kept the leather curtains open despite the rain. Even with the weather, every intersection had its boxtop orator, wearing the white cockade of the Unionists or the blue of the Nullifiers. Around each speaker was a bodyguard, a dozen men gripping clubs. More often than not, there were fewer listeners than bodyguards, but that there was anyone at all spoke of the passions in the city.

"Put the horses under cover, Josephus," he said when the coach drew up in front of the house on Meeting Street where Cheves was staying, "and get yourself something hot to drink."

The butler took his hat and overcoat, and led him up to

the second-floor sitting room where Cheves and Pettigru waited.

"Robert," Cheves said warmly, "I'm glad you could come." A thin man, two inches shorter than Robert and five years younger, his head seemed too large for his body, the more so for his high forehead and great mass of graying hair. He wore small round spectacles set low on his nose.

"I'm glad you finally decided to join us," Robert said. Until the previous summer Cheves had cooperated with the Nullifiers. He inclined his head to Pettigru, warming his buttocks in front of the fire. "James."

Pettigru was a younger man than the other two, spare and intense. "I wasn't sure you'd come, Robert."

"Why not?"

"From some of the statements you've made lately, I thought you might have moved to the Nullifier camp."

Robert bristled. "And I stand by my statements. The new tariff leaves all the worst features of the old in place. The only way to spike Hamilton and Hayne is to get some reasonable adjustment." Those two had come a long way since Vesey, he thought. Hamilton was Governor, Hayne United States Senator. They, with Calhoun, were the prime movers of the Nullifiers.

"Easy, gentlemen," Cheves laughed. "It's the Nullifiers we must fight, not each other."

"There are too damned many people ready to fight," Robert grumbled. "And this time I'm not talking about the Nullification Clubs."

"Perry and Bynum," Cheves said quietly. Robert nodded. Two months before, in the upcountry, the controversy had erupted in a duel. Clark Bynum, Nullifier editor of the *Greenville Mountaineer*, had been killed by Benjamin Perry, Unionist editor of *The Sentinel*.

"You're right," Pettigru said. "But no gentleman should meet one of those Nullifier rabble on the field of honor. It's lifting them to our level."

Cheves made an angry sound in his throat. "If you're going to let your politics fuzz your brain, James, you'll not be much use. Men like Henry Pinckney and Whitemarsh

Seabrook may be fools, but they're gentlemen."

"Next," Pettigru said, "you'll be agreeing with Robert that we must organize associations to counter those infernal Nullification Clubs. Damned Jacobin Clubs, I call them."

"And why not?" Robert demanded. "Those clubs are influencing the vote. People see them. People listen to them. Are you forgetting the election's only three days off? We've no more time to waste."

"The people," Pettigru said fastidiously, "want to be led. We are their leaders. We will lead them."

Robert snorted. "I've never heard such poppycock. Do you agree with this, Langdon?"

"Robert, we might as well remember who we are. Low-country planters. Broad Street lawyers. East Bay merchants. The mechanics are with the Nullifiers almost to a man. I simply don't believe we can organize clubs."

"By God," Robert said, "I'll do it myself, then. I have friends among the mechanics. What's that supposed to mean?" he added as Pettigru laughed.

"Robert, a man of your standing doesn't have friends among the mechanics. Oh, I'll grant you acquaintances. If you'll forgive me, you always have had a peculiar taste for the common people. But friends? They probably think of you as a rich eccentric."

"I'm afraid James is right," Cheves said. "You're a relatively wealthy man, you know. Your steam packets to New York and London. Your foundry. The cotton mill. And you invested in the Charleston and Hamburg Railroad, didn't you? They probably think you're a Unionist because the tariff benefits you as much as it does the Northerners."

"I will be damned," Robert breathed. It was true he had benefited. Many who could no longer afford to buy from Europe with a fifty percent tariff on cottons, woolens and iron goods had bought from him rather than go to the Northerners. But he hadn't pushed his prices up to just under what the imported goods cost, as the Northerners had. "Do you think that's why I'm with you?"

Pettigru shrugged expressively. "Frankly, Robert, I've

no idea why you're with us. The way you talk at times, you sound like a Nullifier."

"I'm a Unionist because we can't win a war."

"*War?*" Pettigru said.

"War," Robert said. "If the Nullifiers win this election, they'll get their state convention, whether they get the Southern convention they want or not, and nullification will become the law of the state. I know Andy Jackson. He won't let it go by. And if he tries to use force, you know the Nullifiers will fight back."

"That would be civil war." Cheves' voice was hollow.

James nodded. "Calhoun told me ten years ago the tariffs would lead to just that. I'm afraid I didn't believe him, then."

"Well, if he wants a war," Pettigru said, "we'll give it to him. If the Nullifiers try to organize a military force, we'll organize one, too."

"So we confine the civil war to South Carolina?" Robert said drily.

"If necessary, Robert," Cheves said. "Surely you see it's better we handle it ourselves if possible? Would you rather have the state occupied by Federal troops?"

"I won't help Carolinian kill Carolinian." He sensed them drawing away. "I thought we were supposed to plan a statement for the meeting at Seyle's Hall on Saturday."

"That hardly seems important, now," Cheves said. "I suppose we've had our heads in the sand about a lot of things. I thank you for pulling them out, Robert. I propose we devote this meeting to planning what to do if the Nullifiers do try to force a military confrontation."

"You're twisting my words," Robert protested. "It's what might happen, not what will. We should be trying to stop a confrontation, not conceding it."

"We no longer control events, Robert."

"Now just a moment," Pettigru said, but Cheves went on.

"For whatever reasons, we can do little more than react to what the Nullifiers do. Robert, we need you in this wholeheartedly. You have considerable experience in military matters."

"This quickly it's military matters." Robert's bitterness increased by knowing he had brought the subject up. He told himself they'd have thought of it themselves sooner or later, but it didn't help. "If you're going to discuss organizing to fight our own people, I won't be part of it. Gentlemen." He turned with a short bow, but Cheves' voice stopped him.

"Don't you think keeping a Federal army out of South Carolina is worth fighting for?"

"I don't think it'll matter to the men who die whether they're killed by a Federal bullet or a South Carolina one. If you'll excuse me." Cheves opened his mouth again, but Robert hurried out.

He was silent at midday dinner, lost in worry. Thomas, eleven, and Carver, nine, ate unnoticing and left to rejoin their tutors. Moira watched him, frowning but wise enough to leave him to himself.

Settling in front of the study fire, he chewed the stem of his unlit pipe. The only solution he could see was a more equitable tariff from Washington. Whether one would be forthcoming was another thing. Insofar as they were doing anything, southern congressmen spent their time orating on the sovereign rights of the states, northern congressmen fulminating on treason. No one seemed interested in finding a way out of the crisis.

There was no chance of a local solution. Cheves and Pettigru might believe the voters would follow them to the polls; Robert knew otherwise. Unless some scandal broke among the Nullifier leaders in the next three days, the election would go their way. He wasn't sure even a scandal could deflect their massive support. The election must be conceded. But then, what could be done? Something must be.

Filling and lighting his pipe, he moved to the window. Rough water in the harbor had driven barges to shelter by the seawall that rimmed the tip of the peninsula, barges loaded with huge granite blocks for the almost-finished artificial island at the harbor mouth. A new fort was to be built there; it was said the fort would be named after General Sumter, of Revolutionary War fame. He stared past the barges, across the whitecapped harbor, and saw none of it.

Once the Nullifiers' States-Rights and Free-Trade Party won the election, they would call their convention to endorse a nullification law—a Nullifier-dominated legislature would pass it immediately—and call for a nullification convention of all southern states. Some southern states had already come out against nullification. Louisiana felt the tariffs protected their sugar industry, and Tennessee was solidly pro-Jackson. The rest would come, though.

If that all-South convention could be stopped from agreeing on a joint nullification policy, however . . . . There had been some talk of a Unionist convention in Columbia, the state capital, in December. He must encourage it. And there were Unionists in other states who must be reached with the same idea.

Puffing contentedly now, he started for his desk to list the men he would write, and stopped as Albert entered.

"Sir, there's a lady to see you. A Mrs. Marie Fourrier Southford." He emphasized the second name slightly.

Robert said in confusion, "I didn't see a coach." The last time he had seen his half-sister, she was two, and in her mauma's arms. He hadn't known she'd married. Or if she had children. She might as well be a stranger.

"Mrs. Southford arrived on foot, sir."

"In this weather! She must be soaked. Bring her in to the fire, quickly. We'll want hot tea. And hot spiced wine. And tell Mrs. Fallon," he added as the butler was leaving.

In a few minutes Mrs. Southford hesitantly entered the study, and he hurried to greet her. Marie was forty-seven, her face careworn. Her gray-streaked hair hung damply. Their mother's violet eyes were all he recognized about her, but he never doubted she was who she said. "It's been so long, Marie. So long. Come to the fire. You'll catch your death. Why on earth did you walk? And when did you arrive in Charleston?"

She let him lead her to the fire, eyes down under his barrage of questions. "I just thought I'd . . . ." She took a deep breath. "Hiring a coach takes money, Robert. Passage from Jamaica took most of what I have. It seems strange not to pronounce your name in the French fashion.''

"I don't understand," he said. "I know Gerard is doing well in Texas."

She gave him a frightened look. "Gerard? Gerard hasn't shown much interest in the rest of the family since he went to Texas. Or in anything in Jamaica."

Moira bustled into the study, followed by Albert and a maid. "Thank you, Albert," she said as he set down the tray he carried. She took a basket from the maid, who left with Albert. "I thought you might be chilled, so I brought a warming pan for your feet, and a warm towel to wrap your hair.''

"Thank you," Marie stammered.

Moira caught Robert's eye, and he jumped into the awkward silence. "Moira, this is my half-sister, Marie. Marie Southford. Marie, this is my wife, Moira."

"You are very welcome in this house, Marie," Moira said.

After a few moments Marie had been settled in a chair with hot tea, warming pan, and the towel around her hair. "Marie, I just don't understand. Whatever else can be said about Gerard, I never knew him to lack family feeling for those he considered family."

She sighed and set down her tea. "Gerard doesn't consider a sister family, Robert. In that, he's like papa. Papa never knew what to make of a daughter. Gerard told me I should have been more careful with my husband's estate."

"I'm sorry, Marie," he said. "I didn't know."

"I'm not," she said defiantly. "Thomas wanted sons, and when I gave him four daughters in four years, he proceeded to make my every waking moment a misery, gamble himself into debt, and drink himself to death. If papa hadn't let me bring the girls back home with me, we'd all have starved by the roadside."

"I'm sorry," he said again, awkwardly. "But surely you inherited part of the Fourrier shipping line when . . . .' He trailed off, wondering if she knew how her father had died. Her face didn't change.

"Papa did leave me a small part of the line, but of

course Gerard was managing the business. I'm afraid he didn't have papa's touch. By the time he left for Mexico, there were only three ships left." She twined her hands together. "A month ago he signed the ships over to me. He sent a letter, a note, really, saying it was the last he expected to have to help me."

"Then your problems are solved," Moira said. "Three ships."

"You don't understand, Mrs. Fallon. The ships have been tied up a dock for almost a year. I had a man look at them. I'm afraid I don't understand such things, but . . . ." She raised her hands helplessly and let them fall.

"The hulls will be fouled," James said. "They'll have to be scraped, new cordage and sails bought. After so long with no one looking after them, some of the ironwork may have to be replaced, too."

Marie nodded. "That's what I was told. But I can't afford to make repairs. Or to hire crews, or pay the—what are they called?—dockage fees."

"Marie," he said slowly, "you must allow me to give you the money. Call it a loan. You are my sister, after all, and you're no more responsible for Gerard than for the moon." She stared at him so long he was sure he'd offended her. Moira often told him he was too direct, but it was obvious she had come to him for help.

"I . . . I can't accept that, Robert. I would very probably never be able to pay it back. Jarrel Stone, the man I had look at the ships, says there's a lucrative trade from Kingston to South America, but even I know there are risks. Even if I was able to repay, I can't imagine you could allow your money to repair Fourrier fortunes."

"Balderdash!" Robert said. "I'm repairing my sister's fortunes."

"Your half-sister." Her voice was so low he could barely hear. "I am half Justin Fourrier's blood, as well. I know there was never anything but hatred and strife between the two of you."

"But not between you and me, Marie. You didn't come here to tell me I couldn't help." Moira frowned at him, and he carefully avoided looking at her. Women always wanted to do things the roundabout way.

"Could I have some of that spiced wine, please?" She took the silver goblet Moira handed her, and drained half of it. "I came to ask you . . . to ask you to become my partner."

"Your partner!"

She rushed on quickly. "There's still just as great a chance you'd lose the money, but if the South American trade is as lucrative as Mr. Stone says, you would make as much as I do. Please, Robert. Either way you share in the risks. If this fails, I have nothing else to pay you with. You must share in the profits, too, or I can't accept. I simply can't." She appealed to Moira. "You understand, don't you?"

Moira patted Marie's hand and shot Robert a firm look. "Men sometimes don't realize we have our pride, too."

He sighed to himself. He was going to become Marie's partner whether he would or no. Not that he'd look askance at extra income. That first set of bank loans ten years earlier had led to others, and no matter how the businesses flourished, there always seemed to be a need for another. Firmly he put a halt to that idea. Once the amount of his investment was paid back, he'd find some way to channel the rest to Marie.

By the time Marie left, he had talked her into letting him move her from her small, none-too-clean inn to rooms in the Atlantic Hotel, and arrange for a coach and driver. She was effusive in her thanks, almost weeping. When the front door had closed behind her, he stared at it thoughtfully.

"It occurs to me, Moira, that I've no proof this isn't some plot of Gerard's."

She drew breath. "Would Marie be a party to a plot against you? Perhaps, but she was shaken by having to ask you for help. I can't believe she's a good enough actress to fake that so well. Is Gerard still plotting against you? It's been almost four years since those two ships were seized by Mexican customs, and you haven't told me of anything since that can definitely be laid at his door. Finally, are you willing to turn your sister away on suspicion?''

Gerard's presence in Texas, discovered through a chance mention in one of James' letters, had been a surprise. But it had explained, in his mind at least, why Mexican authorities had claimed that two of his ships were smuggling. Robert no longer traded with Mexico. Since then he'd kept a sharp eye out, looking for Gerard's hand in every altercation with customs officials, every cargo stolen by another line, every ship delayed. When *Olympic* had blown up in New York harbor in 1829, he had found no connection to Gerard. And steamships did burn.

"I wish I could be sure," he said finally.

"If it helps, dear, she loathes Gerard Fourrier. Whenever she mentioned his name . . . well, I can't explain it. But you can take my word for it."

He had, after all, no real reason not to.

He returned to his study, to his desk, but had listed only three names before the door banged open and Edward sauntered in, another young man behind him.

"Hello, uncle." Edward fell into a wing chair, hooking his leg over the arm. His hair had darkened with age, but it was still a mass of soft ringlets. Two inches over six feet, and slender, only the slight hook of his nose saved him from being pretty rather than handsome.

"You're early." Robert looked at the other young man with a raised eyebrow. "Have we met before? You do look familiar, but . . . .''

The other looked embarrassed. "Excuse me, Mr. Fallon. I'm Edward Hammond. Your nephew and I met a few days ago, at Elger's Coffee House." As tall as Edward, but broader in the shoulders, he wore a sober mien and his dark eyes were serious.

"You don't sound like a Charlestonian, Mr. Hammond. Are you from upcountry?"

"Oh, no, sir. I'm from Virginia. By way of Harvard," he added with a laugh. "My father said I sounded like an Englishman when I came home."

"Didn't know that," Edward said. "I was at Harvard, too." He laughed again. "For about two years. They kicked me out. Setting fire to a privy while drunk. How was I supposed to know there was a fat old farmer in it? I wanted uncle to get me in at William and Mary, but he made me come back here and go to South Carolina College. Had more farmers' sons than gentlemen.''

Robert waited for him to run down. Edward liked to play the languid fool, but there was a sharp mind behind the pose. He'd proven that when he could bother to attend classes. But the pursuits of ''gentlemen''—gambling, horseracing, cock fighting, fox hunting, attracted him more than working. Without letting Moira know, Robert had fulfilled his gambling debts, paid off two girls he'd gotten into trouble—Robert was just thankful the girls had seemed more interested in the money than anything else—and quietly covered a shortage and gotten him into another law office when he had been allowed to resign at the first.

''How did you and Edward meet, Mr. Hammond?'' he said when Edward was finished.

''You don't have to interrogate him, uncle,'' Edward said drily. ''I'm not a virgin girl, you know. Remarkable about the names, isn't it? I call him Hammond and he calls me Fallon, just to keep straight, you see. He's got a fighting buck, you know. Biggest black I ever saw. Bigger than that Kemal fellow of yours.''

''You have a fighting slave, sir?'' Hammond said.

''God, no,'' Edward laughed. ''Uncle doesn't believe in slaves. Should've warned you. No, this Kemal is a big Turk, runs a coffee house. Got no tongue. Ought to get uncle to tell you how this Kemal and he escaped from the Barbary pirates. Damned good story. Say, uncle, is Bets about?''

''Elizabeth is upstairs,'' Robert said. Hammond had dropped several notches in his estimation. Keeping a fighting slave was a brutal custom, one he was glad wasn't popular in South Carolina.

Hammond seemed to sense the change in his mood. ''King was a gift from my father, sir. I think it was his way of sending a bodyguard with me on my travels. And King would certainly rather fight than work. I hope this won't prevent my escorting Miss Elizabeth to the poetry reading.''

Robert blinked in surprise. ''I wasn't aware,'' he began, when Albert tapped on the door and entered.

''Mr. Graham, sir. He wishes to see you.''

''Show him in, Albert,'' he said. He needed a chance to regain his equilibrium. This stranger apparently thought to escort Elizabeth somewhere? Once the sandy-haired Scott was in, and the introductions had been made, Robert said, ''Now what is it, Kenneth? Some trouble with the foundry?''

''No, sir,'' Graham said. ''I came . . . well, sir, Miss Elizabeth indicated she wouldna' mind if I accompanied her t' the poetry reading tonight.''

''You?'' Edward said incredulously. He coughed under Robert's glare, and added lamely, ''You must be thirty-five. Elizabeth's just a girl.'' It was Graham's position as an engineer, Robert knew, that Edward disapproved of. Engineers weren't gentlemen.

Shorter than the young men, Graham faced them with his chin lifted defiantly. ''I havena' spoken of romantic intent. And I'm thirta'three.''

''It seems there's a problem here,'' Robert said.

''Miss Elizabeth,'' Hammond explained, ''has given me the honor of escorting her to the poetry reading.''

''I gave it to both of you.'' Elizabeth bustled into the study, frowning as she buttoned her gloves. At seventeen she was stunningly beautiful, her mass of raven hair surrounding a heart-shaped face with lavender eyes. Her dove-gray dress covered a full bosom above a tiny waist. ''It wouldn't be proper for me to go with just one man, even with Esmerelda for chaperone.''

''Just where did you meet Mr. Hammond?'' Robert said. He tried for an admonishing tone, but she wore a tiny smile, and he was painfully aware how easily she could wrap him around her finger.

''On Broad Street, papa. I was looking for a new hat, and he was with Edward. It was perfectly within the bounds of propriety.''

"Hardly propriety," Robert grumbled. She wrinkled her nose at him, then flashed a smile of triumph as the last tiny button slipped into place. "No offense, Mr. Hammond," he added.

"None taken, sir," Hammond said smoothly.

"Now, papa," Elizabeth said, "you aren't going to be difficult? Why, with Esmerelda, and Edward, and Mr. Graham, and Mr. Hammond, think how safe I'll be. He wasn't going to let me go at all," she said over her shoulder, "because of the altercations in the streets."

"Me!" Edward exclaimed. "I'm not going to any da— to any poetry reading."

"You'll escort your cousin," Robert said firmly. "Supper's not till ten, and you'll be back by then."

"Then it's settled," Elizabeth said. Robert had to smile at the way she managed the three men without seeming to, getting them all started on the way out before he could change his mind. The smile faded when she turned on the point of leaving and said, "Oh, yes, papa. I told Chloe to bring you some warm milk. You'll sleep better."

After they were gone he found himself chuckling. She managed him, too, and as well as her mother did. When Moira came in, he said, "Your daughter takes after you."

"I am surprised you let her go, Robert."

"Perfectly respectable. Esmerelda and Edward are both with her."

She grimaced. "It's too much you let her get away with, husband. That horse, for instance."

"There's nothing wrong with her having a saddle horse, Moira." He was more than a little defensive about that horse. In secrecy, Elizabeth had trained it as a jumper, to his pride, but there'd been an explosion when Moira found out. To divert her, he said, "She's trying to add Kenneth Graham to her string. She'll have no luck there. The man's not interested in anything that isn't iron or steel."

"That's why he came this afternoon," she said drily. "Really, Robert, you are blind, you know. The man's besotted. And she treats him like a new toy. That's another thing. She's entirely too flirtatious, Robert. And so long as you let her play you like a trout, it does no good for me to put my foot down.''

He hadn't heard anything after 'the man's besotted.' ''Graham's sixteen years older than her!''

''Yes, dear,'' she said, so blandly that he drew himself up short.

He was twenty-one years older than Moira, he admitted grudgingly. If his age made no difference to Elizabeth . . . . He liked Graham, personally, and the man certainly had a future. ''I wouldn't object to a marriage,'' he said slowly.

''It hasn't gone that far,'' she laughed. The musical sound warmed him.

He chuckled. ''I practically had her married off, didn't I? Dear, if you'll forgive me, I want to get this list finished before they get back for supper.''

XLIX
Texas, 1832

The cold December wind, racketing down the streets of San Antonio, clawed at the shutters of the Veremendi house. James' fringed buckskins were at odds with the Castilian formality of the room as he sat reading in a massive, leather-upholstered chair in front of the fireplace.

My Dear James,
    Please forgive me for the brevity of this note, but time and events press me. The elections are done, two days and nights of rioting in the streets, of free whiskey and drunks being carted to the polls. The Nullifiers were better organized in the streets. During the weekend prior to the election we Unionists almost came to blows with the Nullifiers in the middle of King Street. Debouching from a meeting at Seyle's Hall, several hundred found ourselves face to face with an equal number of Nullifiers, marching up the street beneath their banner, 'States-Rights and Free-Trade.' In an instant respectable merchants, planters, lawyers and mechanics were tearing clubs from passing wagons, seizing cobblestones, surging toward one another. How odd it was to see Joel Poinsett and Whitemarsh Seabrook, each in his way eager for the coming conflict, putting out all their oratorical ability to avoid bloodshed for the moment.
    No sooner had the election results—a two-thirds majority and more for the Nullifiers—been announced, than their convention was called for November. We must participate, use our small numbers to influence events as best we can, yet I find resistance and even disdain at the idea. It seems the convention will be left to the Nullifiers, the call will go out for a Southern Convention, and the

South will unite behind South Carolina. And now a terri-
fying new word has been added to the oratory.

Secession.

You will remember my surprise at learning that Gerard
Fourrier was in Texas. As a further example of the sort of
man he is, his sister, Marie, has appeared here in Charleston, widowed and destitute, abandoned by Gerard. For all
my suspicion of anyone with the Fourrier name, she is my
half-sister, and I will help her as much as I am able. Remember to keep an eye on Gerard. He is so convoluted he
could well stab himself in the back with his left hand,
plotting against his right.

I must go, James. I send you my affection and my
prayers.

                              With Love,
                              Robert Fallon

It appeared his father needed lessons in proper caution.
This Marie might be his half-sister, but then Gerard was
his half-brother. Discovering that Fourrier was an uncle of
sorts had come as a shock to him.

He tucked the letter away as *Don* Tomás entered the
room. It was his presence, and Elena's, that had resulted in
James being a guest of the Veremendis. The old man,
white-haired but still erect and firm of eye, was frowning
worriedly.

"James, I have been wanting to talk to you." He hesitated. "About the meeting you attended in San Felipe."

In October representatives from seventeen settlements
had gathered in San Felipe, meeting in the unpainted
board building that now served as town hall.

"Is it true that you have sent a petition to Mexico
City?"

James nodded.

The old man sucked in his breath. "Do you not understand this is not proper? You must first obtain permission
to present a petition. This is a very dangerous game you
play."

"We play no game, *Don* Tomás. We asked for Coahuila
and Texas to be separated, and for immigration to be
opened up again. And there was a statement of support

and congratulations for General Santa Anna.'' He felt a stab of guilt at what he was holding back. He had supported stern-faced William Wharton, an exponent of rebellion and independence, against Austin. Austin's shock had been palpable. In the end, he had voted for the petition, but only because he believed it would be rejected for the very violation of form Don Tomás had pointed out.

''That last,'' Don Tomás mused, ''was a good stroke. Santa Anna may well be in Mexico City this minute. Still, nothing is certain. The norteamericanos must learn patience and sacrifice, if they would live in Mexico.''

''Most of us feel we've sacrificed enough.''

The old man snorted. ''You? You—they—know nothing of sacrifice. You have seen the old mission of San Antonio de Valera outside of the town? It is old and abandoned, yet it gleams whitely in the sun. When it was being built, Mexican mothers gave the goat's milk that was intended for their children to be mixed with the mortar, that it might shine to the glory of God. When you can do such a thing and consider it no sacrifice, as they did not, then you will have begun to learn the patience that Mexico demands.''

''There's no time left for patience. Even if Santa Anna has won, there's no guarantee we won't be ordered off our land and out of Mexico.''

''You have no worry. You are a Mexican citizen.''

''Legally, and in your eyes. Others see me as just another yanqui. And it's not just we norteamericanos who think Texas is the orphan of Mexico. Speak to Don Erasmo Sequin. He was at San Felipe.''

Don Tomás was silent. ''I must think on this,'' he said at last.

When the old man had gone, James poked viciously at the fire. He should leave. Already he'd been in San Antonio too long. The restless urge to be somewhere else —anywhere else—was beginning to grow, overwhelming the desire to be with friends at Christmas. Not with friends, he told himself savagely. With Elena. Turning from the fire he saw her in the doorway.

''You are troubled,'' she said quietly.

He managed a bleak smile. "Just one of my black moods. I'm not fit company."

"Then I will be company for you." She settled into a chair, smoothing her skirt. "We will talk of commonplaces."

"If you wish." It was pleasant being in the same room with her. When she was with him, thoughts of leaving faded.

Her smile was angelic; her big brown eyes seemed luminous. "There will be a procession of the children of the town to the cathedral tonight. They will carry candles and sing."

He could see her surrounded by children, their children, in the courtyard of the *hacienda* he had always planned to build beneath the plum trees . . . . No! He had brought Drusilla into his life and killed her, her and Amelinda both.

"James, what is the matter? Do not look at me like that."

Abruptly he realized his smile had become a rictus. It took an effort to smooth his features.

"*Señor* Fallon?" He spun to face the maid who had just entered, and she took a frightened step back. "*Señor* . . . *dispénseme, señor*, but there is a man in the stable who says he must speak with you. He . . . he gave no name."

"In the stable?" Elena said incredulously. "And without a name?"

"It might be important," he muttered, and hurried out before she could say more.

In the stable, a slender, vaguely familiar *vaquero* stood on the straw-covered floor, turning his hat in his hands and nervously watching the men working with the horses.

"Who are you?" James said.

"Antonio Fuentes, *señor*." He stepped closer. James watched him warily. "I worked on the *rancho* of *Señora* Applegate, and after that for *Señor* Fourrier."

"That's no recommendation, Fuentes. What do you want with me?"

"I came to tell you that *Señora* Fourrier wishes you dead." James burst out laughing. The slender man looked pained. "As God is my witness, *señor*, this is the truth."

"Fuentes, I never met *Señora* Fourrier in my life. She wouldn't know me from a fence post." He remembered Fuentes now, though. The man had ridden for Cordelia.

"I would not know about that, *señor*. I know only that she offered me much gold if I would find you and kill you."

"Why you?"

Fuentes shrugged. "I have lived among *los Indios*. I am the best tracker and the best shot of all the *vaqueros* on the *hacienda*. I could have done this thing, but I know that you are a friend of José Escobar, a man I respect much. When I refused, she told *Señor* Fourrier that I had attempted to lay hands on her. I had no chance to tell the truth. He would have killed me. I fled, and because of my respect for José Escobar, I came to find you and tell you."

"I could almost believe it," James said, "if it was Gerard instead of his wife. I could believe damned near anything about him."

"Oh, no, *señor*. The *señora* was most pointed about that. *Señor* Fourrier was to know nothing. The money depended on it, she said."

"Fuentes, I don't know your game, but your cards are bad. Why don't you go back to Gerard and tell him it didn't work?"

"But *señor*," Fuentes began. James turned on his heel and walked away.

Since learning who Fourrier was, he had wondered if the man's hatred of Fallons could ever have been directed at him. There had been the murder charge following on the heels of Fourrier's appearance. Almada's attack, and the gold found on him. When he began to wonder about things as improbable as the Comanche attack that killed Drusilla, and as trivial as the note that had spurred Piedras' attempt to arrest him, he knew his speculations were growing insane. And now this Fuentes claimed it wasn't Gerard, but his wife, who had something against him. He needed a drink.

He was back into the sitting room where he'd left Elena and halfway to the sideboard when he realized the girl was

gone and Jim Bowie and another man were warming their
hands at the fire. Bowie was tall, as tall as James, but the
other man stood at least three inches taller, proportion-
ately broad of shoulder and deep of chest. His long,
strong-jawed face was fine featured, and his frank eyes
watched James closely.

"James," Bowie said. "Elena told me you were here.
Meet Sam Houston, former Congressman, former Governor of Tennessee, soon to be a Texan if I have my way."

"Mr. Houston," James said. He knew of Houston.
Everyone knew of Houston; at one time he'd been spoken
of for the Presidency of the United States—but much of
what he knew was rumor and innuendo. Houston had
married a much younger woman. Three months later she
went home to her parents, and he resigned as governor and
crawled into a bottle. That much he knew as fact. "What
brings you to Texas?"

"Texas Indians, Mr. Fallon," Houston replied. "Comanche, to be precise. They've been causing trouble across
the border in the United States. President Jackson asked
me to try to get them to a treaty meeting at Fort Gibson."

James turned away, filling a glass with whiskey and
downing it before he answered. "Comanche don't believe
in peace treaties," he said harshly. "To them peace is just
the time to prepare for the next battle." He refilled his
glass, sipping slowly as he tried to calm himself.

Bowie leaped into the silence. "Fact is, Old Hickory
had to get Sam out of Washington." A frown creased
Houston's brow. "William Stanbury, Congressman Stanbury of Ohio, accused Sam of fraud while he was governor,
and Sam whipped him within an inch of his life."

"Hardly that," Houston said drily. "I did get carried
away and thump him a bit. I understand you know the
Indians well, Mr. Fallon."

"Thump or whatever," Bowie went on, "the Congress
wouldn't sit still for it with one of their own. They put
Sam on trial, James. Had no right, but they did it. Old
Francis Scott Key himself was Sam's lawyer, and drunk the
whole time. They found him guilty, of course. No other
way, with the Congress being prosecutor, judge and jury

all in one. I guess Andy figured he'd better get Sam out of Washington before he thumped the whole Congress."

Houston's face had grown darker as Bowie spoke. "Mr. Key was drunk only during his opening address, and I've never heard him in finer fettle. I was indeed found guilty, but the fools contented themselves with a letter of censure and a fine I'll never pay." His mouth compressed. "And as for President Jackson—"

"You're thinking of settling in Texas, Mr. Houston?" James said. There was no need to let the conversation erupt in anger.

Houston's face cleared quickly, and he gave James a look of gratitude. "I am considering it, Mr. Fallon. This Texas is quite a land."

"But a troubled one," James said.

"It is that, Mr. Fallon. I understand there's to be another convention to discuss possible solutions."

"In San Felipe, in April." He had the feeling the other man knew as much about Texas' troubles as he did. "Tell me, Mr. Houston, what do you believe the solution is?"

"In this case, Mr. Fallon, I agree with Jim. And," he added with a shrewd look, "if he's told me correctly, with you."

Bowie chuckled. "You see why I want him to stay? Let's face it, James. You and I are nothing but adventurers in most people's eyes. They're not going to listen to us. Sam Houston, though—hell, James, everybody knows Sam Houston. Help me convince him."

James didn't think Houston needed convincing.

"If you do settle here, Mr. Houston, will you be practicing law, or trying your hand at ranching?"

"Oh, law, certainly," Houston said. "I suppose every man wants to own a little land, though. If I stay, I'll probably talk to Mr. Austin about it."

Delegates to the April convention had to be land owners. Houston, James thought, probably didn't want to be seen as coming to Texas to rebuild his political fortunes. "Welcome to Texas, governor."

After one sharp look at James, Houston said, "This talk

is interesting, as talk, but I mustn't forget my purpose in Mexico. Jim tells me you know as much about Indians as any man in Texas.''

''I can name six or eight *vaqueros* who know more,'' James said. ''And they're just the ones I know.''

''Unless one of them is here in San Antonio, you're the man I want. I need someone to be a go-between with the Comanche chiefs.''

Bowie's breath caught loudly. James poured another whiskey before answering. ''I don't deal with the Comanche.''

''But—''

''Sam,'' Bowie said quickly, ''let me introduce you to a man or two who might be able to help you. I didn't realize . . .'' Once more he frowned worriedly at James. ''I'll take Sam over to meet Alvarez and Gallegos, and come right back. You'll still be here, won't you?''

James shrugged. ''I don't have anywhere else to go, Jim.''

Bowie hesitated, but when James didn't say any more, he left with Houston. James barely noticed; he was staring into the fire. The flames changed. Elena's face. Drusilla's. A log split, sap shrilling in the flames like a woman screaming in the distance. Angrily he hurled his glass into the fire and left.

He packed hurriedly, stuffing his few possessions into saddle bags, and went out to his horse. The urge to go was overpowering. Fuentes was no longer in the stable, but the thought of the man made him decide on San Felipe. He still didn't believe Fuentes' wild charges, but it was as good as any other place.

His way took him across the split-log bridge east of town, past the old mission. San Antonio de Valera, *Don* Tomás had said, but most people called it after the cottonwoods lining the irrigation canals that surrounded it. The flames were still in his mind. Flames that had killed Drusilla, flames that would soon engulf Texas. And he would help one as he had caused the other. The pale walls of the aged mission seemed to mock him. Let it be a symbol of

Mexican sacrifice, he thought, this *Los Alamos*. Texans had sacrificed enough. He put spurs to his horse and galloped eastward along the tree-lined road.

L
Charleston, 1833

A crisp breeze whipped around the widow's walk atop the Fallon mansion on East Bay Street, but the January sky was clear, and Robert could study every part of the harbor without difficulty. He muttered to himself every time he shifted the brass spyglass. Three of the seven Federal revenue cutters busily swept across the harbor approaches. Another paralleled an inbound merchant brig, a small boat tossing halfway between. They were taking no chances of the tariffs being evaded. The duties were collected in cash before a single crate or bale went ashore. Well out in the harbor a sloop-of-war lay at anchor with the other cutters. Rumors told of heavier Naval units on the way.

With a sigh he started to turn away, then stopped as a carriage pulled to a stop in front of the house. Edward sat laughing across from Elizabeth and Hammond. She was laughing, too, looking up at the dark-eyed man. King, Hammond's slave, rode the back of the carriage in footman's livery, the red and white looking comical on his six-and-a-half-foot, massively muscled frame. Suddenly Robert jerked up the spyglass, cursing his failing eyes, and peered back down at the carriage. Edward wore the blue Nullifier cockade in his lapel.

It was all he could do not to shout his rage down at the street. He stumped rapidly down the spiral stair into the house, and on down to the entry hall, where Elizabeth was just giving her pale blue parasol over to a maid. She turned a smiling face to him. He stalked across the hall, spyglass

437

clenched like a club in his fist.

"Hello, papa. Have you been up to the widow's walk? It's a beautiful morning, isn't—"

"Where is your cousin?" he cut her off.

"Edward's still with Mr. Hammond, papa. Why—"

"He's a damned Nullifier!"

"Who, papa? Mr. Hammond?" Her eyes twinkled, but he met her gaze sourly.

"Don't play the fool with me, miss."

"Aren't we a bear today. Papa, it's the way with every family in town. If the fathers and uncles are Unionist, the sons and nephews are Nullifier. I think Edward has a point. The way the North—"

"When I need the political opinions of a seventeen-year-old girl, I'll be ready for a rocking chair." He turned away from her hurt eyes. "What about Hammond? I suppose he's one, too. I never see you anymore except with Edward and Hammond. I don't like that, daughter."

"Mr. Hammond," she said tightly, "doesn't believe women are just overgrown children. He discusses politics with me, and art, and literature, and he listens to—"

"Enough!" he shouted. She took a step back, then stiffened her back. "You'll get to your room before I show you just how much of a child you are. To your room, I said!"

Frozen-faced, she dropped a perfect curtsey and glided up the stairs. He opened his mouth to call her back, and shut it with a sense of frustration. Slapping the spyglass against his palm, he strode into the front sitting room.

"Shall I send for your whips, husband?" Moira said wryly. She set down her book and stood up, smoothing the pale gray velvet of her dress.

"Now don't you," he began angrily, but let it fade into a sigh. "I'm not angry with her. And I suppose Hammond is a decent enough young man. It's just . . . Edward's joined the Nullifiers. At least, he's wearing their badge."

"I know," she said. "I've no doubt you were heard on ships in the harbor." Her smile took any sting out of her words.

"I've a perfect right to be upset, Moira. A Nullifier! Even if it weren't for the stupidity of the politics, the thing's a slap in my face."

"You ought to know him well enough to know he doesn't care whose face he slaps."

He shook his head wearily. "Could you go up to her, explain things? I have to be in my study. I'm expecting a man from Hayne." Hayne had succeeded Hamilton as Governor. After Jackson's reelection, Calhoun had resigned rather than remain as a powerless lame-duck figurehead, and had taken Hayne's Senate seat.

"Of course." He had the unpleasant notion she knew he simply didn't want to face his own daughter.

He had no sooner settled gloomily in his study than Albert announced the man from Hayne.

"James Butler Bonham, sir," the visitor said. A handsome six-footer in his mid-twenties, he wore a gold-braided blue militia officer's uniform. Wavy black hair and a ready smile added to his striking good looks. "Officially, it's colonel, but really I'm just Governor Hayne's aide."

"Whiskey, or brandy, Colonel Bonham? Or do you prefer mister?"

"I prefer brandy and mister, sir," Bonham laughed, easing his high collar with a finger. "We're all of us hoping all this military nonsense never has to be used, aren't we?"

Robert handed a brandy to Bonham. "Some of us are," he said drily.

Bonham hesitated, then nodded. "Granted, sir. And some aren't. Some on both sides. Some in Washington."

A few weeks earlier Jackson's call for Congress to give him special military powers to deal with the situation—the Force Bill, it was called by some; the Bloody Bill by others—had been met in South Carolina by the raising of twenty-five thousand armed volunteers. Unionists had raised eight thousand of their own, but for the moment everyone, Federals included, seemed to be waiting for someone else to make the first move. The latest furor had been caused by Jackson's threat to 'hang any man who even breathed sedition and treason from the nearest tree.'

"Colonel, what is it you want to see me about?"

"Mr. Fallon, you hold quite different views from other,

ah, from some of the men you associate with.''

"I'm still a Unionist, colonel.''

"You're also a Carolinian, sir. The question is, what will you do if Jackson tries to make good his threats by force?''

"Threats,'' Robert said disparagingly.

"Winfield Scott.'' Bonham spoke to the air. "Second ranking general in the United States Army. He is already in the city. In the last month Castle Pinckney and Fort Moultrie have been reinforced.''

"And Governor Hayne's boasted that the heavy cannon he's had brought in can pound Castle Pinckney into rubble in twenty-four hours. I'll ask again, colonel. What do you want with me?''

"You have a foundry, sir,'' Bonham said. "You make muskets there. Carolina's biggest problem is the lack of arms. Governor Hayne's personally set up a cannonball manufactory.'' Bonham swirled his brandy, obviously waiting for Robert to comment. Robert sipped from his own glass. "Sir,'' the younger man said finally, "surely it's obvious. The state will pay good prices for whatever muskets you have in stock. And for your future production.''

"I no longer make muskets,'' Robert said. "Too difficult to compete with the English and French. Even the tools were sold.'' He'd crated and stored the tools in a warehouse on the Neck six months previous. He wouldn't make muskets for a civil war. "The last muskets I had were shipped months ago.''

"Damn! Sorry, sir.''

"I understand Congressman Verplanck of New York has put a new tariff bill before the House. If the tariffs are dropped to reasonable levels, there'll be no need for any of this.''

Bonham set his glass on Robert's desk. "But we think, sir, that Verplanck's tariff hasn't a chance. And I fear the President will get his special powers. In that case, there'll be more need than I care to think about. If you'll excuse me, sir.''

For a long time after Bonham left Robert sat behind his

desk. He wanted to believe what he'd said, that the tariffs would be lowered, that the trouble would melt away. Unfortunately he thought Bonham was probably right.

Opposition from the Northern states, whose industry the tariffs protected, might stop the bill, even if they believed the alternative was Southern secession. He remembered his father—Michael Fallon, not Justin Fourrier—telling him how the North had been willing to make a separate peace during the Revolution, leaving the South to England. The seeds of the present struggle had been sown then, during those last two years when the South fought alone, abandoned until they managed to win their own victory.

He'd spoken to everyone in the state who would listen, written everyone in the South he could think of. Aside from Calhoun, he knew few in Washington. The men he once could call on—Jefferson, Madison, Monroe—were long gone.

"Mr. Fallon?" Startled, he looked up at Albert, in the doorway. "Mr. Cheves is here, sir. He says it's—"

Langdon Cheves pushed past Albert. "Robert, I understand Bonham was here."

"Thank you, Albert," Robert said. He waited until the butler had left. "It's good to see you, too, Langdon. Yes, it's a brisk day out, but sunny. Would you like a drink?"

Cheves pushed his spectacles up his nose with one finger. "I'm sorry, Robert. But you must understand a little agitation on my part when I hear Hayne's aide has called on you. In uniform."

"In uniform," Robert laughed. "He wanted muskets, Langdon, and he got the same answer you did. I don't have any."

"No matter." Cheves hesitated. "I might as well tell you. President Jackson sent us five thousand stands of muskets. The last arrived yesterday, in crates marked 'shovels.' They've already been distributed."

"Good God, Langdon. You're still outnumbered three to one. Unless you intend calling on those Federals you claim to be intent on keeping out, all you can do is precipitate a bloodbath. Jackson is just waiting for an excuse."

"Daniel Huger, the damned fool, asked the President to occupy Charleston immediately, and he refused. Does that sound like a man searching for an excuse? The only way Federal troops will leave the forts is if Hayne seizes Charleston. I have the President's word on it."

Robert laughed bitterly. "I'm sure you do, Langdon, but think. Why is he so willing? Already there've been rumblings in the North Carolina and Virginia legislatures against letting Federal troops cross their borders to, oppress, I believe, was the word used, South Carolina. If he makes the first move, he'll be seen as no better than one of those South American 'presidents,' taking and maintaining power by force of arms. But if the fighting begins inside the state, then no matter who fires the first shot, no matter who gains the upper hand, he can send in troops to put down insurrection."

"You can't believe he's that cynical, Robert."

"Look at his history. The way he handled the Florida problem. The Creeks in Georgia. Jackson has always looked to force for solutions. He's always believed that right was on the side of power."

"If it will keep South Carolina in the Union . . . ."

"But it won't, Langdon. Not without Federal troops garrisoning every crossroads. Let one Carolinian be killed by Federal troops, and Hayne and Hamilton will have a vote in favor of secession before he's buried. Virginia's ready to follow, and the rest won't be far behind."

Cheves sighed. "Well, I can't, I won't, watch it happen without doing something. It might be the wrong thing, but at least I'll have tried. I'm sorry, after bursting in the way I did, but I must go, Robert. I'm meeting with Huger and Pettigru. Why don't you come, too? You're still wanted, you know. And needed."

"I can't, Langdon." But Cheves' words rang in his head as he showed the other man out. Doing something, even if it was the wrong thing. Trying. What more was there he could do? Full of uncertainties, he went in search of Moira.

Moira glanced up from her embroidery hoop as Robert entered the parlor. "Elizabeth is sulking in her room," she said, placing the next stitch carefully, "but I think she understands." The last wasn't exactly true. Her mission of reconciliation had met with such a tirade from Elizabeth that she herself had grown angry enough to fetch the castor oil and force a good mouthful down a disbelieving Elizabeth's throat. But Robert didn't have to know that, or that Elizabeth was locked in her room to mend her manners until Moira returned.

The silent way he moved to the fire drew her attention. "Is there something on your mind, dear?"

"Moira," he said, without looking at her, "am I turning into an ineffectual old man?"

For a moment she stared at his back. Then she leaped to her feet, the embroidery hoop falling to the floor. "No! And I'll not have you talking about yourself that way. What's gotten into you? You're the most vigorous man I've ever known, of any age."

"I feel so damned helpless." He stared into the flames, rubbing a hand back and forth aimlessly along the mantel. "Everything I do seems to be flailing to no purpose. I'm drifting with events initiated by other men, without the slightest idea where I'll end up."

Her heart went out to him, but she knew sympathy would be deadly. He had grown old, she realized, without her even noticing it, but the will that suffused him was still as great as it had ever been. She would not let that will die, for she was certain he would die with it.

"What more can you do?" she said quietly.

"I don't know. I've done everything I can think of, short of going to Washington, but . . . ." He threw up his hands and let them fall limply.

"Then go to Washington." When he didn't move, she put bite into her words. "I won't have you sitting around feeling sorry for yourself. Even if it does no good, at least you'll be doing something."

He jerked as if struck, and looked at her for the first time. "Doing something," he murmured. "I suppose . . . I couldn't go till after the first, of course. God knows what it'll be like here then. I'm not sure I shouldn't take you and the children upcountry till after. And everything's almost arranged for Marie . . . . I can't run off." His spirits were visibly sinking.

"It's now you must go, Robert Fallon. Today. As soon as you can hoist the boiler, or whatever it is you do to those infernal steamships. You can do something, Robert. I know you can."

"Perhaps," he said, his voice firmer than before. "But you, and the children, and Marie . . . ."

"Do you think a few men playing soldier can frighten a woman who saw her husband on the battlefield at New Orleans? And remember the stock your children come of. They're hearty enough to survive a little bombast. As for Marie, she's waited this long; a little longer won't harm her."

He touched her cheek, and his smile made her throat ache. "Do you have any idea," he said softly, "how much of my strength I draw from you?"

"Then you but borrow it back again, Robert, for I draw all of mine from you." She wanted to laugh. And to cry. He stood straight, with his eyes full of purpose. It was already drawing him away.

"Calhoun," he said. "I'll make him listen if I have to grab him by the throat. Getting there . . . . *Flying Fish* is due to sail tomorrow. I could move it up. You'll forgive me, won't you, darling? I have to go to the Bridge." The last words were delivered as he hurried out.

His problems were settled for the moment, she thought as she recovered the embroidery hoop from the floor. By the time he returned from Washington, she would have the smaller problem of Elizabeth settled as well.

LI
Washington, 1833

As Robert made his way into the Senate building, he reflected that Washington had changed little since he had seen it last, the night the British burned it. The destroyed buildings had been rebuilt—the one he was in among them—and Pennsylvania Avenue no longer detoured around the marshy stretch where Tiber Creek thrust into the city, but the streets were still muddy lakes when it rained, and the main business of the city still was plotting and sly maneuvering. In the Senate lobby, small groups of two and three men, most wanting to influence legislation —they were coming to be called 'lobbyists' for the way they infested the lobby waiting to corner Senators—stood with their heads together, passing the gossip that fueled the city.

Ahead he spotted Calhoun, spare and towering over the men around him as much by force of spirit as by physical size. His massive head, with its brooding, deep-set eyes, was topped by a mane of white hair, thrown straight back from his forehead. Black broadcloth was the traditional garb of the Senate, but as if to emphasize his rebellious stand, Calhoun's suit was of white cotton nankeen. As his gaze fell on Robert, unadorned surprise crossed his face.

"You're looking tired, John," Robert said, offering his hand.

Calhoun hesitated before seizing it warmly. "So are you, Robert. I'm surprised you're speaking to me. I've had some of your letters quoted in speeches against me on the floor."

"I'm glad you're willing to talk to me. Your friends back home consider me a dangerous eccentric, at best."

"Friends?" Calhoun snorted. "Fools!" Looking around with seeming casualness, he drew Robert to a spot along the wall where they weren't close enough for anyone to overhear. "Those 'friends' of mine have practically drummed me out of the party for opposing their damned secession nonsense."

Robert blinked in surprise. "Everything I've heard puts you squarely with Hayne and Hamilton."

"You know me better than that, Robert. I've never advocated secession. I want to protect the South, but *in* the Union. For months I've been trying to get them to put the whole nullification question off for a year, trying for time to find some solution short of leaving the Union." He sighed heavily. "A despatch rider brought word this morning that some sort of meeting in Charleston two days ago voted to suspend implementation, but only until Verplanck's tariff is settled one way or another. I can't find out whether the meeting was official or not. Hayne and Hamilton were there, but I haven't heard from them. Do you know anything?"

"It must have taken place right after I left." He hesitated, then added, "But the day I sailed, Hayne's aide was after me for muskets for his volunteers."

Calhoun smiled and made a short bow to a passing man, who returned both without stopping. "Then they're still building for a confrontation," he said through his smile. "If they keep on, they'll get it, too. Jackson's spoiling to send troops into South Carolina."

"I told Cheves that, but he didn't believe me. Jackson still thinks like a general. Force is the first solution."

"It may be more than that, Robert. There are persistent rumors that a list of strong Jackson opponents, not just Nullifiers, exists, and that the men on that list are to be arrested if armed fighting begins in South Carolina. My name is supposed to head it."

"Surely you don't believe rumors."

"They come from so many directions, and vary so little . . . . One thing is certain. He wants to punish South

Carolina. He told Senator Wright of New York so flatly, and Wright lost no time repeating it.''

"Then he can't be given the chance," Robert said. "Everyone in South Carolina's afraid the Force Bill will pass and Verplanck's won't. What are its chances, really?''

"That Verplanck's been amended by Uncle Tom Cobley and all till it pleases no one and offends everyone. It'll pass the day I'm elected Senator from Massachusetts.''

"Then why hasn't someone put up another? Surely you have friends in the House who'd propose any bill you want.''

"You never were devious enough for politics, Robert." Calhoun shook his leonine head ruefully. "My name associated with a tariff bill before it reaches the floor is a death knell for it. New England would vote 'no' in a block without waiting to read it.''

"There must be a way," Robert said. "There has to be. If the tariffs aren't lowered—damn it, any drop at all will do—Hayne will get his secession. And Jackson his excuse.''

Calhoun stared silently across the marble-floored lobby, seeing no one. His conversation with a stranger had been noted; Robert saw men eyeing them speculatively.

"It'll have to start in the Senate," Calhoun said finally. "House committees are barrels of snakes. Slow snakes.''

"But don't tariff bills have to start in the House?''

"They must be voted on first there, but there are ways to get around the rest." There was a twinkle in Calhoun's eye, the first true relaxing of tension Robert had seen. "You leave the politics of it to me, and find a Senator to get this replacement bill proposed.''

"Me!''

"You. An outsider, a well-known South Carolina Unionist. You'll be listened to. What I said about me applies here, too. In fact, we'd better not be seen together again in public. Where are you staying?''

"My bags are in a carriage in the street.''

"When you have rooms, send a note to my office.'' With a short bow he was gone, his white suit disappearing into the tide of black broadcloth.

* * *

Robert took a sitting room and bedroom at Mrs. Elias' Boarding House, and began his circuit of the Senate with little more guidance than curt notes from Calhoun. Even private meetings were to be kept to a minimum, Calhoun said, lest Robert be tainted with his stigma.

Washington was as strange as he remembered it, its Senators as changeable and capricious. Thomas Hart Benton had once fought a duel with Jackson—the ball in Jackson's shoulder had only recently been removed—but the intervening years had made him a staunch Jackson man. Missouri had no foreign trade to speak of to be hurt by a tariff, nor industry to be protected, but Benton's words of refusal to Robert had almost been enough to make him forget his refusal to duel.

John Tyler and William Rives of Virginia were split, Tyler anti-Jackson, Rives pro, but even Tyler wouldn't propose the bill for fear of the advantage it might give Rives in their home state. All Robert could get from Tyler was a promise to support such a bill if someone else put it forward.

Felix Grundy and Hugh White of Tennessee. George Bibb of Kentucky. Bedford Brown of North Carolina.

Three days after his meeting with Calhoun, a note and a carriage arrived at Mrs. Elias'. He was summoned to the White House; Jackson's scrawling hand spoke of their service together at New Orleans. It had been he who introduced Jackson to Lafitte, but he was sure it was Calhoun, and not New Orleans, that interested the President.

The White House had been gutted by fire when the British took the city, but no damage remained. Whitewash used to cover burn scars on the exterior walls had fixed the name 'White House' firmly. A lawn with a few young oaks surrounded the building. A black butler showed him to the President's study.

Jackson, an inch taller than Robert, stood in front of the fireplace, a shawl around his narrow shoulders, coughing from time to time into a handkerchief clutched in one bony hand. His long face had never been handsome, but smallpox scars and a saber scar on his right cheek destroyed what chance it might have had. Brilliant blue eyes and a stiff brush of white hair gave him an imposing appearance, though when he spoke it was damaged by a high-pitched voice.

"By the Eternal, Fallon, it's good to see you! Pour yourself a brandy. Right over there." He gestured to the sideboard, then stopped to cough. When the fit passed, he cleared his throat harshly. "Damned lung abscess. They're waiting for me to die, Fallon, but I intend to fool them. I'll bury them all. Too bad Lafitte's dead. That damned reprobate would make it complete if he was here, eh? Be just like old times."

"Old times," Robert agreed, filling a glass. "Can I pour one for you, Mr. President?"

"No, no. Damned doctors won't let me have but one on waking, to start the blood flowing. Fools say it's bad for me."

"You and I have lived long enough to know what's bad for us without doctors."

Jackson coughed into the handkerchief. "Perhaps some of us never learn, eh, Fallon? Here you are, with home and family, come to Washington and dabbling in politics."

"I wouldn't put it that way," Robert said.

"Even the President hears things. One veteran of New Orleans to another, why don't you go back home and leave this to us?"

"It's too important for that, Mr. President. The whole lot of you here in Washington have done nothing. Some sort of compromise tariff could—"

"By the Eternal, I'll see those traitors punished!" Jackson's outburst brought on another bout of coughing. When he was done, he glared at Robert across the handkerchief. "South Carolina thinks just because I was born there, they can defy me, defy the authority of the President, of the Federal government. Well, I'll dragoon them back into line, and if it has to be done with bayonets, so be it. You'd better understand that straightaway."

Robert remembered he was talking to the President, and also remembered how uncontrollable Jackson's own temper was once it was roused. "It'd be much better if we weren't forced back at bayonet point, wouldn't it?''

'' 'We,' Fallon? I hadn't heard you'd joined the Nullifiers.''

"If you have to use force, I don't think any distinction will be possible. Frankly, Mr. President, I don't understand you. A bare two months ago you were admitting that the tariffs were too high. Now all you seem to want is this Force Bill, so you can jam the tariffs down everyone's throats.''

"You've been spending time with Calhoun," Jackson said abruptly.

"I've known him a long time, Mr. President. His role in this isn't entirely what you might believe.''

"Role, sir? By the Eternal, I know his role!'' Jackson began pacing in long, storklike strides. "Back in '18, he'd have had me arrested and disgraced over Florida, just to mollify Spain. If I hadn't crossed into Florida, the South he professes to love so much would still be suffering from the Indians there. And after that, while he was making sly, invidious attacks on me, he still thought to be heir. To be President after me. Oh, he thought he was so sly. He published a pamphlet against Van Buren, never realizing I would know it for an attack on me. He inveigled his wife into snubbing Peggy Eaton, and organizing other women to snub her, after I had made her hostess here in the White House. Sly attempts to undermine me, and he thought I wouldn't see them for such.''

Robert was shocked that Jackson would even mention the Eaton affair, two years past. William Eaton, then Secretary of War, had assigned John Timberlake, a Navy purser, to foreign duty and taken his wife, Peggy, as a mistress. After Timberlake's suicide, Peggy Timberlake became Peggy Eaton, and the scandal had eventually forced Eaton's resignation. To assign blame to Calhoun for Peggy Eaton's snubbing was ridiculous.

"Mr. President, are you saying that you intend to punish South Carolina because you have grievances against Calhoun?''

Jackson whipped around, face rigid. All outward trace of his frenzy was gone, but his voice was shrill. "I mean, by the Eternal, that I will not tolerate traitors. If you get this tariff reduction, you and Calhoun—I know he's in it somewhere—well and good. But South Carolina will submit itself to the Federal government, or I will crush her."

"If a tariff reduction is passed," Robert said tightly, "and you sign it, there'll be no need for crushing."

"The entire doctrine of nullification must be stamped out. I will not allow it to retire, waiting to strike again."

"Nullification will collapse if a decent tariff is passed! For God's sake, only a few really want confrontation and secession. The question is, if such a bill is passed, will you sign it?" Jackson was silent. "In the past you've said the tariffs were too high. Will you sign a reduction?"

"I will," Jackson said heavily. "But only if I get the Force Bill, too. Anything else would be a surrender to the traitors, and that I will not do. I will preserve this nation, Fallon. Without bayonets if I can, with bayonets if I must. But by the Eternal, preserve it I will."

By the eighth of February, Robert was beginning to wonder if he would ever find a willing Senator. Calhoun still kept their communication to brief notes, and he was finding it harder and harder to obtain appointments. The Senate was embroiled with the Force Bill. In desperation he found himself appealing to men who had no reason to want the tariffs lowered; William Wilkens of Pennsylvania, John Clayton of Delaware, Theodore Frelinghysen of New Jersey, and his reception was what he should have expected. A chance meeting outside Frelinghysen's office, though, with Robert Letcher, a Kentucky congressman, took him that night to a musicale given by Margaret Everleigh.

"I find you Carolinian gentlemen so amusing," Mrs. Everleigh said as she showed him into yet another room where jewelry-bedecked women and men in snowy linen and black broadcloth listened to a string quartet playing Donizetti. "You seem to have retained the gallantry of a bygone age." Many of the men talked quietly in small groups instead of listening to the music.

The red-brick mansion was ablaze with spermaceti candles, and Robert mused to himself that his hostess, stout, red hair piled high, dripping pearls, bore more than a passing resemblance to her house. "It's simply that we take the time to appreciate lovely women," he said, smiling. His eyes searched the clusters of men for the one he hoped to meet; Henry Clay of Kentucky.

"Oh, you." She tapped his wrist with her fan. "I would like so much to stay and chat with you, but I really must see to my other guests. But you will listen to the Mendelssohn with me in the ballroom later, won't you?" She gave him a smile and floated away, her eye already on another man, a younger one than he, Robert noted with relief. He had a sudden aversion to Mendelssohn.

At that instant he saw Clay, walking slowly down the hall in close conversation with a short, craggy-faced man with a jutting brow. He hurried after them, pursued by lush Italian strings. Beside his heavyset companion, Clay seemed even taller and thinner than he actually was. His pale gray eyes looked at Robert questioningly.

"Senator Clay," Robert said, "I'm Robert Fallon. I believe Mr. Letcher told you I'd be here this evening to speak with you."

Clay's long upper lip and slight lower jaw made his small head seem topheavy. He opened his mouth, but his companion cut him off. "Fallon?" he said, furrowing thick eyebrows. "I've heard of you and your dabbling, sir. I'm surprised a Unionist of your reputation would be working for the other camp, as it were."

"You have the advantage of me, sir," Robert said coldly. The last week had put his temper on edge.

"Mr. Fallon," Clay said smoothly, "may I present the Honorable Daniel Webster, Senator from Massachusetts. Daniel, Mr. Robert Fallon, of Charleston, South Carolina, is it not?"

"Senator Webster," Robert said. Webster supported high tariffs and higher tariffs—Massachusetts was developing a considerable cotton and woolen milling industry. Putting the proposition to Clay wouldn't be any easier for having Webster there.

"You haven't answered my question," Webster said brusquely. "You supposedly believe in the good of the nation. At least, that's the claim I've heard for you Unionists. Why this meddling in the tariffs?"

"I also believe in the good of my state," Robert replied. "Some tariffs are admittedly needed to protect our industry from unfair competition from abroad, but you must admit, sir, that some Northern merchants are profiteering from the situation."

"You sound just like your Senators, sir. Damned traitors."

Robert took a tighter grip on his temper. "We in Carolina believe Stephen Miller and John Calhoun do a very good job, Senator."

Webster stiffened as if struck, his cavernous eyes staring coldly at Robert. "Henry, if you'll excuse me." Without so much as a nod to Robert, he stalked away.

"Oh, he'll be full of hell now," Clay said.

Robert stared after Webster's retreating back. "If this was anyplace but Washington, the way he just spoke would be cause for a duel."

"We do exercise a certain looseness of tongue," Clay said, smiling, "but you must understand Senator Webster's provocation. He once had, excuse me, a certain contemptuous affection for South Carolina. After all, he made much of his reputation as an orator against your Senator Hayne. A short time back, though, he took on Senator Calhoun over nullification." Clay winced and shook his head. "Webster's flamboyant oratory against Calhoun's remorseless logic. I don't approve of Calhoun's position, of course, but he dissected Webster muscle by muscle."

Robert regretted having missed Webster's dissection. He brought himself back to the matter at hand. "I suppose you know why I want to speak to you?"

"Oh, yes, Mr. Fallon. You've been the subject of quite a bit of gossip the past week or so." There was a smattering of genteel applause from inside the room as a number came to an end. "Let's see if we can find a couple of bourbon toddies before they begin again. Tell me . . . ."

LII
Charleston, 1833

When the schooner *Alice B.* docked in Charleston on the fourth of March, Robert leaped to the rough planks of Carver's Bridge like a boy. The early morning sky held the last clouds of a pre-dawn shower that had washed the air.

Once he had brought Clay and Calhoun together, they had taken off on their own. In four days Clay had introduced the bill before the Senate, Calhoun had risen to support it, and in short order they had used the very objections Robert had raised—about tariff bills having to originate in the House—to get the same bill, word for word, introduced in the House. On the twentieth, the Force Bill passed the Senate; on the twenty-sixth, the Compromise Tariff passed the House. One last ditch had arisen when Clayton of Delaware, with the manufacturers' lobbyists firmly behind him, threatened to get the tariff tabled if every single Southern Senator didn't vote for it. It had been a move to humiliate the Southerners, and all of Robert's persuasive abilities had gone into convincing Calhoun and the others to swallow it. He had sailed on the last day of February, the day before the tariff would come up for a vote in the Senate, and the Force Bill in the House. He hoped to find good news awaiting him.

He saw Morton hurrying down the wharf toward him, for once minus his pen and sheaf of papers. "Any news from Washington, Morton?" he called. "Any word on the tariff?"

"No, sir. But—"

"What about here? Are the Nullifiers still holding off?"

454

"Yes, sir, but . . . ." The lanky Georgian took a deep breath. "Sir, you'd better get home quick as you can."

"Is someone sick?" His breath caught in his throat. "Moira?"

Morton shifted uneasily. "No, sir. She'll tell you about it, though."

Robert broke into a run for the street. If it wasn't Moira, it was Elizabeth or one of the boys. And he hadn't been there. A horse was tethered to a hitching ring at the end of the warehouse. He took it. The owner could claim it later. Or never. He didn't care.

His ride down East Bay Street was a wild gallop, pedestrians leaping from his way, carriages and cotton drays colliding in his wake, frenzied curses following him. He scrambled down in front of his house, leaving the horse to wander free, and dashed inside.

In the entry hall Frank Hill and Albert stood in conversation against one wall, Ben Miller, Lafitte and Kenneth Graham near the other. Kemal, pacing, towered over them all.

"What's happened?" he asked, and was met by silence. His stomach shriveled.

"Sir," Albert said finally. "Sir, I'll take you to Mrs. Fallon." Lafitte grimaced and looked at the floor.

Moira was in her sitting room, lying on the chaise lounge with a compress on her forehead. To Robert's surprise, Edward was there, pacing and casting worried glances at Moira.

At his entrance, Moira gave a sob of relief. "Thank God, you're home. She's gone, Robert. She's gone!" Her eyes were red and puffy, and her mouth quivered.

"Elizabeth?" he said shakily. "Dead?"

"No, no," Edward said. "She's not dead. I keep telling Aunt Moira she'll be all right. This is just a prank."

"If she's put her mother in this state with a prank," Robert began, but Moira cut him off.

"Her bed wasn't slept in last night. No one's seen her since yesterday afternoon."

Robert swallowed a mouthful of bile. "Where can she have gone? If there'd been an accident, surely you'd have been notified. Now let's think about this rationally. She had to leave the house of her own free will, else someone would've heard something. There's that in favor of her being all right.''

"I've already thought of that," she said wearily.

"Yes, but why would she go without telling you? You . . . you don't think she's run away? Surely she's not that foolish." He blanched at the thought of Elizabeth trying to make her own way in the world. She had no skills. She was too hot-tempered to become a servant, and that left . . . he refused to think of it.

"There's been no reason. Not for weeks," Moira said.

"There was something then?"

Moira put her hands over her face, and he dropped to his knees beside the chaise lounge, cradling her, feeling her silent sobs.

"Don't cry, Moira. Don't cry. We'll find her. We will."

"That Edward Hammond," she breathed. "I told her to stop receiving him, so she began sneaking out, saying she was going to Cornelia Pinckney's when she was actually meeting him for carriage rides."

"There's nothing wrong with Hammond," Edward said with surprising heat.

Moira sat up, momentarily blazing with spirit. "And I say there is. He's talked more than one young fool around here into pitting some fieldhand against that brute of his. There's been least one death as a result." The brief flash faded, and she sank back listlessly. "It doesn't matter now, though. She came to her senses two weeks ago."

"It was their own choice," Edward said. "He never forced anybody to pit their blacks against King."

"I doubt the field hands had much choice," Robert said drily. "Why don't you forget about Hammond, and set your mind to where Elizabeth might be?" Edward retired sulkily to the fireplace. "Don't worry, Moira," Robert went on, smoothing her hair. "I'll find her if I have to search the city building by building." Even as she huddled against him he was wondering how he might go about that. Advertise for her, like a runaway? There was a knock at the door, and he said, "Come." He kept on stroking Moira's hair, thinking feverishly.

Hannah entered, somewhat deferential outside her domain of the kitchen, pushing a bony young black woman ahead of her. The cook had gained weight with each passing year, till she was almost completely round, but she still waved her wooden spoon like a scepter and ruled the kitchen absolutely. "Welcome home, Mr. Fallon," she said. "They done told me downstairs you was back. You gots to pardon me for coming up here like this, but this here Anna girl, she seen something last night, and she too much fool to know it any important."

Moira gripped Robert's arm tight with both hands.

Hannah waved her wooden spoon in front of Anna's face, and the young woman jumped a foot, words tumbling out of her mouth. "It was last night, I don't know what time, exactly, only I was going back to the necessary, pardon me, and I seed Miss Elizabeth come down the back stairs carrying a hatbox, only I never thought nothing of it cause Mr. Edward was with her, and I reckoned whatever it was happened had to happen after that, so I didn't say nothing, on account of I didn't think it was important, and . . . ."

Robert had heard nothing beyond Edward's name. He stared at Edward as if he'd never seen him before.

"The girl's lying," Edward burst out. "You going to believe some nigger wench . . . ." He quailed under Hannah's glare, tried to meet Robert's gaze and failed. He finished up muttering at the floor. "She's lying, I say."

"Hannah," Robert said, "would you leave us, please?" He felt Moira's nails digging into his arm, and hugged her tighter. When the door closed, he said, "She's with Hammond, isn't she?" Moira made a sound in her throat, half moan, half growl.

"I told you—"

"Damn you, boy, don't lie to me!"

"I wouldn't do anything to hurt Elizabeth," Edward said angrily. "You know that. Damn it, they're getting married." He shut his mouth abruptly.

"Married!" Moira whimpered.

"You helped my daughter elope?" Robert said hoarse-ly. "With a man like that? Where is she?"

"It's too late, uncle. They're married already. She loves him, and he loves her, only Aunt Moira just couldn't see—"

Robert tried to keep his voice down, but it came out a roar. "Damn you, where is she?"

Edward took half a step back and wet his lips again. "They went straight from here to a minister. Briarwood," he said quickly, as Robert started to rise. "Up on the Neck. You know it. Hammond rented it."

"Get out," Robert growled. "Get out of my sight!" Edward started to speak, took a look at his face, and ran out of the room. Robert discovered he was trembling. "I'll bring her back safely, Moira. I promise."

She stroked his cheek, and he was shocked to realize she was comforting him. To his mind it should be the other way round, but he realized, not for the first time, there was considerable iron in her. He got up, but she caught his hand.

"Robert, send Albert and Frank Hill to me. Please? I must talk to them."

"I'll send them," he said. "You rest."

When he reached the bottom of the stairs, his face was stone. Lafitte, Albert and the others gathered around him, waiting. "Elizabeth has eloped." His voice was so hard none of them moved except to breathe. "The man's name is Edward Hammond, and he's a bad sort. If she's lucky . . . if she's lucky he actually does intend to marry her, but I intend to bring her back if I have to kill him. I may anyway."

"By damn, we are with you," Lafitte said, and Albert said, "If he's hurt her, Mr. Fallon, you won't have to kill him. We'll do it." Kemal growled and brandished a fist the size of a ham.

"Wha' are we waiting for?" Graham's voice almost broke. "He could be . . . she might need us this minute."

"Albert," Robert said, "Mr. Hill, would the two of you go up to my wife, please, and stay with her?" They started to protest, but he silenced them quickly. "She asked for you in particular. I think she might be afraid to be alone, without a man about. I would appreciate it if the two of you would look after her till I get back with Elizabeth."

The two men shared a look. "Very well, sir," Albert said.

"We'll take care of her, Mr. Fallon," Hill said.

They went past him up the stair. "The rest of you," Robert said, "come with me, and we'll get a brace of pistols apiece. There are horses aplenty in the stable."

The coach carrying Marie Fourrier—for so she had always thought of herself, even when married to Southford—was forced to stop at the Fallon carriage drive by a knot of horsemen galloping out. Through the window she could make out faces as they passed, though none of them spared a glance at the coach. Robert Fallon's was a shock. She hadn't known he was back in the city. And from the look on his face, he knew at least some of what was happening.

She opened the trap in the roof. "Briarwood. Quickly!"

As the coach lurched forward again, she settled back. The damned fool was ruining everything. She hadn't prayed in years, but now she began to pray in earnest.

It wasn't fair, Edward Fallon thought. He paced the second-floor drawing room, nervously eyeing the door. Hammond wasn't a bad sort, and if he had an occasional nasty streak, well, it wouldn't harm Elizabeth to be taken down a peg or two. It wasn't as if Hammond would actually hurt her. He certainly hoped they had gone straight to a minister the way Hammond said they would. If he knew her, she wouldn't let him get away without marriage for long, but what did it matter, so long as they loved one another, and they both said they did?

Of course, Uncle Robert wouldn't see it that way. Being her father, he'd likely never noticed what a toothsome piece she'd become. Why, there'd been a time or two when he wished she wasn't his cousin. His overtures in that direction had been slapped down pretty sharply—he'd lived a month in agony waiting for her to tell—but he had managed to bore a hole from his dressing room to hers when he came back from Harvard. God, sometimes she'd flaunted herself as if she knew he was watching. And here they were worrying because she'd eloped. It was a damned good thing she had, before she got herself in real trouble.

He became aware of the door opening and snatched up a fire iron. Damn it, he shouldn't have stayed in the house. Then he saw it was Albert, and the ridiculousness of his position, poker held like a club, half-poised for flight, washed over him, changing his fear to rage. "God damn you! What do you mean barging in here without knocking?" He became aware of Frank Hill behind the butler; he was vaguely aware that Moira had some connection with the man, from days before he owned half the fishing boats in Charleston. He sometimes wondered if Robert's wife had cuckolded him with Hill, but now his anger simply spilled over. "And you! What are you doing, lurking about? We don't need any fish, fishmonger!"

"Mrs. Fallon wishes to see you," Albert said coolly. "In Mr. Fallon's study."

Edward opened his mouth to blast the man for disrespect, but a needle of fear stabbed him. "Is my uncle with her?"

"Mr. Fallon left ten minutes ago," Albert said. "Mrs. Fallon did say right away."

Edward lowered the poker, and thrust it back in the holder. "Very well, Albert. You may go." The butler made no move. "I said you may go, Albert. I know my way around this house."

"Mrs. Fallon said I was to return when you did."

Edward grimaced. The man was probably fool enough to think he had to stick to the letter of her instructions. He contented himself with checking his tie lingeringly in the mirror above the sideboard. "Lead on, Albert," he said finally, and followed the butler out of the room.

Hill fell in behind them without a word, and Edward had the uncomfortable feeling of being under guard. Why didn't he just walk on out the front door? He certainly didn't have to subject himself to Aunt Moira's tongue. It wasn't, he told himself, because the two of them might stop him. Preposterous to think that a butler and a fishmonger would lay hands on a gentleman.

They entered the study. Moira was just turning the last key to lock Robert's safe, and there was a stack of banknotes and a leather pouch on the desk.

"A little peculation, auntie?" he said. "Buying yourself something you don't want Uncle Robert to know about? I hope he doesn't find out." He essayed a laugh, but it felt awkward with the two wooden-faced men behind him. "Listen, auntie, do we need these two? Couldn't you send them off on an errand, or something?"

Her face was expressionless as she took the chair behind the desk. "There is thirty-seven hundred dollars there. You're going to take it and leave Charleston tonight. In fact, you're leaving South Carolina, and you're never coming back."

He chuckled, but she didn't flicker an eyelash. "That isn't even a good joke, auntie. Remember, I come into my inheritance in a few more months. Tell you what, when I do, I'll give you thirty-seven hundred dollars. You can buy yourself some trinket or other."

"I'm not joking, Edward. I'm saving your life. No, the truth of it is, it's Robert's life that I'm saving. If you're here when he comes back, it's killing you he'll be, and I don't think he could live long with that."

"You're exaggerating," he blustered. "Of course, he'll be mad for a bit, but he always comes around in the—"

"You fool!" she spat. "Do you think I don't know that man has . . . has had his way with my daughter already?"

There was a growl behind him that lifted the hair on the back of his neck. He took a quick step to one side, where he could see both Albert and Hill, but he couldn't tell which had made the noise. They watched him with cold eyes. For the first time since learning Robert had gone, he began to feel uneasy.

"If not for the love I bear Robert Fallon," Moira went on, "I'd be cutting your throat myself this minute. And if you refuse the offer I'm making you, I'll be doing it still."

He scrubbed his hand across his mouth, eyeing her the

way he would a rattlesnake in his bed. "You've been waiting for this, haven't you? Plotting to steal my inheritance."

"Don't be a fool, Edward."

"I'll be a rich man! You can't throw me out, you bitch!" The world seemed to explode, and he found himself on the carpet, Albert standing over him. He touched his face gingerly. "You struck me," he said in disbelief. His voice turned shrill. "I'll have you hung for striking a white man!"

Then Hill was helping him up, the hands still scarred from his years as a fisherman brushing him off. "Sorry about that," Hill said. "Should've known you'd object to a black hand." Edward had just time to see the big fist coming, and he was on the floor again.

"My nose!" he groaned. "You broke my nose!"

"Stop this!" Moira said. "I don't want him beaten to death."

"I can have him fed to the sharks in the harbor before Mr. Fallon gets back," Hill said.

Edward stared wildly from one to another of them. They meant it. "You can't murder me! I'm Edward Fallon, God damn it!"

Moira pushed the money nearer to him. "The choice is yours," she said calmly.

If he pretended to give in, they'd let him go. He could catch Uncle Robert on his way back from Briarwood. Uncle Robert had always stood up for him, no matter what. Damn them, he'd see them all pay for this. "I'll take the money," he croaked. God, his nose hurt.

Hill hauled him to his feet again; Albert stuffed the money in his pockets. Despite himself he was grateful for the support. He didn't think he could have stood unaided.

"We won't hurt him, ma'am," Albert said to Moira; Hill added, "We'll just see him to a horse."

From her frozen face Edward didn't think she cared if they took him out and hung him. He let them half-carry him out, relishing the thought of bringing her down. His first fantasies about women had been about her. God, it would be almost as good as bedding her to see her broken.

She'd always hated him, always been ready to leap on everything he did. She . . . . He realized they were taking him out the back way, down the brick stairs leading to the stable.

"I can walk," he said, but they continued to drag him. "I said I can walk!"

They turned suddenly, slamming him against the brick wall of the kitchen building. "Albert and me had a talk," Hill said, "after Mrs. Fallon told us what we were fetching you for."

"And we figured," Albert said, "maybe you weren't smart enough to believe Robert Fallon will kill you."

Edward struggled futilely. "I don't know what you're talking about. Let me go. I agreed to her terms."

"A bit too fast," Hill said. "So this is what we're going to do to make sure. The two of us know men who'd cut your throat for ten dollars cash money. We're going to let them do it." Edward struggled again, briefly, subsiding when Albert's fist in the pit of his stomach set him gagging. "The fine Mr. Edward Fallon is well known around the city, and if he's seen in the city thirty minutes after we leave you, he'll die here. Do you understand me, Mr. Edward Fallon?"

Edward suddenly wished he could vomit. "I understand," he managed. "I said I'd go, didn't I?"

They backed away from him so suddenly he had to clutch at the bricks for support. "Just you remember," Albert said, and abruptly they were gone in the night.

He hung there, dazed, willing himself to wake and find it all a dream. The pain, the blood trickling down his face, told him it was no dream, though. Damn it, they *had* broken his nose. Broken his nose, thrown him out, stolen his inheritance. His inheritance. He fumbled in his pockets. The money was actually there. Three thousand seven hundred dollars. That wouldn't support him long, not the way he liked to live. And that raised the question of where to go. New York was his first thought, or Boston, but there were people in the North who knew him, people who'd be all too ready to pity him when his money was gone, and dole out charity for which he would have to be properly grateful. Damn them, and damn their charity.

He had no idea how long it was since Albert and Hill had gone. How much time did he have? He lurched into a stumbling run for the stable. By God, he'd take the best horse there. The best horse. Robert had a bastard son who'd done well—gotten rich, by all accounts—beginning with nothing but a horse somewhere in Mexico. What he could do, Edward surely could. Let them think him dead somewhere, then, when he'd made his fortune . . . . He croaked a laugh, and looking over his shoulder, hurried on to the stable.

Briarwood was a large brick farmhouse set among oaks near the Ashley River, a broad porch across its front. As the party of men turned into the drive, a scream drifted from the house. Heedless of the others, Robert spurred ahead and leaped from the saddle at the foot of the wide brick stairs.

Before he set foot on them, King appeared around the corner of the building. The huge man advanced with a warily outstretched hand. The shoulders of his livery seemed ready to burst. "My master don't want no visitors," he said in a guttural voice. Another scream echoed from inside, and King grinned broadly. "He entertaining."

"Damn you!" Robert pulled one of his pistols, and the big man tensed, but before either could move Kemal jumped down from his horse, facing King. He motioned Robert to go on. King was an inch the taller, and fully twice as massive.

"You ain't too little," King laughed, "but you look too old. Get out my way, granddaddy." He swung a fist that staggered Kemal, but when he started past the Turk clutched at him, pulled him to the ground.

"Forgive me, old friend," Robert whispered, and hurried by into the house. He heard Lafitte, Miller and Graham arriving, but there was no time to waste. Yet another scream rang down the halls, and another, till they filled his heart.

Snarling he went up the stairs, following the screams,

blanking from his mind what had to be behind them. A door loomed in front of him. He kicked it open, and there they were. Hammond, naked, rolling off the bed, rolling off Elizabeth. She lay naked and weeping, her wrists tied to the head of the bed, bruises covering her breasts and thighs.

Through his horrified state and the keening scream he knew was his own, he caught a glimpse of movement and dodged as Hammond fired. He felt a solid blow low on the left side, but his answering shot was almost an echo. A blue hole appeared in the center of Hammond's naked chest. For a moment the man stared incredulously at the blood that began to fan across his stomach, then sank to his knees.

"My blood," Hammond said. Trickles of it appeared at the corners of his mouth. "I never thought . . . . Damn you, Fallon!" He said the name like a curse. "How do you like your daughter being a whore? You can't kill all of us. Sooner or later—"

The muzzle of Robert's second pistol slammed his words back into his mouth along with broken teeth. Robert pulled the trigger caressingly. Hammond's eyes had a second to bulge before his lifeless body was thrown sprawling on its back.

Graham had already cut Elizabeth free when Robert turned back—Miller had his eyes discreetly averted—and was wrapping a blanket around her. She pushed away from him, shuddering and sobbing. "Get away from me! Don't touch me! Don't look at me! Leave me alone!"

Robert started toward her, but Miller grabbed his arm. "No, captain," he whispered.

Graham's face worked furiously as he stared at Elizabeth, huddled in the blanket with her back to him. "Lass," he said quietly. "Elizabeth, I love you."

"You don't know what he . . . what he . . . ." She broke down in sobs.

"I dinna' care, lass. You're the same woman now you were a week ago, and I loved you then. How can I na' love you now?" He put a hand on her shoulder, but removed it hastily when she shuddered.

"Give her time," Robert said softly. He wanted to cry. The time he had wasted with fools in Washington for fools in South Carolina. They could all go to hell. He should have been there to protect her.

"That Kemal," Lafitte said, bustling in, "he break that big black's neck. I never see no fight like . . . ." He caught sight of Elizabeth, and his face twisted in pain. "Oh, by God damn, Robert, I am sorry. God damn it to hell!"

"You killed him," Marie said from the door. The men all leaped as if the dead man had spoken. "I knew you would."

Robert heaved a sigh of relief. Another woman was just what Elizabeth needed. "Thank God you're here, Marie. Did Moira send you?"

"He was my favorite, you know." She moved past him to the body as if she didn't see anything else. "After my daughters, of course."

"What are you talking about?" Robert said. "Marie, are you all right?"

"You were the one who killed him, weren't you? It doesn't matter. It was you, no matter who pulled the trigger." Carefully she closed the dead man's eyes. "He was just supposed to keep an eye on me, be my protection, but he always had an eye for pretty women, and he always wanted to do things his own way."

Robert's voice was a whisper. "What are you saying, Marie?"

"Don't you know him?" she cried. "I was sure you would when he was fool enough to go right up to you. Don't you recognize your own nephew? Not Edward Hammond, Robert. Edouard Fourrier. Lucien's son. You remember your baby brother, Lucien, don't you?"

"Oh, my God! Why, Marie? There was no hatred between us."

She smoothed the dead man's hair into place. Her voice was preternaturally calm. "He liked to listen to stories of the wars against Napoleon, as boys will. From his father. From Gerard. Gerard was his hero. He would have done anything for Gerard."

"I didn't mean him, Marie. You. Never by any stretch of the imagination have I ever done you any harm."

"Harm, Robert? You killed my father. Or your wife did; I never did get the straight of that. But I can't count that, can I? Given time enough I might well have killed papa myself, what with the way he insisted on gratitude for every little favor. Just like Gerard. When he came home he insisted my girls fetch and carry for him, clean and make his bed. He wouldn't allow anyone else to do it. I think he just wanted to show me my proper place, put me in the right frame of mind to accept what he told me to do." Her voice had taken on a dreamy quality. "Poor Edouard. Poor Marie."

"So it was all lies," he said. "Everything you told me. But why? It doesn't make sense. Not for this." His gesture took in the entire room, Elizabeth shuddering in her blanket, the body.

"Oh, no, Robert," she said. "It was the truth. Or most of it was. I do live on Gerard's charity, and he makes me crawl for every penny. When Melissa married, and Amanda, I had to beg, literally on my knees, for their dowries. Poor Lucien's no use. He really has lived in a world of his own since his wife died. And then Gerard told me if I wanted dowries for Jocelyn and Beatrice I must do exactly what he told me. It's not as if we were close, you know. I don't . . . hate you, exactly—or I didn't—but I certainly don't love you either. What would you have done?"

She took Edouard's head on her lap, careless of the blood.

"The ships, Marie."

"Oh, yes. The ships. He was such a handsome young man, wasn't he?" He thought he'd need to prompt her, but when he opened his mouth, she said, "Everything about the ships is exactly as I said. Truth. Exactly. It's just that when the ownerships were recorded, you would have been the sole owner. My name would appear nowhere. Women shouldn't be allowed property, after all. Gerard is a firm believer in that, except for that wife of his. I think he's a little afraid of her. What was I talking about? Oh, yes. The ships. You would be the owner, and when they were found trying to smuggle slaves into the United States, slaves in very poor condition, you would have been destroyed.''

Destroyed indeed, Robert thought with a shiver. Social and financial ostracism, stiff fines, a jail sentence. He'd have been lucky if his family hadn't had to change its name.

"Why doesn't he open his eyes?" Marie asked plaintively. Robert felt his hackles rise. "He's badly hurt, isn't he?"

"She's gone mad," Miller whispered, and Elizabeth looked up fearfully.

This was what it came to, Robert thought, he and Gerard playing out an enmity formed before either of them was born. Edouard dead. Marie mad. Elizabeth.... Fuel enough there for the next generation on both sides. Cause enough for his sons to hunt Gerard's, for Gerard's grandsons to hunt his.

"Let's get out of here," he said. "Ben, will you remain with Mr. Lafflin until I can send someone for . . . ." He gestured to Marie, crooning a lullaby now to Edouard's body. Miller nodded.

"Sure, by damn," Lafitte said. "And when we get back, you tell us what happened up there in Washington, eh?"

"Washington can go to hell!" Robert snapped, and ignored the hurt on Lafitte's face. He knew the former pirate was only trying to take his mind, if only for a moment, off the horror of the room, but he didn't care about any of it any more. He crossed the room and put his arm around Elizabeth, wincing when she stiffened. "Come home with me, Bets," he said, and after a moment she let him lead her out. Tears streaming down his face, he wept unashamedly.

LIII
Texas, 1833

The San Felipe town hall, a long box of rough, unpainted planks, was so crowded that April felt more like August. The lone door was closed, and the oiled-paper windows held in the heat. The buckskin-clad men crowding the chairs and split-log benches stirred the heavy air with palmetto fans as a frock-coated man orated from the council platform.

" . . . And I say," stern-faced William Wharton declaimed, "the history of Texas is one of oppression by Mexico City. You all know the entire region of Texas has but one representative in the Coahuila-Texas legislature. You all know . . . ."

"If he's going to tell us what we all know," James whispered to Erasmo Sequin, "I'm stepping out for a breath of air."

Sequin grinned and stilled his fan for a moment. "I fear my gray hairs compel me to show more respect, even to such a recital."

James grinned back and made his way down the side aisle. He nodded to a bedraggled-looking Bowie, surrounded by three gesticulating men, and jerked his head toward the door. Bowie shrugged resignedly and turned back with a show of listening. Ben Milam got up, though, and followed James outside. Horses deepened the pawing holes at the hitchrails.

"Fallon," the lean, leather-skinned *ranchero* said, "you're on Houston's committee, aren't you? Drawing up a constitution?" Ten years older than James, Milam had been one of those who had gotten an *empresario* grant just in time to have it canceled by Bustamente's law.

"I think they put me there because they couldn't think of any place else."

"Maybe. But you know this Houston. Leastways, you seem to be siding with him against Austin."

"I voted for Wharton," James said carefully, "and so did Houston, but I'm not turning against Austin."

"Didn't mean to say you were. Houston, though. He's pretty well set up for a man who's only been in Texas a few months. Bought a league of land down on Karankawa Bay and got himself elected to this convention in short order. What's a man like him doing in Texas in the first place?"

"Ben, Houston is the only man in Texas well enough known in the United States that he won't be branded another Haden Edwards or James Long. And you better believe we're going to need men, money and supplies from the States before this is done."

Milam eyed him shrewdly. "You don't think Santa Anna'll make any difference?" Early in January Santa Anna had marched into Mexico City, placed Pedraza back in the Presidency for the few remaining months of his term, and promptly been hailed as the savior of democracy and elected Pedraza's successor.

"I'd sooner trust a rattlesnake," James said. "This petition won't get any further than any of the others." The convention's purpose had been to draw a petition for redress of grievances, and if the supporters of Wharton and Houston had managed to gain a measure of control, that purpose hadn't been entirely forgotten. David Burnet had chaired a committee to frame the petition, and Austin, Sequin and James Miller had been chosen to carry it south. "You tell me, Ben," he went on, "from your experience, what do you think the Mexicans will do?"

"I think I'd better go on back inside." At the door, though, he hesitated, finally looking back over his shoulder. "Keep your powder dry, Fallon. Maybe we will need it, after all." He disappeared inside.

James decided to take his air strolling through the town. San Felipe still straggled along a single street rutted by carts and horses, but the log cabins had been replaced by buildings of sawn pine, though unpainted and weathered. Only thirty families lived in the town proper, but Groce's was no longer the only store, nor Smithwick's the only blacksmith shop. The town was the center of commerce and social life for a thirty-mile radius.

He spotted Houston on the porch of the single-story Virginia House hotel and started towards him, slowing when he realized who Houston was talking to. Elena Velasquez, in a russet silk traveling dress, an ivory lace shawl draped around her head, looked in his direction, and it was too late for him to turn around. The sign promising guests "Clean Beds—No Rats or Fleas" creaked in the breeze as he stepped up on the porch. Elena's black-clad *duenna* adjusted her charge's shawl.

Houston, in buckskins like James, but with a curly-brimmed white beaver hat in his hand, broke the silence. "James, *Doña* Elena tells me she's going to Monclova."

"*Sí,*" Elena said. "*Señor* Bowie has sent Ursula and the children to the mountains there for fear of the cholera, and she wrote asking me to come also. It is good to see you again, James."

Her big, melting brown eyes tugged at him, but he hardened himself. He hadn't even been back to San Antonio since December for fear she might be there. "This is a long way out of the way for Monclova." The words came out harsher than he'd intended, but if it made her go away . . . .

I have not seen you since before *Navidad,*" she said softly. She seemed barely aware of the others. "*Papá* is much disappointed that you have not visited."

He stifled a pang. "I've been busy."

"Too busy to see *papá?* Or José? Or *Señor* Cameron? Or me?"

"Busy. Sam, for Christ's sake, would you tell her I've been busy?" Houston grinned and held up his hands; James made an exasperated sound.

Elena's smile included Houston in a conspiratorial way. "You are like a wild horse, *mi* Jaime, frightened of the touch of a hand. Do not be frightened of me."

"Frightened! What are you talking about?"

"Once, as a little girl, I told you how I felt. Perhaps you do not remember."

"I remember," he said, and saw by the light in her eyes the admission was a mistake.

"I said them as a child, but I believe them as a woman."

"You . . . ." He was suddenly very much aware of Houston's scrutiny. The *duenna* didn't speak English, but her eyes were suspicious. "Excuse me, Sam," he said, and grabbed Elena's arm, pulling her a few paces down the porch. The *duenna* clutched at him, muttering, but he shook her loose. Under Elena's soothing she subsided to angry murmurings under her breath, but she remained a single pace away, looking at James as if she would go for his throat.

"Yes, James?" Elena said when she turned to him. "You wish to say something to me in private?"

"Da . . . girl, this isn't right. It isn't seemly!"

"If I were seemly, *mi* Jaime, you would continue to escape me. I have no wiles to ensnare you in. And you are too much *hombre* to waste your life with drinking . . ."

"Elena—"

" . . . and gambling . . ."

"Girl—"

" . . . and chasing loose women. I will not let you waste it so."

Vaguely he realized their voices had risen until they might as well not have moved away from Houston. "Damn it, girl, I won't be pitied!"

"I do not pity you, *mi* Jaime, I love you."

"But I don't love you," he said brutally, and saw her flinch. "You're Drusilla's baby sister, and that's how I see you. A little girl playing with dolls, a little girl who won't let go of a childish infatuation."

"I do not believe you." Her voice shook.

He felt as if he were drowning in her eyes. "Believe me," he said hoarsely. "Go away. Don't you know all you do is remind me of things I want to forget? Leave me alone!"

She stumbled back, the back of her hand pressed to her mouth, then turned and fled. The *duenna* glared at him and darted after her. He gritted his teeth against desire, pounded his fist on the porch rail.

Houston put on his white beaver and pushed it back on his head. "You were hard on the young lady, James."

"For her own good," James said.

"Her own good?" Houston echoed softly. "You know about such things, do you? Hell, James, it's plain as a picture you're in love with her."

"You talk too much, Houston."

"Why don't you marry the girl, James?"

"In case it's missed your notice, there's a war coming. Hell, Sam, you and I are helping start it."

"Seems to me a lot of people get married during wars. Have children, too. A sort of instinct toward leaving something behind. Seems a good instinct, to me."

For a moment both men were silent, then Houston said, "How about a bite of dinner?" and James nodded.

They made their way across the street, dodging carts and horses, to the New England Retreat. A few minutes later they were seated at a table with a red-checked tablecloth, plates of baked beans and fried fish and a big pot of coffee before them. After they had eaten a while in silence, Houston spoke.

"Travis is ready to work with us, if he can find time out from dancing with the ladies."

"You'd better watch Travis," James said over his coffee. "He doesn't trust Mexicans, especially since Anahuac, and that may cause trouble. Bowie tells me he's already offended Erasmo Sequin, and him we do need, if we want any support from the Mexicans."

"You and Bowie," Houston grumbled. "You know you're both suspect. Too close to the Mexicans, some say."

"Some fools," James snorted. He refrained from saying they were numbered almost exclusively among men who'd been in Texas less than a year. After all, Houston was in that group as well. "Some of them are the most dangerous of all. They think independence will mean they can kick Mexicans off their land. Fredonia all over again."

"You're exaggerating, James. No one of any importance believes that."

"Perhaps, but . . . ." He stared as Gerard Fourrier came out of one of the private dining rooms at the rear. "I didn't know he was in town."

Houston twisted around to look. "Fourrier? He got in yesterday. I've been talking with him. He seems to have a good grasp of the situation."

"He should. He played both sides against the middle with the Fredonia business."

"A lot of good men were involved in that, James. You and Austin, too, I recall hearing."

James opened his mouth to explain what he meant, but at that moment Fourrier stopped by their table. The look he gave James was sharp, but his smile was ready.

"Good day, Mr. Houston." A slight twist of the mouth. "Mr. Fallon."

"Mr. Fourrier," Houston said; James kept silent. "Won't you join us?"

"I'm afraid not, Mr. Houston. My wife wants to return to our ranch, and we're leaving in just a few minutes."

James smiled to himself at the Anglicized word "ranch." Fourrier had always spoken of his *hacienda*. Well, "ranch" would be more popular with Houston.

"That's too bad," Houston said. "Your advice will be missed."

Fourrier's thin smile was appreciative. "Kind of you to say so, Mr. Houston. We must humor the ladies, though, eh? Gentlemen?" His bow included both men, and he strode out of the restaurant.

"Who was he meeting?" James said. At Houston's questioning look, he added, "A man doesn't eat alone in a private room."

Houston shrugged. "Maybe whoever it was left by the back way."

"We'll talk later," James said, crumpling his napkin on the table. "My appetite's gone, Sam. I'm going to walk for a while."

As he reached the porch, Fourrier passed in his carriage, a beautiful dark-haired woman beside him. That must be his wife, James thought, the woman Fuentes claimed wanted him dead. He couldn't remember ever seeing her before. Just then she saw him, and such a look of hatred passed across her face that he suddenly believed Fuentes' story. An incongruous thought of snakes flickered through his head. Her look was certainly reptilian.

As the carriage rolled on by, James saw a fat, scruffy man climbing onto a horse across the street, and all thought of Fourrier's wife went out of his head. It was Nat Coffee and San Felipe. He was sure that Coffee had sold guns and whiskey to Indians, and smuggled slaves, too. He hurried back to the town hall and met Austin coming out.

"The heat in there is intolerable," Austin said, mopping his face.

"Stephen, Nat Coffee is in town."

"Here? You're sure? I'm afraid this convention is drawing all sorts of riff-raff."

"Is that all you can say? Damn it, he's supplying guns to the Indians."

"You've never been able to prove it, James."

"I've never been able to get my hands on him. Well, he's here, now, and I'll bet he'd break wide open if he was questioned. He's got as much backbone as a jellyfish."

"Why don't you go to Houston?" Austin said acidly. "Why don't you and Houston arrest him?" His high forehead was creased with anger.

James sighed. "Stephen, you know there was nothing personal in the way I voted. I just don't believe petitioning will get us anywhere."

"I expected Bowie to vote with Houston, but not you. Bowie's still just an adventure, for all his marriage, and his cotton mill. You mark my words. Houston's here for what he can get. His political career in the United States was destroyed, so he means to feed his ambitions on Texas."

"He doesn't dislike you," James said quietly. "When he saw you were being pushed aside, it was him got you named to carry the petition to Mexico City."

"Trying to get me out of the way." Austin's voice was bitter. "Perhaps permanently."

James was silent for a moment. "I thought you believed

in the petition, believed a peaceful solution was possible."

"I don't know," Austin sighed. "I just don't know. I'm trying to talk Sequin and Miller into staying behind. There's no need for more than one of us to stick his head in the lion's mouth."

"Then why should you go, either? Damn it, Stephen, it's a foolish risk."

"We must try, James. I must." He shook his head wearily, then fumbled in his coat pocket and brought out a letter. "I almost forgot this. The post rider was going to take it to San Antonio, but I saw your name. I didn't know you had relatives in South Carolina."

"On my father's side," James said vaguely, breaking the seal. "Excuse me just a minute. I haven't heard from . . . from them in months." Robert Fallon's usually strong hand showed signs of strain.

My Dear James,

As I write to you, the streets of Charleston are filled with jubilant people claiming victory. Only yesterday a convention of Nullifiers repealed the Nullification Ordinance, under fear of the Force Act, men who should know better say. But it is enough for Unionists to flaunt white cockades and say God and Andy Jackson have smitten the Philistines. On the other hand, the same day the Force Bill was signed, so was the Compromise Tariff. So many Nullifiers believed that this signified a triumph of their views that they, over the objections of their leaders, repealed the ordinance. Even so, before they did so they nullified the Force Act. A last bit of bravado, the Unionists say, not seeing or not caring that the passions still remain. The seeds are in place, and everyone, in his own way and for his own reasons, will help them grow. I have reversed a decision and had the tools for making muskets put back into the foundry. If conflict comes I must side with my neighbors, wrong-headed though they be, rather than outsiders who are even more wrong-headed. But it will not come in my lifetime, I think. You will see it, though, and Thomas and Carver will bleed in it. God is truly the cruel God of the Old Testament. I hope that the convention your last letter spoke of—it may be over by the time you receive this, I realize—finds a peaceful solution to your problems, at least.

As for personal news, old sins have returned to wreak their havoc with me. Gerard Fourrier's machinations have nearly destroyed me, and though he probably sees the attempt a failure, I fear he has done better than he knows. A nephew dead, a sister mad. And yet we will all of us survive. I wonder anew at the strength in Moira. Elizabeth has been bedridden these past weeks, yet through the love and patience of Kenneth Graham—you do not know him, but the depths I have discovered in him, also, surprise me— she will recover. I am sure of that now. There was a loss, one who went away, but I will not speak of him again. Old sins. Old sins.

It is the legacy of our blood that the road never be smooth, and yet we are driven to follow it just the same. Take care on your journey, my son. Learn from yesterday, plan for tomorrow, but do no let today pass you by. Grasp it tight and live it with all the strength in you. That, I fear, is the sum of the wisdom I have gathered in my life. Live today without weeping for yesterday or fearing for tomorrow. God be with you, my son, and peace and happiness your portion.

Robert Fallon.

James stared at the pages after he finished, then raised his head. "Stephen, do you think I'm a fool?"

"No more than the rest of us. Why?"

"If you were in love, would you marry her before you went to Mexico City?"

"I would," Austin said promptly. "A man can always find reasons to deny himself happiness. As soon as he gets one out of the way, there's always another. You want to tell me what you're talking about, now?"

"I'm a fool," James said, as if that were the answer. He saw Houston approaching from the direction of the New England Retreat, and shouted, "Sam! Has Elena left for Monclova yet?"

A smile appeared on Houston's broad face as he answered. "I think so. But her coach can't have gone more than a few miles."

"Elena Velasquez?" Austin said. "James, what's going on?"

"Houston'll explain." James broke into a run for the stable, shouting back over his shoulder, "I'm getting married!'' He could apologize to her, make her understand. Damn it, he'd force her to understand. Storm clouds were rising over Texas, and over the United States, as well. But whatever happened, he was through living in the past. It was today was important. He laughed as he ran. However tomorrow looked, today was bright and clear.